SOON SHE WILL BE GONE

JOHN FARRIS

SOON
SHE WILL
BE GONE

A TOM DOHERTY ASSOCIATES BOOK

NEW YORK

SOON SHE WILL BE GONE

Copyright © 1997 by Sand Dog Productions, Inc.

A Forge Book
Published by Tom Doherty Associates, Inc.
175 Fifth Avenue
New York, NY 10010

Forge® is a registered trademark of Tom Doherty Associates, Inc.

Book design by Judith Stagnitto Abbate

Library of Congress Cataloging-in-Publication Data

Farris, John.
    Soon she will be gone / John Farris.—1st ed.
      p.   cm.
    "A Tom Doherty Associates book."
    ISBN 0-312-85375-0 (acid-free paper)
    I. Title.
    PS3556.A777S63   1997
    813'.54—dc21   96-53281
                                           CIP

First Edition: July 1997

Printed in the United States of America

0 9 8 7 6 5 4 3 2 1

To Margaret Pasante

Night is the nature of man's interior world.

—WALLACE STEVENS,
A Word with José Rodríguez-Feo

SOON SHE WILL BE GONE

ONE

ELECTRA-GLIDE IN RED

It had been a frustrating day for Sharan until she heard, or thought she heard, the sound of her stolen motorcycle. After that, thanks to her impulsive nature, the day quickly got a lot worse.

She was in the Laundromat of the modest shopping center across from Skinner's Texaco and the new branch post office on East Fourth Street. The spin cycle of the washer she was using had finished, and she was separating the few things she didn't want to go into the dryer when the familiar sound of a Harley engine running too rich on idle caught her attention, like a bee sting at the base of her neck. The carburetor might well have been the used S and S Super B she'd been jetting, a trial-and-error process, on the Sunday when her iron was swiped. It was now Wednesday afternoon, and her outrage was still fresh.

Sharan sprinted out of the Laundromat and stopped, shielding her eyes from the sun with her hand as she scanned the street. Continuing to hear the motorcycle (there was nothing else in the world that sounded like a Harley) but not seeing it—then, *there it was,* coming slowly around from the rest room side of Skinner's, as cruddy as a motocross bike from hard use but still with the distinctive, not-so-common customized X-Sportster front end, the chromed bullet-style turn signals looking like dirt daubers' nests from splattered red clay. For several seconds she couldn't quite believe it. Not three miles from her front porch, and there he was riding around Tombetta, Georgia, all gall and brass and wearing a black helmet with a bronzed face shield that mirrored the sun as he turned his head.

Sharan didn't recognize him, but his style was familiar. He wore low-cut biker boots, Levi's torn across one knee. His black T-shirt was a souvenir from a death-metal concert. There were blue stains of tattoos on his sunburnt forearms. He had that small-time, redneck, dropout look.

He might have noticed her. Rider and Harley were motionless for a few moments. The engine stumbled but didn't die. A mail delivery Jeep pulled out of the post office driveway and turned left, momentarily blocking Sharan's view of the Electra-Glide thief.

"Hey!" Sharan hollered. And took off running.

Simultaneously the Harley's engine revved and he headed up Mulhern Street, backfiring, black smoke erupting from the twin exhausts. Past the low stone wall of Greater Gethsemene Baptist Church and cemetery, disappearing from sight as Sharan reached the pump island on the Mulhern side of the Texaco station.

Some Mexican bricklayers were drinking Pepsis in front of Skinner's while one of them shimmied under their pickup truck to look for a source of trouble. No help there, Sharan decided. There was a dark blue Dodge Caravan with no one in it parked by the pumps, the door on the driver's side open. Keys left in the ignition. Sharan hesitated, dismayed and angry, adrenaline turning her blood to rocket fuel. She looked at the Mexicans.

"That guy stole my motorcycle! I am borrowing this vehicle! *Comprende*? I'm going after him, and I *need* to *borrow* the vehicle! Tell whoever owns it, it's an emergency! *Emergencia!*"

Maybe they understood her, probably they didn't. Sharan unbuckled her fanny pack and hung it on the pump beside the van. Her wallet was in the fanny pack, forty-two dollars and her driver's license in the wallet. SouthTrust Mastercard, not quite maxed out. Whoever owned the van, she thought, would surely appreciate her motives in this crisis, realize that her intentions were honorable. Sharan had nine thousand dollars tied up in her motorcycle, which was all the transportation she owned.

Meanwhile the Electra-Glide thief was putting more distance between them.

Sharan jumped into the van and took off after him, past the old cemetery with its weather-riddled, hand-hewn tombstones lopsided all over the hill, through a shady tunnel of oak trees that enclosed the narrow blacktop, out into the sun again at the crest of the hill and the intersection with Gun Club Road. The Electra-Glide thief had found the lumpy surface of Mulhern tough going and had turned west, toward Stone Mountain. Gun Club was two lanes with a turn lane down the middle, and there was traffic. The tires of the van screeched as Sharan ignored the blinking stop light and a delivery truck halfway through the intersection.

"Way cool," the kid in the backseat said.

Startled, Sharan glanced over her shoulder and thought, *Oh, no.*

He was eleven or twelve, husky, with one of those Dutch-Boy haircuts severely buzzed around the ears. He was wearing a little-league uniform, smudged here and there with Georgia red clay. Her quick wide turn had sent him sprawling across the middle seat of the van. He looked up with a flush of apprehension, tooth edges showing white as eggshell, his eyes locked on her; but he seemed determined to be a good sport.

"Hi," Sharan said, smiling tensely and returning her attention to the road, a live wire of guilt and consequence snapping sparks in her breast. Nothing much to do now but get on with it.

"Who're you chasing?" the kid said.

"Somebody who stole my motorcycle."

"Are you a cop?" he asked, making an effort to give her some legitimacy.

"No. Not anymore."

In the rearview mirror Sharan saw him sit up and lean forward, as if he had just noticed what was unusual about her.

She had the van up to sixty on a straight stretch of road, using the turn lane to pass slower vehicles, gaining on the motorcycle. The huge bald dome of Stone Mountain was off to the left, about three miles away, but looking much closer in the clear air, a red cable car riding high in the unclouded sky.

"What's your name?" Sharan said.

"I'm Jesse."

"Are you going to be late for your game?"

"No ma'am, we played this morning."

"How did you do?"

"Two for four. I had a double. You're driving kind of fast."

"I'm a good driver, Jesse."

"What are you going to do when you catch him?"

"I don't know yet. Get my bike back."

"Is that a bionic hand?" Jesse said. His head appeared between the seats as he stared at the prosthetic device on the steering wheel. "It almost looks real."

"Bionic? Not quite, this one runs on batteries and nerve impulses. It's a pretty good hand, though. I can do all kinds of things with it. Pick up a needle if I want to. You'd better sit back and fasten your seat belt."

Less than half a mile to the intersection with U.S. 78, and a long light that had just turned red. The Electra-Glide thief was slowing. As yet he hadn't turned his head to see if he was being followed. Sharan slowed down, too, but stayed in the empty turn lane. Now she gave serious thought as to how she was going to handle it, thinking how nice it would be to see a cop approaching the intersection on 78. Unfortunately the van didn't have a phone, so she couldn't call for help.

"What's *your* name?" Jesse asked.

"Sharan. Sharan Norbeth."

"There's this boy in fifth grade at school, he's got, like, part of his arm is missing, but he was, like, born that way. Were you—"

"No, I lost the hand, Jesse. I mean it was cut off. Do you have your bat with you?"

"I've got a couple of bats. Cut *off*? Jeez."

"Pass one up here to me, would you please, hon?"

"Sure!"

The Electra-Glide thief had stopped for the red light at 78, behind a Ready-Mix truck and a couple of cars. A county crew with backhoes was working on a utility cut beside the road, separated from the traffic lane by a line of orange-and-white striped barrels. No escape for the thief in that direction. A rebuilt seventies sedan partly primed and partly repainted had pulled up behind the muddy red motorcycle, bass cannon booming, three teenage boys cutting up. The thief had not left much room between himself and the Ready-Mix truck. Sharan stopped in the turn lane to the left of the thief, took the metal baseball bat in her prosthetic hand and got out of the van. She walked around the front end and through the cloudy heat of the Ready-Mix truck's exhaust to the right-hand lane and planted herself in front of the Electra-Glide.

"You're in possession of a stolen motorcycle. I know, because I own it. Switch off the ignition and stand aside. Do it *now*."

His face was invisible behind the face shield of his helmet. For several seconds he was motionless. Then he gunned it and tried to drive between her and the right front fender of the van. Sharan stepped nimbly aside, hands halfway up the taped handle of the well-used bat, and hit him on the front of the helmet as the Electra-Glide roared by, jolting him in a backward somersault out of the saddle.

The Electra-Glide struck the high bumper of the Ready-Mix truck and flipped wide open across the turn lane, then went skidding to the opposite side of the road, shedding chromed bolt-ons and an exhaust pipe. Sharan glanced at her bike, fearful of fire. How much was she going to be out of pocket trying to get it up and running again? There was a high deductible on her insurance, at least five hundred dollars. Angrily she turned to the thief and pinned him to the asphalt, fat end of the bat pressing against his solar plexus. His face shield had popped off. He had a nosebleed. He was dazed from the impact and from the hard fall. She still didn't know who he was: friend of a friend of somebody who lived at the mobile home park, maybe. She kicked his feet wide apart and leaned on the bat until he hollered. Sharan was as lean as a bicycle racer but strong, five feet ten inches tall, her height giving her good leverage. He'd hurt his shoulder. One thing was for sure: there was no fight in him.

"Just stay put until the cops show up and sort this out," she told the Electra-Glide thief. She glanced up then and saw Jesse grinning at her from the van. She grinned back, but halfheartedly, perspiration running down her cheeks while traffic piled up and passersby gaped at the scene, searching for meaning, as if it were impromptu theater, or a religious tableau.

Ryan McClendon lingered inside the garage of the Chevron station at one corner of U.S. 78 and Gun Club Road watching the incident play itself out, drinking canned iced tea and mopping his forehead. No breeze and the afternoon temperature in the low nineties. A fire truck showed up first, who knew why, maybe because there was a station only a couple of blocks away and the wrecked Harley was smoking. Then two units from the sheriff's department, paramedics and an ambulance, followed by state cops, who had a hysterical woman with them. Apparently the mother of the kid in the baseball uniform, the way she hugged him and carried on. The kid kept saying in a disgusted voice, "Jeez, *Mom*." It was an interesting scene, but violence is always interesting.

For the most part he kept his eyes on the tall woman with the prosthetic hand who had done such an efficient job of relieving the redneck-type of a motorcycle that didn't look worth fighting over in the first place. Ryan liked the fact that she stayed calm, even when, inevitably, two of them escorted her to a squad car. No handcuffs—but of course there was no point in attaching a shackle to a prosthesis.

He'd made his usual weekly visit to his grandmother at the nursing home in Loganville and was heading back to his office in downtown Atlanta when the front end of his Lexus started to shimmy. Pulled into the Chevron where the problem was diagnosed as an improperly seated lug nut on the right front wheel that had nearly sheared off. Two mechanics were still trying to drill what was left of the nut off the wheel bolt.

As the sheriff's deputies were seating the tall woman in the back of the unit he tossed his empty Fruitopia can into a barrel and sauntered to the edge of the road, taking out his ID. He showed it to the overweight deputy sweating behind the wheel of the unit.

"Ryan McClendon, United States Attorney for the Northern District of Georgia."

He glanced at the woman behind the thick grillwork separating her from the front seat. Her head was up, but she wasn't studying anything. She seemed drained of energy, damp bruised-looking eyelids half-closed. She was a strawberry blond, lanky but not awkward-looking, kind of a tomboy beauty, but certainly no kid.

"Where're you taking her?" Ryan asked.

"Jail, partner," the deputy said, looking from the wallet card to Ryan himself, squinting a little in the merciless sun.

"It's not an idle question, deputy, and don't be taking that tone with me."

His own tone of voice caused the woman in the back seat to look at him, mildly curious.

"Sorry," the deputy said grudgingly. "She's going to the Jubilation County sheriff's office. This is Jubilation County, which I reckon you didn't know, Sir."

"What's she charged with?"

"Couldn't tell you."

The woman said in a clear unemotional voice, deeper than he had expected, "They'll likely start with theft by taking and kidnapping. But I didn't know the boy was in the car, or I wouldn't have—" She made a fist on one thigh and grimaced slightly, commenting on her rashness and subsequent folly. She was one of those few redheads, he had noticed, who could lay on a tan and not resemble a speckled trout.

"What's your name?" Ryan asked her.

"Sharan Norbeth."

"Norbett?"

She spelled both names for him, carefully.

"Do you have a lawyer, Sharan?"

"No. Maybe. I'll probably call Kennesaw Wilkie." She took a deep breath that turned into a sigh. "But he's probably off fishing somewhere."

A hard-eyed woman deputy came toward the unit, saying to Ryan, "Sir, step away from there, please."

Ryan asked Sharan, "What did the guy on the bike do to you?"

"It's my iron. He stole it."

"Sir, I don't want to have to tell you again—"

Ryan smiled at Sharan Norbeth and stepped back from the sheriff's car.

"Accept some advice. Don't open your mouth again unless there's counsel with you."

"Thank you," Sharan said. "But I've been there." She turned her head slightly to look at him through the side window. Her eyes were so bright her sandy lashes seemed to disappear in that blue inquisitive blaze. The woman deputy gave Ryan a brush-back stare before getting into the front seat. He passed his handkerchief, which was now a little soggy, over his sweltering forehead and watched as they drove east toward whatever the seat of Jubilation County was. He couldn't remember; Georgia had more counties—159 of them—than any other state in the union except Texas. Obsolete little fiefdoms in which pissant politicians quietly munched away at the tax dollar.

The Electra-Glide had been moved from the eastbound lane of Gun Club Road to the side of the Chevron's garage pending impoundment by the sheriff's department. Ryan looked it over while he thought about Sharan Norbeth, wondering what it was, beyond her considerable physical appeal, that he found so memorable about her. The artificial hand came as a shock, of course, but after a few minutes it wasn't something he dwelled on or pitied her for. She had committed what under the circumstances should be simple assault—no criminal purpose—but if the biker's injuries turned out to be severe it could go to aggravated. One to twenty in this state. She had reacted with dignity to the consequences, no defensive tantrum or shrill accusations. She had made what she considered a necessary explanation and refused to say more. Obviously Norbeth possessed a temper and a maverick sense of justice, but also she had a sense of self-worth. *Thank you, but I've been there.* Been where? In the joint? Or maybe she was talking about a background in law or law enforcement—her expert handling of the Little League baseball bat, only a half swing, not trying to take his head off, and her correct usage of "theft by taking" according to the Criminal Code of Georgia—Ryan began to feel a resonant excitement. He just might have found the right woman, he thought, for someone who could do him a great deal of good when the next vacancy occurred in the Federal District Court, his next step on the way to the Supreme Court of the United States.

In the garage they were nowhere near finished with his car. Ryan decided to put his waiting time to good use by establishing a relationship with the District Attorney of Jubilation County.

TWO

LEAVE IT TO CLEAVER

Coleman Dane left his office at the Justice Department in Washington shortly before seven o'clock and took a government jet from Andrews Air Force Base to Atlanta's Peachtree Dekalb Airport. ETA 10:20 P.M. He was accompanied on the trip south by a staff assistant named Fitzie, whom he appreciated for her brains and loyalty, and a former FBI official who had helicoptered, courtesy of the Justice Department, from his centuries-old retirement home on the Potomac River in southern Maryland to meet Dane.

"How are the renovations coming along?" the Deputy Attorney General asked, when they were airborne.

"Put it this way," Dayton Emmons said. "It would have cost about half as much to tear the house down and rebuild from the original plans."

"What, and lose all that historical significance?"

Emmons smiled painfully and accepted a cold Amstel from Fitzie. Coleman Dane was drinking premium Scotch, one ice cube, no water. He had taken off his loafers and loosened his tie. He wasn't interested in fashion: long ago he had adopted English traditional tailoring and stayed with it. Dark gray suits, shirts with spread collars and French cuffs. Dane was a rawboned, intense man with the workaholic's look of chronic impatience, one of those apostles of high seriousness whose dedication to the law of the land took precedence over personal ambition, which was tempered by the fact that he had been born rich. He was forty-four. Divorced. Two kids. Probably at the height of his career, Emmons thought. The ongoing conflict between personal and legal ethics and the DoJ's complexity, a medieval sprawl of largely unassociated departments with no central control, had discouraged many good men at the executive level. The average stay for deputy or assistant directors in the department was less than twenty months.

"How's Misty?" Emmons asked.

"Good. Real good. Bone marrow reports are all positive. She'll be six months in remission come Labor Day."

"What's the cure rate these days? About seventy percent?"

"Something like that. All we can do is pray."

"You should bring Misty and Griff down for a weekend before school starts. Dot keeps asking. We'll do some clamming, just putter around."

"Yeah, that would be great for them. I'm definitely going to do that, Day." Tugging at his tie, massaging closed eyelids. Dayton Emmons smiled sympathetically. The grind. The pressure. He knew. He was a little more than twenty years older than Dane, but already harboring a fortune in artificial body parts.

"Would you like a sandwich, Day? Fitzie loaded up from the commissary before we left."

"Rare roast beef on rye, touch of mustard," Emmons said to the discreetly posted Fitzie.

"Boss?"

"I don't know. Don't think so, right now. Bring me my laptop before you get busy in the galley, Fitz." He fidgeted in the wide leather seat opposite Emmons, unable to make himself comfortable. Emmons, white-haired and with a sailor's indelible tan, sprawled smiling in his own chair, beer in hand, a little drowsy at five hundred miles per hour, the somber red light of sunset on his brow.

"We may have a way in," Dane said finally, energized by the arrival of his ThinkPad. He turned his chair to a fold-down table and opened the portable computer where they could both see the color screen. He tapped away at the keyboard. Dayton Emmons reached into his shirt pocket for glasses that corrected his astigmatism.

"Pretty woman," he said in response to the sharp images—full face, right profile—on the active-matrix screen.

"Her name is Sharan Norbeth. Age thirty-five, single. Right now she's cooling out in a holding cell at the detention center in Jubilation County, Georgia. She's seen her lawyer, but they haven't transferred her to the jail. I don't want her there yet, anyway."

"What did she do?"

Dane told him.

"So?"

"The man she busted with a baseball bat may be an innocent party, as he claims, although it's fair to say he knew the bike was stolen."

"The kidnapping charge is bullshit," Emmons said thoughtfully. "Has she been in trouble before?"

"She got aggressive with a guy who had been romancing her. Tossed him into a fountain at the mall where she works sometimes. He claimed personal injury."

"Sharan has a temper."

"Her ex-suitor pressed charges. Misdemeanor battery. After the bargaining-down she paid a fine and did some weekend community work."

"One prior? What's she looking at currently? Did she cross a state line with the kid or the van?"

"No, but the van was a government vehicle. The boy's father is a soil scientist with the Department of Agriculture. Which gives me—"

"An edge." Emmons nodded. "Why her?"

"Sharan Norbeth is an amputee. Right hand and wrist, a couple of inches of forearm. She wears a prosthesis, courtesy of the U.S. government."

"She was in the service?"

"Comes from a military family. Army of the Cumberland, Seventh Cavalry, AEF, Big Red One." Dane tapped the keys again. "Her father was a career noncom. Two tours of Vietnam with a Ranger unit. One of two hundred and thirty-nine Medal of Honor winners in that war. Posthumous. Threw himself on a grenade to save some of his men. It's astounding how many Medal of Honor winners had the balls to do that."

"Her father's medal entitled Sharan to a free ticket to West Point."

"Class of Eighty-three. She was recruited by the Military Police, then joined the CID two years later. Undercover work in Germany, until—Jesus, Day, I'm telling you. Sharan Norbeth is just what we've been hoping for. Better. She has investigative experience."

"How did she lose the hand, Cole? Accident?"

Dane was silent for a few moments. He had returned Sharan Norbeth's image to the computer screen. "A drug bust didn't quite go off as planned. Some Albanians were operating a butcher shop in Old Sachsenhausen for cover. Maybe she got a little careless. Maybe one of the Albanians took her by surprise."

He glanced, a little sulkily, at Emmons, whose eyes were closed in contemplation.

"You're grinding your teeth, Cole."

Dane relaxed his jaw muscles. "I can tell what you're thinking. Post-trauma syndrome. Night sweats. The horror."

"She must have had psychological counseling."

"I don't have those files yet. I'm getting them."

"Under the circumstances—"

"You think she's wrong for it."

Dayton Emmons looked out, at dark blue clouds filled with a celestial light. "I'd have to talk to her. Events already indicate she's impulsive, too much of a risk taker. That may be what got her into nearly fatal trouble in Germany. There's bound to be a lot of anger. How does Sharan Norbeth really feel about herself? Right now she's sitting in a detention center cell hating the world. Almost as much as you do, Cole."

Emmons smiled as Fitzie brought him his sandwich on a tray. He ate most of it while Coleman Dane rigidly digested his analysis of Dane's motives.

"I hate that son of a bitch Dix Trevellian," Dane said finally. "I wake up nights thinking about him. Getting away with it. I want him. I'm going to get him. Whatever it takes, whatever I need to do—"

"Whoever you need to use," Emmons suggested, unnecessarily. "If I were Norbeth's lawyer—"

Dane's lips had thinned to an incandescent white line. "He's an old country warhorse. The best he could hope to do for her is two years."

"She won't serve a day's worth of that time, Cole. She's attractive, she had reasonable cause."

"Two years. Then I'll push for Alderson. Five on top of two. The Justice Department will come down on the back of her neck if she won't cooperate with me."

"Listen to you."

"I'm not waiting any longer. It's been almost three years. I'm bringing it to Dix Trevellian. He's going down, I swear it. All I need—"

"This isn't rational of you, Cole."

It seemed to wound Dane momentarily, to be thought irrational.

"I've considered the action very carefully. I'll be with Norbeth every step of the way."

"I promised your father I'd keep you out of trouble, but you're making it difficult. Two billion, and their money just keeps flowing in. Think about the protection it buys Dix Trevellian. Not that he needs it. For all his excesses, he's very clever when it comes to murder. If indeed there have been any murders."

"Felicia is dead."

"We don't know for sure."

"Doll Gaffney said she was no longer on the earthly plane."

Emmons shifted uncomfortably in his seat.

"Christ, Cole, a psychic—"

"The Bureau's used her," Dane said, not defensively but with a heads-up earnestness that denied refutation. "Police departments from Seattle to Memphis. She's pretty damn amazing. Felicia is dead, all right. My sister is ... dead." The word discharged so much blocked emotion he suffered a temporary attack of hiccups. Fitzie brought him a six-ounce bottle of Evian. He drank all of it slowly, and was calmer, but bleak. "All the others, probably." He looked frankly at Emmons. "I can't care as much about them. I only think about Felicia, and what she overcame to go on living, and how he—he took all the love she had to offer him, then *disposed* of her like garbage."

"You know what you really want, Cole. A body this time. And her blood still wet on Trevellian's hands."

Dane shook his head as if the image depressed him. "I *can* protect her. It doesn't have to be that way."

"What about the political implications? The Trevellians can apply a lot of pressure on the tender parts."

"I've already briefed AG. The operation's okay with him, as long as it's NMF." No memos filed. "The Director needs to be on my good side, since I'm about to go to bat for him before the Finance subcommittee on the digital telephony matter." Dane tried to look as if he hadn't surrendered his pride. "I've learned how to use my clout, Day."

"Your case would have to be built like a brick shithouse."

"I'm good at what I do. Let us not forget."

"It's high-octane stuff," Emmons reminded him, and was silent, thinking about his role in the risky scenario. "I can brief you on Norbeth, after I've had a couple of sessions with her. But who can predict? When I've explained Dix Trevellian to her—"

"That's why I invited you along."

"—based on everything I learned while I was running VICAP, then—tell you what my hunch is, Cole. Once she knows all that can be deduced about Dix Trevellian's personality, she'll be happy to do the time at Alderson or anywhere else, thank you very much."

The women's holding cell in one wing of the Jubilation County De-
tenion Center hadn't been designed for overnight stays. It was ten feet
square, with only an eight-inch-square window in the steel door, steel
bench seats bolted to the walls and worn smooth by a lot of restless
bottoms, a seatless toilet but no sink. Sharan had the cell to herself.
They'd brought in a cot for her, a small pillow and a blanket. Sharan
lay on the cot with her running shoes off and her left hand behind
her head, looking at the door. The cell shared a wall with the jail
laundry and another with the kitchen. The hall outside was quiet, a
blessing. She wondered if Bessie Chick had picked up her laundry in
town, and if Kennesaw Wilkie had gone by the mobile home park to
feed her cat, as he had promised. He seemed a little more vague and
prone to forget things since the last time she'd seen him. But at the
age of eighty-one he was better than the public defender of Jubilation
County, whoever he might be. She wondered if she might not have
reacted differently to the day's principal event if she hadn't spent part
of the morning arguing a disputed bill at the telephone company,
which had cut off her outgoing service.

She could hardly think about the trouble she was in. That
would be a lot like thinking about hell, when she was six years old.
She couldn't cope with the possibilities right now, defend herself
against the fear.

Couldn't sleep, either. They'd taken her Seiko along with her belt
and West Point ring. She didn't know the time, but the sky had been
dark for quite a while.

So the kid she'd bopped wasn't the thief, but he probably knew
who was. A gang of them, maybe. No trick to stealing a motorcycle,
even a big one. All you needed was muscle and a pickup truck. There
was no such thing as a foolproof security system, when the thief had
the leisure to work on it.

She didn't know why they were still keeping her on hold. Maybe
the jail was overbooked. First-appearance hearing tomorrow. How
much bail depended on the judge. She'd lived in the area going on
two years. A lot of friends from the Rising Fawn Mobile Home Community would vouch for her. That was a comfort. According to a
friendly deputy who had passed the word back to Sharan, they'd
called and come by the sheriff's office in the other wing since hearing
about her arrest. So had some of the guys from Prexy's Hawg Heaven.
Harley owners were the best damn people on earth. Maybe the judge

would release her on her own recognizance. Of course she didn't have steady employment. Sharan marshaled points in her favor. West Point graduate, twenty-second in her class, purple heart. So how to handle the judge—tears and regrets, a plea for leniency? It hadn't been murder. No real harm done. *Just let me out of here, I'll be good.*

Ham and cheese sandwich for dinner, potato salad with too much dill, but not bad for jail food. Never eat cold potatoes on a nervous stomach, however. She was going to have to try to move her balky bowels again before long, even though that was difficult for her, hunkered down peasant-fashion over a lidless toilet.

When she was agitated and uncomfortable, Sharan usually thought about faces. She had total recall of great portraits by great painters. Courbet, whom she'd fallen in love with the moment she laid eyes on his darkly soulful self-portrait in the Musee d'Orsay. Classically handsome, with the deeply romantic eyes of a youthful genius, a laborer's large, strong hands. Renoir's buxom, contented young women. Gauguin's brawny Tahitians. *Someday I want to do that . . .*

Sudden, overwhelming sorrow. Sense of failure, sense of doom. Her eyes burned wetly, and she closed them. *Defend yourself against the fear.* No, she would not feel bad about what she had done. Popped him just right with the baseball bat, otherwise he would have flown away again on her motorcycle. MP training, some kendo for sport, expert with any kind of club. She remembered the face of the boy in the van, impressed, grinning at her. His name was Jesse. She'd seen the exact same face somewhere else, not too long ago. The guileless bright eyes and snub nose. Haircut was different, though—Billy, Wally—sure, that was it. He looked just like the kid who'd played Wally on *Leave It to Beaver.* The old shows still around on one cable channel or another. Wally and the Beav. And their parents were— hold on a second—June, and, um, Ward. The famous double entendre. June to her husband: "Ward, you were a little hard on the Beaver last night." Then there was the obsequious blond boy with the ferret eyes. Eddie, the conniver, almost like one of the Cleavers himself. All of them more familiar, more kin to Sharan than her own messed-up family . . .

She dozed and dreamed herself among them. Impeccable June-mom, dinner on the table promptly at six, didn't smoke didn't drink didn't go out on dates in order to make car payments during the long stretches when she was left alone with the kids, or slug it out with her old man when both she and the Sarge were on a toot. Two adorable brothers who would never never wind up in juvenile court or one detox center after another, and finally: Dad, wholesome, humane, wise; she could curl up in his lap after supper and tell him all the secrets of her day, all the bitter bad hateful things, too, and he wouldn't get upset. He'd know just what to say to make all the hurts better, to make her laugh. And he would sternly discipline the boys when they got rowdy, invaded her room, did mean things like hide her hand where she couldn't find it, so that she had to use her left hand, the clumsy uncooperative left hand. Going sinistral meant using the other side of her brain, which caused severe headaches, such intense emotional anguish it would be a relief to die . . .

How did it happen? She and the Beav fooling around in the backyard with Wally's sharp tomahawk, that's how. Hold the balloon at arm's length, and— Oops. No blood this time, as in some of her other, more realistic nightmares, the silly little hand just lying there palm up in the green grass. Beav tried to put it back on with airplane glue but got it backwards. Ho-ho, leave it to Cleaver. Sarge was going to be real upset with both of them when he came home for supper; but of course she never saw him again. When he did come home it was in a closed coffin and there was this big to-do at Bragg, his Medal of Honor, the neatly folded flag in Mom's lap (Mom looking badly in need of a beer) and ritual guns firing crack-crack-craaack into the cemetery air . . .

The door to the holding cell was unlocked.

"Sharan?"

She raised up groggily from the cot. It was the deputy who had brought her supper at seven-thirty, a crew-cut kid with an interior lineman's neck and upper body who reminded Sharan of her brother Lyle. There was a woman deputy with him, a homely country girl with tobacco-spit freckles all over her face.

"Are you taking me somewhere?"

"Jest over to the courthouse," the woman said.

"What's going on?" She heard the courthouse clock tolling, but lost track. "What time is it?"

"Five minutes to midnight. That old clock has been sounding off early since Jesus made corporal."

"Why—"

"You need to come with us, that's all I know."

"Could you give me a few minutes? I have to—"

"Surely," the woman said, nudging the other deputy, and they withdrew, leaving Sharan to wonder why she needed to be appearing at the courthouse in the middle of the night. She shivered; too much air-conditioning. Tried to move her bowels. Knots in the colon. Painful. Thirty-five years old. She was already a pitiful wreck.

The courthouse was a block away. There was a freight train sitting on one set of tracks that diagonally divided downtown Tombetta. A single pickup truck moving slowly on their side of the street as Sharan walked between the deputies. Otherwise they were alone. The night was muggy and still. They had given her a cherry Coke to drink in a paper cup. Sharan let a piece of ice melt on her tongue. The deputies complained about the discomfort of having to wear protective vests in the summer's heat. Lightning flickered in clouds higher than the Himalayas.

Lights in two windows on the second floor of the courthouse, south side. Black custodian polishing a brass stair railing inside. He didn't look at them as they walked up the marble steps, scooped out nearly an inch in the middle from a hundred years of use. Echoes beneath the rotunda's dome. Down a hall. Shadows behind the pebbled glass of a door. County Prosecutor. Sharan's pulse was faster. They went in.

A stout fortyish woman with dyed black hair was eating from a paper plate of microwaved Krystals at the receptionist's desk. She looked up at Sharan without expression. A young man, probably still in his twenties but balding, was at the water cooler. He looked around, a little red-eyed, as if he was up well past his bedtime. Wrinkled tan suit, knit tie askew—Jubilation County probably the last place in the civilized world where knit ties were still a fashion statement. Sharan thought she had seen him at the sheriff's office when she was brought in.

"Hi," he said. "I'm Roy Starks, District Attorney for Jubilation County."

Sharan sighed. "Is my lawyer here?"

Starks looked a little surprised. "Mr. Wilkie? No. Do you want him here?"

"That depends. What am I—"

"There are some people down from Washington who want to talk to you, Sharan."

"Washington?"

"The Deputy Attorney General of the U-nited States," Starks said, making an effort not to sound reverential.

Sharan stared at him.

"I'll let them know you're here," said the woman who had been eating Krystal cheeseburgers. "By the way, I'm Fitzie."

Sharan nodded as if that explained one of the essential mysteries of the universe. Fitzie licked her fingertips and went to one of two office doors off the reception room, opening it enough to get her head inside.

"They're using my office," Starks explained to Sharan. He honked into a handkerchief, as if the blades of the creaky ceiling fan had stirred up an allergy.

"Do you want to tell me what this—"

"I don't know," Starks said, with a shrug and a bemused smile. "Would you care to have some water?"

"No." Murmurs from the District Attorney's usurped sanctum. Fitzie turned and beckoned with a smile.

"Right this way, please, Miss Norbeth. That name's English, isn't it? Names are a hobby of mine. I'm kind of a nut on genealogy."

"It's Welsh," Sharan said. She was more confused than intimidated, and now with a surge of blood to her cheeks. Her eyes flashed but she said nothing. Fitzie held the door for her, smiling. Sharan went in.

Both window shades pulled down. Single lamp with a metal shade on one corner of the desk. Window air conditioner on low, but still noisy. One man, sixty or so, sitting in an armchair in a shadowy corner with his tanned spotted hands, lighted like the centerpiece of an altar, folded on his midriff. Hard to make out his face, which was above the oval of lamplight cast his way.

But the man behind the desk was easy to see. Lean; about six-two; slicked-back graying hair; black, wide-awake, searching eyes. High cheekbones, deep brackets around his mouth. He had the warrior look. Not necessarily a soldier. But someone with an avid interest in territory. The territory of the ego, maybe. His suit looked like money.

"Please sit down, Miss Norbeth. I'm Coleman Dane. This gentleman is Dayton Emmons."

Sharan looked at the shadowy man, then at the cracked red leather in the offered chair directly in front of the desk but angled a little to the left. She moved sideways into the chair, then turned it squarely to the desk. Feet on the floor, back straight, hands in her lap. She looked only at Coleman Dane. He, obviously, was dealing.

"You're in a great deal of trouble right now," Dane said after a few moments.

"Why are my troubles worth your time?" Sharan asked him.

Dane reacted with a slight contraction of his brows and a quick glance at his partner, barely moving his head. Most women would find him handsome, Sharan thought. But he would be hard on all of his women. A glint of amusement at her reply? He seemed to be approving of her, as if she cared.

"Speaking frankly."

"Please do."

"I see you as someone who can help me with an ongoing problem I have."

"What do you know about me?"

"Everything that's a matter of record. Of course—" Another flick of his gaze toward the shadowy man. "—we'll want to get better acquainted."

Sharan's mouth was as dry as if it were packed with gauze after dental surgery. She tried to work up some spit. Pulse fast, blood zinging to her temples. She hated the way Dane was studying her, as if she were a trophy he had already pursued and shot.

"What is it you want me to do?"

"Investigate a possible criminal act. Or acts."

"What do you mean, 'possible'?"

"We have no evidence that a criminal act has taken place. We only strongly suspect."

"*We* being the Justice Department?"

"Among other government agencies, here and abroad."

"The FBI? Treasury?" Dane's expression gave nothing away. "I did undercover work for the CID. Drug cases. I was good at it. But that was—almost seven years ago. I'm retired."

"We know, Sharan."

"Everybody makes that mistake. Calling me *Share*-un. I'm used to it. But the correct pronunciation is Sha-*rahn*. My mother named me for the Vale of Sharan in Connemara. She was born there."

Dane listened gravely.

"I assume you have the FBI and your own investigators to work up the case you want to prosecute."

"The situation is complex. Unexplained disappearances in widely separated locales, involving citizens of several countries, lacks a necessary imperative, particularly when there's no task force involved, a common authority to designate a primary suspect."

"I'm on partial disability. Nine hundred sixty-seven bucks a month for the rest of my life, plus medical. A new glove every couple of years, the latest in SOF technology. If I had lost both hands, I'd get twice as much. Fortunately I was only half-stupid."

"How did it happen, Sharan?"

"That's better, but not quite. Hit the last syllable a little harder. Sorry. I don't talk about it. Not to you, or anybody else."

"I understand."

"Are we going to continue this?"

"Are you in a hurry to go back to jail?"

"No."

"Then we'll continue."

Dane opened a folder with a Justice Department seal on the cover.

"August 10, 1987. Almost ten years ago today. Full moon. A twenty-seven-year-old actress named Thursday Childs failed to show up for rehearsal of an off-Broadway play at a Sheridan Square theater. No trace of her was ever found." Dane paused, raising an eyebrow. She'd been waiting for that. He seemed to be the sort to raise one eyebrow inquiringly. It looked like kind of a neat trick. Sharan didn't say anything. There was a photograph attached to the page he'd been reading from, but she couldn't make much of the face from where she sat. Blond kid with a fluffy hairdo.

Page two.

"Astrid Wulff," Dane said. "West German distance runner, silver medal winner in the two-thousand-meter race at the eighty-four Olympics. Disappeared while training on a foggy morning near her Black Forest home. April 17, 1988. New moon. Has not been seen since then."

Page three.

"Kerry Rogers. Full-blooded Cherokee and a gifted violinist. En route to Edinburgh, Scotland, from London on 29 December, 1989. One day after the new moon. Reportedly she left the train when it stopped at Nottingham. Vanished."

Sharan suppressed a shudder.

"May 28, 1991. Buenos Aires, Argentina. Full moon. An internationally known theatrical designer named Caterina Chiado left a party at the flat of a friend in the Recoleta. She left alone. It was raining. She was observed accepting a ride from someone in a white Mercedes Benz, someone she apparently knew, but Señora Chiado was never seen after that."

Page five.

"Robin Smallwood. Novelist and poet. Trevellian Prize winner for her memoir of growing up black in a Jamaican mountain village. Left her apartment in Philadelphia on July 14, 1992, to walk to a veterinarian's office two blocks away, and hasn't been seen since. The moon was full that day."

Dane paused then, a hand to his forehead, mouth pursed in deepening brackets. He turned to what seemed to be the last page in the folder.

"Felicia Dane. Explorer and ethnobotanist. Trevellian Prize winner, 1993. Last seen on the corner of Eighth Avenue and Fifty-fourth Street on her way to Carnegie Hall, the night of December 2, 1994. Snow on the streets, but the sky was clear and there was a new moon."

"Felicia Dane?"

"My sister. Two years younger. We were—always close. She's probably the most courageous person I've ever known in my life."

"But now you think she's—"

"Dead? I'm convinced of that."

"And the other women, too."

"I have no doubts."

"Why? Is there a connection?"

"Persuasive, in my view."

"I wonder if I could have a drink of water."

Dane nodded, got up and went to the office door. Sharan shifted her attention to the other man. He was smiling at her.

"Don't you talk?" she said, a little crossly.

"I haven't meant to be rude."

"What is it you do? Are you with the Justice Department?"

"I'm retired from the FBI."

"Women disappear all the time."

"Unfortunately, yes."

"But these women—they were all well-known, weren't they? Trevellian Prizes—that's big-time."

"They were all quite accomplished in their respective fields."

"They had—they have—families? People who care about them? Who are still looking for them?"

"Yes," Emmons said, a little sadly. "Thousands of hours have been devoted to some of these cases. I couldn't say how much money—most of it for private investigators. Local authorities have these tremendous caseloads. They lack manpower. Often they lack motivation in the event of a mysterious disappearance. They want tangibles—a ransom note, a body. People do walk away from their lives, start over with a fresh perspective, a new lover."

"Is that what you do now? You're a private investigator?"

"Only a consultant. My family and Cole's family have known each other since before the turn of the century."

Dane came back with two small paper cups of water, one for himself.

"Sorry, there wasn't anything larger."

"Thank you. This will do."

He sat down behind the desk again.

"The best investigative talent money can buy," Sharan said with a glance at Emmons, but her attention was focused on Coleman Dane. "So what is it about me that had you rush down here from Washington?"

Dane crushed his empty cup and dropped it in a wastebasket.

"Six women, all of them accomplished and attractive to the same man, himself charismatic and possibly a genius, but erratic and apparently subject to a compulsion we have no name for. 'Serial killer' doesn't really get it."

"Oh, God."

"Thursday Childs had hereditary arthritis that eventually would have made her a helpless cripple. Astrid Wulff was a hemophiliac. Kerry Rogers was born with Ehlers-Danlos syndrome, a connective tissue disorder, which coincidentally gave her the long and spiderlike fingers that helped her play so beautifully. Caterina Chiado survived a plane crash that killed a hundred and twenty people, but she was severely crippled during her escape from the wreckage. Robin Smallwood was stricken with Stargardt's disease when she was eight years old. Stargardt's is an incurable, genetically caused degenerative eye disorder; one in ten victims also becomes deaf." Dane paused, and there was something more than expressionless about him: static, enduring, oddly menacing in the fullness of his grief. "Felicia—my sister suffered severe exposure on Aconcagua in Argentina, which cost her part of a foot and the sight of one eye. She wore a black patch, which didn't diminish her beauty. It seemed to make her that much more desirable to the man who, we believe, had affairs with all six of them."

"Please don't tell me."

"Who apparently is very attracted to women who are beautiful, talented and flawed in some profound way."

Sharan sat there for longer than she knew she should, then got up with an expression of pain. "Would you excuse me? I'm having some problems and I need to find a bathroom."

"That door right there."

She barely got herself ready when her bowels let go in a torrent they probably could hear through the closed door. When it was over she put her head down, tingling and cold, feeling exhausted and near tears.

After ten minutes there was a knock at the door.

"Coming."

Dane had thoughtfully brought her another cup of water.

"You've put it together by now, haven't you? What do you say, Sharan?"

"What do I say? *Never.* It's crazy. I wouldn't do it."

Dane tapped a pencil eraser against the desk blotter, smiling, benign but uncompromising.

"How does it work, Sharan? The artificial hand, I mean."

"It's a sense-of-feel prosthesis. Transducers on the thumb and forefinger control a small servomotor that operates a cuff around the residual arm. Pressure from the cuff tells the brain how much pressure is exerted by the thumb and finger. I also have a hot-and-cold sensory system: thermopile electrodes operating off two nine-volt batteries. But I still don't do much with the new hand. When I was struggling with less sophisticated prostheses I switched over to being left-handed. It's the hand I paint with now. In fact, I didn't paint at all until I was left-handed."

"The right hemisphere being the imagistic brain. Visual and spatial abilities. Also the site of the oblique intellect. Insight, intuition."

"You know more about it than I do." She drank some water. She wasn't sweating, her skin was too cold. She felt nauseated.

"I'm not prepared to take no for an answer, Sharan."

"I'm sorry about your sister. But this—is *not* something I could carry off. For one thing, I'm not particularly good with men."

"You don't like men?"

"I didn't say that. I just don't have much confidence in relationships these days."

"How's it going with that Ranger instructor from Benning?"

It was an interrogation technique she would have employed herself, not so long ago. How quickly they could get to know you, and know just how to use what they knew. She refused to reveal annoyance and shook her head negligently, her Carolina accent thickening a little, more brown sugar added to the slow-cooked sweet potato.

"JimTom? Well, it's been off and on, mostly. He wanted to get married, but I—"

"Don't have any confidence in relationships. That's good, actually. To be a little nervous, uncertain. It's disarming."

"You know you can't force me to do this. You don't even have jurisdiction."

"I've got a piece of you, Sharan. Enough to get you four or five years at the Women's Correctional Facility in Alderson, West Virginia. There's no early release in the Federal Penitentiary system, Sharan. You do at least eighty-five percent of your time."

"A piece of me?"

"That vehicle you stole—"

"Borrowed."

"Stole, was government property."

This was news to Sharan. She put a hand to her forehead, rubbing slowly, eyes turning bleak.

"You'll never prove intent. We'll let a jury decide."

Dane shrugged. "Okay. And while you're tied up in state and federal courts, figure a year at least, postponements and so forth, you'll be out on bond and under house arrest. You know what that's like, don't you? Think you can keep up the payments on your doublewide with your government disability check?"

After a considerable pause Sharan said, "I count for shit, don't I?"

"You're very important to me, Sharan," Dane said soothingly. "The most important person in my life right now."

Sharan drew a long breath.

"I think my lawyer should know about this conversation."

"That old fuddy-duddy? Sure. Tell him anything you like."

"I'll be getting a different lawyer. Somebody who's not afraid to play hardball."

Dane looked amazed. "With us? With me? I don't care who you hire, my dick is bigger than his dick."

Sharan said, exasperated, "Take me back to lockup."

"Okay. The deputies are waiting outside. No problem. Try to get a night's sleep while you think it over."

"I won't think anything over."

Coleman Dane looked at Sharan, and looked at the door. She got up slowly.

"I mean, you just come whizzing down here from Washington, expecting—"

"But I was never here. You never spoke to me. Sharan Norbeth, who's that?"

"The most important person in your life, sixty seconds ago."

"Oh," he said, smiling, as if he had just remembered, or she had rekindled his interest.

"It's what I resent most, the wham-bam-you're-screwed routine."

"I promise you. We'll never be out of touch. You'll be as safe as churches."

"Some wannabe Aryan Brothers burned one down in my neighborhood two weeks ago."

"Bad analogy." Dane lowered his head, revealing the beginning of a bald spot. "Well, good night again."

"Does he work for the government?" Sharan said.

Dane looked up, then at Emmons, and back to Sharan.

"Six women missing, in four countries. That means, accepting the hypothesis that there is one man responsible for these disappearances, that he gets around. Enjoys some sort of prominence. A government official, international businessman, maybe an entertainer."

"He's an architect. Offices in all four countries."

"Well off, possibly rich."

"I'm rich. He's in another universe from me. Family money."

"Jet-setter. Huge ego. A lot of women. But no bimbos. He's interested in achievers. Sports, the arts. He doesn't feel threatened by women with brains. Or does he?"

"Do you want to sit down again, Sharan?"

"No. I want to go home."

"Okay," Dane said. "You can go home. Federal marshals will watch over you the rest of the night. At nine tomorrow morning you'll be driven to the courthouse for your first-appearance hearing. Prosecution will accept your counsel's recommendation that you be released on your own recognizance. You'll be nolle prossed immediately after your court appearance. Do you know what I'm talking about?"

Sharan said with a shrug, "I go free, but you have the right to refile anytime within sixty days. Should I have a change of heart."

There was silence in the office. It lasted. They studied each other, from a fresh point of view, newly linked together in a chain-gang of consequence.

"There's something else I—require."

Dane smiled slightly and leaned back in his swivel chair, arms clasped behind his head.

"Do you know who Jules Brougham is?"

The name seemed familiar to Dane. It took him several seconds.

"Brougham Gallery on Fifty-seventh?"

"Yes."

"What about him?"

"I want a show of my work there."

"Uh-huh. Well, that could take some arranging."

"I know you'll find a way. You're the great arranger."

"Some purpose to this, other than feeding your artistic ego?"

"Think about it," Sharan said. "I don't travel in the same circles as our guy. But I'll bet Jules Brougham does."

Coleman Dane looked at Emmons, beaming now.

"What'ya say, Dayton? Can I pick 'em? Isn't she something?"

Sharan paused with her hand on the doorknob.

"Good night," she said, "Mr. Dane. And fuck you."

She didn't wait to see his expression change. Maybe it didn't change at all. He already knew she was afraid of him.

THREE

COMANCHE
FORGET-ME-NOTS

Dempsey Wingo had been drinking fairly steadily for the better part of two days when he got it into his head that he needed to crash his ex-wife's party at Trevellian House.

He was pissing between parked cars in the gutter outside Barefoot Perkins' tavern when the idea came to him. Sometimes he got his best ideas while relieving himself. And a few of his worst. The obscure street, in the least civilized part of the West Village, was almost deserted. Nobody would have paid attention to him anyway. There was no street etiquette to violate in this neighborhood, the only rule being mind your own business and watch the back of your neck. Dempsey had no problems with muggers or the randomly violent. By daylight he was formidable; at night he could be scary. Six-two, about 230 these days. Smoothed-down raven hair, center-parted, two wings framing huge cheekbones. He had an icon's spacious brow, a chin like a butcher's block. In between his youthful good looks lingered, much diminished by adventuring and betrayals of the soul.

Barefoot's tavern was the latest and most remote of several he had visited, seeking the company of artists who weren't painting and writers who weren't writing. Inactivity brought out the craziness in most of them. Brooding on their lack of inspiration, shuffling through the assortment of available women in places like Chumley's and the Horse, arguing esthetics, picking fights with one another. The downtown Art Scene. Locations and the names of the dwindling supply of

Village bars changed, but not the Scene. Have a few belts, close your eyes in any of the watering holes and hear Hart Crane or the young de Kooning or Jack Kerouac. The air so rich and warm with bullshit you could grow tomatoes in it.

What Dempsey heard now was familiar laughter as a couple of literary groupies came out of Barefoot's with their catch of the evening, Peter Troy, a young novelist with good credentials from the MFA crowd. Promotable looks, prestige publisher, impressive notices from reviewers who had come up through the same farm system as Troy to what passed, these days, for the literary major leagues. Two novels and a book of poetry before he was thirty; now he had dried up. Dempsey had talked with him earlier. The kid wasn't a drinker, his was a controlled-substance generation, but he was paying homage to a sturdier tradition. He had actually read Fitzgerald, a talent that may have scared him. At the moment, in the clutches of the sex debs, he looked abnormally pale and sounded incoherent. It was only a little past eleven o'clock. Dempsey had the notion that the sex debs might not appreciate just how bad off Troy was, and before the night was over feed him something that would put him in cardiac arrest.

So he zipped up and sauntered over to the women who were trying to keep Troy on his feet and said, "Hey, thanks, I'll take him now."

One of the debs had thick glossy hair like warm tar, a provocative petulance and eyes drowsy with carnal mischief.

"He's with us."

Dempsey said, "I promised his mother I'd have him home in time for Vespers."

The other deb said, "Vespers was hours ago, like, at sunset. I was born Catholic. So forget about it, you don't even know his mother."

She had the blonde stubble of a drastic haircut and hydrangea-blue eyes. She wore a tight tube top through which her nipples and nipple rings showed plainly. She looked about as clean as a sink trap.

"Not kidding you, I guess, Cuddles. But he's coming with me anyway."

Peter Troy raised his curly head slightly and said something that sounded like "shitless."

The dark-haired deb said, "Don't I know you? You been around the Deshazio Gallery lately? I work there."

The other one said after a thoughtful reappraisal, "No, he's a writer. He wrote a play or something. Won a prize. That was a long time ago, wasn't it, dude?"

Dempsey felt an unexpected ache in the dry bones of ambition. "Yeah, a long time ago. Want to hand the kid over? He's not going to be very entertaining the rest of the night."

"Fuck you, Maggot Eye," said the first deb. "What, you looking to get into his pants?"

"Shitless," Peter Troy said earnestly, as if he were struggling to communicate the essence of a brilliant idea.

"Let's not be hostile," said the second deb.

"No, let's not," Dempsey said agreeably.

"You could come with us if you want. Have some laughs. I'm Nickie Rae, and I'd like for you to meet Chantal, my roommate."

"I'm a performance artist," Chantal said, posturing a little.

Nickie Rae accepted the cue to establish her own creative identity. "I was, like, with a band, you know, but now I'm doing poetry."

Peter Troy held himself erect for five full seconds and said clearly, "To be recognized as a poet is to be shitless in the outhouse of fame."

"Finally got that out," Nickie Rae said admiringly.

Maybe, Dempsey thought, the boy had genuine talent after all.

"If we're gonna be a foursome," Chantal said to Nickie Rae, "you take *him*." She shuddered superstitiously. "I don't like the looks of that eye, man."

"Stop talking about my eye," Dempsey advised her. "Nothing wrong with it. It just happens to be a different color from the other one."

"It looks like a fucking pea. What's that from, defective genes or something?"

"But I'll bet a lot of women get turned on by it," Nickie Rae said diplomatically. "You know?"

"No defective genes in my family. My great-great-grandfather was Quanah Parker."

"That sounds like the answer to a Trivial Pursuit question."

Peter Troy's knees were mush. They were having a hard time getting him to stand up, and beginning to look as if he wasn't worth the trouble.

Dempsey scooped the medium-sized Troy out of their grasp and piled him on one broad shoulder.

"One of the last of the great war chiefs," Dempsey said. "Cochise. Geronimo. Crazy Horse. Quanah Parker."

"You putting him in your car?" Nickie Rae asked. "Better make sure he barfs first. That's us, the No Radio sign. Also the Stolen License Plate sign. Also no windshield wipers. I mean, why drive a good car in the city? Like, forget about it."

"Where do you sweeties live?"

"Twenty-sixth and Ninth. It's called the Palm d'Or."

"You lead, I'll follow," Dempsey said, having no intention of following them anywhere.

He put Peter Troy in the front seat of his Bondo Special, a twenty-year-old Plymouth that had once been blue but was now, in the gritty poisonous-looking light of the city street, a shade of purple. He settled into the bead-covered seat behind the wheel and started the engine, the one thing about his Bondo Special that made it worth stealing. The chromed V-8 thrummed, the car trembled.

He was pulling away from the curb when a big new Suburban with a rack of lights mounted at the roofline came roaring around the corner from Seventh Avenue, as startling a sight in the urban dreariness as the Batmobile. Dempsey had a premonition. Although he drank a lot, he never got very drunk. And he seldom forgot there was a price on his head.

"Trivial Pursuit," Peter Troy said, in another moment of semilucidity.

"I don't think so," Dempsey said, with another glance at the oncoming Suburban. "If they're who I think they are, these guys are damn serious." He hit the gas and took off, back tires biting into the old Nieuw Amsterdam paving bricks, leaving stripes ten inches wide.

Dempsey made a wrong-way left turn onto Christopher, then a right onto Hudson, heading uptown, not much traffic at this point. He didn't have anything in mind except to keep as much distance as possible between himself and the Kreggs while he ditched them.

"Kafka," Peter Troy said. He was tilting one way on the seat, then another, crowding Dempsey as he turned abruptly off Hudson into the heart of the Village, the rack of lights on the Suburban blazing in his rearview mirror as the Suburban zigged and zagged in pursuit. Dempsey pushed him away and went south on Bleecker. Troy's eyes were open, but he was as unfocused as a blind man.

For a few moments Dempsey had lost the Suburban in the Village maze, the tight little tree-lined streets of walkups and townhouses. He turned again, catching the curb, bouncing off, just missing the rear end of a car parked illegally close to the intersection. Wrong street. There was a block party ahead, still going strong. Barricades. Dempsey looked for a driveway, catching sight of the Suburban again, southbound, clearing the intersection. He slowed and swung into a driveway, blocking the sidewalk, and killed the lights.

"This has been swell of you, old man," Peter Troy said. He'd been reading Fitzgerald, all right.

"No problem."

"Peter Troy. And you're?"

"Dempsey Wingo. We met earlier." He saw the Suburban again, backing up, stopping in the intersection. They weren't sure. Then the rear doors opened; two men jumped out, looked around, conferred. The Suburban drove away. The men split up; one of them, on the small side but with the same slightly hunched, loping stride that characterized all of the Kreggs, including the women, headed down the middle of the street toward the driveway Dempsey had appropriated, looking around, not seeing the Bondo Special right away. He was wearing a flat-crowned black hat with a wide brim and a fringed black shirt.

"I think I'm living at the Dakota now," Peter Troy said.

"I'll be a few minutes," Dempsey told him. "Why don't you take a nap?"

"Didn't we meet at Slim Churchward's house in Amagansett? I believe that's where I was in July. Or was I at Tanglewood?" Troy looked around, sweating, his mind suddenly on a different tack. "Cockroaches," he said uneasily. "Big ones. The woods were full of them."

"You and White Lady must have been on bad terms that week," Dempsey said. "Lock your door." He got out of the Bondo Special, leaving the motor running. He glanced at the street scene. Rhythms of the night, paper lanterns like coy moons among the trees. A Zydeco band. The boastful, lusty music, falling somewhere between a chantey and boogie-woogie.

If he'd been cold sober he wouldn't have tried it, opting instead to join the crowd at the block party, maneuver his stalker into a doorway, a cellar stairwell. Or take him to the dark rooftops. Instead he did the stalking.

The young man had a walkie in his right hand. He froze when he saw Dempsey coming, spoke urgently into the walkie, backed up, spoke again. His blond hair came down from beneath his hat like water over a spillway, reaching his shoulders. Little mean gleam of blue eyes in the bristly face. He had no fear in him. He switched hands with the walkie and, still backing away, went for the reserve knife in the sheath between his shoulder blades. Dempsey skinned his first, right-handed, left hand yanking off his two-inch-wide leather belt, giving it a quick windup. The sterling silver rodeo buckle weighed a pound and a half, and the belt was three feet long. He popped the young man below one ear as quick as a rattlesnake, which splintered his jawbones before he went sprawling between two parked cars.

The walkie he'd lost his grip on lay in the street, saying, "Woodrow? Where're you, goddammit?"

In stride, Dempsey scooped the walkie up with two fingers, pressed the send key and said, "You want him, come get him."

Somebody was running already, footsteps not far away. Dempsey closed in on Woodrow, who, in spite of shock, was trying to scramble up. Gristle-tough, like all of the Kreggs. His hat had fallen off. Dempsey picked him up one-handed by the back of his collar and ran him headfirst into a wrought-iron fence. The fence reverberated like a dull bell; dogs barked inside the brownstone. Woodrow's head was partly jammed between curlicue bars of the fence, one peeled-back ear hanging him up. Dempsey's Green River hunting knife, hand-honed with Washita and Arkansas stones until the edge was quicker than a scalpel, took the ear off with a stroke. He immobilized Woodrow between bars with a hard shove, turned and caught a glimpse of a second Kregg running in the street toward them. Two days making the rounds with no pretense of caution, he'd all but invited this confrontation. Dempsey's blood was up; he made a keening, singing noise deep in his throat, something ancestral. Ominous. Using the hood of a Lexus as a springboard, he came down in the street in front of the man.

Mordecai Kregg's weapon of choice was a bullwhip, wrapped around his right shoulder. He unlimbered the blacksnake with practiced speed and cracked it, catching Dempsey on the arm near his left elbow. Dempsey winced, lowered a shoulder and dove, cutting Mordecai down at the knees.

There was a screech of brakes in the street behind them as the Suburban reappeared. Dempsey also heard the deep, perfect-pitch revving of the Bondo Special's 454-cubic-inch street rod block.

They floundered in the street like two drowning men, but Dempsey, on the attack, had the advantage and also the edge, which was quickly against Mordecai's throat. He smelled, as most of them did, like chew tobacco and bad teeth. Dempsey wasn't thinking, only reacting. Both of them yelling simultaneously. Mordecai still holding the whip as Dempsey, sinews popping, knife under Mordecai's chin, dragged him backwards and away from the Suburban, oncoming, slow, the lights half-blinding both men.

"Drop it, drop it, drop it!"

Mordecai let the blacksnake slip from his hand.

"Tell them to get away, get away, get away!"

"Goddamngoddamngoddammmm!"

"You want your throat cut I'll do it I'll fucking do it call them off you son of a bitch!"

"Godgodgodgogogetout of here he's fucking you're fucking cutting me!"

"Why the fuck don't you people stay in North Carolina where you fucking belong!"

The Suburban started backing up as Dempsey dragged Mordecai farther down the street, his left arm locking Mordecai's left arm so that it was straight up over his head, left hand pushing Mordecai's head sharply back, the exposed throat scored red now from the inadvertent action of the knife blade, skin deep but a sixteenth of an inch from the carotid artery, which was running as full as a storm drain in a hurricane. Pulses pumping, heart jumping, skin flushed from exertion and an evil helpless rage. They were both enraged, stoked, in bondage to the luck of the moment.

Dempsey heard screams, a call for police. It was a respectable neighborhood, all high-priced homes, architectural significance, pretty little gardens tucked away. He looked back, saw no one—but his Bondo Special was on the move, bouncing out of the driveway, backing into the curb across the street, then backing toward him, gaining speed, veering into parked cars, returning to the curb on the other side. Almost out of control, as if a chimpanzee were learning to drive. Or a bombed-out Peter Troy.

Mordecai Kregg was trying to dig the heels of his boots into the street surface. Dempsey dragged him between two parked cars. The backing-up Bondo Special nearly ran over Mordecai's outstretched legs. He grabbed the tailpipe of a Volvo with his right hand. Shrieking. The Bondo Special hesitated. Dempsey reached up with the Green River knife while shifting into a full choke hold with the ulna of his left arm cutting off wind and blood supply. He fileted Mordecai's scalp with a single curving motion of the blade and yanked off a goodly handful of yellow hair, a scalplock. It took him eight seconds. Blood streamed down over Mordecai's face, flooding the hollows of his disbelieving eyes and running into his open mouth. At some point while he was being scalped the fight left him and his body went slack.

Dempsey abandoned Mordecai, leaping over him with the scalplock in his knife hand. He yanked open the front door of the reversed Bondo Special and crammed himself inside.

"Hit it," he said.

"What did you do?"

"Tonight I have counted coup on my enemies. Now kindly get the fuck out of Greenwich Village before they swarm all over us."

Peter Troy punched the accelerator with a nervous foot and steered erratically toward the Suburban, which was trying to maneuver into a blocking position at the intersection. Dempsey reached out and grabbed the wheel, sent the Bondo Special veering to the curb, and over it. They rode the sidewalk around the corner and halfway down the street, tearing away a couple of little picket fences protecting the trunks of sycamore trees.

"Straighten it out."

The Suburban wasn't following. More Kreggs had piled out and were going to the assistance of Mordecai and Woodrow Kregg. There apparently was no limit to the supply in Simon the Rock County, where three Southern states met in mountainous sublimity.

Peter Troy crunched into a fireplug.

"Sorry, I—"

"Get out of there and let me drive."

He pulled Troy from behind the wheel. They struggled awkwardly to exchange seats.

"Hold this."

"What—"

"It's a scalp, what does it look like?"

So far there were no cops. The Kreggs weren't likely to call for help. They handled their own problems. As for Dempsey, if he wanted this bullshit to stop short of some real pain and suffering, he knew he had to take the initiative.

Peter Troy said, "Who were those men? Were they trying to kill you?"

"Kill me? No. They wouldn't go that far, although they'd probably enjoy it if they had the option. I've made them look like assholes a couple of times. So they'd party with me. That probably is an option. Slice open my back, the backs of my thighs, rub in the rock salt, hang me up in the smokehouse for three days."

He got his bearings eastbound on Great Jones Street, headed uptown from the Bowery. Peter Troy's eyes were closed. He made little sounds of internal discomfort.

"Need a drink?"

"Yes."

"I know where there's a swell party."

"You do?" He was smelling the blood on the scalplock he held gingerly in his lap. His nostrils pinching together, then flaring. He still looked excessively pale for someone who hung out in the Hamptons during the summer.

"My ex-wife's place. Trevellian House. You've heard of the Trevellians."

"The Trevellian Prizes? I was introduced to Esther Trevellian at Saul and Gayfryd's—she's one of the most beautiful—but—she couldn't be—"

He looked at Dempsey with a faint doubting smile.

"That's my ex-wife. Don't look so stunned, you'll hurt my feelings. The fact is she's still crazy about me."

"I didn't mean to—"

"No offense taken. Where're you from, Troy?"

"Illinois. Rockford, Illinois."

"I'm from Oklahoma. The part that was left to the Comanch and the Kiowa after everybody stole us blind. That place is still open." Dempsey pulled over at a bus stop, opposite a liquor store on Park Avenue South. "What do you want to drink?"

"Uh, anything. No wine."

"Loan me twenty bucks. I want to buy some flowers, too." He winked at Troy, a hand with dried blood on the fingers extended in a way that didn't allow for refusal. Troy swallowed a couple of times, patting himself down until he found his wallet in a pocket of his wrinkled cotton summer blazer. He extracted two tens.

"You're a writer?"

"Playwright."

"Would I know—"

"I won an Obie for *B-Movie Boxcar Blues*. That was eleven, almost twelve years ago. I got an Obie and married one of the richest women in America, the same month." He took the money from Troy. The mismatched eye made Troy uneasy. There were fitful lights in it, like fireflies trapped in an old Coke bottle. His other round eye was dark brown, or even black, and blandly intimidating. "I meant what I said. She's still crazy about me. I'm looking forward to having you meet Esther. The fact is, I probably love her, too, although I still don't think that arrow in my back was an accident."

"Arrow?" It sounded like madness. Paranoia, for sure.

The car door slammed. Troy watched Dempsey stride across the street to the liquor store. He had disdain for traffic, for any trajectory but his own. It was partly the big shoulders. But he walked as if his purpose were chaos. Vehicles slowed, there was no angry blowing of horns. The drivers watched him warily, withholding curses, their celebrated New York scorn.

Troy thought about getting out, hailing a cab. But he wasn't sure his legs would hold him up that long. He also had the feeling that Dempsey Wingo would be angry about his desertion.

Momentary blackout. Then Dempsey was back with a fifth of citrus-flavored vodka and six long-stemmed red roses wrapped in crinkly green paper.

"I got these for four bucks," he said, "at the Korean's there. Close-out price." He handed the vodka to Peter Troy. "I'll take that scalplock now."

Troy watched him unwrap the roses, then rewrap them with the scalplock among the thorns. He placed the roses on the back seat of the Bondo Special and smiled at Troy.

"Comanche forget-me-nots," he said. "Open that bottle." He drove uptown again, toward Grand Central.

"What sort of relationship do you have with your ex-wife?" Troy said eventually, thinking about the scalplock.

"Complex. It's a complex relationship. To tell the truth, I get along better with other members of the immediate family. I suppose that's one part of the trouble I have with Esther." He drank from the bottle of vodka and passed it back to Troy. "You getting any work done?"

Dempsey ran a red light at Park and Fifty-seventh. Troy shrank back in his seat, sweating, clinging to the fruity vodka. When he was able to drink without spilling any on himself he had a nip. He was in that netherworld between flashes of understandable reality and alcoholic befuddlement. The furious semicrazed action of the midnight street, speed and momentum, unnerved him. So did his companion. Literate but savage. The still-lurid smell of blood. Had he also murdered the man whose hair he had lifted? It was plausible, Troy thought, that they would both wind up in jail before the night was over.

"I *have* been having a few problems with the new book."

"What's the setting?"

"The setting? New York. The Ionian Islands."

"What do you call it?"

"The Saboteurs."

"Beautiful people drifting like ghost ships through ambiguous lives.

Celia and Richard, Amanda and Julian. Never quite rich, but always with enough money to do themselves in. Booze, dope, sex. The sacraments of ennui. Endless conversations in symbolically desolate settings. Long descriptive passages but no firm sense of place, a cultural and social matrix in which the characters can breathe and evolve. The characters are replicas of replicas. They have no toenails."

Feeling unfairly condemned, Troy said, "And how is *your* work coming?"

"I am my work, in a manner of speaking."

"You've got the yips."

"You said it."

West on Seventy-ninth, the Bondo Special missing by an eighth of an inch the fender of a yellow cab turning right off Park.

"Camel jockey," Dempsey said dismissively of the turbaned cab driver. "There it is. Trevellian House."

Peter Troy, who had just acquired and was renovating a corner apartment in the Dakota with a view across the park of Trevellian House, had never been inside. The modern addition had been constructed above a staid limestone mansion originally built in 1909. The addition was twenty-eight stories, a dark obelisk of ebony volcanic rock and bronze worked like wicker to frame vertical windows occuring irregularly the height of the tapering shaft. Rose-colored glass sheathed the apex of the obelisk. The design had won both an AIA gold medal and condemnation for Dix Trevellian. A critic in *Rolling Stone* had described the obelisk as a "black phallus rudely mocking the sensibilities of the supposedly liberal, oh-so-rich denizens of the East Seventies."

Troy mentioned this. Dempsey said, slowing to look over the circular drive of the mansion, lined tonight with limousines and a dozen parking attendants dressed like British equerries, "That sounds like Dix. Everything he does is on the verge of being unmannerly or just plain outrageous. He mows you down with his enthusiasm. That's why I like him."

"What's inside? Apartments?"

"A few. Office space, mostly. It takes a lot of people to give away all that moolah."

Dempsey turned blithely north on Fifth Avenue, a one-way street southbound, encountering no traffic in the lane closest to the curb. He made a right turn at the next block, paying particular attention to the security people on duty at the brightly lighted entrance to the obelisk's underground garage on Eightieth. He passed the garage and made a left turn into a driveway across the street. A high iron gate blocked further progress. The mansion where he was illegally parked was also owned by the Trevellian Foundation. Dix Trevellian had his New York offices and workplace on the third and fourth floors. The Greek Revival portico was lighted but there was no traffic in or out of the building.

A black man with a large head on a short but powerful body, walking two shimmering borzois and a putty-colored shar-pei, had crossed Fifth Avenue from the park side and was coming down the wide sidewalk toward the Bondo Special.

Dempsey said to Troy, "Stay put a minute." He got out of his car.

"Mr. Marlowe Hare," he said with a wide smile as the dog-walker approached him.

"Oh, my. My, my, my. Mr. Dempsey Wingo. Here you is."

"That a surprise to you, Marlowe?"

"I allow it may be. On account of all the fluctuations in progress." His own smile, enhanced by diamonds, did not conceal his anxiety. The two borzois, looking like skeleton keys with silky hair, wagged their tails, having identified Dempsey. The shar-pei, which appeared to be crouched inside the plush coat of a much larger dog, he hadn't seen before. It was indifferent to Dempsey's presence.

"Yes, sir." Marlowe Hare breathed with a soughing regretfulness. "There's been fluctuations aplenty tonight." The walkie he had with him crackled momentarily, and Dempsey heard a female voice, unrecognizable. "Not twenty minutes ago it was Miz Mardie herself went running out, down to St. Vincent's hospital, it would seem."

"A couple of the Kreggs needing repairs," Dempsey said, with a slight repentant down-tilt of his head. "All I did was defend myself, Marlowe."

"Yes, sir, I appreciate that's how it must have been."

"I need to see Esther tonight."

"Oh, my. My, my," Marlowe said nervously, his well-developed chest expanding against the buttoned vest of his three-piece lavender suit. The walkie crackled again, some security-guard conversation on the open channel.

"Understand where I'm coming from. I want to stop all the nonsense. Tonight it was an ear got cut off, they sew it back on, no big deal. Maybe Mordecai needs plastic surgery on his head where I took scalp. He'd of put out my pretty green eye with that mule-popper of his, never give it a thought. He's meaner than his sister, if that's possible. Anyway, shit. I've had a gutful of the Kreggs tracking me around

town, ruining my social life. Esther can put a stop to it if she wants
to. All I need do is convince Esther I'm not hiding her little brother
from her. I'm in a mood to be convincing tonight. So get me inside,
Marlowe."

Marlowe Hare had the look of a man whose blood has suddenly
run cold. One of the Russian wolfhounds began to bark.

"The fluctuations," Marlowe said. "Oh, my, no. No, no! I don't
even want to think of such a thing."

"He's been in touch, but I don't know where to find Scott. That's
the truth. Do you know me for an honest man, Marlowe?"

"Yes, sir. And I always liked you, Mr. Wingo. But what does it
matter? There's always severe fluctuations when you come around.
And Mr. Wingo, I don't want you to feel badly when I say it's obvious
you been bending your elbow in a few places already tonight."

"Maybe I don't look so good," Dempsey conceded, aware of the
hailed-out left knee of his Wranglers, which had happened while he
was scuffling with Mordecai Kregg. And there was stiff blood from
Mordecai's scalp on the front of Dempsey's blue workshirt. When
had he shaved last? Didn't matter, he'd never been able to raise much
of a beard. But there must have been an odor about him, of barroom
smoke and neglected hygiene, the acrid sweats from an adrenaline
high. Fuck it, he only wanted to talk, he wasn't going to make love
to her. Ever again.

He looked down at Marlowe regretfully, his vision hazy from
weariness and the pain of loss. Divorced eight years. He hadn't had
so much as a glimpse of Esther in many months, even though he knew
where she'd be showing up around town—Lincoln Center, MOMA,
high-profile charity events at the Plaza or the Pierre—but her face
was the last thing he saw most nights before he fell asleep, drunk or
sober.

The dogs were restless; one of them stepped on the toe of a black-
and-white wingtip shoe. Marlowe Hare spoke softly to them, while
not avoiding the plea in Dempsey's eyes. But he had to deny him,
with a slow, side-to-side movement of his unfinished-looking, totemic
head.

"Sorry, Mr. Wingo. You knows I just can't do it."

"Send her out to me, then," Dempsey said.

"What's that?"

"I'll be over there, by the park. Tell her to come by herself. She's
not afraid of me, anyway. Esther doesn't know what fear is. Tell her—
I can find her brother for her. It's what I do for a living now." Mar-

lowe Hare began to shake his head again. "Tell her that, Marlowe. He's been sending me E-mail messages. Long letters. They haven't made much sense, but at least Scott is communicating with me. I'll find him."

"Is that on the level, Mr. Wingo?" Marlowe said, with a hesitant flashing of the diamonds in his two front teeth.

"I swear it on my sainted mother's grave."

"Then I'll tell her everything you just said to me."

"Thank you, Marlowe. And I could use another favor. See that boy in my car?"

"Yes."

"His name is Peter Troy. He's an important young novelist, but I'm afraid he's about one drink away from the screaming d.t.'s. Open-heart surgery without anesthetic may be more fun that the screaming d.t.'s."

"Oh, my, yes," Marlowe Hare said softly.

"See if you can get some black coffee into him, ship him across the park to the Dakota, which is where he lives. It won't be a problem?"

"I was on the road with Mr. James Brown for two and a half years. I guess I know how to deal with sensitive artistic folks."

"You're a good man, Marlowe," Dempsey said. "There'll be two tickets to my new play at the box office for you. It's guaranteed to happen. Once I get past the second act. The second act is always the ball-breaker."

"Good luck to you, Mr. Wingo."

Dempsey returned to the Bondo Special and opened the left-side back door. Peter Troy's head lay back against the seat; his face was filmed with sweat and he breathed harshly through his mouth. Dempsey picked up the Comanche forget-me-nots in their wrapping of waxed paper and took them with him. Marlowe Hare was speaking to someone on his walkie. He flashed a hopeful smile as Dempsey went by him.

After midnight there wasn't much happening on upper Fifth Avenue; traffic consisted mostly of southbound out-of-service taxis streaking through the open lights past the grandeur of the Metropolitan Museum of Art, more taxis on the Seventy-ninth Street transverse that cut through Central Park to the west side. There were a few dog walkers, equipped with pooper scoops, in the well-lighted vicinity of the museum. A Con Ed crew was working at the corner by the Stanhope Hotel. The park itself, at this hour, was no-man's-land, dark and wild as the forest sauvage.

Dempsey leaned, arms folded, hands in his armpits, against the wall that fronted the park, the roses by his feet. There was no breeze and the city hadn't cooled off much from ninety-degree heat that day. Nevertheless he felt a chill, centered around his heart, and he had begun to get the shakes. He didn't want to think about where he'd been lately, and what he was trying to do to himself by making the bar scene again. Introspection, more often than not, depressed him. His depressions were the same as being buried alive; violence or obsession snapped him out of it, but violence bred vengeance and created legal problems, while obsession served only to grind away a little more of his soul.

While he waited for his long-lasting obsession with Esther Trevellian to take shape from the shadows of his psyche and become theater once again, he looked at the obelisk which Dix, the architect, had created. There was something forbidding and enigmatic about it, symbolic of the Trevellians themselves.

The family always had had money, from Reconstruction on. They were Philadelphians who had moved south to exploit whatever opportunities were presented in desolated Dixie. Cotton land and carpet mills became the basis of a fortune that totaled about one hundred million dollars at the time Esther took control of the family enterprises, then handed over fiscal responsibility to her younger brother Scott. It was Scott, combining Zen sensibilities with the wordless egoless logic of the computer, who multiplied the family's worth twenty times, in slightly less than a decade. Scott sold the carpet mills for cash, constructed computer models for timing the rock-and-roll currency future markets, rode a strong yen to the limit, took his profits and began buying deepwater oil leases in the Gulf of Mexico when the government could barely give them away. Now the family controlled thirty-two percent of all the deepwater leases in the gulf, where oil and gas reserves were estimated to be in excess of ten billion barrels; sublease agreements with an American and a French company that had begun drilling operations from billion-dollar platforms would soon be worth approximately one million a day to the Trevellians.

All of this information Dempsey had gleaned from the latest annual report in *Forbes* magazine on America's richest people.

Scott Trevellian probably didn't know or care what his business intuition and financial skills had meant to his family; at the age of twenty-nine he had been overtaken by another horseman of the Apocalypse, namely paranoid schizophrenia. All attempts at treatment had failed. For at least a year, in spite of Esther's efforts to locate her brother, he had been missing. This was not public knowledge. Esther Trevellian was often photographed but never gave interviews; Dix was an enigma the equal of his art, a dark force with a glib and toothy smile for the paparazzi who congregated by the watering holes of the world's social gadabouts.

He waited, propped against the old stone wall, for his ex-wife to appear. Listening to the siren songs of New York night, the rattle of dangerous taxis on the lumpy thoroughfare. He was forty-eight years old. Feeling the hard years on the rodeo circuit in his often-broken bones and joints. His mouth, his throat, were thick with thirst. If he'd brought the bottle of vodka with him, then probably he'd be drinking. Dempsey's father had romanced the bottle after a midlife divorce, drunk up the cattle and lost his ranch on the Salt Fork of the Red River; he had two sisters who were alcoholics. But Dempsey had never craved strong drink. He drank when it was there. If it wasn't handy he didn't miss it. A dozen feet away two women dressed in black walked by him. Willowy, hair very short, they moved with the incomparable self-absorption of ballerinas transiting the urban stage on which he had no more relevance than a prop tree. The setting, in fact, required him: his look of displaced raggedness, of seedy obsolescence.

His vision was hazy; he saw concentric rings of color around every street lamp and traffic signal. He rubbed his closed eyes gently and when he looked up she was there, alone, on the corner of Fifth and Eightieth, watching him from within her particular, lambent aura, sleek but not excessive in her party dress, a cocktail sheath that looked to be made of chainmail hammered thin as silk and that shimmered in a spectrum somewhere between copper and gold.

A bus raced by, heading downtown, brilliantly alight, a single face in one window like a dark thought in an otherwise empty mind. He digested the murky fumes from the bus, rubbed his eyes again and pushed the wings of his hair back from his face with the hard heels of his palms. He looked up. Esther had crossed the street and was standing at the edge of the brick sidewalk beside a row of vending devices for the *New York Times* and numerous sexually oriented tabloids, photographs of women bizarre in their proportions, agape with erotic dementia.

Esther, as burnished as an angel, held a beaded clutch purse large enough to conceal a handgun. He guessed it would be her old favorite .44 derringer, or a no-nonsense snubnosed Smith with a hammerless frame.

"Badman José," she said. Her pet name for him, once upon a time. He had sported a bandito mustache then.

"You never change." His voice was raw, as if filtered through ground glass, the compliment distorted, somehow derisive.

"You never learn, José," she said. There was no anger in her voice, not even a tone of reprimand. It was a regretful statement of fact.

"What is it I'm supposed to have learned by now?"

"Not to come around."

"Old grudges that never die."

Esther said, dropping the mild banter and the nickname, "You know I don't have anything against you, Dempsey. I'm simply not interested in seeing or talking to you."

"So you're not here at the moment, and I'm having an hallucination."

Esther smiled. The light wasn't good where she was standing, a careful distance away in leaf-shadow, but he saw no changes in her face, no sign of that certain age creeping in. She had seldom, in Dempsey's memory, changed her hair style. Her hair was thick and dark and framed her face like a lyre, curving up slightly from the shoulders toward her jawline. She didn't care for makeup, except for eyeliner, because her eyes were large and dark brown and filled with a gypsy allure. Her other features were fine, perfectly turned out, one oblique curve after another, her expression serene. But her eyes made one think of wiles and hidden daggers; they struck at the heart of a man, challenging the predator and devastating the weak.

"I have the feeling you may not be far from some sort of hallucination, Dempsey. You don't look to be in the best of shape."

"I work out like an Olympic athlete. I took on a couple of the Kreggs tonight and came out the winner."

"Yes, I heard. What started it?"

"Your long-standing order to run me out of town. Just can't seem to get me out of your mind, right, Esther?"

"You have a habit of intruding where you're not wanted. Attempting to continue relationships that ought to have ended. You're an old, bad story, Dempsey. As persistent as a skin disease."

This little flare-up made him smile. Esther closed her eyes briefly, an expression of resignation or annoyance. Dempsey said, "As for family relationships: Scott still seems to need me."

She had a way of masking avidity with the fingertips of one hand spread lightly on her forehead, the cupped palm partly concealing her downcast Romany eyes, like a phony medium trying to gauge the worth of a fish looking for enlightenment.

"You've heard from him. And the Badman doesn't lie."

"Neither of us ever lies. That's why we turned into raw meat for each other."

"Stop it, Dempsey," she said with a little nervous tapping of one gilded shoe against the bricks, still not looking at him. "Has he called you? From where? What did Scott *say*? Why is he hiding from us? We love him. He knows that."

"He doesn't value anyone's love. How can he? He's a schiz."

"Why should he trust you?"

"How should I know? Maybe he thinks I own a share of his delusions."

"I don't know what you mean. Are you going to tell me—"

"Look, Esther, he communicates by E-mail. Long discursive messages, arguments, essays that I can't—haven't been able to interpret."

"How would he have your E-Mail address?"

"I gave it to him, the last time I saw him. Here." Dempsey turned his head, indicating the park behind him. "Fourth of July, a year ago. The Sheep Meadow."

Esther made a fist and tapped her head in exasperation. "You could have let me know."

"Yeah, well, I didn't."

"How did he look? What did he have to say?"

"He has most of his hair, but it's gray now. It looked as if he had trimmed one side with scissors without the help of a mirror, then forgot about the other side. I'd say he's down to about a hundred and fifty pounds, but he didn't look undernourished, just consumed to the bone. No physical problems, no nervous tics, only that look of spiritual wasteland in the eyes. He was wearing a pink cotton V-neck sweater that was too big for him, baggy gray twill pants and yellow work shoes that had a lot of dirt on them. Laces untied, maybe one of them was broken. He had a backpack with some books in it. He was wearing one of those laminated religious cards you can get in Hispanic storefront churches, the Bleeding Heart, on a pull chain around his neck.

"I can remember every moment of our lovemaking, Esther. I know every muscle and bone in your body, and how you used your body fucking. Fucking me. Your beautiful biting teeth, folds of my skin and flesh between your teeth, God. I feel your heartbeat in broad daylight. I taste your pussy. I hear you scream. More than once you passed out, pale from ecstasy, glaze of spit on your chin. I think about how sex turned mean as a bullfight even as we became more desperate for each other. For dominance. I don't flinch from that, because I'm still trying to understand. To know you completely. Know what you could never explain to me, or anyone else."

"For Christ's *sake*, Dempsey. Can't we stick to the subject? The subject is *Scott*. Did he come up to you? Was he—making sense that night?"

"I saw him first. I was tagging a couple of Trinidadians who I thought would probably lead me to the guy I was looking for, a fugitive and bail jumper wanted for deportation by the INS. This one was worth twenty-five hundred to me. Anyway, when I recognized Scott I gave up the tag, because I knew I'd pick up the fugitive later, they're all creatures of habit and dumb as dogshit to boot."

"Scott recognized you?"

"He even seemed glad to see me. For a few minutes. He said he had a place to stay. He said he had a job and was eating vegetarian meals. He said he loved the sunsets on the river. He said he didn't watch television because sooner or later the characters on *Melrose Place* or the politicians on C-Span would casually start talking to him, telling him more secrets about his family he doesn't want to know."

Esther shook her head impatiently. "You told Mr. Hare you could find him."

"If I put my mind to it. Why do you suppose all the investigators you've hired haven't been able to track Scott down?"

"No driver's license, no credit cards, no bank account. He never renewed his prescription for Risperidone."

"Without a paper trail they're fucked."

"Damn you, Dempsey. Stand there and taunt me, why don't you? What do you *want*?"

"To see you again."

"Forget that. Did you print out the E-mail from Scott?"

"Yes. Cooperate, Esther. We'll put our heads together and study the messages he's left me. Look for clues maybe only you will recognize. He must want to be found. Something's on his poor possessed mind, other than disembodied voices. But he's wary of tipping off the wrong people, of course."

"You still haven't explained why he would trust you," she said, worlds of suspicion in her peppery gaze.

"What about this? Scott sees me as a fellow victim of the Trevellian family psychodrama."

"There's nothing wrong with my family. I'm very proud of everything we've accomplished, in spite of tragedy."

A dark blue Lincoln Town Car had made a turn from Eighty-first Street onto Fifth Avenue and was crossing all lanes as if out of control, heading in their direction. Dempsey had a hunch who was in the car as Esther turned her face to the street.

"Keep her out of this," Dempsey advised. He glanced at the wrapped roses, then stepped sideways and ground the petals into the sidewalk. The Comanche forget-me-nots no longer seemed appropriate, considering the progress he thought he was making with his ex-wife, and the arrival of Mardie Kregg.

She was dressed almost like a cop, in dark blue skirt and royal blue blouse, with epaulets but without a badge or shoulder patch. Mardie was small-breasted, but massive in thigh and shoulders, and she had the hands of a bare-knuckle brawler, several knuckles either freshly scraped or scabbed over. The rest of her skin was unusually fine, with a hint of healthy pink. She had reddish bangs, eyes the color of earthworms and a thinly bridged nose. It had been a pretty face, but now was drawing into the pinched mean aspect of someone who had made a religion of grievances and feuds. Like most of the members of Mardie's Carolina clan.

"What's goen on here?" she demanded of Esther.

"Nothing, Mardie."

"You're talken to him. And my poor brother sufferen tonight, half his scalp tore off."

"Mardie, I can handle this."

"Ought to be down on his knees, beggen for his life."

"Mardie, go on."

"Sorry son of a bitch."

"He can help me find Scott. He's seen Scott."

"Cain't believe you swallowed that."

"Go sit in the car, Mardie. I won't be long."

"If he makes a move."

"No, it's okay."

Mardie said vehemently, "Don't you know what you want? You said, Never want to see him again. Do somethen, Mardie. Now you tell me, *don't* do hit. Look at him. That's a bum standen there. Cain't you see you're maken a mistake?"

"Maybe I should be on my way," Dempsey suggested.

Esther glanced at him, frowning, then looked back at Mardie Kregg, asserting her authority in some way that was invisible to outsiders, even to Dempsey, who had puzzled over the relationship of the women during his hectic years of marriage and was still none the wiser. The bond was not one of blood but had been forged through ordeal.

"We'll discuss it later, Mardie. Wait in the car."

Mardie, knotted and baleful, turned her ire on Dempsey.

"I'll wait. But hit ain't over. Dempsey Wingo, your day of reckonen is near."

Mardie turned and stalked to the Lincoln, slamming the door once she was inside.

"Why do you keep her around?"

"You know why."

"All that fanatical devotion is sexual, you know."

"Don't be a fool."

"They love it, don't they? Code of the hills, the offended honor, self-righteous bloodletting. *You* love it. Turmoil and intrigue. The spoils of vengeance. It's something dark in you that traveled over the Carpathians to a more civilized world three centuries ago."

Esther laughed.

"Now I'm a vampire? That bloodline's only a trickle. One of my lordly ancestors ravished a gypsy girl. I'm Catalonian, not Roumanian. Passion and fortitude, hon."

"I don't know just what you are, Esther. I've got a screw loose in my head from thinking about you."

She nodded, as if that wasn't news, but no fault of hers.

"Just help me find Scott."

"There's a health food restaurant on Fulton Street near downtown Brooklyn called Sun Ra. Suppose you meet me there for lunch. One o'clock Saturday."

"Brooklyn? That's where you're living now?"

"Maybe," Dempsey said, aware that a front window of the Lincoln was halfway down. "Goodnight, Esther."

"Hokay, José," she said, with a little gesture that may have been conciliatory as she turned and walked to the Lincoln.

He felt the breaking of a contact, pop of sparks around the heart, fading dismally in his over-expanded chest. The fudging of his blood, a sense of unworthiness and anxiety at being worthless. Esther could do that to him, merely walking away. Dempsey was aware that he might have made a mistake, a case of refreshed lust overwhelming what remained of the hunter's cunning and caution. Whatever Scott Trevellian's reasons for avoiding his family, in spite of his illness there was always a chance they were very good reasons.

FOUR

MAMA'S GOT THOSE
STALKING-HORSE BLUES

After the court proceedings, following which Sharan Norbeth was released on her own recognizance, Dayton Emmons, the retired Federal Bureau of Investigation official, took Sharan to lunch at a Red Lobster. Deputy Attorney General Coleman Dane had flown back to Washington at two in the morning.

"What did you do with the FBI?" Sharan asked Emmons.

"Behavioral Science programs. Violent Crime analysis. Victimology."

"What's that?"

"Background and psychological makeup of murder victims, particularly victims of serial killers."

"Serial killers. Did you catch any?"

"Quite a few."

Sharan had a crabmeat salad and iced tea. Emmons ordered a filet of grilled flounder dressed with lemon juice, and took several pills with his meal, smiling apologetically at his luncheon guest. Sharan had no comment.

"Your health is good?" Emmons asked her. "Do you stay in shape?"

"Tai chi. Kendo."

"You were quite a marksman in service."

"I don't own a gun now. I can paint left-handed but I don't think

I can shoot left-handed. I never enjoyed it much anyway. It was part of the job. So are you going to give me some idea—"

"Before you're so much as introduced to Dix Trevellian, you'll know more about him than most married people know about their spouses. Or ever hope to know."

Sharan trembled slightly and complained, "It's too cold in here."

"I know you're afraid. But you've been trained to deal with fear."

"What if I'm not his type?"

Emmons smiled slightly. Below the table Sharan squeezed her left knee painfully. Her expression was impassive. Her heart sounded as loud to her as a cheap alarm clock.

"There's nothing, not even circumstantial evidence, to indicate he may have murdered those six women."

"Only three of them are legally presumed to be dead," Emmons reminded her.

"But all vanished. No trace."

"As for circumstantial evidence, Dix Trevellian is the best link between the women. He had affairs with three or more of them. The other link is proximity. He was at least temporarily in all of the countries at the time of the disappearances."

"Has he been questioned?"

"Certainly."

"Alibis?"

"Yes."

"Polygraphed?"

"In the latest instance, the disappearance of Felicia Dane. At his suggestion, perhaps because he was a classmate of Cole's at Princeton."

"He passed."

"Yes, he did."

"Who did the testing? FBI?"

"Independent consultant."

"He knows he's a suspect," Sharan said. "The Deputy Attorney General has a personal reason for investigating him. Then I show up. Too neat, isn't it? If I were Dix Trevellian, I'd be—"

"Highly suspicious. Of course. He's very bright, possibly a genius in his field. Well aware of his superiority to most of us mortals. Infatuated with his cleverness. He'll look very carefully into your background. I think he'll be stimulated by the potential danger you represent. But the psychological imperatives outweigh native caution in the case of some highly organized and intelligent killers. The organized killer doesn't strike at random. He has relationships with each of his victims. He takes trophies, something that, long after the deed, will remind him of his—accomplishment." Sharan's face was a study in dismay and disgust. "Nothing very big or even valuable. A keepsake as trivial as a monogrammed hairbrush, a scarf. That's one of the things you should be looking for. He may reveal a trophy to you, represented as something else, carefully monitoring your response. If he decides you may be investigating him, I think he could become enamored of the possibilities, perhaps even help you. Up to a point."

"They keep it way too cold in here."

"You won't be on your own, Sharan. You'll be watched day and night. The latest surveillance techniques."

"The last time I went into something like this—" She made a slow fist of her prosthetic hand on the table. "He hates women, of course. That's a given."

"Hatred is a by-product of some deep trauma, an inadequacy he can't deal with."

"Not very good in bed?"

"That may be a little too pat. We've seen letters to Dix from Robin Smallwood and Caterina Chiado that raved about his prowess."

"I don't plan to find out It will not go that far. The idea of touching him at all nauseates me. What does he look like, anyway? Do you have a recent photo?"

Dayton Emmons opened an attaché case on the banquette beside him, and took out two VHS tapes, which he placed on the table near Sharan.

"Introduction to Dix Trevellian. Do you have a VCR? Good. Once you've studied these, we'll talk about your impressions."

"When am I going to see Dane again?"

"I don't know. He's busy in Washington."

"He'll stay in touch, though."

"With you?"

"Yes, with *me*. His stalking horse."

"Oh." Emmons stirred an envelope of artificial sweetener into a glass of San Pellegrino water, watching her as if the light in the restaurant had changed where it fell across her pretty, clenched face, or a flaw in his vision had cleared up. "Yes, I'm sure you can count on that. You'll be hearing from Cole."

An impromptu celebration of Sharan's release and vindication became a neighborhood lawn party at the Rising Fawn Mobile Home Park.

Rising Fawn was one of the nicer parks around, with shade trees and a willow-cooled pond that didn't shrink to a mudpie during the droughts of summer. Most of the units were smart-looking double-wides with porches or decks added on, central air and garden plots. The drives, though laid out in a monotonous grid pattern, were paved and kept in good repair. The septic tanks seldom backed up. The residents who weren't living off pensions and social security had steady jobs and drove late-model pickup trucks. By contrast, there was a Tin Can Alley across the pond and behind a sagging barbed-wire fence, filled with small trailers and campers, many of them rusting through in places where hailstones as big as eyeballs had left depressions that collected rainwater. In Tin Can Alley, which the local cops called "Felonyville," screaming domestic disturbances were routine. Felonyville averaged three shootouts a year. The pizza delivery establishments in the area would not accept phone orders from residents.

As it turned out, the Electra-Glide thief Sharan had run to ground, one Ray Gene Pruitt, was related to a two-time loser who worked at a parts store in East Tombetta and lived with his common-law wife and an assortment of dingy-looking blond kids in Tin Can Alley. Barely a hundred yards across the barbed wire and pond from Sharan's address, site number 72. He would have seen her working on the Harley out behind her double-wide, and schemed to get his hands on it. At least that was the theory of Dardy Jeff Kimbro, who had a country music band that played local engagements and once had opened for Charlie Daniels at the Crystal Chandelier in Kennesaw.

"Probably been spying on you right along," Dardy Jeff said.

Allison, Dardy Jeff's long-running girlfriend, said, "I hope you keep the blinds shut on that side when you get naked."

"Learned that a long time ago," Sharan replied. There were twenty residents of Rising Fawn, and friends of residents whom she knew only slightly, sitting around on various pieces of aluminum and vinyl lawn furniture in front of Buddy and Kay Combee's double shorty. They had eaten buffalo wings and fried catfish; diced chicken-and-corn-and-sweet pepper salad; pickled beets and green beans and cole slaw. Two washtubs held wine coolers and long-neck Buds. Harryette Brigham had baked blackberry and peach pies. There was homemade ice cream to go with the pie. Everybody had refused to let Sharan chip in.

Dardy Jeff was sprawled in a big hammock, endlessly tuning his Stratocaster between draughts of Bud.

"Did much damage to your iron?" Allison asked Sharan.

"I've been afraid to go down to Prexy's and look at it."

A bug zapper hanging beneath the metal awning of the Combee's trailer juiced a hardshell beetle with a particularly savage popping sound.

"See the size of that sucker?" Allison murmured. She was a copperhead with a lush body. She was doing her toenails in purple lacquer. Occasionally Dardy Jeff would reach out and squeeze a cheeky half-moon where her short-shorts left off. "Now, you quit," Allison said each time. Olin Apworth and Elmo Dowdy, Jr. were arguing about the efficacy of pine and bay bush sprays for disguising a deer hunter's natural odor. Mary Berk was helping Eunice Keeter choose a Powerball number. There was a Braves game on TV. Kids laughed and battled each other for the truck-tire swings on the playground.

"When you fixin' to marry me, Allison?" Dardy Jeff whined. They had been keeping steady company for two and a half years.

"The hasty heart is always in divorce court, son," Allison said.

It was all very familiar and comforting to Sharan, who had drunk her share of the beer, enough so that her head and eyelids felt heavy. But the good company and the quantity of beer, which had twice sent her off to the bathroom, hadn't coped with her downhearted feeling of being at the mercy of cold and ruthless people. All she could think about was the midnight scene in the County Prosecutor's office. She wanted to wash Coleman Dane out of her mind, but wherever she looked, even if she was in the middle of laughing at some tasteless joke of Dardy Jeff's, she couldn't get rid of Dane, her vision of his haggard good looks. She couldn't explain her silences and worsening mood to anyone, either.

The bug zapper flashed. "Lordy," Allison murmured, "that'un must have been one of your lovebirds, Miss Lucy."

"Just because your mother was hitched five times," Dardy Jeff complained.

"I don't count it as five, because after all she was married twice to Booly Thurman."

"The bull rider?"

"Bullshitter was more like it. You'd say to her, 'Mama, *why?*' And she'd all the time be getting this loony look in her eyes. 'Cowboy butts drive me nuts.' That was my mama—rest her soul."

"Whatever happened to Booly?"

"Oh, some Brahma kicked him in the chest and ruptured his aorta. They said the blood was coming out of his mouth like a firehose."

"Well, I reckon he was better company for your mama than your own daddy was."

"You mean Dr. Frankenstein?"

"Why did you call him that?" Sharan asked.

"Because he kept us all in stitches."

One of the kids came bawling to his mother with a bloody lip. Rose Coralian got out her Tarot cards. Philip Luckmire, who weighed four hundred pounds, tried to convince Idalee Chisum to go skinny-dipping in the McClearys' above-ground pool.

Sharan got up a bit unsteadily, stretched and yawned. "Believe it's time for me to get some shut-eye."

J. C. Winborn called to her, saying, "You know you can have the borrow of my Taurus this weekend, Sharan. I need to be at the Georgia Dome for the Buckmaster expo."

"That is so sweet of you. I really do appreciate it, J.C."

Sharan checked her telephone message machine. Her younger brother Lyle had called from Wyoming and left a number where she could get in touch with him. He was probably in need of a loan. She'd paid the disputed part of her phone bill, leaving her with a hundred and thirty-three dollars in her checking account, but she wasn't in a mood to talk to Lyle. He was always investing in schemes he heard about in barrooms, then wondered why he wasn't rich. Dale Upshaw had some leftover house paint for her, and said he would drop it by the space she was currently using as a studio, next to a DUI school in a nearly defunct shopping center on Mt. Patmos Road. JimTom Coburn hadn't called, but that was to be expected. He was involved, along with some other instructors from the Sixth Ranger Training Battalion, in a weeklong Special Operations Command exercise in Florida. The last message was from a guy named Zach who said he was a friend of Critter's; they had met, Zach claimed, at the graduation ceremonies for new Jubilation County firefighters, and would she like to go with him to see Travis Tritt at Lakewood Saturday night? Sharan barely knew Critter, and belatedly placed Zach: he had one of those faces destined to show up on a post office wall. No thanks. She erased the tape and sat in her living room surrounded by all of the cheap bright furnishings that had come with the double-wide as part of a distress sale, Bonkers the cat making a nest of her lap.

Chet Atkins was playing plucky ruminative mood guitar on the Bose stereo system which JimTom had given Sharan on her last birthday. Never a perishable rose or a drop of perfume from pennywise JimTom. He always spent too much on her—practical stuff like the Bose audio equipment, or a camcorder—which, although he was not in the least devious, JimTom may have reckoned he would also be able to enjoy once Sharan agreed to marry him.

Right now she had an ache as if she missed JimTom, but the ache may have been a part of her overall distress, a need to be comforted and petted. Pensively roughing up Bonkers' fur while he snoozed didn't fully satisfy that need. She thought about calling her mother, but it was not yet eight o'clock in San Diego, full daylight still, and she was probably out of the office, showing properties. After Sarge's death in Vietnam, Caitlin had done an about-face while the glow of her late husband's heroism had continued to cast her and the family in a favorable light. She cut out the heavy boozing, revised her memories of a marriage that had been pretty much an ongoing brawl and earned a broker's shingle while the death benefits lasted. Always gregarious, she became a good saleswoman. Her next marriage, to a fat canny California native with his own realty company, had put Caitlin on easy street during the boom years for residential property in the Golden State.

Sharan's relationship with her mother was tenuous. They could be chatty together, but there was always the underlying strain, as if from a rite of unspoken censure. Sharan had never been fully forgiven for misapplying what her mother, in her California incarnation, called her Life Force, by opting for a military career—which was largely nigger work—and nearly getting herself killed as a result. Already in her midthirties, an unknown artist with little income. *Stuck without a spare in the breakdown lane of life*, Sharan thought, her humor jaundiced tonight. Her mother also was put out, as she so candidly expressed herself, that Sharan preferred the rural south to Southern California, where, Caitlin explained, she could hope to meet some really interesting men with "professions."

She had taken a couple of aspirin but she was jumpy from the beer and unable to fall asleep. The presence of the cassettes atop her VCR nagged her. She wanted to look, she didn't want to look. As if seeing his face would confirm an essential fascination with the distortions of humanity that had originally charted her course in police work. Viewing the tapes would be better done by sober daylight, Sharan reasoned. When she had a firmer grip on herself.

The telephone rang.

She let it ring, waiting for the answering machine to pick up.

"Hello, Sharan. Have you seen the tapes yet? I'm interested in your reaction. Call me back when you've reviewed them. I'm at this number." He spoke slowly and carefully. The abrupt tone, the Establishment edge of honed arrogance, was gone from his voice. He sounded a little drunk. She pictured him sitting on the edge of a bed with the knot of his tie pulled down, his socks off. Probably had long bony feet. His hair might be a little mussed. "Call whenever. I want to hear from you."

There was a pause. He didn't hang up.

"By the way. I saw Dix Trevellian tonight. He asked me if I still thought he killed my sister. He was smiling when he said it."

Coleman Dane was having dinner at Pamplona with the White House counsel when Dix Trevellian walked in with his party of twelve, an eclectic but convivial group that included a member of the royal family of Belgium and a Supreme Court Justice. But Dix obviously was hosting. Dane's appetite vanished before they made eye contact. He lost the thread of his conversation with Aaron Brannen.

"Stunning," Brannen murmured, misinterpreting Dane's interest in the members of the party, who were being seated in a semiprivate alcove of the Spanish restaurant. He thought Dane was eyeing the princess.

"Yeah."

"Do you know her?"

"Do I know—? Oh. Haven't had the pleasure."

"That Dix Trevellian?"

"Uh-huh."

"You were saying?"

"You work for a man who insists on hearing the bad news first, as long as it's happening to somebody else."

A waiter poured more of a Marques del Puerto '87 for them. Dane's eyes were fixed on Trevellian's party. He knew personally, or professionally had something on, most of them. A couple of the women were strangers. Dix's date was a high-priced society whore, a tawny fornicatrix with hoodoo in her eyes. Dix Trevellian had tightly curled, prematurely platinum-white hair, dark brows, sherry brown eyes, a dark tan, a slight gap between his front teeth. He seemed always on the verge of becoming overwrought. A man of emotion, hunger, ambition. He was not physically large, but like the embodiments of his imagination, everything about him seemed outsized: gestures, embraces, affections, laughter. Dane saw Dix as a lavish ass. But there wasn't a woman in the dining rooms of Pamplona who wasn't intrigued by him.

Brannen coughed to claim Dane's attention.

"I can't honestly say the President is losing sleep over the subcommittee investigations. A DNF memo was, unfortunately, misinterpreted by an overzealous FBI official."

"AG is entirely sympathetic although of course blameless, it wasn't on his watch. But he *is* taking heat from Jackson Mustoe and Cal Hartridge. To examine the spin from their dugout, our president is the first since Lyndon Johnson to employ a special ops unit of the Bureau for political purposes. Which can be interpreted as a disregard for the rights of ordinary citizens."

"A corpus of irrational fears coupled with seriously muddled legalities."

"Just the way the politicians have always liked it. Apropos the President's penchant for Do-Not-Files, there's an old Chinese proverb: 'Eagle with loose feathers falls near the nest.' "

Brannen grinned and devoted his attention to an *aperitivo* of duck livers and truffles. Dane ate a scroll of Serrano ham, dark red and sliced thinner than parchment. He looked again at Dix Trevellian, who had engaged the full attention of Pamplona's *enologo*.

"Our thinking is, if the President addresses the matter he's giving it credence, and if he fails to address it he's open to charges, baseless though we know them to be, of nonfeasance."

"Got one for you. Who said, 'If we believe in absurdities, we shall commit atrocities'?"

"Kierkegaard? No, wait. Joe Stalin."

"It was Voltaire. You buy the cigars. I chatted with Director Harms this afternoon. Internal investigation, no mention whatsoever of the President; a couple of junior officials take gas and Mercer Gramling opts for early retirement. I eat humble pie before yet another Congressional subcommittee."

"Mustoe and Hartridge may not be in a conciliatory mood."

"Appointment to Assistant U.S. Attorney in Los Angeles for the subcommittee's junior counsel whom Mustoe is currently fucking. Pending the President's approval, of course. And I hear OSHA has decided to delay the criminal suit against Cal Hartridge's brother-in-law—you know, that little matter at the Pueblo Seco dam site where ten workmen were killed."

"Umm. How long a delay?"

"Until there's an appropriate time to dispose. Say, after the next election."

Brannen considered the proposals, and nodded. "Okay, double or nothing. 'There is no crime of which one cannot imagine himself to be the author.' "

"Goethe. I took four years of German at school. Excuse me, would you, Aaron? I'll be right back."

Dane made his way to the table for twelve. He smiled and nodded and paid his respects to the Supreme Court Justice, a slight, dismal man with the tiny eyes of a lobster behind thick eyeglasses. The Justice was famous for his long-standing grudge match with the Articles of the Constitution of the United States. Dane loathed him.

Before Dane got around to Dix Trevellian, the architect excused himself and, accompanied by Raoul, the Pamplona's wine steward, left the table to investigate the restaurant's cellar, a privilege of the favored few. Half a minute later Dane followed them, down a flight of iron stairs and into a cool grotto stocked with 18,000 bottles.

"Hello, Cole," Dix said, finally acknowledging him with a relaxed smile; then he went back to scanning the labels of bottles of Rioja Raoul removed from the bins with murmured provenance.

"Hello, Dix."

"Another scorcher today. Washington in July."

"I know, I live here."

"I was in Cairo and Luxor last week. Now that's heat. Have you been to Cairo?"

"No."

"Haven't seen each other for a while. Last October, the Princeton Club, wasn't it?"

"Four Seasons."

"Oh, sure. The Four Seasons. You were with—what's this, Raoul, a 1982 Valbuena? They still exist? I can't believe my eyes."

"We have only the one bottle left."

Dix showed his trophy to Dane. "*Rioja Gran Reserva* from the Vega Sicilia region. You know northern Spain, around the Ebro River?"

"I don't travel all that much. Raoul, would you mind leaving us alone for a few minutes?"

The *enologo* gave the Deputy Attorney General a sharp blue glance through the spiky spillover of his gray eyebrows, then looked at Dix, who nodded.

"Tell my guests I have something very rare for them, Raoul. The Valbuena. Such finesse. *Vinos Españoles son tan despreciados.* The whites from Cataluña can hold their own, too."

Raoul nodded to a bin where the vinas sol were stored and left the wine cellar. Dix stood a few feet from Coleman Dane holding his bottle of rioja with a faint perplexed smile.

"You look kind of worn down, Cole."

Dane said nothing.

"I'm sorry about Felicia. I'm so very goddamned sorry. I really cared about her, whatever you want to believe. I'd do anything to help you find her."

"Start by telling me where and how she was buried. Thrown somewhere, into a hole in the ground or a backwoods river? Boxed up in a landfill? Nothing left, nothing at all, in a fucking limepit?"

"Cole, Cole."

"Shut up."

"You had better listen to me. Your grief. Okay, I understand. But you're the one who has to understand. This kind of harassment—it's obsessive. You still think I killed your sister?" Dix grimaced, or smiled; it was hard to tell which. Afterward Dane would remember his reaction as a smile.

"Tell me about it, Dix," Dane said in a soothing tone of voice. "You're dying to tell someone, aren't you?"

"That's crazy. Around the bend, man. You better get help. I say this as a friend. A classmate. But no more allegations. You're going to ruin yourself with these allegations."

"I'm never going to give up, Dix."

"Stop threatening me. Fair warning."

Dane stared at him for several moments, his face drawn tight on one side as if from neuralgia.

"She traveled all over the world, Cole. In spite of her handicap. She knew and was loved by a thousand people. She had other men. Maybe Felicia—"

"Maybe she what?"

"I don't know. I've thought about her so much. Please believe that. Thought about—what might have happened. I have no answers. It's tragic."

"Do you think about the others as much as you do Felicia?"

"All right. You've said enough. That's it. If you won't be reasonable then you can deal with Wilton Hardesty."

"Warp-Speed Willie? Get off it, Dix. You're not filing suit for harassment or anything else. Because you don't want a word of this in print. You don't want the media bird dogs sniffing in your tracks. You're stuck with me. I grind slowly, Dix. But I grind exceedingly fine."

He had been moving leisurely toward Dix Trevellian, Dix yielding, although reluctantly, until he had no place to go, his wide shoulders against an eight-foot wooden rack filled with bottles. His eyes never left Dane's face. He showed a tolerant smile. The too-red lips, pimiento, in the lotion-basted sun-darkened face. The nose and nostrils of the bull-epicure, slight oiliness in the tightly packed whorls of his silver hair, did women really get off on the likes of Dix Trevellian? Dane reached out and took the rioja from Dix's right hand.

"Good stuff, huh?"

Dix, wary of his apparent change of mood, nodded.

"What does it go for?"

"About four hundred dollars a bottle, when you can find any."

Dane stared at the rioja for a few more seconds, then shifted his hand to the base and savagely struck the neck of the bottle against a stone corner of the wine cellar. Glass flew and wine spattered. His hand and crisp French cuff were soaked. There was wine in his eyelashes and on his lips. The odor was as sharp as cat piss. At least he didn't have to smell Dix's Hermès cologne anymore. He wiped his mouth on his other cuff, blinked and turned to Dix Trevellian, whose eyes were crinkling at the corners in disbelief at the sacrilege, handed him back what was left.

"Tell Raoul to put it on my bill," Dane said.

The telephone woke Sharan up at two-thirty in the morning. She had turned the machine off. On the fourth ring she answered.

"You didn't call me back. You're avoiding me. Don't avoid me."

The only way she could tell he was drunk was by the lengthy pauses between clipped sentences.

"Time out," she said, groaning.

"No time-outs. You work for me now. You will always be available. I will always be available to you. That is the nature of our pact. So what do you think of him?"

Sharan sat up. She had fallen asleep on top of the counterpane of her bed, wearing yellow Jockeys-for-Her with white Clorox blotches on them, and gym socks. Bonkers the cat stirred, a gray puffball snuggled against the arch of her right foot. There was striped moonlight on her stomach and bare breasts. She turned over on her right side and pushed hair away from her ear.

"Sharan?"

"Well, he's charming, self-assured, very good-looking. Some Latin blood, I'd say . . ."

"Roots of the family tree on both sides of the Pyranees. Catalonia, Loungeduc. Some of them were Cathars, persecuted for heresy in the 12th century. They made their way up through the Dordogne and across the Channel to England in the late 17th century. There's a bastardized eastern European connection, gypsies I've heard."

"Dix Trevellian could certainly play the part. He has the kind of sexual arrogance women eat up, to their everlasting regret."

"But you're not vulnerable."

"To him? Under the circumstances? Are you nuts? He's not married, I take it."

"Never has been."

"He's a sportsman. Big challenges. Endurance road races, trophy billfish, helicopter skiing. I think I like his work. The fantastic white spiral house cut into the rock of that mountain in North Carolina, like a perfect seashell preserved intact from a diluvian age. What's it called?"

"Cloud Horse Mountain. The family vacation retreat for more than a hundred years. The original, a log house, burned down, was burned down, twenty-five years ago."

"Arson?"

"Dix's mother set it on fire while her husband and his mistress were in bed. That's the story. Nothing was ever proved."

"Why not?"

"Family business. And the Trevellians are a closely knit clan. Dix likes the limelight, Esther, too, I suppose, but they don't talk about themselves."

"Who is Esther?"

"Dix's sister. She's thirty-nine. Esther runs the Trevellian Foundation, which gives out the big-money prizes every two years. The other sibling is Scott. Three years younger than Esther. He's been diagnosed as paranoid schiz."

"You said you saw Dix Trevellian tonight."

"We run into each other from time to time."

"That must be—hard for you."

"I lost it tonight."

"Is that why you're drinking now?"

"Was drinking. Bottle's empty. And so to bed. I've got a seven-thirty breakfast with—I can't remember who. It's on the computer."

"Lost it how?"

"Nothing actionable. I broke a bottle of Dix's favorite rioja. Deliberately. And then I—"

It was a good connection. Sharan could hear him swallow. And take the deep breath of someone trying to keep his gorge from rising. She felt a slight pang of sympathy.

"Then you?"

"I was going to twist the jagged end of the bottle in his face. I saw how it could happen. God, it was like lightning in my veins. I saw the blood spurting. It lasted a fraction of a second. Never happened. I've been angry in my life. But not like that. It—I'm still—"

"Scared?"

"Don't put words in my mouth. I don't like the taste of them."

"Oh, sorry."

"Start losing control at my age, everything goes. A man's life can burn up in a flash. What good would it do Felicia?"

"I need to know them all. Their histories."

"See Day Emmons. He'll be around. He's still assessing you."

"I'm probably going to disappoint him."

"Take my advice. Don't disappoint either of us."

Sharan's scalp tightened. She had to do some deep breathing herself.

"Don't hang up."

"How did you know I was about to hang up?"

"He's coming to see you tomorrow."

"Mr. Emmons?"

"No. The one you asked for. Jules Brougham."

"Jules Brougham is coming to Georgia to see—? *How* did you—"

"Couple of phone calls. No problem. As it turned out, the U.S. government owns him. The government owns a lot of people. Far more than you could imagine."

"Including me."

"Which is something you don't want to forget."

"I'm hanging up now," Sharan said coldly.

"Wait. What size are you?"

"Size? You mean clothes?"

"Yes."

"Seven, most things. Why?"

"Fitzie's going to do some shopping for you. Dressy New York–type outfits. I'm assuming you don't have a closetful of cocktail dresses already. We'll do something about your hair the next time I see you."

Sharan didn't hear the last couple of words Coleman Dane spoke to her. She had already thrown the portable handset of her phone against the window blinds, crumpling a couple of the thin metal slats and letting in more moonlight. It was the end of sleep. She burned for the rest of the night with a rueful blue flame.

Jules Brougham was a short pale man with an aging monk's tonsure and grapelike bulges beneath each sad eye. His face had density, sobriety, the dignity of fine suffering lines. In high summer he wore a silk suit with a vest, a striped shirt and a subdued necktie, both Turnbull and Asser, very large precise knot emphasizing the frailty of his throat. If he noticed the heat he didn't comment, except to remove his suit jacket. Sharan put the jacket on a wire hanger and hung it on a six-penny nail protruding from a section of water-stained wallboard in the abandoned store she had cleaned up and was using, free of charge, as her studio. She had thumbtacked to big rectangles of white foamcore all of the drawings and paintings she wanted to show the art dealer.

"Portraits," he said. His lips continued to move, quiveringly, after he spoke, like the lips of Oriental actors in badly dubbed Kung Fu Theatre movies.

"Yes, sir. It's basically what I'm interested in. Faces. Of course the settings are important, too. Would you like a cold drink of something? I'll just run across the street to the Shell Mart."

"Fine," he said, in a fog, or a funk, as he moved slowly along the wall, his pale eyes watering a little in the brightness. He dabbed at them with a Stars-and-Stripes handkerchief. "Whatever you're having."

Sharan stayed away for fifteen minutes, as long as she could stand the suspense. When she returned with the drinks he was sitting in a folding metal chair, the only chair in her studio, gazing at the gallon cans of paint stacked to the ceiling against the back wall.

"Housepaint," he said, accepting a bottle of cranberry-apple juice. "You use housepaint."

"Yes. Most of it left over from painting contractors I know. But I can get almost any tint I want, color-computed, from Sherwin-Williams or Sears."

"And drawing paper? Everything on drawing paper?"

"I like the texture of the sixty-pound bond. Doesn't wrinkle. I prime it first."

"Where have you studied, lovey?"

"I took a couple of courses at the Art Institute in Atlanta a few years ago. But mostly I learned by doing."

"I see. I wonder how you achieve some of your painterly values. For instance, the sky behind those children running in what seems to be terror from their playground."

"Oh, that," Sharan said, fidgeting. "I bought some paper doilies at Hallmark and soaked them in pans with different shades of blue, then applied them a layer at a time."

"Doilies from Hallmark." Jules Brougham sipped his juice and looked at the portrait wall again. "And who has influenced you?"

"Chagall, Gauguin, Rousseau. In a nutshell. Probably Hopper, for composition. Contemporary artists, Kate Kretz would be at the top of my list. Her sleeping women knock me for a loop."

"Where have you shown?"

"Oh, nowhere. A couple of church bazaars."

Jules Brougham almost permitted himself to smile. "So you're not a household name, even in this little corner of the world."

"I guess not."

"Just where am I? It's barely an hour since I stepped off the plane at that monstrous airport, and into my limo."

"Jubilation County."

"*Jubilation* County? Hush my mouth. You're virtually an artistic recluse. That can be useful. The fact is, you have talent—" He waited for Sharan to react, but all she did was hold her breath for a dozen seconds, "although your art is perilously close to illustration. What saves you, I think, are the primitivist elements and the tension you impart—what you have hidden, what you don't say—while flaunting your gift as a colorist. Talent is everywhere, of course. If one is to achieve distinction, that is, if you are to become marketable, the approval of the Culturati is required. We will need to work all of the levers." He blotted his forehead with his Old Glory handkerchief, sighing. "And time, apparently, is of the essence."

"What's the Culturati?"

"A somewhat derogatory but convenient term for those gallery owners, curators, collector-patrons and critics who provide the proper aura; who define what art is, and what it is not; who is, and who is not. For the ultimate gratification of a much larger group of wealthy but often insecure aficionados who collect art because it either reflects or enhances their self-images: the Vulturati, as it were. My contracts are verbal. Brougham galleries pay expenses for insurance, shipping, storage, exhibitions and catalogues. My fee is fifty percent. I am worth it. By the way, I have never represented a woman artist. The comment this move generates should be invaluable."

"I'm going to have a show?"

"Eventually. The buildup takes time. The show will be in the spring of next year. By then your success will be a *fait accompli*. Your prospective patron has already been designated. Fortunately it's someone of whom I approve."

"Do you mean Dix Trevellian?"

"Esther Trevellian. She is, in her unobtrusive manner, one of the world's most influential women. Her artistic judgment, which I have played a part in shaping for nearly twenty years, is beyond reproach. A nudge from Esther, and you're in the permanent collection of MOMA, LACMA, the Whitney, any number of contemporary exhibits in good museums from Mexico City to Helsinki. Her pet critics will respond. Favorable opinion in *ArtNews*, the *Voice*, the *Observer*. Last and always least, the *New York Times*. You're about to become the art world's equivalent of the three minute egg. But if you are to have lasting value, we must avoid overcooking you. Nothing is more damaging to a young artist than the cult of celebrity."

"Mr. Brougham?"

"Jules, please."

"If I had sent some slides to your gallery, would you be here now? Saying what you're saying?"

"I don't know. I see the work of hundreds of new artists each year. I have a business to run, and many well-established clients who continue to sell nicely even in a depressed market. Unknown artists constitute a risk. I might have overlooked you."

"I see."

"Never devalue good fortune, honeychile. I am here. I like what you've shown me. The possibilities are interesting. I haven't fallen in love yet. Whether you will continue to evolve as an artist remains to be seen. Meanwhile, I have an obligation to do my best."

"Who are you obligated to?"

"Some questions should not be asked."

"You were about to get slam-dunked in tax court?"

"This is very arrogant of you."

"No, sir, I don't mean it that way. You probably don't even know who's working your levers. But I know. It's all kind of overwhelming to me now. I never really thought I'd be talking to you, Jules. I only wish the circumstances were different."

His quagmire eyebrows came together in a frown. "You seem very anxious. Who is this person to whom we both may owe so much?"

"I guess it's like you said. Some questions shouldn't be asked. For instance, what am I doing, and why am I really doing it? I enjoy painting. I never gave much thought to being a big success. Now how can I possibly trust success, if it does happen? People I don't even know yet will approve of me because you approve, because you don't have any choice. Two days ago I thought I knew who I was, that I'd finally come to terms with my life, with *this*"—holding up her flesh-colored prosthetic hand—"so that I could get married, have a couple of kids before I'm too old, which is practically *right now*. And then I get slam-dunked. By a guy who did it because he could. I'm nothing to him. I'm a means to an end, and I'm an obligation to you. That is such a downer. It kills. See, I have to believe. In somebody, something. In myself. Or I'm no good for it. Painting, solving murders. That's what you all have to try to understand about me."

Sharan stopped when she ran out of breath. Her face felt moist. She was, surprisingly, calm. Purified, as if she'd sung with all her passion a favorite hymn in church. Hadn't known she was going to do it, but what a relief. He could put her outburst down to artistic temperament, neurasthenia, whatever. Maybe he'd change his mind and get up and walk out of her studio now, to the aloof idling limo, its dark, tinted windows, interior coolness. He was watching her. He had never looked away. His long melancholy face had seismic quivers, consequence of his age, that she hadn't paid much attention to. Now they seemed indicative of some momentous psychic event, perhaps a just and withering wrath.

"I was going to leave for New York this afternoon," he said. "Perhaps I should stay over for another day while arranging for insurance and shipping of your work. That will give us the chance to get better acquainted. Next week I hope you'll join me in the Hamptons. August is the best month there. We'll go sailing with my grandson and his family."

With one hand he made the motion of a boat rocking on the waves, looking at Sharan, a shy charmed smile, pixie lode of gold in several small teeth.

FIVE

SOCIAL HOUR OF THE LOST LADIES

The estate where Scott Trevellian worked as a gardener in exchange for lodging and other privileges that gave him the wide-ranging but anonymous use of his computer and computer accessories was located on a bluff opposite one of the widest points of the Hudson River, near the village of Verplanck. A nineteenth-century Georgian manor house and a fin de siècle iron-and-glass conservatory were sited on twenty acres of flowing lawns, crushed-brick walkways, abundant but not formal gardens, arbors of roses and grapevine and fruit orchards. The estate was owned by a Japanese investor who visited it twice a year. Scott had been friendly with the investor's oldest son, Hideo. While they were students at Harvard they had gone backpacking and whitewater rafting together. Three months from graduation Hideo had been stabbed through the neck in the men's room of a Cambridge student hangout by a crackhead who wanted two dollars from him.

All the staff and gardeners, except for Scott, were Japanese. They spoke little English. Scott was fluent in Japanese, but he never let on. Limited communication and a complete lack of socializing suited him fine. When he needed money for personal effects, bus fare or CD-ROMs, they cashed a check for him up at the house. The check was drawn against a numbered account at a Luxembourg bank.

He lived in one of the rooms behind the conservatory. There were six small bedrooms, all plainly furnished, installed for the use of more servants than were currently required on the estate. Periodically and according to a plan known only to him, Scott changed rooms, going from the northeast corner of the conservatory to the southeast corner. Often in good weather he took his bedroll and telescope and stayed outdoors, never in the same place twice, but always within sight of the river and the excursion boat—airily musical, flush with light—that came up the river from the city to dock at the Bear Mountain landing. He enjoyed the sunsets while he waited for the boat to appear, particularly when the orange sky was engulfed by thunderclouds, staccato flashes of lightning. It reminded him of the crackling displays over Cloud Horse Mountain, the home he had loved until Esther contaminated it. This happened when he was eleven and she was fourteen. Dix had designed and built a new house according to one of the precepts of his hero FLW: the house must be *of* the mountain, not on it. Dix obviously understood the symbolism of what he was building (Scott had seen photographs of the architectural model and shuddered in horror), but Dix's knowledge of the evil contamination was incomplete. Or else Dix was implicated, and didn't care. Both had plotted against him—Esther and Dix—so that was that. Nothing more to be said. There was no language that could adequately express Scott's disgust and sorrow.

The midsummer work on the estate of the Japanese gentleman was not extensive or tiring for Scott. He had no responsibility for keeping up the lawn or trimming the centuries-old boxwood. Instead he pruned, sprayed and fertilized beds of gloxenia, daisies, rose vines and ivy; the snow-in-summer, portulaca and climbing wisteria. He also tended a small vegetable plot he was allowed to have near the conservatory, where he raised blemish-free cabbages, tomatoes, carrots, strawberries and blackberries. Marigolds planted between the tomato plants kept the sucking insects away. Apples and pears were ripening now in the orchards. In winter he relaxed his rules about eating food that other hands may have touched. He had discovered a macrobiotic grocery in a blue-collar Peekskill neighborhood slanting down to the river on a cobbled street, twenty minutes by bus, ten minutes of walking, a grocery that one of the Lost Ladies, his favorite, had implied he could trust.

Plenty of time to read these days, but he had a hard time concentrating on a book. Any book. He found himself paying more attention to the margins on each page, the white spaces between lines. It seemed to Scott that something must be there, some extra-textual message that had to do with the mathematics of the page's composition. So many characters per line; perhaps every third character significant in the pattern he was trying to discern. Or fourth, or tenth. Try arranging them differently—a page of *War and Peace* soon became an acrostic nightmare. He was better off with his computer, imparting notes, his diary, to secret sources, until ghostly feedback, the electronic susurrus, deadened him to the point of sleep.

There were cedars in one of his favorite places on the estate, so old and huge it took a stiff wind rising from the river canyon to get them moving, rolling like combers against the dusky flickering sky. The motion of the cedars was reflected in the strong, frost-proof glass alloy panes of the conservatory. The Lost Ladies held their social hour in the empty conservatory during the long twilights when the atmospherics were right.

Some nights they accepted him, some nights he was not wanted. He had to be exceptionally clear to remain in their presence; that is, free of the influence of cacodaemons who delighted in turning every sensory experience—birdsong, church bells, sunlight on dusty pond water—into lessons in the dynamics of hell. When images of sublime beauty became thorns in the eye, great music discordant, and innocent laughter raised blisters on the heart.

The sheltering cedars and the fresh winds of twilight after an internally stormy day could clear him. Lying on warm earth with the river darkening below, the air scented with cedar and, more elusively, rosemary, his thoughts purely visual and unconfused by language, he achieved a low-level state of bliss. Lengthening out, fingertips receptive, secure in his skin. When his mind was tumbling out of sync his body warped into a lumpy humpbacked troll thing, a bag of bubbling pus.

But, given the rightness of the hour, the sky with its unthreatening pyrotechnics (rain usually fell elsewhere, in brilliant torrents), the timeliness of the excursion boat, his own limpid mood of surcease and sensation of floating, the ladies would make their presence known to him.

They had not been acquainted, he knew, before they died; since they had begun to assemble, tentatively at first, beneath the barrel-vaulted glass roof, friendships had developed out of shadows and shared pain. They were like sisters now.

Robin. Her meticulously braided and beaded hair, nearly waist-length, was the color of raw hemp. Tight round black glasses hid her eyes. Unmasked, the eyes were olive, almost the shade of muddied water. Huge laughter, a show of polished uneven teeth, offset her damaged stare. She could still make out the brightest colors, and wore them. Folklorist, mountain witch, she made a circle of the others around her.

Astrid the athlete and compulsive bleeder prowled with suppressed quickness beyond their circle, dark short hair slicked back from a widow's peak on a narrow pensive face, her long bones in a minimum of flesh like sheathed rapiers.

Kerry had the attenuated body of a malnourished waif with radium seething in her joints, but her face was full and cheeky. Her eyes had the sweetness of dark cherries. She had been separated from her music, but on some nights Scott heard an exalted sonata in the troughs of the river wind, and Kerry's face was alight with memory, hearing it, too.

Thursday Childs, the actress, competed with Robin for attention in their set, with her crafty pouts and platinum flourishes. Hands all but shut in her lap as if her joints were made of toy-gauge oxidized metal, her fingertips on fire. There was envy in her appraisal of Astrid's nervy stalking.

La Doña Caterina was, like Astrid, largely aloof, but she could be prodded by the mischievous Robin until she joined in the social hour. Then she had showbiz-bitchy opinions about everything. Her eyes were set deep in wells of Latin melancholy, her lips were broad and flat and cruelly passionate. Although she had been untouched by the fire on the crashed plane, the leap she had taken to avoid suffocation had so damaged her legs and hips she walked only with the help of four-footed aluminum canes.

Felicia, Scott's favorite, the one who had been most kind to him in life and after, also used a cane to get around, a sturdy driftwood shillelagh that had been a gift to her grandfather from Sean O'Casey. Felicia was, by far, the most beautiful of the ladies, not withstanding a patched eye blinded by unendurable rays at one of the ultimate heights of the world, and a foot reduced by frostbite, now resembling a mandragora. She was a creature of superior breeding, refined by self-imposed hardship. Classic features without commonplace flaws are a waste of genetic draughtsmanship, the resulting beauty a monotone. Felicia had sun crinkles and lips that tended to flake even in mild climates. Intelligence and conjecture sparkled in her dark uncovered eyes. Her expression was never passive, never dull, although she might be tired or in a reverie.

Felicia understood his chaos. She was also concerned about the arrival of the seventh sister.

He knew nothing about this one. At times during the summer it seemed to Scott that definitely there was someone else, female, hanging around inside the conservatory, even on glum sultry afternoons when the others had not yet assembled. Her flame low and with only a slight turquoise tint, no firm shape to it. Indecisive, as if she had taken a shortcut into a blind alley, or had been misdirected to the exclusive constellation of the Sisters. A few days would go by, no further appearances: she was not one of them yet. He would forget about her. Maybe it wasn't going to happen again.

Then Felicia would give him a nudge.

You have to find out.

After the social hour, when the others had dispersed to volleys of thunder and the wind that rattled insecure panes in the ground-floor line of conservatory windows, the ones that could be opened, only Felicia remained visible sometimes, depending on his energy level.

He would walk around in manic bursts, or slump on the terra-cotta floor, eyes raised to the glass ceiling of the entrance hall, a Gothic vault between the lower, barrel vaults, where lightning sometimes arced sensuously from the tip of a filigreed rod, a white-hot writhing in the sky.

It must not happen again.

What can I do? What he meant, and Felicia realized this, was *I don't want to do anything.*

As long as they keep coming, none of us who are here already can leave.

You come and go now.

Like migrating butterflies. But, sky or earth, it's all limbo, Scott.

Who is she?

I don't know. None of us do.

In a burst of lightning that scorched through the center of his brain he saw Felicia in torment, and was sorry.

You're the only one who knows, she said.

I'm not.

The only one who knows why *it's happening.*

No one would ever believe me. I bear the mark of Bedlam. I said once—I think I said, "I know where Felicia is." I shouldn't have said that.

Maybe it didn't matter.

You know better. Why don't you leave me alone? Go with the others now.

Words to that effect. The arguments differed in language and intensity. Until the night Felicia put an end to arguing by coming up with a new idea.

He didn't easily accept new ideas. Yet there was a certain chilling appropriateness about it that cut through the instinctive barriers raised in his mind. He wanted to tell her he was afraid. But fear was such a prevailing condition of his life—smothering, gaseous, unnameable fear—that it was almost a relief to have something particular he could dwell on, a revenge play of his design, enacted with the help of his computer. His sanctuary apart from Bedlam. And there was always the possibility that it might do some good.

Scott ate unsalted tomatoes and carrot sticks for dinner one night not long after Felicia had explained her idea. Then he began to rummage, as if the computer were a magician's trunk, in his cyberspace attic, probing weak defenses, appropriating the contents of electronic mailboxes, his own identity secret as his queries shunted from blind to blind around the world: Kobe, Adelaide, Bergen, Cartagena, Calgary. Appointments were set up, precise instructions relayed, funds transferred in near-silence and isolation. Until at last he was ready to bring up the lights on the stage he had set.

Let the play begin.

SIX

THE DEEP BLACK STARE

Concourse A at Hartsfield International Airport in Atlanta is usually crowded, except during the off-peak travel hours from around midnight to six in the morning. The rest of the time, particularly in summer, it's a jam-up of humanity jostling for their cut-rate seats on flights back to the old hometown or to vacation spots across the continent. Business persons. Tousled hearty-looking foreign tourists wearing sturdy hiking shoes. Kids of divorced parents handed over to airline personnel for trips to distant moms or dads. Old folks in wheelchairs looking slack and depleted, like dying fish who have washed in on a toxic tide. The occasional movie star, that face of epic celebrity, igniting a flash-fire of interest and awe as he proceeds under heavy escort to his flight.

Lew Carbine is smaller than he appears onscreen, but aren't they all. There are two airline officials and two bodyguards with him, the kind who look as if they've done hard time as bouncers in surreal after-hours clubs. The bodyguards are on their toes, theatrically watchful. Deranged snipers are a possibility. Lew is darkly tanned and still pumped from his most recent workout. His shirt barely accommodates a sculpted torso that looks like solid bronze. His slacks have that pleated flaring forties look. Legend has it that Lew needs a lot more crotch room than the average male. The leather of his black boots, like his sultry Sicilian locks, has a buttery gleam. The boots have two-inch heels. It seems, at any moment, that Lew's distant, slightly weary gaze will shift and he will ceremoniously encourage the recognition of himself by onlookers. Exchange smiles. *How ya doin'*. But it never happens.

His girlfriend is an inch taller than Lew can manage. She looks pale and moody behind dark glasses apparently designed to protect her eyes from nuclear explosions. She cradles a Yorkshire terrier in one thin lanky arm. She and Lew walk side by side but there is an apartness implicit in their relationship, as if they never waste energy making small talk.

A flurried few moments, then they have swept by, leaving a little thrill in the minds of those who glimpsed Lew.

Sharan, looking up from her Coke and burger, thought, *Is that what it's going to be like? These people with their money and vanity swank and virtuoso aplomb?*

Dayton Emmons, accompanying her on the flight to Washington, said, "Rumor has it that Esther Trevellian and Lew Carbine were lovers once upon a time. That she helped him with his career."

"Oh."

"What do you think of him?"

"Viscerally? Intellectually? I suppose he's worth all the millions they pay him per picture. I don't know much about those things. I'd say he wears women the way women wear fur coats. There's something unspeakably gluttonous about a man like that—Sharan, stop," she said in mock exasperation. Nervous and far too talky this morning.

"My daughter would have said something like that," Emmons observed.

In the four days they'd spent time together he had said next to nothing about himself, while revealing, little by little, just how much he knew about Sharan. Apparently Dayton Emmons had access to every detail of her life that was on file somewhere, from grade school on.

"What's your daughter's name?"

"Oh, she isn't with us anymore. Mary Ellen died when she was thirteen. Church camp bus went out of control on a mountain road. One of those things. But you're a lot like her. How you observe your surroundings. The ways you express yourself, sometimes with just a shrug or that wry, put-upon squint."

"Do you have other children?"

"Three boys. The last one's just beginning med school. We have two grandchildren." Of course he had photos with him. "Sibby, that's the blonde, lives in Portland, Oregon. Bob is with the field office there. Dot and I don't see as much of them as we'd like."

"Will I see you again? I mean, after we get to D.C.? Or am I being turned over to Coleman Dane like a laboratory rat?"

He looked sympathetic. "I probably won't be seeing you, Sharan. Because of my connection to the Bureau there's a risk involved, for you. But I'll be following your progress very closely. I'll be available for advice if you need it."

"You know I'm going to need it."

"Your record with the Military Police and the CID was exemplary. You just couldn't pull the trigger once, when maybe you should have."

"It doesn't keep me awake anymore. I'm over it. Funny. I wasn't peeing in my pants. I wasn't scared. I just couldn't pull the trigger. He didn't seem—worth it, somehow. An undersized man, eyes close to his long nose. I was watching the gun that had malfunctioned. Never saw the knife. Special chef's knife, they make them in Japan. Twenty-five hundred dollars apiece. Sharper than Excalibur. The Japanese get the most out of steel, don't they? Didn't see it, barely felt it. A slight jar when the blade went through my bones above the wrist. I still have that knife, buried in a trunk somewhere. I suppose you know they reattached my hand and wrist. But it took too long getting me to a hospital where they could do the procedure."

"I know. Infection set in."

"Bet you don't know the name of my first boyfriend."

"Ronnie. You were fourteen. Did you kiss him?"

"I *lived* for kissing him. Mr. Emmons—couldn't you ask him for me? Please. Just get me out of this." Seeking to employ his fondness for her.

He shook his head, regretful but firm.

"I've tried to persuade him, Sharan."

"God *damn* it. What kind of man *is* he?"

"He hurts deeply, Sharan. Hates deeply, too."

She put down the uneaten half of her burger; it was already giving her gas. "I thought I was hungry. Maybe I should have had a salad."

Emmons looked at his watch. "It's about that time."

Sharan covered one of his hands with her own, looking him hard in the eyes. In distress her own eyes turned cobalt-blue.

"I never loved my father. I respected him, but I never loved him.

When I lost my hand I thought, Jesus and Mary. I don't have to feel guilty anymore."

"Yes, Sharan. I know that, too."

Sharan had been to Washington only once, when she was a teenager. A reunion of Korean War vets, her father's Army Raiders unit. He had been a teenager himself in Korea. Sarge was being honored posthumously, a last sprinkling of stardust for the Medal of Honor winner. They visited Sharan's great-uncle Bert, a World War Two general, now living at the Soldiers and Airmens' home. They went to the zoo and to the White House. The President was on vacation. They met the Vice President, who gave Sharan a glass paperweight with the presidential seal embedded in it. She still had it in a trunk, but not the trunk in which she kept the Japanese carving knife.

A car and driver were waiting for her at National Airport. The driver was at the gate, holding a sign with her last name printed on it. Sharan and Dayton Emmons had said their good-byes before deplaning.

The driver, a sandy-haired kid in a black suit, took her carry-on luggage and she followed him, quaking, to the parking garage where he'd left the Cadillac sedan. Washington was sweltering under a glary, threatening sky. Instead of crossing the river they drove south and then west, to one of those office parks with fountains and low, sharply angular, stepped-back glass buildings dreamily reflecting trees and sky. She could see swans on a lake dyed emerald-green from her fourth-floor quarters in the Embassy Suites Hotel. In the distance windshields sparkled on the Beltway. She was, according to the receptionist who had signed her in, just outside the city limits of Alexandria, Virginia. Her suite was prepaid. There were no messages.

Sharan unpacked. She took off her skirt and blazer and blouse and hung those up, put on a jogger's bra and featherweight Dacron shorts and spent an hour at tai chi in front of the picture window. Riding the Horse, Carrying the Tiger Back to the Mountain. She drank tomato juice from the minibar and took a nap. When she woke up it was raining, tropical ferocity, solid gray outside except for lights that had come on in the watery dusk. It was too cold in the room. She put on the bathrobe furnished by the hotel and lay down again, staring at the textured ceiling. After a while she got up, opened her portfolio, took out a pad and colored pencils and drew, recalling the face of a red-haired little girl she had seen on the plane. The light wasn't good and her hand wasn't steady. Why didn't he phone her?

Local news on TV. A Washington she wasn't familiar with. It looked more like Southwest Atlanta. Gunfire in the projects. Rapists, drug dealers, child molesters. Squalor, despair, heartache. The drone-like eyes of children brutalized by their environment. No blazing salt-white monuments visible from this neighborhood.

The arrogant son of a bitch.

Eight o'clock. The rain stopped, the sky cleared to a faint rose shade just before dark.

Three paintings bolted to the walls. A Dubuffet knockoff that left her cold, a reproduction of a Corot landscape, some bright confettilike doodlings, after Miró. She ate a handful of Macadamia nuts. She decided to take a bath. Watch a movie. Lew Carbine's latest was available on pay-per-view. She had seen a trailer for the movie four or five months ago at the TenPlex near her home. In it the actor wore a tight-fitting futuristic outfit with a codpiece. Incredible thighs. Too much eyeliner. But that codpiece.

Somehow, someday, she was going to get even with Coleman Dane. If she lived long enough.

At twenty past eight, as she was running water for her bath, the concierge called and told her there was a car waiting for her on the rear motor court.

So what was she supposed to wear, goddammit!

Sharan settled for the best dress in her wardrobe, a clingy black number with gold cuff links and hustled downstairs.

The car was a pearl-gray, top-of-the-line Mercedes sedan that looked as if it had just been whisked off a showroom floor. The driver was a bald brown man who wore a houndstooth sport coat and jodh-purs with his highly polished boots. He had a polite smile but was disinclined to speak, even when Sharan introduced herself. She wondered if he thought she was nothing more than trade for the night.

They drove south to Prince William County, then northwest on a secondary road. Sharan saw a sign that said Manassas. The driver took a lane through rolling hill country, horse farms. A few lights, an occasional pickup truck or horse van to squeeze by on the narrow lane. The driver made a phone call. Left, right, left again. White fences. At the head of a horseshoe drive there was an illuminated two-story Tidewater-style house of weathered old brick with carefully trimmed ivy accents. Two large barns, a manager's bungalow and a carriage house on the property. There was a blue-and-silver, Italian-made, very expensive Agusta MKII helicopter on a circular pad to one side of the brick house, away from the barns and the outdoor equestrian rings.

Coleman Dane met her personally at his front door. He was wearing gray athletic shorts and a Gold's Gym T-shirt. No shoes. He had a pair of well-used sixteen-ounce boxing gloves over one shoulder.

"Hello. Just got in myself. Monthly grilling on Capitol Hill. Senate Judiciary Committee. Expanded wiretap authority. Last year it was pay phones." He was spitting it out, like a volcano spitting out leftover brimstone. "Now they want all telephone equipment to be manufactured with a device that provides instant tapping capability. I have to try to justify every abuse of citizen's rights the Feebies think up, whether I like it or not."

"Do you?"

"I taught Constitutional Law before I was appointed, if that gives you a clue."

"May I come in?"

"Oh, sure." He opened the door wider, giving her a critical once-over. "What are you dressed up for?"

"I didn't—"

"Cook's night out. If you're hungry, James can nuke a pizza. We have them in the freezer for when the kids are here. Millie kept the house in Georgetown. I usually put up at my uncle's apartment at the Shoreham. But the farm's better for our meetings."

"Which you don't see as an abuse of my constitutional rights."

"Still a little on edge, Sharan?" he said, rubbing a deep-set fatigued eye. Without his shoes, they weren't far apart in height. She didn't reply. "I was just about to work out. Care for a drink?"

"No."

"Slip out of those shoes, be comfortable. Have a look around the house if you want to. I'll be in the gym."

Since she'd been invited, she took the tour. Shoes off. The house had two wings. Twelve-foot ceilings in all rooms, at least six fireplaces. The choice of decorations seemed to have been a woman's: silk roses everywhere, which Sharan hated. Fuddy-duddy. Worcester Bengal Tiger and Blind Earl porcelains in the formal dining and the informal breakfast room were more to her taste. So were the George III mahogany furnishings she saw in several rooms. The art collection was substantial, ranging from Mary Cassatt and Boudin to modern Southern-themed painters like Wolf Khan, Wadsworth Jerrell and Carroll Cloar.

James, the man who had driven her from the hotel, had changed clothes and was now wearing a white buttonless jacket over his striped shirt and suspenders that held up a pair of red golf slacks. He was polishing brass in the butler's pantry.

"May I get you something to drink?" A little more friendly, as if he had decided she wasn't there for entertainment purposes.

"Coke, I guess. No, I've been drinking too much cola. Orangeade, or something like that. How long do his workouts usually last?"

"There's no telling. Most nights, when he don't stay in town, he won't get in 'til half past eleven. Then at two in the morning, Mr. Cole still be at it. That speed bag just a blurrin' like a hummingbird's wings."

James juiced an orange and added spring water in the kitchen, an expanse of quarry tile, bird's-eye maple–topped cooking islands and a colonial brick hearth with wall ovens on either side.

"How long have you worked for Mr. Dane?"

"Oh, fifteen years next January."

From a kitchen barstool Sharan looked out at the lighted swimming pool, a couple of magnolia leaves floating on the surface like deflated amphibians, and the white Palladian-style pool house.

"This is delicious, thank you."

"What I add, just that little touch of cherry heering."

"I'll have to remember that. How long has he been divorced?"

"Almost two years. Not long after Miss Felicia up and disappear without nobody have the slightest notion how or why. Foul play has been suspected. Lord, she was a lovely woman. Then little Misty taken sick. Now, you got to be on your toes at that Justice Department. Mr. Cole work like a big dog guard a cathouse. His beeper gives him no peace. I'm reminded of a picture I seen once, at the National Gallery it might have been, the poor man chained to a rock, his face a study in torment; and once a day a vulture come to tear out another chunk of his liver."

"What's the matter with his daughter?"

"She has leukemia. Lately it's done much better, but the good Lord only knows."

"Is there a bathroom handy, James?"

"Yes, ma'am, up the back stairs there, the one between Misty and Griffin's bedrooms is closest."

Misty had a lot of computer equipment; Griffin was a horseman, roly-poly in his formal riding habit, one bedroom wall nearly filled with blue and red ribbons, built-in shelves of trophies. Sharan by-passed their common bathroom and continued on to the master bedroom, which, along with a paneled sitting room that Dane used as a home office, took up the second floor of the west wing of the house.

Maybe it had been an amicable divorce. Dane had kept on display throughout his bedroom numerous family photos that included his ex-wife, and two framed portraits of her alone, one in which she wore a high-fashion veil that covered without concealing her face and long neck. The veil added a mystical dimension to Millie Dane's somewhat severe, hard-nosed beauty. Southern Italian, Greek, difficult to pin down her ancestry. She looked as if she never took crap from God, man or Yeti. But in softer, more youthful images, her smile, as she gazed at her husband, was close to rapture. There was an ease about him, one arm draped companionably across his wife's shoulders, that reminded Sharan of how close to burnout, or an awesome collapse, he might now be.

There were three land-line telephones beside his bed, one equipped with a scrambler. Reading material. Six weekly magazines and several insider-type newsletters. He belonged to a best-sellers-on-tape club. Lawbooks, piles of legal briefs, current events and biographies in the sitting room, which had an overload of framed photos of Dane with the high and might-be's on five continents. A collection of presidents' signatures and personal notes in a fireproof viewing case. A photograph of a Gothic-style dorm with a casement window and a couple of grinning faces in the window, circled in red. The faces had been painted on bare buttocks. College hijinks. One shelf of a bookcase held the handwritten journals of Felicia Dane. And a single small photo of his sister, framed in gold. Spotlighted. The shelf seemed uncomfortably like a shrine. Sharan looked at the photo for a long time. She had the feeling that they could have been friends, that she had missed something by not knowing Felicia.

Harvard Law Review in Dane's bathroom. And several *Penthouses*. Women in big-assed rutting positions, looking back over their shoulders, the goodies plumply displayed like small garroted animals. She would have thought he'd have a preference for more intellectual or artistic pornography. Oh, well. Busy man. No time for subtleties. Maybe while he was having his morning coffee and shaving at the same time. Sharan smiled but her head had begun to ache. What else was gleanable here, without expanding her area of investigation to closets and cabinet drawers? He took vitamin E and vitamin C and used a prescription nostrum to retard hair loss, or promote new growth. A losing effort so far. There were many loose hairs in the soap and sink basin, his brushes were full.

Sharan used his toilet and washed her hands and went looking for Dane. Found him by tracking the nonstop patter of a speed bag being worked below the master bedroom suite in the west wing. While she had been roaming around his quarters she was conscious of the sounds of the timing bag, greatly muffled, as if her traced and retraced shoeless steps were accompanied by his heartbeats.

Speed bag, heavy bag, free weights, benches, a Nautilus machine, a sauna, mirrors on three of the gymnasium walls. He had taped his hands and wore ring shoes. He was pouring sweat, his hair flat as an oil slick. He had fast hands, and Sharan thought of her older brother Ted: great athletic ability but no ambition other than to drive a forklift days and get high nights, until drug testing became mandatory for all but the most menial jobs. Dane had the same athleticism, the look on his face that of a conductor before a world-class orchestra, hearing nuances beyond the range of most human ears.

She sat on a padded weight bench, knees together, and studied him until he stepped back, hands dropping, chest heaving, blinking sweat out of his eyes. She threw him a towel. He blotted his face and tucked the towel around his neck. His shirt was soaked, his cotton shorts stuck to his butt in back and clung to his jockstrap bulge in front. Sharan thought, not deliberately, of codpieces.

"What kind of shape are you in?" Dane asked her.

"I exercise."

"Do you run?"

"Not much. It's boring."

"I thought I'd do a couple of miles now."

"Don't mind me," she said peevishly.

He turned his eyes on her, the deep black stare.

"Okay. It can wait. We need to talk anyway. What kind of martial arts course did they put you through at McClellan?"

"Throws, blows, come-alongs."

"Have you kept up with it?"

"Some things you don't forget. I'm basically one-handed now, so I wouldn't rely on judo in a deadly situation."

"What would you rely on?"

"Club arts, I suppose."

"What's that?"

"Baton. Riot stick, whatever you want to call it."

"If you happen to have one with you. They're about two and a half feet long, aren't they?"

"Well, I wouldn't need a bona fide hickory or bamboo club. I could improvise. A length of PVC pipe, one of those tall pepper shakers, I don't know. A copy of *Time* magazine."

He wiped a drop of sweat from his eyelashes, and smiled. Sharan wondered if she'd seen him smile before. It wasn't like the coming of the dawn, only cynical amusement.

"*Time* magazine? You could hold off a grown man with *Time*?"

"*Newsweek. U.S. News.* Any magazine."

He began to peel the tape from his hands, yanking it off in long soiled strips, looking down, still faintly smiling.

"*Penthouse*," Sharan said.

Dane glanced up, thinking about why she might have thrown that in. Then he knew. He looked momentarily uncomfortable. "Well. Did you enjoy your exceptionally thorough tour of my house?"

"It was something to do."

"Mil and I bought the place eighteen years ago. It belonged, a long time back, to General George Patton. My wife, ex-wife, used to ride a lot, but she has a problem with a hip joint. Some hereditary defect, she'll need to have it replaced in a year or two."

He gathered up the adhesive tape from the floor and carried it to a wastebasket beside a water cooler. Then he drew water into a paper cup.

"Why did she divorce you?" Sharan asked.

"I was never home. That old story. We never knocked heads or anything. She just got fed up. I think Mil's ready to marry again. I get these vibrations from the kids. It could be any of three guys I know Mil's been seeing. But of course the kids aren't talking. They never tried to manipulate either of us, the way children of divorce usually do. In fact, we may be more of a family than we were before, because of Misty's illness. My daughter has leukemia."

"I know, I'm sorry."

"She's a hell of a fighter." He drank a second cup of water, slowly. "You cut your hair."

"A little. Too short and I look like a scarecrow."

"You get along okay with Jules Brougham?"

"Yes."

"That's it? Yes? You got along?"

"He's going to make me a star. He says I have talent."

"I'd like to see some of your pictures."

"Paintings. I paint. I'm an artist. I don't just draw pictures."

He didn't reply to her testiness, except for a wan grimace. But he might have been thinking of something else.

"Why don't you get out of that dress?" he said.

"Excuse me?"

"I need to know. Can you handle yourself? If it gets rough, what happens?"

"You send in an FBI SWAT team, isn't that the arrangement? I'll be as safe as churches, or reassurances to that effect."

"Trevellian gets around. He's in Cairo, he's in Kuala Lumpur. He has projects, some in conjunction with other architects, in a dozen countries."

"There is *no way* I'll leave my native soil with that man."

"You may be jetting off with Dix in the middle of the night to Cloud Horse Mountain to visit his mom. Or to San Francisco for a late dinner in Chinatown. Vegas for high-stakes baccarat with the Sultan of Brunei and Steven Spielberg. It's their lifestyle. They have planes, helicopters and yachts."

"I'm going to be wired, aren't I?"

"Betcha. The latest trouble-free, no-maintenance gadgets. They run on solar power, lunar power, DNA for all I know. You'll be monitored by satellite. Every conversation you have with Dix, every breath you take will be stored for retrieval if you happen to leave a zone of direct transmission."

"Including my last breath?"

"The louvered door there is a changing room. Plenty of clean sweats."

"You're serious."

"Uh-huh."

"This is awkward for me."

"You'll do it anyway. Won't you, Sharan?"

The stare.

In the changing room she put on Fila track warmups she found in a locker. She still had a headache. She went barefoot into the gymnasium and paused at one corner of a square made from four blue tumbling mats. Dane handed her a copy of *Time* magazine, one of the thin ad-shy summer issues.

"You're not ready," she said.

"What do I need?"

"Head gear. Foul protector. Those sixteen-ounce gloves laced up high enough to protect your forearms. Got any knee and elbow pads?"

"I think there's some of Griffin's skateboarding stuff around. What do I need all the padding for?"

"You don't. As long as you don't mind bone bruises, earaches and peeing blood for three days."

He tilted his head slightly. She thought he was going to laugh at her. Instead he may have thought about the kid on the stolen motorcycle. Sharan bounced on her toes in various places on the mats, finding the footing satisfactory. She stopped and turned her attention to the magazine, rolling it up tightly from the stapled side. She wrapped each end with adhesive tape to maintain compactness. Dane found some of the protective equipment. After he put it on he sat down with the pillowlike boxing gloves. He didn't wrap his hands. The left glove went on first.

"Where did you learn to box?"

"The manly art is a tradition in our family. What do you want me to do, I mean, pull my punches, or what?"

"No."

"I don't have headgear for you. Wear mine."

"No, you'll need it. If you duck the wrong way."

He looked skeptically at the rolled magazine she was holding in her left hand, about two inches showing between thumb and forefinger, the rest of it lying snug against the inside of her forearm. Her other three fingers gripped the makeshift club lightly.

"I'll need you to lace these gloves," Dane said.

Sharan put the magazine down and helped him. On his feet, he tucked in his chin, pawed the air with the cumbersome gloves. Circling, good footwork, smart powerful jabs. Sharan retrieved her copy of *Time* and watched him detachedly.

"Now I'm ready," Dane said, facing her.

"No, you're not."

Stepping toward him with her left foot, head back and protected by the prosthetic hand, she flicked her makeshift club with a quick turn of the wrist and caught him below one knee with a force that hobbled him, enough pain to cause him to drop his guard. She lashed again at the new target, the base of his throat. Easing up this time, not wanting to crush his larynx. As he was choking and sinking to his knees she rapped the bridge of his nose backhanded, hard enough to let him know she could have splintered the bone if she'd wanted to, then stepped back with her club tucked up along the forearm, watching him.

"Jesus. Christ." He coughed and almost threw up. "It's *paper*."

"What matters is density and velocity, Cole. Pounds of pressure per square inch. It's all in the wrist. That skinny rolled-up magazine is really traveling on impact. Human bones are ridiculously easy to break; a small amount of torque can wipe out a wrist or elbow. As little as eight psi of direct force can snap the femur above the knee."

His headgear was lopsided. She kneeled beside him and took it off. Then she raised his head in her two hands. He was sweating again. There was a little trickle of blood from one nostril. Sharan wiped it away. His upper lip was bristly; he was one of those men who probably needed a touch-up shave after twelve hours or so. The deftness of her fingertips after the swift beating created confusion in his flesh she could read like a medium reads tea leaves. It was her own confusion she was unprepared for, and found intimidating. She let go of him.

"Set me up, didn't you?" He had a raspy breath. The look he gave her hinted at admiration.

"Yes," she said. "I set you up, Cole."

"For what?"

When she didn't answer him, he nodded slightly, having made up his own mind.

"Can you help me out of these gloves?"

"I don't know," Sharan said, thoughtfully rocking on her heels, seeing another drop of blood worm its way down her long upper lip. "Maybe I'm safer with you like this."

Dane started to smile, then looked alertly past her, and Sharan turned her head.

James had come quietly into the room, holding a cell phone.

"Sorry to disturb you, Mr. Dane. Seemed as if you ought to take this one."

Dane nodded, rising. Sharan stood with him and untied both gloves, pulled them off his hands. He brushed past her to take the phone from James. Sharan dropped the gloves on the mat and walked another way, found herself looking into a slightly tarnished, rimless mirror on one wall, staring at herself as if she had suddenly become someone she didn't recognize. She bowed her head, prosthetic hand pressed against one temple.

Dane didn't say much to whomever had called him. Asked terse questions in a low voice. She glanced into the mirror again. His back was to her until he had finished the conversation.

When she saw his face again, her skin prickled.

"Something's happened," he said.

"Oh, no. Your daughter?"

"Not that."

He put the phone down and came silently toward her.

"Dix Trevellian apparently went berserk tonight. He maimed a whore and attempted suicide."

Sharan had to think how to breathe. "Yes?" she said.

"Accounts are sketchy. They'll stay that way. Massive damage control underway by the Trevellian family machine. Not a breath of scandal will escape to the media."

She waited for the relief she hoped would come now, the canceling of obligation.

"James will drive you back to your hotel. Nothing's changed, Sharan." His eyes were neither cruel nor conscienceless, but implacable. "As long as Dix is still alive, then nothing has changed."

SEVEN

SUMMONING THE
GOBLINS

Esther Trevellian had finished her computer chat with the wife of the Chancellor of Austria, a member of the Board of Directors of the Trevellian Prize Committee, and was thinking about turning in for the night, when Mardie Kregg came into the ninety-foot bedroom of Esther's suite. Mardie wasn't ready for bed either, although she'd probably been taking a shower. Her hair was damp and lank. She looked as if she had dressed quickly. Loose-fitting action clothing: short-sleeved safari jacket, baggy pants, jump boots. She had a remote radio with her.

"Dix," she said.

"Drunk?"

"I don't know. Lot of commotion over thur. Somebody screamen."

"Security report to you?"

"Dix has everybody locked out of the workroom. He's on the roof."

"Oh, boy," Esther said. She took off her scarlet silk chinoiserie robe and was carelessly naked. It wasn't meanness on her part, Mardie knew; sometimes she just forgot. Mardie simply looked away. They had been lovers in tender adolescence, and Mardie's own carnality and attending guilt had precipitated a long-lasting nervous breakdown. Mardie was now, would forever be, celibate, for the continuing good of their relationship. Flesh to her mind was merely the Lord's clay. Or mud, as the case might be.

Esther was aware of thunder outside.

"Raining?"

"Not yet. Hit's moven in across the river. What you want to wear, Esther?"

"Lightweight jogging. No shoes. If he's on the roof, I'm better off without shoes."

"Could start to rain anytime," Mardie warned, going to one of the walk-in closets. Esther had four. Sportswear, casual, executive, formal. Computerized inventory. Styles, designers, colors, location, the dates when each article of clothing had been worn, and the occasion.

"I'm coming," Esther said. "I need to pee. Do you have the skipper software for the workroom locks?"

"Hit'll be thur when we get thur."

"Nobody goes in yet."

"Screamen bloody murder," Mardie said, hearing a report on her radio.

"I don't care. *Wait for me.*"

They took Esther's elevator to the Trevellian House subbasement below the parking levels, where an electric cart and driver were waiting. He drove them through the tunnel beneath Eightieth Street and up an incline to another elevator in the four-story mansion. A lot of cross talk on the remote radios from security people.

Esther said irritably, "Mardie, tell them all to shut up."

The fourth floor of the mansion, 3500 square feet, had been extensively renovated for use as Dix Trevellian's New York workshop. In reception glazed red tile alternated with library paneling from a three-hundred-year-old English house that had been half destroyed in a fire and purchased by Dix for the wealth of its remaining features. A Frank Stella painted aluminum sculpture occupied a third of the reception area.

Mr. Marlowe Hare, wearing a chalk-striped, double-breasted, burnt-orange suit and a brown fedora, had been out walking Esther's borzois when he heard the screaming. "Quiet in there now," he said.

"Who was screaming?"

"Sounded like a woman, Miss Esther."

"Get us inside," Esther told Mardie Kregg, her eyes narrowing slightly as lightning lit up the panes of the A-frame skylight overhead.

Mardie was already behind the old Swiss convent table that served as a reception desk, tapping on the computer keyboard. The computer absorbed the skipper instructions. In six seconds the override took effect, locks clicked and matching paneled doors glided open.

"Oh God, oh God," the woman moaned softly. They couldn't see her when they entered the workroom, which had been blitzed. Drafting tables overturned, architect's lamps smashed, black ink splattered in a rage on the floor-to-ceiling drawing of a Berlin opera house project that took up eight curving feet of wall inside Dix's personal studio.

"I guess he was overdue," Esther said regretfully to Mardie.

"Here she is," Marlowe Hare called to Esther.

The woman had crawled under a light table, twelve feet long, that held models of architectural projects: an airport terminal in South Africa, the new Chilean embassy in Washington. All broken, smithereens. A sturdy gnarled walking stick lay on the table amid the litter. The woman was young, dark-haired. She looked as if Vandals had visited her body, left her flinching and deranged. Her left arm was broken, the jagged ends of the radius bone protruding through bruised bloody flesh just above the wrist. She was wearing a black eye patch and a trench coat. The resemblance, Esther thought, with a prickling indignation about to flash into fury, was an eerie one. But, kneeling near the young woman, she noted that the patch covered the wrong eye.

Details.

"Oh God. Don't let him come near me."

"What's your name?" Esther asked her.

"Oh God." She had vomited all over the trench coat.

"The sooner you talk to me, the sooner you'll be in the hospital."

"I never hurt so bad. He tried to kill me."

"No, he didn't," Esther said, pulling the eye patch, which disgusted her, off over the woman's head and throwing it away. "Or you'd be dead. Now tell me your name."

The young woman—she might have been only about nineteen—rolled her shocked eyes. "Kimberlea."

"I don't mean your working name."

"Mary . . . Ascencios."

"Who sent you?"

"The pain is bad. It is so bad. I can't look at it. He broke my arm. Then he just threw me."

"Whose string do you belong to, Miss Ascencios? Donnerly? Sally Queens?"

"Donnerly."

"Thank you." Esther straightened and walked Mardie away from the model table, where Dix had laid out party favors and treats: a Baggie containing prepared base, glass pipes of different sizes, his gold Dunhill lighter, cotton swabs and a quart of 151-proof rum. "Send her out to the Island. Private hospital. She'll need surgery. Call Hershbein at Shady Knolls. I want her out of the country by dawn. Some place restful and remote. Lac St. Jean, or maybe Prince Edward Island. Nursing care as long as she needs it. Full-time security."

"How about her family?"

"If she had any kind of decent family she wouldn't be whoring."

"How much do we pay her?"

Esther stared at her long enough to give Mardie, who in the better part of her lifetime had had plenty of opportunity to become hardened to Esther's moods, a case of the flutters. "We don't pay," she said, spacing the words, emphasizing none. Esther turned and walked back to Dix's studio, climbed a spiral stairway of iron covered with tanned saddle leather, opened a hatch and emerged onto the roof of the mansion, where the west wind, laced with a light rain, blew in her face.

"Is that you, Esther?"

She looked around, saw him. Perched, like a goddamn fool, on the copper cupola with the lightning rod. Smoking base, or trying to, his back hunched against the wind. Feeding his breakdown, courting insanity with the base. Summoning his goblins. He was twenty feet above the main skylight over the workroom, twenty-five feet from the limestone floor of the parapet walk that encircled the various roofs and chimneys. Esther reckoned she could get up there easier than Dix had managed, in his agitated state. But at any moment the low thunderous sky moving across the Hudson from Jersey might loose a charge at the mansion's lightning rod. Of course she knew from experience that it was the discharge traveling upward to the leader that registered on the eye as bolts of lightning, repeating several times a second in an ionized channel of air. Dix would feel the discharge sizzling on his skin an instant before he flashed and parts of him, his kidneys, the end of his nose, charred like matchheads.

On the other hand, there were those victims of lightning who survived without losing digits, without serious scarring. Esther had only the burn scar, like a purple patch on an innertube, under her right arm, the arm that had been raised to the sky on Cloud Horse Mountain. Except for the partly melted barrels of the shotgun she'd been defiantly brandishing, which she had kept as a souvenir (with very few exceptions, Esther never discarded anything), there was no other visible reminder of her ordeal. By the time Esther was twenty she had overcome all the tiresome speech defects, her efforts leaving her with a slightly lower register, a softness of voice as soothing as old-fashioned patent medicine. Much later new techniques of brain-scanning and wave analysis had determined just what else had gone awry in her head at the instant she was struck. Knowing that she no longer had a small gland the size of an almond in one hemisphere of her brain was of no practical value to Esther. But her inability to experience fear from the day she was struck by lightning often had been useful.

"Time to come down, Dix," she said, looking up at her brother.

"Come down to what? It's all shit, Esther."

"What is?"

"I try and try. The inspiration is always pure. The dynamics are perfect. Then what happens? Look at Trevellian House. Is it the best thing anyone's designed since the pyramids, or is it what that asshole Havelock Blore says it is—a monstrosity?"

"Trevellian House is magnificent. You'll always have your critics, Dix. It's against the rules of your profession to be famous before you're sixty. The critics can't stand your success. Nevertheless you're a phenomenal success."

"I can't tell anymore," Dix moaned. "After the first pure moment, I lose my vision. I see it wrong tonight. I see it all wrong. I want to puke my guts out, it's so fucking wrong."

She'd been through it all before, how many times? With Dix, with an occasional protege of hers. Drunks, philanderers, devils—great artists in everyday life were like acrobats trying to walk with their shoestrings tied together.

"No, it isn't. You're a genius. There hasn't been anyone like you since da Vinci. But please. You have to live in your body, Dix. You can't keep abusing it and expect to have those wonderful soaring moments. The pipe steals your soul. Throw the pipe away and come down. It's going to storm."

"She took me by surprise. I didn't mean to hurt her."

"The prostitute? You ordered her, didn't you?"

"Are you *crazy*? She's not the one I asked for. Did you see her? She came in with that eyepatch and shillelagh, shit, she was the image of Felicia Dane. I'm telling you, Esther, my heart nearly stopped. Then I just fucking lost it."

"Oh, I see. The girl was someone's little gifty."

Dix began to sob.

"I guess I blacked out again, Esther. I can't remember. I have such a terrible headache now."

The wind was gusting. A virulent black cloud the length of Manhattan Island loomed through the vertical city's smoky nimbus across Central Park. It contained galaxies of lightning, like a dangerous universe aborning.

"I'm coming up there, Dix," Esther said.

"Esther!" Mardie Kregg called warningly from the hatch. Esther paid no attention.

The steep roofs were covered with overlapping barrel tiles, but there were handholds—an angle of gutter, the edge of a skylight, rusty cables that served unknown purposes. Then a short inclined iron ladder to the cupola where Dix sat crying in his shirtsleeves. He had put down his devil's glass dick. The first thing Esther did was fling it toward the street.

"You promised me."

"But it picks me up, Esther."

"You're just exhausted. You try to do too much. Then your nerves."

She put an arm around him. His head went to her breast.

"I've been throwing up for two days. I want to work, and I can't. And this happens."

"Don't worry about the hooker."

"He sent her, didn't he? He threatened me this week. I didn't tell you."

"Who?"

"Coleman Dane."

"Threatened you how?"

"We were in the cellar of Pamplona in Washington. He broke a bottle of Valbuena that Raoul was saving just for me. Then he—he made a gesture toward my face with the broken edges of the bottle."

Esther didn't reply, but held him tighter.

"He said, 'Tell me. You're dying to tell someone, aren't you?' "

"Tell what?"

"How I killed his sister. What I did with her body. Imagine hearing something like that! I was choosing wine for dinner."

Esther wondered if it was freebase paranoia. But he probably hadn't smoked enough; she could barely smell the fumes in his silvery hair.

"Not that again," Esther said dismissively.

"I said he was crazy. Around the bend. You should have seen—the look he gave me."

"Cole's not going to bother you anymore, Dix." She bit down on the next word. *"Promise."*

"But Esther." His eyes were bewildered. "Sometimes I have to think about it. The accusations." He writhed, possibly surrounded in his imagination by hooded men with iron instruments of torture.

She pressed two fingers against his mouth. "Stop this."

"You know how I get," he mumbled. "Can't take the pressure sometimes. I just need to forget about them."

"That's for the best."

"But—"

"You haven't murdered anyone, Dix. There haven't been any murders. How many times—?" Esther's eyes were cheerless in a face paled by lightning. She looked up. The storm very near now. Esther breathed heavily, feeling oppressed. She pushed a slender thumb hard against her front teeth, childhood habit, and chipped polish from the nail. The flakes tasted bitter as old blood on the tip of her tongue. Someone would have to pay for this night, and right away. She knew just where to start. "Okay, we're going down. Get on the ladder, behind me. Don't look. I'll guide you."

Dix held fast to her a little longer, as if she were taking away a treat.

"What is death like, Esther? You were there, for a few seconds. Did you see the face of God?"

Esther smoothed her brother's brow; a straightening-up gesture, as if invisible laurel were askew.

"There's no God, Dix. There's just us. And we have to love each other, do for each other. That's all. That's how we get through this." She smiled. "Til we all make it over to what Mardie calls 'the huther side.'"

After Dix's personal physician had put him to bed following the appropriate injections that would keep him peaceful for the next forty-eight hours, and oblivious when he awakened, Marlowe Hare drove Esther and Mardie through streets awash in sweeping rain to Sage Donnerly's house in Turtle Bay. By the time they got there, the power was out on the East Side at midtown.

Candles burned in Sage's third-floor parlor, which was decorated with no sense of harmony or serenity. Stained glass, porcelain birds and animals, staid and gloomy nineteenth-century landscapes, busy, busy fabrics on too many overstuffed chairs and loveseats: an example, Esther thought, of how a little bad taste, implemented with enough money, could get completely out of hand.

In addition to her porcelain pets, Sage Donnerly had two live dogs that trotted at her heels, miniature dachshunds named Porgy and Bess.

"Esther Trevellian. How delightful to meet you."

Esther didn't say anything. Nor did she introduce Mardie Kregg. The madam's hard old eyes shrank a little in the flickering light as she absorbed the fact that business was to be conducted. But for what other purpose would the famous Esther Trevellian call at one-thirty in the morning? Sage settled herself on a loveseat, one dog at her plump elbow, the female on an ottoman, facing her in adoration.

"May I offer you something to drink?"

"Fine."

"I don't have alcohol in the house. My late husband was opposed. Tea? Ceylonese. From the Isle of Serendip."

"Fine."

Sage summoned the Indian houseman who had let them in, and gave instructions. He had slicked-down silver-gray hair and eyes that smouldered deep in his head like those of a mad monk in a ruined temple.

"My late husband and I traveled often to India. At the time we were in the import business."

"Yes, I know," Esther said. "Supplying the pedophiles in U.N. delegations with ten-year-old quiff from East Africa, Pakistan and Calcutta."

"Several of our proteges have married extremely well in this country. One of them is a Ford model. Compare her success to the fate of so many female children in India, those allowed to survive at all once their sex has been determined in the womb."

"The Trevellian Foundation spent six point two million dollars for shelters and clinics in four Indian states last year."

"Perhaps you've come to me for a donation. I have many charities, of course, but one can always do a little more."

"I was thinking in the neighborhood of two hundred thousand dollars."

Sage Donnerly's eyebrows rose slightly, even as she smiled. Her upper and lower lips lacked symmetry; as a result her smiles were off center, conveying mean amusement.

"If only I had the resources for such a worthy cause."

"You could sell the house," Esther suggested.

When she continued to keep a straight face, Sage Donnerly sputtered with laughter. Porgy, the dachshund at her elbow, put his paws on her shoulder and licked her face anxiously. The other sausage dog whined.

"Oh, my dear," Sage gasped.

"Let me tell you who the money is for. It's for one of your girls, Mary Ascencios, a.k.a. Kimberlea, who is getting out of the life."

Sage Donnerly carried a Baggie of dog treats in a pocket of her green silk lounging pajamas. She gave one treat each to Porgy and Bess, rearranged some small pillows on her loveseat, settled down to business.

"What about Kimberlea?"

"You sent her over to my brother tonight. He was trying to work up a party, I suppose."

Sage nodded. "There was a special request on the computer. His usual dates at the end of the week are LaShondra and Shawleen. In tandem. A little show, but straight sex. Tonight we were requested to supply costume. A scenario was included in the order, which had to be followed to the letter."

The lights came back on in Turtle Bay. A window air-conditioner started up.

"What was the source of the request?"

"I'm sure we didn't keep a file."

"Oh? Not even for billing purposes?"

"The account was prepaid, by wire transfer."

"From what bank?"

"My accountant may know."

"I wish you wouldn't hold out on me, Sage. Let me tell you what happened. A dirty trick was played on my brother tonight. Someone had one of your girls, pretending to be a former lover of Dix's, go to his office. We're talking about a woman who disappeared almost three years ago, hasn't been heard from since. Dix was extremely fond of her."

"Oh."

"Imagine his shock, then his anger at being treated so cruelly. Yes, Sage. I had to talk him down from the roof of the mansion. If I had been out of town, who knows? Fortunately he didn't do irreparable damage to Mary Ascencios. As I said, two hundred thousand ought to be sufficient. What you do now is, you write me a check. I'll see that she gets the money. Then you comb your records for the name of the person who set my brother up."

"Of course this—distasteful business indirectly reflects on me. Although we take utmost precautions. Never a hint of scandal. I am rigorous in my standards. As for Mary Ascencios, I'm distressed, needless to say. I *would* like to help. But it was your brother who— am I right in assuming?—is responsible for whatever injury—"

Esther said, "Mardie?"

Mardie took a Glock automatic from the shoulder holster she wore under her safari jacket and put it in her lap. Sage Donnerly did a slight double take by way of comment, not taking the gun too seriously. Her parlor. Her house. Mardie reached into an inside pocket for a black box, like a cigar case but thicker, and opened it. There was a silencer for the Glock inside, socketed in velvet.

Sage Donnerly said, "Really, I—"

With the silenced Glock Mardie shot the dachshund on the otto- man. In one ear, out the other. The dog plopped on the carpet at Sage's slippered feet. Sage screamed, sounding like a high-pressure gas leak, and snatched up the whimpering Porgy in her arms. The Indian houseman pushed a tea cart into the parlor and looked at the dead dachshund. He didn't look at anything else. His dark seamed face was as still as a ritual mask. He knelt, wrapped the dog's body in a hand towel and carried it out of the parlor.

Sage, Kabuki-pale, looked as if she were going to faint. Porgy licked her jowls frantically.

Esther said, "Why don't you serve the tea, Mardie?"

EIGHT

SPLITTING THE LARK

Max said you were looking for a ride?"

Sharan glanced up from the truck-stop booth where she had been sitting for the better part of an hour with a barely touched BLT and a glass of iced coffee.

"Yes."

"Where you headed?" the woman asked her, looking from Sharan's faded blue eyes to the prosthetic hand in her lap.

"It doesn't really matter," Sharan said, after trying to frame a more positive answer. She shrugged in apology.

The woman nodded. She looked to be about forty, a feisty half-pint with a petite face and a waist that was smaller than the diameter of her head. She had about an eighth of an inch of white-blond hair, full lips rendered slightly clownlike by cordovan lipstick. She wore a tank top and jeans, a do-rag and a nose ring. She had tattoos on both shoulders—a screaming eagle and a dove. The two halves of her personality, Sharan presumed, liking her.

"Well, I'm going to Charlottesville and then I'm going to Beckley," the woman said. "Pet food and feminine hygiene products. No livestock. I don't haul shitters unless I'm desperate to make a payment. Beckley's in West Virginia."

"West Virginia sounds okay."

The woman put out her hand. "I'm Patty. Patty Hornwood Trikonis Howington Rudasill. Three-time loser, but you chalk it up to experience if you've got any smarts."

"Sharan. I really do appreciate—"

"Honey, you don't have to say a word. That's a West Point ring you're wearing, isn't it?"

"Class of Eighty-three."

"I'm impressed. We need to be making time if you're finished with that sandwich."

Patty drove a blue Freightliner truck with sunset cloud motifs painted on the sides of the sleeping compartment behind the cab. The trailer that completed her rig belonged to a trucking company in Fairfax, Virginia.

"I'm independent and aloof," Patty explained. She adjusted the Airflex passenger seat for Sharan's weight ("I think I'm about one twenty-five; I haven't eaten much lately.") and checked her Qualcomm console for messages routed by satellite. The truck had impressive electronics, good stereo, a CB radio and a cellular phone. The sleeping compartment behind them contained two bunks, a refrigerator and a two-burner stove. Home on the road. Patty edged onto the four-lane southbound, moving up through the gears with a right arm that looked as strong as bridge cable. Once they were rolling she pointed out the children's photos on her sun visor.

"Left to right, Sal, Burt and Cady. Not a one of them that favors me. But all their hearts belong to Mama, I'm proud to say. I want to ask what happened to your hand, but I don't pry. You don't care to say a word all the way to Beckley, it's cool. Cry your eyes out, won't bother me. I don't see that you've been wearing a band of gold, but I expect it's a man all the same. Traveling light, nowhere in particular. You have people?"

"My mother lives in San Diego."

"But you don't want to go to San Diego."

Sharan said, staring down the road, "I haven't thought that far ahead. I got out of the shower, I was drying off, and it just came to me, Okay, that's it. It's getting too complicated. I can deal with the pressure of the—the assignment, that's like old times, but a relationship, with him? I mean, where did that come from? My God. No."

"Just had to get out, and fast." Sharan nodded, but had no more to offer. "It don't matter if you want to tell me, or not. I'm a good listener. Advice for the asking. What kind of music do you like? George and Tammy? Hal Ketchum?" Patty sang a little of "Mama Knows the Highway." "Nothing worth listening to on the radio anymore. That dirtymouth nigger stuff you can't dignify to call it music. Patsy Cline. That says it all. I've got the New Testament on CD if you're needing spiritual sustenance. *The Bridges of Madison County*, which is my all-time favorite work of literature. She did right, you know. Didn't go off with that photographer and abandon her kids. But oh, the heartbreak. Saw the movie four times. Clint Eastwood. *That* says it all. I'd like to meet him sometime. I just want to hear three words out of his mouth. 'Patty, let's fuck.' You'd see me again about the time cows give root beer. Did you have a big fight? He didn't smack you around, did he? I never allowed that. It's the shame of our sex. I always have an icepick handy, like Sharon Stone in that movie *Basic Instinct*. There's one in my boot right now. Mess with me, man, I'll let air in your eyeball."

"I didn't see it coming. I thought I could trust myself. But there's something about him—it's been driving me crazy."

"In love with the wrong guy?" Patty asked astutely.

"It can't be. I mean, if it's love, where've I *been* for thirty-five years?"

"Oh-oh, I think I know what you mean. Ben Trikonis was probably the meanest most selfish bastard I ever hope to see. Guess what? Couldn't keep my hands off him. Sex all night, then at the breakfast table he'd say something so trashy and hurtful I'd want to shove the waffle iron up his ass. Pardon my seamy mouth, it's from hanging around truckers half my life."

"He isn't mean. I met mean in the military. Nothing bully-casual about it. Really profound, organized meanness. Instructors who wanted to destroy you, because you were a woman where they thought a woman shouldn't be. I took their crap. It made me stronger. I intend to stay strong. I doubt if he can find me, if I don't want to be found."

"You think the guy is the type who wants to destroy you?"

"He will if he has to. Nothing personal. He might even feel bad about it. But he's relentless. How could he say, 'Nothing's changed?' *Everything* changed, out of the blue, blink of an eye, bullshit bullshit bullshit: can't he realize that, or doesn't he want to?"

Patty glanced at her, understanding little of it but smiling sympathetically.

"He could be compassionate. Loving. I know it's there. I saw it, in a photograph. He grinds his teeth sometimes. I think it's partly because he hates his job, he's only at DoJ because of the power base he needs now. His daughter may be dying. All right. I'd like to help him. But I don't want to feel this way. I'm so fucked up it isn't funny."

"Hey, babe. You did the right thing. You're young yet. Give yourself time. You've got nothing *but* time."

Sharan gnawed her salty lower lip and rubbed her eyes. The sun was low. Patty put Tammy Wynette on the CD player, called home, chatted with the kids. After a while Sharan, worn out from thinking too much, drank some orange juice from the fridge and napped in the lower bunk with an Appalachian star quilt over her.

She woke up hearing Patty say, "That's goofy."

It was nine-fifteen. The western sky was clear above the darkening hills of central Virginia. Some bright stars had appeared, but they were few and far between, as if God had decided to charge for them. Patty said that they were ten miles north of Charlottesville.

"What's wrong?"

"Well, a few miles back a Smoky pulled in behind me, and he just stayed there. Minute ago another 'un came on from the side road, and he's in front, pacing me it seems like. No bubbles. Wonder what they're up to?"

Sharan got up and sat in the passenger seat again. She looked down at the blue-and-gray state police car in front of the Freightliner, feeling a pain low on one side as if her gut had been sectioned with barbed wire.

"Oh-oh, bubbles just lit up on both cars. Smokey wants me to get off. And there's *another* one waiting down there at the crossroad. Jezuspleezus, what's goin' on? I hope they ain't going to shake down the box and find something that'll have me behind bars for the next thirty years."

"They want me," Sharan said.

"Whoa, babe. You got any dope on you? I never thought to ask, you never looked the type."

"No."

"Then why all the attention? Lord, look now. There's a helicopter. What the hell *is* this, *Real Stories of the Highway Patrol*?"

"I told you," Sharan said. "He's relentless."

Sharan stepped down from the cab of the Freightliner with her rucksack and fanny pack, flinching at the minicyclone the deluxe Italian helicopter was kicking up as it settled down on a knoll less than a hundred feet away.

"Sharan Norbeth?" one of the state cops asked her.

"Yes."

"Come with us, please."

Sharan looked back at the Freightliner cab, thumb of her left hand up.

"Thanks, Patty! I'll be okay."

"You know how to get ahold of me on the satellite!"

"Thanks again."

A cop was waving Patty back to the road with his flashlight. Sharan went up the knoll to the helicopter. The door was open. She tossed her rucksack on the deck and made her way to a rear seat, upholstered in black glove leather.

Dayton Emmons was in the seat next to her.

Sharan strapped herself into the harness as the helicopter lifted off. Emmons indicated he was a little hard of hearing. Sharan put on a headset like the one he was wearing. Voice-activated microphone. Tears of frustration stung her eyes.

"I don't get a cut dog's chance, do I?"

"I know there's a lot of tension between you and Cole. It will have to be resolved."

"How did you all do it? I suppose I'm just lousy with little electronic fleas."

"The suite you were staying in at the hotel, and the ones on either side, are permanently leased by the FBI. Modifications have been made in the configurations of some rooms."

"In and out like bandits? I should have expected that. Microphones, cameras too?"

Sharan choked on the notion of constant surveillance. Just how oblivious could she get? She'd been a professional herself. Dayton Emmons handed her water in a squeeze bottle.

"Where are we going?" Sharan asked him.

"To the country house."

"If I could have a little time. I really can't face him right now."

"It's a matter of necessity. By the way, Cole's children have come for the weekend. There was nothing he could do. Millie had plans."

"I don't want to meet his children."

"That can't be helped. Sunday you'll be in the Hamptons."

"So soon? My God."

"Jules Brougham's famous Sunday brunch at La Fondriere. His Easthampton home. Sounds pretty fancy, but 'La Fondriere' is French for 'the bog.' "

"Movers and takers," Sharan said ungenerously.

"Dix Trevellian is usually a fixture, but unfortunately you probably won't see him there. We haven't been able to learn what his status is. Something very serious happened to him. We have inside information, of course. We know most of it now."

"He went nuts."

"More like a breakdown. It's periodic with Dix."

"Yes, and then he kills a woman or two. The more helpless, the better."

"That doesn't describe Sharan Norbeth, does it? Cole told me about the exercise in club arts you put him through. He was bragging on you."

"Was he?" Sharan was thinking about something else Emmons had said. "What did you mean, you have inside information?"

"Someone who works for the Trevellians also works for us. He's valuable and trusted, even by the notoriously suspicious Mardie Kregg."

"Just a minute."

"What's wrong, Sharan?"

"You're not going to tell somebody who works for the Trevellians about *me?*"

"It may be to your advantage."

"Let me decide that. Absolutely *not.*"

Emmons was silent for a few moments. "All right. We'll re-think that part of it." He reached out and took Sharan's left hand in his own. She tensed and gave him a bitter look. He smiled.

"Better let me have this now," he said, thumb and forefinger on her West Point class ring.

"My ring? Why?"

"For one thing, it isn't yours. It's a duplicate from the Bureau's Rapid Prototyping Facility at Quantico. Contains a powerful miniaturized transponder, part of a tracking system that links through NSA satellites."

"How did you—I never take my ring off!"

"Except on those occasions when you have your nails done. The day before you left Georgia."

"Bambi Christine's been doing my nails for—are you telling me you bribed—"

"We paid off her son's orthodontia bills," Emmons said gently. "You know there's always a way, Sharan."

"I suppose this is only the beginning," she said, feeling more intensely violated as she removed the substitute ring. "Next we'll all have coded transponder implants at birth to take the place of infant footprinting."

"As a matter of fact—"

"Forget it! Don't tell me! Whatever happened to land of the free?"

"A theoretical concept in a highly integrated, technically complex society. Our combined computer capacity at DoJ now has more units in it than there are cells in the human brain. There's a story that's been around about a telephone engineer who has a recurring nightmare: any day now all of the telephones in a worldwide automated system are going to ring simultaneously, and when we answer, something will be there that we don't want to hear at all."

"Just blow us weak creatures off and be done with it." She had to laugh, but it hurt her insides; and such laughter left her feeling grim.

Emmons accepted the ring from Sharan. "You won't be wearing this on the job. We have a cross instead, Mexican silver, very beautiful. And a beautiful piece of microphone-on-a-chip technology. The broadcast range is a third of a mile."

Coleman Dane was riding with his son in the Grand Prix ring when the helicopter returned to the farm. Two black horses on shadowless balding turf beneath floodlights. Sharan could see Cole's white shirt clinging to his back as his horse cantered through a figure-eight course. All Sharan knew about horses was that when their ears were pinned against their necks they were in a lethal mood. Her own ears might still be fiery red, but she was able to admire, from a height of a couple of hundred feet, the coordinated action of horse and rider. His talent for control. Griffin Dane looked up as the helicopter came down, but his father paid no attention. He might have looked up too, Sharan thought. His talent for totally pissing her off.

James the houseman met the helicopter, wearing plaid slacks with his buttonless wrinkled white houseman's jacket.

"I saved supper for you," he said.

The helicopter took off again, with Dayton Emmons. Sharan followed James to the kitchen, rubbing an eye that had some rotor-blown dirt in it. In one of the bathrooms downstairs she washed out her eyes and brushed her hair. She avoided looking at herself in the mirrors on every wall and the ceiling, but there seemed to be an uneasy crowd of her. In the kitchen she ate an escarole salad and baked oysters with an orange-and-curry sauce. Cole Dane's daughter Misty was on a chaise by the swimming pool, reading and jotting down things in a notebook. The girl had a softer version of her mother's face. She wore a red bandana to partially hide the fact that her dark hair was just beginning to grow back. Chemo had imbued her with an unearthly translucence, emphasized by the pool lighting, though she didn't appear frail. She had a good figure; her body hadn't puffed up from the drug protocol.

"How old is Misty?" Sharan asked James.

"Just turn fourteen, Saturday last."

The girl said, over the kitchen intercom, "James, could I have a cold beer?"

Sharan looked at James.

"She won't drink but a little of it. Just the idea of having it, you see. Because when she's legal to drink beer— We give her what she ask for, if there can't be no harm. Why not?"

"Let me take it to her," Sharan said.

Misty glanced up when Sharan approached. Her eyes seemed as big as plums, perhaps because of the absence of shielding eyelashes. Thin shadows of eyebrows were reforming on the bony ridges. There was a scab at one corner of her mouth, another on her chin. Her expression was blank, perhaps calculated. On her left arm she had an implanted IV secured with an armboard and a heparin lock. The IV, Sharan assumed, was for drug reinforcement during remission. Hunched on the chaise with her knees up to prop her book against, she was like a slightly damaged doll someone had tossed on top of a box of attic discards.

"I'm Sharan." She placed the beaded bottle of Rolling Rock and a Pilsner glass on a two-wheel, glass-topped cart where Misty could reach them. The girl gave her no further coverage. Sharan sat in an Adirondack chair with a striped seat cushion, watching her, feeling numb in several places. The night's blue mood. A breath of wind overflowing with summer's grainy fragrance. Sunflowers by a corner of the white pool pavilion. Van Gogh. Beauty and mutilation, catastrophes of the spirit.

After a while Misty said, not raising her eyes from her school lit book, "Everybody wants to know what it's like, but they're afraid to ask. I'll tell you what it's like. Heinous. I was on a cancer floor for seven weeks. I had radiation and blood transfusions. Spinal taps were the worst. I puked and puked. My pee turned brown. I had these big ugly ulcers that wouldn't heal. My hair fell out. My gums bled. I screamed at everybody. I was not a little trouper. Are you fucking my dad?"

"Were you this rude to total strangers before you got so sick?"

Misty, after an interval of surprise, hunched her shoulders slightly. "No."

"Doesn't become you. I went through the dumps too, when they told me in the hospital there were complications and they'd have to take my hand off again. And I, uh, would have to learn to do without it."

Misty turned her book facedown in her lap and sat up, interested in Sharan's prosthesis.

"What can you do with that thing, I mean, does it work like a real hand?"

Sharan held out the prosthesis. Misty took it hesitantly. They shook.

"Hey. How do you do that? God, it felt so weird. When the fingers were tightening, I was afraid it would crush my bones or something."

"Nope." Sharan gave the short course in prosthesis design. Misty studied the artificial hand, holding it as another child might hold a fallen bird. She touched fingertips to fingertips. She looked inside. Nothing complicated there, no stainless steel imitation bones, gears, or levers: a sleekness and simplicity of design, some wiring, an ordinary nine-volt battery, available at any Wal-Mart store. The prosthesis might have seemed to Misty a tangible reward of the debilitating medical process, while her own chemically spiked blood seethed from the effort of dampening a lethal wildfire.

"Want some beer?" Milly asked.

"Sure."

Misty shook the Rolling Rock bottle, then poured the Pilsner glass half full and licked up the foam that brimmed over. She handed the bottle to Sharan.

"So why're you here?"

"Just visiting."

Misty licked up the rest of the head of beer, disgruntled, suspecting subterfuge.

"Have you known my dad very long?"

"We're business acquaintances."

"Oh. Have you met my mother?"

"No, I haven't."

"She's getting married again. He used to be Secretary of State. Now he consults, or something. Every time there's a crisis somewhere, he goes on *Nightline* to explain what the government ought to do about it. A real know-it-all. He gave me diamond studs for my birthday. I want a navel ring when I can get pierced without bleeding to death."

"What are you working on there?"

"English. I need to do some catch-up so I can be in ninth grade, where I belong, when school starts. I missed half of the eighth grade because my white count wasn't high enough. You don't teach school by any chance?"

"No, I'm a painter."

"Well, so you're like *artistic*. I have to find the meaning of this poem? I like poetry, but this one's a toughie."

"Let me have a look."

Sharan read the Emily Dickenson poem to herself, frowned, then read it aloud.

"Split the Lark—and you'll find the Music—
Bulb after bulb, in silver rolled—
Scantily dealt to the Summer Morning—
Saved for your Ear when Lutes be old.

"Loose the Flood—you shall find it patent—
Gush after Gush, reserved for you—
Scarlet Experiment! Sceptic Thomas!
Now do you doubt that your Bird was true?"

When she looked up from the page Misty was crying.

"I think I get some of it now. It's what my parents are doing to me. They don't mean to. But love is selfish. Isn't that what Emily says?"

"Maybe she's also being ironic. Music, love—it isn't something tangible you can put away for later. The beauty of it is now, or it's memory. Don't split the Lark. Accept the gift."

Misty wiped her cheeks on the back of one hand and reached for her pencil. "Irony means—"

"Oh, in this case it would be, making a point by not concluding with what you seemed to be saying in the first place."

"Thank you," Misty said, busily writing.

Coleman Dane walked out of the house and across the terrace, down two steps to pool level. He had showered and put on navy slacks and a chambray shirt. His hair was wet as a diver's and combed back from his high forehead. He had a drink in one hand. His body language read, not cool.

He kissed his daughter. "Hi," he said to Sharan. "Nice to see you again."

Sharan smiled. "That's irony, too, Misty."

Misty looked puzzled, eyes going from Sharan's face to her father's. His jaw was lumped on one side. He ground his teeth, caught himself at it, and relaxed, regarding Sharan with the reflective generosity of her confessor for the evening. Sharan looked deliberately blank. Misty's expression changed as revelation made her instinctively hostile. She closed her notebook.

"I'm going to play computer chess for a while," she said to her father. "Because you, *obviously*, are not going to play with me tonight."

"I need to talk to Sharan," he said. "I'll be up at eleven to help you with your IV."

"Griffin can do it."

"Don't you want that beer?"

"Nothing has any taste. Cold isn't cold, wet isn't wet. Oh shit. What's the point?"

Dane made grinding sounds again. "I love you, Misty."

Misty, under the spell of adult ambiguities, glanced at Sharan, smiled weakly, then snapped at her father, "I told you you should chew gum, you won't have any teeth left." She went into the house on quick thin legs, her moppet's bandana red as a gash.

"She's really a good kid. Refuses just to veg, although I couldn't blame her. What was she crying about?"

"Misty read a poem that got to her. It got to me, too."

"I've never been able to read poetry, since I was force-fed Walt Whitman and Milton in prep school."

"It's an acquired taste. Whitman's not so bad, a footloose old guy with mice in his beard, weeping at sunrises. What are you drinking?"

"Why?"

"Good God, I'm just trying to make conversation. Find a topic that doesn't have to do with rage and betrayal. I spent last night in a place where FBI spooks walk through the walls."

"Oh, that." He sipped at his drink, watching her with the slightly glazed look of someone thumbing through a memorandum of failed possibilities. "Scotch," he said. "The Macallan. One ice cube. It's a ritual with me."

"Like grinding your teeth."

"That's probably a neurosis. Want another beer?"

"No, thank you."

"Well, why don't we sit down?"

"How long am I staying?"

"Until Saturday."

Sharan looked at a surveillance camera mounted out of easy reach beside the doors into the house.

"Standard home security," Dane said.

"Will you be locking me up at night?"

"I don't think you're going to take off again," he said, sitting at the end of the padded chaise. He motioned to the Adirondack chair. "I get a crick in my neck when I have to look up for any length of time."

Sharan sat down, arms across her breast, attitude of tournament watchfulness.

"Obviously we've both been under a lot of stress."

Sharan nodded.

"You know, I've been thinking. Wondering. If we'd met under different circumstances, would we like each other better?"

"Why don't you answer that? It may give me a clue as to how perceptive you are."

"No."

"No?"

"There's something to be said for a head-on collision. No time for subtleties. You're dazed, you taste blood, the adrenaline cooks. It was still cooking last night, when you had your turn. James interrupted something, didn't he?"

Sharan turned her face aside, a gesture of deflection that raised a confirming smile from him.

"Let's don't do this," she said.

"I understand that it's not the best possible time."

Sharan let her arms drop.

"Oh, boy, what you don't understand."

He stopped sipping and drank down the rest of his Scotch.

"You're a very spontaneous person. Impulsive, I guess. You have a lazy lingering smile with a vocabulary I haven't begun to learn. You want something from me I want to give to you, but I'm afraid I never learned how. I know I need to learn, before it's too late."

Sharan intercepted a look that wasn't meant for her; it was aimed at his recent past.

"What was life with Millie like?" she asked, and was surprised to hear herself speak at all.

"Emotional and intellectual combat zone. You have to enjoy the game, I suppose, on some level. But it kills spontaneity. In or out of bed. There's nothing retrievable from our marriage, but we maintain a certain cordiality. We were both brought up to be respectful of people we don't really need anymore."

"Your daughter wants you to be with her tonight. Where am I bunking?"

"James will show you. Door locks from the inside only."

"What does that mean?"

"Gesture of trust on my part."

Sharan glanced at the surveillance camera again, with one of the smiles he claimed to like so much.

"I'd say I would get about half a mile."

"You know I must have your help. There's no other way, Sharan, or I wouldn't try it. Having said that, I'd like for you to forgive me."

He had no more whiskey, so he chomped on an ice cube. His busy jaw bulged with muscle, but his eyes looked less tired. He watched her.

Sharan shook her head, perplexed and amazed, then stood and walked toward the house.

"Sharan?"

"Do you like peanut butter sandwiches?"

"Toasted, with chocolate milk."

"Then maybe I can forgive you. But slowly. Let's get the kids and stuff our faces."

The four-poster bed seemed crowded with dreams left over from other people. Deep in the night Sharan woke up and was thirsty: all that peanut butter. A couple of hunting dogs barked in their kennel by the stable, then settled down in the profoundly quiet country night.

She went downstairs in the jogging outfit she'd slept in and found Dane, in an office on the ground floor next to the kitchen. In a space within the office, a soundproofed, brightly lighted space behind glass. Nothing in there but a functional typist's chair on casters, a desk, computer equipment, steel cabinets with combination locks on them. He sat in the chair, his back to Sharan, facing the video screen. Dark-haired woman on the screen, the earthy eyes of a pagan soothsayer. Video feed, transmission problems, her face blurred by electronic chaff as sand-laden winds have blurred the Sphinx. But the woman was recognizable as Esther Trevellian, whose likeness Sharan had seen in *People* magazine. Sharan couldn't read her flawed expression. Nor could she hear a word that was spoken by either of them.

Sharan leaned against a wall of the outer office with her arms folded, not as composed as she made herself appear.

After a couple of minutes the transmission ended. There was a message on the screen: did he want to save? Dane popped in a digital tape cartridge. The blank screen revealed an image of Sharan behind him.

He turned off the lights and came out. He wore a short robe and was fetchingly bare-legged.

"Dogs wake you?"

"Old four-poster beds intimidate me. I keep wondering who died in them. Who broke whose heart in the intimacy of the bedchamber. Wasn't that Esther Trevellian?"

Dane nodded.

"Do you know her?"

"Let's go to the kitchen. I'll warm up some of that store-bought chocolate milk while you brew your tea."

Outside they strolled around the pool. The lights were out. There was a three-quarter moon overhead.

"You never said you knew Esther Trevellian. Up kind of late, isn't she?"

Dane yawned and loosened his tight jaw muscles. "It's eight-thirty in Paris."

"Oh, she's in Paris."

"Popped over on the Concorde for a couple of days."

"The way some people live. What did she want?"

"We're having lunch next week in New York."

"Why?"

"She'll ask me nicely to let up on Dix."

"Do you think she knows her brother is homicidal?"

"She has to know."

"And she won't do anything about it?"

"Keep a close eye on him. I'd say she's genuinely sorry that six women are dead. She wouldn't want it to happen again. But she'll go on protecting Dix. I suspect Esther would do it even if she didn't think he was a genius. She's obsessively loyal to her family."

"Obsessive? It's insanity. You seem to know a lot about her."

He was silent, working up to something, sipping chocolate milk.

"Why are we pacing like this?"

"I had an affair with Esther Trevellian. This happened two, almost three months after Felicia disappeared. I was neglecting everything: the firm, wife, kids. Drinking like a maniac. Esther called often. She'd been a good friend of my sister's, even before Felicia won her Trevellian Prize. Esther and I met, we walked on the mall, those end-of-winter days, long walks while I wrung myself out. She has that wonderful quality, the eternal listener. A heaven-sent ear. It came to be that there were only three of us: me, my sister, Esther Trevellian. And Felicia had vanished. Esther can subtly and surely close you off from everyone else, until even your dearest friends seem trivial: irritating and unimportant. In Esther's league everyone is a powerfucker, but her game is more oblique. I was a partner in the D.C. firm founded by my godfather. Then came the opening at Justice. The appointment. Nothing I'd wished for, just the quiet machinations of Esther Trevellian. I think she's had hundreds of lovers. More than a few of the names would amaze you. Men and women. Royalty, moguls, artists, the cream of the world's social criminals. But there's no stink of decadence about her. No one smirks when her name is mentioned. What gossip there is acknowledges that she's the best at her game. Muted envy and admiration. Because of the Prizes, she's the absolute ruler of a large society of status-seekers. When Esther comes on to you, she makes you believe you're the first man she's ever wanted. It was as if we were inventing sex together. That nearly forgotten adolescent astonishment refreshed in the blood, the vigor. Until Esther, I was a faithful husband. Adultery is losing your virginity for the second time."

"Did you fall in love with her?"

"That's the other side of her nature. You can drown in Esther, like a sacrifice in a Mayan well. But you can't love her."

"Who'd want to? She sounds grotesque."

Sharan was quaking, though the night was still and mild, illuminated by a Perseid shower they watched in silence. Lightstorms of the spirit.

"I guess I've been trying to warn you," Dane said. "There's more to this than Dix Trevellian."

"You ought to stay away from her. Unless of course—"

Sharan stopped to put her nearly empty mug on the cart with the two big wheels beside the chaise. When she straightened they bumped casually; he put a hand on her shoulder, took it away.

"I got over Esther. Once it was obvious where my investigations were going."

"But if Esther knew about, or suspected her brother too, why did she put you in the Justice Department?"

"She gave me the power to be powerless, if she so decided."

"I don't get it. Maybe I get it." Sharan stepped away from him, looked back. "What does she have on you, Cole?"

"Not what you're thinking. Let's just say that all who have known her wear Esther for life, like a tribal mark, a stain of superstition. We become a part of what is good about her, and what is bad. Most of all we never want Esther to be unhappy with us. The initiation fee will be forfeited, maybe in blood."

"Are you afraid of her?"

"I might be. If I hadn't found out what real fear is. When Misty got sick."

Sharan felt the rub of the moon against the nape of her neck, hallucinatory.

"I don't have a four-poster bed," Dane said. "I gave ours away after Millie and I divorced. The bed I sleep in now has no history. No ghosts, no bad dreams hanging around."

"Did I ask?"

"I just thought it might be on your mind."

"I have a lot on my mind. I'll work it out. See you in the morning, Cole."

NINE

THE RETURN OF
BADMAN JOSÉ

The excavation going on beneath downtown Brooklyn had been suspended for a while, due to lack of money and volunteer efforts. But about half of the old Court Street station of the Long Island Railroad had been restored. It was a project of the Empire State Historic Railway Association, of which Dempsey Wingo was a board member as well as a patron. Dempsey liked old things as much as he did hidey-holes where, except for occasional craftsmen, he had no visitors. Court Street station, more than a hundred and fifty years old and long forgotten by all but a few railroad buffs, was in the middle of a bluestone tunnel with a vaulted Roman-style brick ceiling. The half-mile of tunnel and the station were tight and dry, except during nor'easters, the air usually breathable. There was little standing water and not enough heat to breed mosquitoes or waterbugs, no food supply for rats. The temperature in the tunnel was about fifty-five degrees year-round. In addition to the old railroad tunnel, this part of underground Brooklyn was a hive of utility runs, steam and gas line tunnels, abandoned water tunnels—some of them twelve feet in diameter—subway and Long Island Railroad tunnels, and a complex of passageways beneath the Long Island Teaching Hospital, four square blocks on the Carroll Gardens side of Alantic Avenue.

Dempsey entered and usually exited by way of a manhole on a block-long mews in Carroll Gardens, wearing a stolen Brooklyn

Union Gas Company badge and a yellow hardhat. He handled the 350-pound manhole cover like a bottlecap. Down below he had electricity from a Nottingham connector on a streetlamp pole, a Railway Association telephone line for his computer modem and an ultrasonic toilet. He showered at the gym on Atlantic Avenue that he belonged to. It was so quiet most of the time he could hear his mortality whispering through the chambers of his heart.

Cobbles had been removed from a wall of the gas company tunnel to allow access at the bulkhead of the railroad tunnel, which Irish laborers had spent months cutting and constructing in 1844. The rails were long gone. A lot of soot had been cleaned from the brick vault overhead. There was no draft through the tunnel, so an odor of men's cologne lingered in the air when Dempsey returned from a futile day of bounty-hunting in the warrens of Spanish Harlem and East New York.

He drew his knife without a thought and listened, back against the rough-cut stone of the tunnel, eyes on the station platform that would have been illuminated by gaslight a century and a half ago. Seeing a shadow, someone walking around inside the station. Then hearing music, from his Beach Boys collection. "The Sloop John B." And a sing-along voice, the falsetto a little creaky with age. Welcome home, Badman.

Dempsey put his knife away and trudged along the ridges of the tunnel floor to the station platform.

"Somebody, I say somebody must've installed a tweetie bird in mah Bondo Special." His voice produced an echo.

"Yes, sir. I am the guilty party, Mr. Wingo."

Marlowe Hare smiled in a conciliatory way. He was wearing a jacket with the colors and striping of a rattlesnake watermelon, a gold Borsalino with a black band, pleated gray flannel slacks with twelve-inch-deep cuffs and yellow vinyl boots on platform heels.

"Should I expect more company?"

"Oh, no, sir. And begging your pardon, Mr. Wingo, it has been a long afternoon's wait. The quiet does get on a man's nerves down here."

Dempsey checked an explosives meter for the presence of lethal gas, a common hazard in all the tunnels, then threw himself carelessly into a hammock he'd bought for ten dollars at a Salvation Army outlet and gestured towards the refrigerator.

"Let's have us a couple of beers."

"Exemplary, Mr. Wingo."

"I suppose you did it the night I was up there visiting."

"That's right."

"Esther tell you to Lowjack my car?"

"No. I took it on myself, Mr. Wingo."

"You puzzle me, Marlowe. I thought you were a dog walker. Takes a certain amount of expertise to home in on a rigged vehicle."

"I've been many things in my lifetime. Oh, yes." He flicked off the caps from a pair of Heinekens, handed one to Dempsey. He adjusted the sharp creases in his slacks and sat on a recently refurbished bench, its antique walnut gleam matching the tones of Marlowe's amiable face, like a crude wood carving with diamond-studded teeth.

"Finding my car is one thing," Dempsey said, sucking on his beer and watching Marlowe with an interest he hadn't felt before.

"I knocked on some doors in the neighborhood, til I located somebody knows you by sight. They seen you a couple of times get out of your car and go down in the manhole with your hard hat on. Now, I thought that was a curious thing to do. So I did the same. Got dirtied up some, but I used a little of your bottle water to clean my jacket while I waited for you. No hurry. Today being my day off."

"So you decided to run some sort of shuck in your spare time."

"No, no. Oh, my, no. Nothing like that. Wouldn't want no harm to come to you, Mr. Wingo. I know there's bad blood between you and the Kreggs, so you needs to be careful. Never did understand how that came about."

"Mardie did her best to bust up my marriage to Esther. From day one. Mardie always figured she had a prior claim, going back to the time she pulled Esther away from her daddy's grave after she was hit by lightning, and breathed life back into her. You know the story?"

"No, sir," Marlowe said, leaning forward on his bench with quiet expectancy.

"Scott told it to me."

"Oh, yes. Mr. Scott." Marlowe's eyes went momentarily to the computer occupying a big rolltop desk in what had once been the stationmaster's pen, behind a brass-and-walnut railing. The computer was on. Dempsey had E-mail waiting.

"The Trevellian family had a summer home on Cloud Horse Mountain. Tongue-and-groove log construction, built in the 1890s. I think it was supposed to be the largest log house anywhere. I've seen pictures. Dozens of rooms, porches, tremendous views. Teddy Roosevelt stayed there when he hunted black bear in the Smokies. So did some crowned heads of Europe who enjoyed the sporting life.

Twenty-five years ago the house burned down. Esther's mother started the fire, because her husband was in bed with his mistress and she wanted to kill them both. Mrs. Trevellian probably underestimated what a tinderbox the old place was. She got caught in the fire herself and was badly burned, crippled for life, although she managed to get out. Her husband died of his burns. The only one who escaped with a singeing was Esther."

"Miss Esther was in the house, too?"

"In her father's bed, Marlowe."

"Oh, Lord!"

"I'm afraid so."

"Just fourteen years old!"

"They've always been with us, Marlowe. The sensually precocious. The *jeune femme fatale*. A compulsion to please, and to control, in combination with beauty, allure and sexual appetite, can produce a fascinating creature. fascinating in the darkest sense."

Marlowe took off his Borsalino and placed it on the bench beside him, rubbed the back of his neck with a pale blue pocket handkerchief that had a flamingo embroidered in one corner.

"But Esther is beyond contrition and above wickedness. It isn't possible to hate her. Instead the hate settles in a man's own bones. I think her daddy may have been fortunate. They mated, he went up in flames. Esther wore a long black veil for three days after he was buried on their mountain. That's all she wore. She grieved beside his cindered remains, a shotgun in her hand to stand off anyone who tried to come near. After she fired a few close rounds, no one did. Except Mardie Kregg. Mardie was a year older than Esther. They'd never been friends, probably hadn't spoken. The Kreggs were back-hollow people, living off shine and ginseng and petty theft. But Mardie was touched by the fascination. She crept as close as she could like a dog on her belly, worshipful, kept watch day and night. Scott said an incredible storm broke over Cloud Horse Mountain, at dusk on Esther's third day, her vigil that seemed destined to end only when she died of starvation. The sky was so full of lightning, said Scott, it was like a windshield after a bad wreck. Where did you get the tweetie you put on my car, Marlowe?"

Marlowe shook his head as if coming out of a deep malaise.

"Oh, you know, one of the stores that sells them snooper things."

"You didn't know I was coming. But you had one handy."

Marlowe mopped his face with the blue handkerchief, eyes squinted almost shut in furious thought.

"Who gave you the tweetie bird, Marlowe? It was Esther's idea, wasn't it?"

"Yes, sir, I reckon," Marlowe finally admitted, in a constipated voice.

"There are lots of tunnels down here, Marlowe. I could take you on a tour. But you know something? You have to be careful not to get lost under the city. You might never find your way home again."

"I never told a soul you were here, Mr. Wingo. I don't intend to. See, I'd like for you to get a message to him. To Mr. Scott. Without anyone else knows."

"What message?"

"That's a story, too, that I needs to trust you with."

"I don't know where he is. Esther and I put our heads together, went over the E-mail I have from Scott. There's never been a return address. There weren't any clues as to his whereabouts. What do you want him to know that Esther shouldn't know?"

"So much talking builds a prodigious thirst."

"Help yourself to another beer, Marlowe, while I see what's on the computer."

"Yes, sir."

Dempsey got up and went to the rolltop desk, clicked the icon to retrieve his mail.

hello BaDmaN

I watched a Japanese gentleman in pink
knickers and white golf shoes practicing
wedge shots on the west lawn. He would hit
the ball perfectly true, getting good loft
and backspin, taking up a teacupful
of turf each time. Each shot traveled about
thirty yards. Then he would walk to where
the ball lay, and hit it back to where he
had been before. The solemn exactness
of backswing. Wrists hinged. Feet a little
together on the slant of the lawn. Good
follow-through, the setting sun glinting
on his glasses as he turned his head
to watch the high arc of the ball. He used

only one ball, instead of lining up several
to hit one after another. It seemed
a very Zen thing to do.

Tomatoes are best when they are loaded
with juice yet firm in the palm of your
hand like a girl's sunwarmed breast.
The first deep bite releases juice and many,
many seeds. Suck slowly, adding a little
oregano and powdered garlic, until only
the skin is left, shriveled but
untouched except for the original gash
made by the teeth. Thus
do love and hunger end in nakedness.

I know now that the angels of the black
wind will not release me to a kindly
death.

It is not enough to say she was a whore.
It is not enough to believe I'm sorry.

I live under the surface of things,
but always afraid of the tolling deeps,
the crouched and truculent beast.

I own many cursed lives, but only one
shadow. It, too, is cursed.

My name, my sin, my hope, all cursed.

Thursday's Child had far to go.
The rifleman was the first to know.
Now there is dark where there was light.
Now there is dark
Now there is dark
Where the hand of blood
leaves its filthy mark.

We shall all drown

in our dry white mansion
of the lost Southern sea.

Dempsey became aware that Marlowe Hare was reading over his
shoulder.

"My, my," Marlowe said in a state of perplexity. "Is it Mr. Scott
saying all that?"

"Yes, it's Scott. Not quite as elliptical as he usually is. But more
depressed."

"What do you suppose he's trying to tell you?"

"I'm not sure," Dempsey said, printing out the E-mail message.
"How long have you worked for the Trevellians, Marlowe?"

"It's almost seven years now."

"Seven years. So you arrived about the time Scott went off the deep
end."

"Well, he was having his good days and bad days. Stayed in bed
for long spells, said he was working on his inventions. Inventions for
what? To protect his brain waves from being stolen, nonsense like
that. People on Wall Street, he said, could pick up his brain waves and
use his ideas to cause a relapse of the entire world banking system.
Those times he went out—and sometimes nobody'd hear from him
for days—he wore a baseball cap lined with aluminum foil. Miss
Esther was at her wit's end. She had him visit psychiatrics. Mr.
Scott, he sat in their offices counting backwards from ten thousand
or some other juju number, smiling, not saying nothing else. She
hired private detectives to follow him around so he wouldn't get
taken advantage of. He gave 'em all the slip, then turned up with a
peyote cult in Colorado, or deckhand on a lobster boat. Miss Esther still wouldn't commit him to no hospital. Thinking she could
take care of him herself. She has the patience of a saint, but you
know you just can't deal with skizzerfrantic folks. They hears too
many voices."

"Marlowe Hare being one more voice with a message. What's the
story you have to tell me, Marlowe?"

"I'll be the soul of brevity. Mr. Scott has a six-year-old son which
he ain't never laid eyes on."

Dempsey nodded, silent for a while, finishing his own beer.

"Who's the mother?"

"Miss Miranda Leland."

"Name doesn't mean anything to me."

"I started in to work for the Lelands about ten years ago, when I

got tired of being on the road all the time with the likes of the Isley
Brothers and Lionel Richie and the Godfather his own self. Mr. Leland made his money in auto parts, he had a chain of stores, and Mrs.
Leland was in the socialite business. I never could stand working for
them. You know what they say, the size of a man's pile has everything
to do with how big a asshole he is? Excuse my French. But Miss
Miranda was a joy to know. She was sixteen when we got acquainted,
and I reckon if it hadn't been for that sweet girl I would have left their
employ long before I did. Well, she went off to Columbia University
and I went to work about the same time at Trevellian House. As fate
would have it, I was the one who introduced Miss Miranda to Scott;
being how it was we were both in the Big Apple, she had kept in
touch."

"Love at first sight?"

"Yes, sir, for both of them."

"Couldn't Miranda tell he was squirrely?"

"Not right away. As I said, good days and bad days, and he was
careful not to see her when the fluctuations set in. Also he kept Miranda a secret from the rest of his family. They'd leave the city, go
away for quiet weekends in the Adirondacks or by the shore. Who's
to say her love wasn't a big help to Mr. Scott? I think it was. Fear's a
big part of what bothers them, the skizzerfrantics. I know that much."

"Yeah."

"But when she did find out, when he couldn't keep from her how
bad he was inflicted, Miss Miranda hung in there. She thought that
maybe together they could lick that terrible illness. But something she
said or did, could've been just a innocent remark she don't even remember, set him off, and he did a major vanishing act."

"Major vanishing acts seem to go on around that family all the
time," Dempsey said, thinking of something in Scott's latest E-mail
that had triggered a little snare of curiosity.

Marlowe gave him a quick look with some depth to it, a troubled
recognition of truth, then looked away, unwilling to comment. "Miranda couldn't eat," he resumed, "couldn't do her college studies, she
was in tears half the time. I had a feeling it wasn't a good idea for her
to go see Miss Esther, but she didn't listen."

"Esther didn't take a liking to Miranda."

Marlowe had a long swallow of beer. "I suppose that's how it was.
You need to understand Miss Esther's feelings. Her brother having a
mental breakdown, whereabouts unknown, and then a young lady
show up saying as how they've been slipping off together weekends,

and how she loves him with all her heart, and Miss Esther maybe coming to the conclusion Scott would be better off without that particular fluctuation."

"What did she do?"

"Oh, she wasn't ugly to poor Miranda, that's not in her nature, is it? Only it wasn't but a day or two after that Miranda's folks got wind of the fact she'd been neglecting school and carrying on with a crazy man, and they snatched her home quick."

"Sure they did. Then it wasn't long before Miranda found out she was pregnant."

"Yes, sir, that's exactly how it was."

"End of Act Two. I've written a lot of plays, Marlowe. Even though I can't find a producer anymore. Shut out of the business, you might say. Who knows? Maybe they're just bad plays. Or maybe somebody's holding an old grudge against me."

"What's that, Mr. Wingo?"

"Forget it. Go on about Miranda Leland. I'm kind of interested in this."

"All right. Not that much more to tell. Miss Miranda have her baby, in Europe, where her papa and mama pay for her to stay."

"I hope you're not going to tell me Miranda hit the skids and went wandering around the Continent in rags with her infant in one arm, taking fixes in her other arm."

"Oh, no. She finished her education, and works today for a big export company in Amerstadam, Holland."

"The almost-happy ending. Except she still pines for Scott, and hopes for the best." Dempsey picked up the E-mail from the printer tray. "This is what Scott is now, and I can tell you from having seen him myself not too long ago that there is no hope. He's cursed. He says as much himself. Seeing his kid won't matter."

Marlowe said, "You have cause to be a cynical man, Mr. Wingo, that I know. But shouldn't this be a matter for Mr. Scott his own self to decide?"

What to make of Marlowe Hare? Dempsey thought, although not very deeply. The separated lovers sounded trite but maybe authentic. So Miranda bore the love child, now six years of age and curious about who his daddy might be. There was also the question of a two-billion-dollar fortune, expanding yearly by, assuming a conservative investment approach, twelve to fifteen percent, or approximately one hundred million dollars more than the Trevellian Foundation was able to give away, either in biannual prize money or as balm for Third

World needy. So much money might be considered a burden that Miranda, and Marlowe in his humble turn, were willing to help them with to the benefit of themselves as well as the new heir.

"What's his name?" Dempsey asked.

"The boy is called Timothy."

"Is she here, Marlowe?"

"Miss Miranda go back and forth. All part of her job."

"Like I said, I don't think I can help. Everyone has reasons for wanting to find Scott. He has his reasons why he doesn't want to be found. It may be that some of those reasons would make sense."

"Not sure I know what you mean."

"Why should he feel cursed? I don't know, his brain is a witches' cauldron nearly all the time. But that bit about the Japanese golfer is realistically observed. Amusing. Scott has his calm moments. He liked the sunsets on the river, he told me, that evening I ran into him in the park." Dempsey gently pressed an eyelid closed, relieving the botched symmetry of his gaze. One eye saying stop, the other go. Or, one eye peace, the other mutiny. The mutinous green eye stared at Marlowe Hare, who looked away as if lucklessly transfixed. "Sunsets on the river," Dempsey mused. "Marlowe, do you know who Thursday Childs is? Or was?"

"No, sir, I don't recall the name."

"My first produced play was a big success. Ran a year and a half off Broadway. *B-Movie Boxcar Blues* is still being acted around the country. Colleges, community theaters. My second play was *Honeymoon at the Ghost Town Hotel*. Two characters, unless you count the giant gila monster, who might also be God. Anyway, Thursday Childs was cast as one of the leads. Loretta. A tart with heart. Our other lead, the rifleman, had been in a Scorsese movie but his career was just a speck on the horizon at that time. Two weeks into rehearsal Thursday didn't show up one morning. No word to anyone. She totally vanished. It's still a mystery. She was just a kid. Twenty-six or -seven. Lived in the Village with a couple of Broadway gypsies. Strange that Scott would refer to her today; it's been I think ten years. Her disappearance wasn't the death knell for *Honeymoon*, of course; we recast the part. But then things went from bed to worse, if you can stand the pun. I mean, the play never got on. It was Esther's money. She withdrew her backing after the fracas, and I got tossed in the can."

"What was that all about, Mr. Wingo?"

"Esther and I were still married. In the lower depths of obsession by then. She'd made one attempt to kill me. Or maybe it was Mardie Kregg. That's another story. This one has to do with Caribino. Our other star. He liked to be called the rifleman. Obvious reason. I found him in bed with Esther after a forty-eight-hour rewriting binge. Second act, always my big weakness. I do great first acts. Anyway, they were blowing coke up each other's asses with soda straws, that kind of thing. As a result of my immediate objections, she was unconscious for nine hours. Esther's incredibly strong for a woman, she hunts deer with a longbow and the kind of arrowheads that were around before Attila the Hun. But she has a glass jaw. I bundled up the rifleman and drove him to Dutchess County in the back of my van and buried him alive in a refrigerator carton."

"My *Lord*, Mr. Wingo!"

"Just wanted to scare him, Marlowe. I didn't tromp the dirt down hard like I should have. And I left him a garden hose for breathing purposes. Stopped off on my way back to Manhattan for a few belts to ease my sorrow. Two days later I remembered rifleman and just did remember where I'd put him and went back to dig him up. But some kids out playing in the woods with their setter dog had heard him hollering for help through his air hose."

"So you didn't go to Attica for the rest of your natural life."

"Esther fixed that beef. But that was the end of us, finally. Three hellacious years. Where is she now, Marlowe?"

"Miss Esther?"

"No. Miranda Leland."

Marlowe Hare looked unsure.

"You want me to help, fine. First I talk to the lady, have a look at the boy."

"Why, Mr. Wingo?"

"That's my condition. Take it or leave it."

Marlowe ran the possibilities with laborious thoroughness, head down, eyes on the scarred old station floor, making grumbling sounds in his throat. A kind of lament.

"Marlowe."

"She'll be at the Plaza. The next week or so." His chest pumped up and his large head rose like a parade balloon. "Let me talk to her first, please, Mr. Wingo."

"Yeah, get her prepared for the Badman with one green eye."

"You know where he's at, don't you?" Marlowe said with a hopeful gleam.

"Within commuting distance of the city. Right now that's all I'm sure of. But I've found men with not much more to go on. I'll show you out, Marlowe. You need to pull that tweetie off my car while there's enough daylight to see what you're doing. There's somebody I should pay a visit." Dempsey grinned. "He makes twenty million a picture now. But I'll bet he still can't go to sleep at night without leaving all the lights on."

After seeing Marlowe off Dempsey returned to the underground rail station for a light supper of canned corned beef and crackers and another beer. While he ate, he watched a movie from one of his collection of vintage B westerns. Gene Autry in *Public Cowboy No. 1.* The plotline was routine, filler between musical numbers, but God how Gene could sing. "Old Buckaroo, Good-bye" always brought tears to Dempsey's eyes. Dempsey sang along, but he had a voice like a ruptured walrus.

When the movie was over he made another copy of Scott Trevellian's latest E-mail and put on some western clothes. A double-breasted shirt John Wayne had worn in *Liberty Valence*, which Dempsey had paid several thousand dollars for at an auction, and an old high-crowned Boss of the Plains Stetson that once belonged to Tim McCoy. He took his spurs with him but didn't put them on. It was hard to drive while wearing spurs.

Two lanes of the upper deck of the Verrazano Narrows Bridge had been closed to traffic after the rush hour for the benefit of the film company that was shooting an action thriller called *Wolfpack*, starring Lew Carbine and a sex deb named Livia Kane, making her feature debut, after a sensational modeling career, as a mute but savvy hit girl who wore next to nothing during the course of the film. This according to an advance puff piece for *Wolfpack* that Dempsey had caught on CNN.

Thirty production vehicles ranging from ten-tons to honeywagons took up most of one lane on the Brooklyn side of the bridge. Dempsey had no trouble passing through the police line, thanks to a film company sign displayed on his windshield, which he had swiped two days ago from a production assistant's van that was parked in front of a Bensonhurst spaghetti joint. Such special privilege IDs were always useful to Dempsey, when he had to leave his car somewhere in a hurry.

The crew was busy setting up props for a sequence that may have been shooting for several nights, and which called for the burned-out hulks of police cars and a crashed helicopter. Dempsey parked. The lower bay was as golden as honey in a hive, the sky turquoise. A cruise ship white as an ice floe steamed south beneath the bridge. Twenty-k HMIs mounted on Condors were warming up. Extras and bit players costumed and made up like disaster victims, shepherded by PAs with walkies, filed off a bus. Dempsey put on his spurs and then his ten-gallon hat, receiving curious glances from extras who had no access to scripts; they probably wondered what part he was about to play.

Dempsey grinned and clumped toward a sixty-foot customized star bus with darkly tinted picture windows and a raised roof. His spurs jingled. He looked seven feet tall. He looked movie. Nobody bothered him until he got to the bus, where a bodyguard stood outside the rifleman's door, gobbling a chili cheese dog as if they fed him only once a day.

"Yo, podner. Where you going?"

"See the rifleman."

"Not now, podner. He's in makeup. Who you with?"

Dempsey heard laughter aboard the bus. "Tell him Dempsey."

"Lew can't be distoibed," the bodyguard said, semireverently, catching a drip of cheesy mustard on his chin with a forefinger. "He's with Livia and Mr. Highburn."

"Dickie Highburn directing this?"

"That's right, podner. You know him?"

"I knew him when he was directing off-off and hustling the five A.M. trade at the Mineshaft. I'm already a little sick of hearing you call me 'podner.' "

"Whoa," the bodyguard said, hunching his big shoulders a little. "Whoa now, you don't want to come on like that to me."

"I guess it depends on how long you're going to keep me waiting. You got some on your tie."

"Jesus," the bodyguard muttered, glancing down. He had a hard cleft chin and some minor knife scars on his face, which didn't make him look tough: they made him look like an inept asshole in a knife fight. Dempsey grinned peaceably at him.

"Club soda will take that mustard right out."

"You think so?"

"Always works for me and Heloise. While you're cleaning your tie, why don't you tell Lew I'm here?"

More laughter inside. The bodyguard said, "Maybe they're taking a break right now; I'll see."

He came back with his tie off and his too-tight shirt unbuttoned at the collar. All the goombahs splurged on expensive tailored shirts, Dempsey thought, but they couldn't forgo the fettuccine Alfredo, so the shirts never fit worth a damn.

"Lewie looked like somebody dropped a piano on his toes when I told him youse outside."

"I'll bet."

"He said come on back anyway."

Dempsey followed the bodyguard, past members of the fringe entourage looking bored as they leafed through magazines or watched a movie on the VCR or played blackjack while waiting to be useful to Low Carbine. Dempsey's spurs jingled but didn't hang up on the thick carpet. A door was opened. He heard the tag line of a joke Dickie Highburn had been telling. "By the way, your pussy's in the sink." Livia Kane had a throaty laugh, Dickie a high enthused giggle. Lew's laugh came up from the belly in gusts. He was semireclined in a barber's chair with his back to the door, wearing a black silk jockstrap while body makeup was applied by his personal makeup artist, two assistants and a specialist in realistic-looking wounds. Lew was playing with a Captain Kirk doll. The doll said "Warp speed, Mr. Sulu," and other things when Lew pulled the ring attached to its back. There were blowups of Kirk, Uhuru and Spock, adoringly signed to Lew, in the star's dressing room. Lew was a big *Star Trek* fan.

"Jesus. I don't believe it," Lew said, catching Dempsey's eye in the triptych of mirrors he was facing.

Dickie Highburn said, "Well, Dempsey Wingo. It has been *forever*. Been keeping your pecker dry, dear old thing?"

Lew said, "Tell you where he should've been. In a federal slam."

"Why's that, Lew?" Livia Kane said, looking Dempsey over in amusement and astonishment. Her wide sensual face was bruised and smudged for the camera; she wore a torn shirt over bare breasts, ragged denim short-shorts and combat boots.

"Son of a bitch kidnapped me one time and buried me alive out in the boondocks."

They thought they were being had. Dickie Highburn sucked in a breath and said, "Naughty, *naughty*."

Livia said, "I've been tempted to do the same thing myself, Lew."

"No. I mean, for real. This slimeball actually stuffed me in a refrigerator carton with my hands and feet tied and fucking *buried* me."

"Whatever for?" Livia asked, falling into a pose in her blue suede director's chair. Women who didn't automatically shrink from Dempsey were inclined to act out their awe while taking the temperature of whatever sexual currents might be flowing. She had aquamarine eyes Dempsey thought he definitely could go for.

"Dear God, what a fright. Did you dirty your knickers, darling?" Highburn asked Lew.

"I buried him in what he had on when I found him in bed with my wife," Dempsey said.

"It had to be something like that," Livia concluded with a hint of glee. "Right, Lew?"

"He told me he was sorry," Dempsey said. "Until he ran out of spit and his tongue wouldn't work anymore."

There was an awkward silence. Lew continued to stare at Dempsey by way of the mirror. The special FX makeup guy glued a latex contusion to one of Lew's thighs. Once in place it looked like the real thing. Dickie Highburn drummed his fingers on his leather script cover. Livia studied Dempsey like a panther breathing in deep shade. He smiled at her.

"Well," Highburn said, "if we're all clear on how the scene should go."

"Sure," Livia said. "It's blat-blat-blat with the assault rifle, then I pick up the RPG launcher, and it's *boom!* and then the stunt guy goes smoking over the side into the net. Then I kiss the blood off Lew's lips and he says the funny line."

"Priceless, darling," Highburn said, getting up to give Livia a kiss. His hair was like a coat of ash, all that remained of a spontaneous combustion that hadn't made it past his ears. Late in the shoot his eyes were battle-weary, but game.

"How's my makeup?" Carbine asked.

"Almost finished here, Lew."

"Livia, would you get the countess the fuck outa here? Let her sleep off her jag in your trailer."

He was referring to a woman, aristocratically thin, who was curled up asleep on the carpet in one corner like a neglected house pet. Livia sighed, saluted and went over to give the woman a hearty shaking.

"Girlfriend! On your feet. Lew wants his privacy."

"I got a few minutes, don't I, Dickie-pie?" Lew said.

"You've got all the time you need, Lew. We don't want it to be merely great. We want it to be stupendous."

Dempsey said, "I read in the papers you were thirty over and the knives were out."

Highburn said with a convincing show of good cheer, "That's the picture biz, lovey. But doomsday predictions are like bad sex: everybody comes too soon." He shook hands with Dempsey. For a little guy he had a powerful grip. "When can we expect another play from you? It's been much too long."

He seemed to mean it. Dempsey said, "I've got a few things in the works."

Livia, chuckling and coaxing, had the tanglefooted countess up and was guiding her out of the stateroom. The countess had a black eye, which somehow didn't detract from her appearance. Dempsey had the impression, given the shape she was in, that she might not be recognizable without it.

Dickie Highburn followed them out. Two of the makeup artists packed up. Lew scowled at the third until he got the point.

"Tell Binks give me ten, then he can dress me."

"Right, Lew."

When they were alone Lew Carbine got up from his barber's chair, looking critically at his body from every angle available in the mirrors. "It's been a pain working with that fag, but Christ he can shoot action as good as Peckinpah did it, and Sam was the master. I can send out for a beer if you want something. I don't drink. Two ounces of the hard stuff shows up under my eyes the next day. You need a job? I've got this script, three or four writers been on it, forget about it. We paid one of them two seventy-five just to add a couple jokes. But it's still shit, and I want to go in October."

"I don't need a job."

"Like your shirt. The Duke?"

"Yeah."

"But what's with the fucking spurs? Man, you were always hard to figure out. Comanche Irish Mex blood, what a combination. Scare the tits off a *strega*. I thought *Honeymoon* would take a Pulitzer, that's how much I loved your play. You would've been the next Albee. Too bad it never got on. I guess technically you could blame me."

"I don't blame you for anything, Lew. The back of my neck gets a little red when somebody calls me slimeball."

"Hey, no offense, man, it's how I talk. I call my best friends Slimeball. Just kidding around."

"See much of Esther these days?"

"We run into each other. London, Cap Farat. The Hamptons. She calls to say hello, why don't I buy so-and-so because he's the next

David Hockney. That kind of thing. Social. Nothing's going on. You know how she is."

"Yeah. Esther enjoys doing things for people, out of the goodness of her heart. Financed your boxing script, made you a star. All in a day's work for Esther."

"You hold that against me? Listen, I was respectful. She was your fucking *wife*. But she wouldn't leave me alone."

"You poor bastard."

"I mean, when she makes up her mind, cha-ching! She'd have the cassock off and the Pope out of his Jockey shorts before he fucking knew what hit him." Lew crossed himself superstitiously. "I was twenty-eight. Not much more than a kid. It wasn't happening for me. I had, I had a lot of *anger*, man. Then it was like, Esther Trevellian, coming on to *me*. Jesus. Lew Caribino lived in a fourth-floor walkup on Avenue C. Lew Caribino was so broke he had to jack off to feed the cat."

"Save it, Lew. I'm not mad anymore."

"Life takes some funny bounces," the rifleman said with a philosophical knitting of his brows. "So what'd you want to see me about? I need a little time to prepare. Four more days of this turkey, some closeups at the studio. I mean it'll make money, the Asian market is very big for Lew Carbine; *Shootout* did thirty-five in Japan only. Huge."

"Do you know what happened to Thursday Childs?"

"Huh?" Lew went to his refrigerator and opened it, stared inside. He scowled. "Fuck. This is *yesterday's* carrot juice. Where's my—" Lew slammed the fridge door, strode across the stateroom while gesturing vaguely for Dempsey to sit down somewhere and yelled through the closed door to his entourage about the carrot juice crisis. Dempsey could imagine the scene outside. The horror in their eyes. The mad scramble. He yawned. He was bored with Lew Carbine. He took a folded sheet of the copied E-mail from a pocket of his shirt and handed it to the rifleman.

Carbine unfolded it. He was one of those poor readers who had to read aloud, even to himself.

"Thursday's child had far to go . . ." He finished the doggerel, then looked up at Dempsey, puzzled.

"Where'd this come from?"

"Scott Trevellian."

"Scott—? Oh, the financial whiz. Went nuts, didn't he? Multiple personality disorder, something like that."

"He's schizophrenic."

"Too bad. So—what's this supposed to mean to me?"

"Scott seems to be saying that you know what happened to Thursday Childs."

Lew shrugged. "Everybody knows. She disappeared. Lived in a crappy neighborhood, like I did. So some psycho probably got hold of her."

"Were you fucking Thursday Childs, too?"

"I don't know. I guess so."

"You *guess* so?"

"Oh, man. You know. First week of rehearsals, we went out, had some laughs, it was like a get-acquainted fuck, that's all. She had nice lungs, I remember."

"What else do you remember about Thursday?"

"Kinky kid. Some strokes with a suede flogger, then up the old bum chute, as Dickie would say. Want to hear my definition of sodomy? Backdoor foreplay."

"Do you ever have anything else on your mind?"

"Okay, okay. Thursday Childs. Good actress. There was something wrong with her hands and her neck. Severe arthritis. She chewed aspirin all the time. Gave me acidosis just kissing her in rehearsals. What're you getting at? Man, I got a big night's work ahead of me, so maybe—"

"Am I making you nervous, Lew?"

"You? Make me nervous? I'm Lew Carbine. Lew Carbine gets twenty a flick, three-picture guarantee. He eats with presidents. He gets blow jobs from royalty. You're ex-everything, Wingo. You couldn't keep your rich wife. You can't write anymore. Cocksucker. You're walking around, courtesy of Lew Carbine. I'm very connected, man. I could have had you whacked. Any night of the week there's ten guys at Gargiulo's would do me the favor. Why don't you think about that? I owe you. I couldn't hold my shit, cocksucker. I heard the dirt hitting the top of that carton and *I couldn't hold my shit!*"

A pert face appeared in the doorway. "Oh-oh, is this a bad time?"

"What do you want, Jiffy?" Lew said sourly.

"Oh. Well, Mike's over at the catering truck and they were stocked up on carrots like you asked for, so it'll just be—"

"*Organic* carrots."

"Sure, Lew. Everybody knows that. Organic carrots. We're on top of it, Lew."

"Yeah, so thanks and get the fuck gone, Jiffy. Tell Binks two minutes, I'm ready." To Dempsey he said, "Want to know why we call her Jiffy?"

"I can guess."

"You want her? Jiffy's got a lower jaw that unhinges like a snake's. Forget about it, Jiffy's the best. After she does you, you can hang around the set. *No problemo*, pussycat. Only I really need to get in character here. So if there's nothing else—"

Dempsey sat down on a sofa amid pillows on which Lew's mother or some other devout relative had embroidered pious homilies, and crossed his right leg over his knee. The sterling silver spur on his boot flashed in the light. The buckaroo-style rowels, twelve of them, were as sharp as the day he had taken his spurs from the presentation box. He idly flicked the jinglebobs, pear-shaped pendants hanging from the rowel axle, making cowboy music. He looked benignly at the rifleman.

"Think back. Maybe Thursday said something to you before she disappeared, didn't sound important at the time."

"I don't want to think about that gimpy little broad! I didn't know a damn thing about her. It was ten years ago. I was trying to learn a Texas accent for your fucking play. Get out of here before I call my security director."

Lew Carbine turned his bodybuilder's back on Dempsey, flexing a little, exhibiting the sharply cut muscle groups. He bent over a dressing table, more or less mooning Dempsey in his jockstrap, and took some jewelry from a case. Small gold object on a thin gold chain. Dempsey had a look as Lew was slipping the chain over his head. Dempsey unbuckled the handy spur on his boot, got up swiftly, moved in behind the rifleman with a forearm across his throat and shoved the spur rowels between the cheeks of the rifleman's ass, tugging lightly upward. Lew's back arched and his mouth flew open in horrified anticipation of serious damage to his rectum.

"Where'd you get it?"

"What? What the fuck? Let go of me, you asshole!"

Dempsey increased the pressure of the forearm across Lew's throat.

"One more time. What are you doing with the trinket? I'll ease off now so you can explain. Simple words, softly spoken. Where did you get it, Lew?"

"You mean . . . my good-luck piece?"

"Yeah."

"Always . . . had it."

Dempsey tugged a little harder on the spur. The rifleman rose on his toes.

"Holy God . . . don't."

"Who gave you the good-luck piece?"

"I think it must've been—"

"Come on, Lew. Your lucky piece! You know who gave it to you."

"Yeah, it was—right before I started *The Big Shot*, at the training camp in Jersey. He was on the set that day."

"Who?"

"Him. The one who sent you the E-mail. Scott Trevellian. Now get that spur out of my ass!"

"Sure, Lew," Dempsey said. He withdrew the spur, spun the rifleman around, and hit him low in the gut with his left hand. Lew collapsed slowly, holding himself, speechless.

"That's for your memory," Dempsey said. "May it improve with age. Because I don't think you're telling me straight."

Lew spewed vomit on his carpet. Dempsey reached down and took hold of the slender chain, broke it and palmed the good-luck piece, a twenty-four-carat gold charm of a woman's cupped, supplicant hand, slightly worn but precisely detailed, about five-eighths of an inch long and a quarter of an inch across the palm.

"I'll tell you where I saw this last," Dempsey said. "It was the day after we cast Thursday Childs in *Ghost Town Hotel*. I bought the charm in India about twenty years ago. It's Canaanite, eleventh century B.C., made its way to the Malabar coast and was buried for three thousand years in an amphora with a thousand gold Hadrian coins and some other jewelry. I paid two large for the little lady's hand. I gave it to Thursday. For luck. Some luck she had. Look at me, Lew."

The rifleman raised his head slowly. Tears marred his made-up eyes and cheeks. He gasped for each tiny breath. His eyes were red with fury.

"Why would Scott Trevellian have the charm, months after Thursday disappeared?"

"Would I know? Maybe she balled him, too. Maybe she hustled him for rent money, you know . . . what rehearsal pay is like. She could have sold it to him. Ask the schiz. What are you muscling me for? You've done it. You're fixed. Canceled. Forget about it. I smell dead meat."

Dempsey smelled fear. He grimaced in contempt.

"Sucker punch. God . . . I think you ruptured me. How am I going to finish the picture?"

"I'll tell Mr. De Mille you're ready for your close-up," Dempsey said, and walked out of the stateroom, past the rifleman's entourage. They'd heard the scuffling. No one made a move. They watched Dempsey, and maybe a couple of them looked secretly pleased.

"A little stomach disorder," Dempsey told them. "Nothing too serious."

He got off the bus. The bridge lights were muzzy in artificial fog and smoke. There was a stretch limo parked twenty feet away. The rifleman's bodyguard stood beside it chatting with Mardie and Mordecai Kregg. Mordecai was wearing a turban of bandages on his healing head, where Dempsey had partially scalped him. Mordecai stared, then made a move in Dempsey's direction, a hand under the black jacket he was wearing. More threat display than anything, Dempsey figured, but with Mordecai you could never be sure.

Esther Trevellian got out of the limousine and said something to him. Mordecai stopped short. They were all watching Dempsey now. He waved.

Esther came over to him. She was wearing a midnight-blue dress that was elegant as hell without being ostentatious. She paid a fortune for simple elegance and exclusivity. Dempsey had seen couturiers grovel like kicked dogs when she passed on some of their creations. The good old days.

"Well, José."

A stunt coordinator with a bullhorn called, *"We're ready to do the gag. Background players, do not deviate from your assigned positions or your asses will be severely overcooked."*

"Hi, Esther. Hard up for something to do?"

"Lew invited me to watch some of the filming. What's that you have there?"

"My spur?"

"No. In your other hand."

He opened his hand and let her see the gold charm.

"How interesting." She touched the charm with a forefinger, looked thoughtfully at Dempsey.

"Lew has one like that."

"This is Lew's."

"His lucky piece?"

"We are going for picture," another amplified voice said.

Dempsey flung the small gold hand and the chain over the bridge railing.

"Why did you do that? It might have been valuable."

"The way you two looked in bed together."

"Oh, don't start pouting, Dempsey. It's such old news."

"Did your brother Scott have a thing for Thursday Childs?"

"The actress?"

"Who disappeared."

"What have you and Lew been talking about?"

"That, among other reminiscences."

"Scott and Thursday Childs? I have no idea. Dix, I think, was interested in her. During the short time she was in rehearsal. Why does it matter?"

"Scott has the notion rifleman knew what happened to the kid. I mean, what really happened."

Esther put a hand on his arm.

"You heard from him again? Did he say—"

"No." Dempsey took the copy of the E-mail message from a pocket. "Here. See what you make of it."

She reached for the E-mail. He held it back momentarily, staring at her. He smelled the scent she always dabbed on the inside of her slender wrist. It did something to his pulse rate. Esther smiled faintly. He ran a finger down her taut inner arm to her elbow, and she winced.

"What's the matter?"

"Sore muscles. Archery practice. I've been neglecting my bow."

"Going after deer? Or should I come down and wear the horns again?"

Esther greeted that with indifferent silence.

"Going hot," an amplified voice advised.

He let her take the E-mail. She held it nearly at arm's length to read.

"Eyes failing, Esther?"

"I've always been a little farsighted," she said, disliking the reminder that physically she might be less than perfect. "You know that. And the light's not so good here."

"Hot and ready!"

Lew Carbine appeared in the doorway of his bus, larger than life, bulging with exaggerated bronze muscle, like a Southern general's courthouse charger.

"Fuckhead. You're done. You're done walking. I'm calling it. Lie down, you stopped breathing already!"

"Background action! Roll cameras . . . roll sound . . ."

The bodyguard came running.

"Boys, boys," Esther said, taking over, and she gently pushed Lew back into the bus, followed him with a perplexed glance over one shoulder at Dempsey. Perhaps a slight smile. Her lips formed the words Call me.

"What happened to Lew?" the bodyguard said to Dempsey. "You try to push Lewie around?"

"*Action!*" the Second Unit director called. There were several *thumps!* from FX propane mortars. Orange blossoms of flame tinted the fog. Stunt players were flung around by air rams, their shadowy figures lifeforms tumbling in primordial soup. Shouts. Gunfire.

A few minutes with Esther, and Dempsey felt undone by the pure paranoia of his raging nerve. Her scent raised blisters in his nostrils. Animal instinct. He wanted to put the goombah down with one punch, see if he could still do it. But it was the wrong guy, and he wasn't even angry. He shrugged off whatever trouble was rising to a boil and walked away, shaking the spur in his hand, jinglebob jinglebob, ignoring the silent staring Kreggs by the preposterous stretch limousine, Carbine's taste no doubt. Another time for the Kreggs. He had Esther to think about.

An assistant director was calling for first team. A scum of black powder smoke and effects vapor hung over the Verrazano Bridge, obscuring the lights of Jersey City and lower Manhattan, far up the bay.

TEN

SACRED FIRES

Bless me, Father, for I have sinned. It has been five months since my last confession."

The priest opposite Sharan waited, his head slightly bowed, dark plump hands folded on the blond oak table. He was a young man, probably younger than she was, with a rapidly balding head, only a close-cropped spearhead tuft in front. He wore two small gold earrings in the lobe of his left ear. He was from Nigeria, and he had a British accent, a theatrical voice contrasting with the utter blandness of his features and personality. She'd been hoping for someone paternal, but without the misogynistic edge that surfaced like a shark's fin in a few of the elderly priests.

"Go on."

"In the past five months I've missed Mass three times. I used the name of the Lord profanely. I was in jail because I lost my temper. That wasn't entirely my fault, because my motorcycle was stolen." She took a breath, the sunny air of the closed bookish study salted with incense and the odor of breakfast bacon from the kitchen down the hall. The familiars of rectories everywhere. "Do you need to hear about that?"

"Whatever you want to tell me."

"I think it's more important that I, I have to confess, I've recently had sex with a man. Since my last confession. I knew I didn't really love him. It was just, uh, one of those relationships that gets to that stage, because I'd been going with him for about a year. So I had sex with him. I haven't told him I don't love him. I need to do that, I feel skunky because I haven't already. I'll give him back the Bose system he gave me for Valentine's Day because he must have spent a fortune on it."

She took a breath, changed her position a little in the chair, changed it again.

"There's another man—I'm kind of mixed up about."

"Is he married?"

"No, divorced. I'm not having sex with him."

"Do you love him?"

"It's just that I'm—drawn to him. He's so angry and so lonely. His daughter has leukemia. His sister was probably killed by a madman. What I have to do is find out, try to prove, who did it."

"You?"

"Oh, I'm qualified. Trained. I was an investigator, criminal investigations, for the Army. I didn't volunteer to do this. He blackmailed me, which he could do because he's with the Justice Department."

"How do you mean, he blackmailed you?"

"Threatened to put me in a Federal prison because of the motorcycle thing. I mean, the van, but I was only borrowing it. I suppose, technically, I took the law into my own hands. I put a guy in the hospital who it turned out didn't actually steal my bike. So I was in trouble. I'm nolle prossed, it's still hanging over my head." The young priest looked lost. Sharan shrugged and plunged on. "Would he still use it? I'm not sure. A couple of nights ago he asked me to forgive him. As if he's afraid I may be killed. Or else he knows something he doesn't want to tell me."

"In spite of all this, you remain attracted to him."

"I know I'm not perfect, but I never imagined I'd get into a situation like this."

"It may be time to think about what God expects of you."

"Yes, Father."

"There may be a gray area in your relationship with this man, but in the eyes of God there is no 'gray area' when it comes to sin and your personal salvation."

"I know, Father."

"According to you, he has great civil power, which he doesn't hesitate to use wrongly, although his motives, at least from his point of view, justify his actions. There's no one you can appeal to?"

"No."

"Is he Catholic?"

"No, Episcopalian or something. I don't even know if he goes to church."

"Still, it would not hurt to let him know he is accountable for his own sins. I'll talk to him, if you'd like."

"You might make him uncomfortable. You wouldn't change his mind."

The priest sat back, closing his eyes as if acknowledging the impasse, her helplessness.

"What else do you want to tell me?"

Sharan said with her own eyes downcast, "That's about it."

"For your penance, fifteen Our Fathers and fifteen Hail Marys. Morning mass twice a week for four weeks while you reflect on the sacred implications of your involvement with any man, and pray for guidance in all relationships. I'll pray for you as well. By the way, that's a beautiful cross you're wearing. Keep in mind always what it means to you."

In the church she lit candles for Sarge, and for each of the women who had disappeared from the face of the earth: for Thursday, Kerry, Astrid, Caterina, Robin, and Felicia. Seven flickering flames in banked wells of smoky rosebud glass. Why red? she wondered, as she had first wondered as a child. Wasn't it the color of the devil? She sought the soothing blue eyes of the Madonna.

Hail Mary full of grace the lord is with thee. Blessed art thou amongst women, and blessed is the fruit of thy womb, Jesus.

One of the two men in the surveillance vehicle parked in front of an Olive Garden restaurant four hundred yards from Immaculate Heart of Mary Church picked up the receiver of the car phone and said, "Reception here is just about perfect."

"Okay," Coleman Dane said. He was standing beside his own car, the pearl-gray Mercedes, in the parking lot of the church, which was surrounded by two acres of lawns and flower beds on a knoll overlooking a busy suburban Virginia highway. Sprinklers were crisscrossing the lawns, fleeting veils of droplets in sultry air. One of the sprinkler heads, misaligned, poured a thin stream of water onto one of the many stained glass panels of the sanctuary that leaned tentlike toward a cupola and a sculptor's cross, massive, that dripped weldings. Naked rusting steel, militant as a warship. Dane folded his cellular phone, put it away and waited.

Twenty minutes later Sharan came out of the sanctuary. Low heels,

a short-sleeved pinstriped cotton shirt with a paisley vest, short charcoal skirt that flattered her long legs. Her hair was shorter, styled,
blowing a little in the misted breeze across her forehead, catching sun,
looking coppery from the tint they'd used at the salon. That on-target
stride of hers. Army brat, beast barracks, you could never completely
smooth the regimen out of her. Every time he saw Sharan, there was
something new to excite his interest, or his mania.

Something in the way he smiled at Sharan caused her to clutch at
the silver cross she was wearing.

"Damn! I forgot to turn it off, didn't I?"

"Yep."

"I'd better get used to this." She looked resentfully at him. "Did
you hear my confession?"

"No. I didn't hear anything. Did you tell him about me?"

"Yes."

Dane shrugged. "In my family religion was a social necessity. Grace
before meals. Our minister wore a wine-dark vest with his clerical
collar. He had the gestures and the irritating complacency of a good
English butler. There was a bible in our library, on a stand. Massive
thing that smelled of moldering leather nibbled by mice. Nobody ever
opened it, to my knowledge. We didn't talk about God the way we
didn't talk about our money. We assumed both would always be there
for us when needed. Do Catholics still believe in hell?"

"Fervently."

"Felicia was a convert. I went with her a few times, but I was
disappointed. They'd done away with the mysteries of Latin. There
was a lot of folk guitar and neighborly hand-holding. The drama was
missing, the threat. The great storming head of God we all must have
buried somewhere in the subconscious."

"Can we go?"

"You've got a case of nerves this morning."

"Of course I do!" Sharan almost yelled, going up in smoke.

He put his arm around her and kissed her. She kissed him back,
head buzzing, heart still faintly burning from remorse and the sacred
fire of penance.

"I'll be in New York in three or four days. We'll talk tomorrow.
After Jules Brougham's soiree."

The wind had shifted. Some drops from the lawn sprinkler fell on
their fascinated faces, which were only inches apart. Dane held her
more tightly.

"Just don't leave me alone too long," Sharan said, with a slight disconsolate lift of her shoulders.

Sunrise at Cloud Horse Mountain.

At three thousand feet fog lay below the summit in long dense folds, obscuring the valleys and the funicular station at the edge of the small town that was the seat of Simon the Rock County. Above the fog line the green mountain shimmered wetly, and there were deer in the subalpine meadows. Higher, hawks soared from rocky bluffs. The windows of the seven-level house that clung just below the summit of Cloud Horse Mountain like half of a wentletrap seashell took on the pale light of dawn. All the glass of the house would, according to the later angle and fierceness of the sun at more than six thousand feet, darken appropriately to maintain interior temperatures at optimum levels.

Dix Trevellian stirred in his bed, half-conscious, artificially calm, body nearly inert. Wondering where he was. Then, a little later, thinking that something may have happened to him he should be concerned about. It was a not unfamiliar awakening. Creative bingeing along with excessive travel combined to throw him out of orbit, tapped fields of electric disorder in the brain. The epilepsy of genius. No mad thrashing and gnashing, but a separation of personality, the sober and hardworking Dix cast off like a ghost that unhappily followed the social whirligig, the obsessive lover and gambler and risk-taker, to inevitable oblivion.

Too much of this lately, Dix said to himself. His scalp itched. He raised his head from a therapeutic pillow and rubbed cautiously, not wanting to pull out hair that might not grow back, and knew by the shape of the window-wall in the bedroom that he was home, on the mountain. He was naked. He had an odor, and a thirst. The blue silk top sheet slid off his body to his lean waist.

By the window—convex sandwich glass that would neither bow nor shatter in one hundred-mile-per-hour winds—a young woman in nursing blue, white stockings and white shoes uncrossed her legs and set a magazine aside.

"Good morning, Mr. Trevellian."

Irish accent, but Esther recruited them from all over the globe and paid huge wages: personal physicians, nurses, housekeepers, executive secretaries, pilots, seldom employing anyone, other than vital security people or numerous members of the Kregg clan—a different matter altogether—for longer than a year. All of them, by contract, forbidden ever to say anything about the Trevellians. Dix didn't recall having seen this one before, but the road out of oblivion was filled with gaping holes.

"I'm Liadan," she said, approaching the round bed. "Would you like for me to run your bath now?"

"How long have I—"

"You've been here for six days, Mr. Trevellian."

"Asleep?" he asked, frightened.

"Oh, no, sir. Not all of the time. You took your meals. You sunbathed. You chatted with your sister on the video phone."

"I did? I don't remember. Good God. What did they give me this time?" He winced, searching for a recent memory. What he got was an image of half-naked, dark-brown people swarming over an immense scab of refuse in broiling sun. Dust dust dust, a stinging miasma of sand from the desert and particles of dried human shit from the unwashed streets. Rain as scarce in their land as the mercy of Allah. Somebody wanted to put buildings on that leveled trashpile. "I was in Cairo. Wasn't I?"

"I don't know, sir."

An impulse of panic was efficiently blocked by whatever combination of drugs—tranquilizers, hypnotics—had him feeling that his skin was not quite in contact with the rest of his body. He rubbed the pelt of his chest. He didn't feel bad. He felt . . . spookily calm. And, aside from a middling thirst, incapable of want. Dix pulled off the sheet and regarded his genitals. Almost always he awoke with a stout erection. Nothing this morning. The Irish nurse Esther had in place to oversee his latest rehabilitation looked away with her hands clasped, chin lifted, a Madonna pose in the mauve and crimson morning light. Assurance and piety. She had blue eyes and a high lucent forehead, a mouth shaped for laughter with a generous lower lip divided by a vertical crease, each glistening half like segments of a mandarin orange. Lips that were bound to arouse him, sooner or later; right now he felt intimidated, deprived of swagger, a deconsecrated fertility figure. One of these times the script docs would permanently unhinge his brain with their knockdown concoctions. A little cloud of guilt obscured his view of the Madonna. Stopping him when he was out of control was like trying to stop an elephant stampede. Esther had always done the best she could.

"I'm an architect," he said, wanting Liadan's approval, if nothing else. "I designed this house when I was twenty-six. My design has won a lot of awards. I don't think it's exaggerating to say that next to Fallingwater and Casa Malaparte, Cloud Horse is the best known house of the twentieth century. Purity of form has always been my standard. What I do can't be talked about, objectivized verbally I mean. My work has to be seen, and felt, as part of an environment."

"Your house is a pure amazement, sir. Never have I seen anything to equal it. I'm required to take your temperature and your pulse. If you'd cover yourself at this time, sir."

He pulled the sheet back over him. She performed her nursing chores and went briskly away to run his bath.

Have to get her into bed, Dix thought lazily, but it was a remote reflex with no thrill involved, his penis lying like a dead mouse atop his testicles. Those emaciated Egyptian scavengers were scrambling through his brain again, rags on their heads and bundled about their loins. The flies, the sun-charred stench. It impacted the sinuses, settled in the taste buds as a reminder that lingered for days, out of Egypt, beyond Paris, home again. But the eyes, ravished, retained even in sleep an afterglow of desert light, a source of inspiration as powerful as the textures, the morphology, the ancient sensuality and spiritual mystery of Egypt. A new Cairo to rise there. His designs in competition with the world's best architects. The most prestigious commission of his career. Couldn't get a hard-on. Today, last week, last month. His creative steel unwhetted while he rejected one influence after another as unworkable or passé: Islamic, constructionist, neoclassic, Corbusian, traditional Euclidean progressions. Finally working all night three nights in a row, stoking on pharmaceuticals, and worse, when the energy ran low. Then Felicia Dane showed up. Real, or a freebase figment? Unprepared for a storm of raw terror. Dead or undead? Squeezed her arm to find out. Screaming, both of them.

. . . Then what?

What did you do then?

"Sir?"

He had gasped for air; he was shuddering. Dix smiled at the nurse. The smile felt strange, out of shape on his face.

"I'm feeling a little flat," Dix confessed to Liadan. "And I've got work to do, as soon as I've had my bath and some breakfast. Could I get a pickup shot? B-twelve or something?"

"I'll speak to Dr. Dorji."

The name was new to Dix. "Dr. Dorji? Where is he from?"

"The Himalayas, I believe, sir. He's with your mum right now."

Dix felt a definite chill at the mention of his mother. "How is the old girl?"

"She's fighting a rather severe infection. Her temperature was quite high for several hours last night. But Dr. Dorji told me she's resting comfortably now. What clothes should I lay out for you?"

"I'm going hiking later," Dix said, staring at her, thinking that he just might take Liadan back to New York with him. Warden, his valet of the last twenty years, was growing cantankerous in his sixties, probably a little senile; time for that retirement cottage in the Cotswolds. Dix thought he could use a valet who was also a practical nurse, who had blood-rich cheeks and hips that moved with the deftness of dance. But if she were looking after his health, choosing his wardrobe and also—yes—fucking him, they might as well be married. Which was an unrealizable fantasy. Esther would send Liadan packing in a hurry.

There was a video phone in the bathroom. Chin-deep in suds, he conferred with one of his secretaries to see what he had missed during the past week. Although it was Sunday morning, he set up a vid conference with all four of his office managers for two o'clock. London, Buenos Aires, Frankfurt, New York. There was a mass of material in his Cloud Horse Mountain office that the computer had been downloading around the clock. Two more of his secretaries were en route on a company plane to help him get back on track. He felt a slight revival of his competitive instinct. He was going to ace that Cairo commission. Maybe his design associates had come up with something useful to get him on a roll.

Breakfast was green tea, fruit compote and oatmeal. He ate in one of the spacious sixteen rooms below cliff level, chambered between gracefully curving steel ribs that anchored the house to the mountain. A hivelike effect, with service elevators and a spiral staircase behind the rooms for access to summit level, which was capped with a massive sculpted white concrete roof, the design borrowed from another type of seashell, the angel wing. The scope and drama of the house could best be appreciated from the air.

From where he sat as his picked at his food, Dix watched the fog thin out over the Keenashee Valley and the river gorge five thousand feet below. The river was low and almost placid at summer's end. In spring it was an exhilarating rockbound flume lasting more than three miles. A nearby mountain, fireswept a few dry summers ago, was greening again. He remembered how it had looked, glowing like a live coal in the night. There was always something interesting to see from any window of the aerie. Sharp-shinned and red hawks, next-door neighbors in their cliff nests, so close one could watch the chicks hatch without binoculars. He'd been worried about driving the hawks away permanently during construction. Like his sister, Dix was a devoted conservationist. He threw back the fish he caught. He hunted with bow and arrow. But after the blasting was over, the hawks and other wildlife had gradually returned to that part of the mountain, which the Trevellians had owned in its entirety, seven square miles of wilderness preserve, for more than a century.

Dr. Dorji dropped by and introduced himself. Cambridge education, Harvard Medical. He was looking after Elnora Trevellian for a year because Esther had promised him funds for a health-care facility in his native Bhutan. He'd been on Cloud Horse Mountain for three months and was a little bored, in spite of the scenery that reminded him of his home, diversions that included horseback riding and trout fishing. He had off one weekend a month to get laid in Atlanta. But he wanted the Trevellian Foundation money. The simple equation that kept civilization in gear. If I have it, and you want it, and if you're not strong enough to take it from me, then you will do what I ask. Some people asked more nicely than others, of course. Esther always graciously assumed the role of the one who was indebted.

The doctor spent considerable time pondering Dix's pulse. Part of the folk medicine he had learned from his father, who practiced only the traditional *gsopa rigpa*. Too much stress, he said. Dix could have told him that: he was on the A list of overachievers. Dr. Dorji had a remedy at hand, a mixture of bitter-tasting herbs pressed into a homemade wafer Dix had to chew. Dix got it all down with orange juice and his morale soon improved. He didn't feel good yet, but he felt okay. He was in a mood to chat with Esther. Sunday morning, third week in August. She would be in East Hampton, along with just about everybody else in the world who mattered.

Video hookup, twenty-one-inch screen. There was a spanking breeze from the blue Atlantic that tangled Esther's hair, strands of darkness making a floating flirty mask for her steady eyes as she spoke to him from the terrace outside the living room. The East Hampton house was another of his designs, just a simple retreat with emphasis, like the best of the Italian villas he'd visited, with terraces and small private gardens off each bedroom, all with views of the sea.

"Hello, Trouble," Esther said.

He knew to speak circumspectly about the amok event that had netted him more than a week of sleep cure.

"Do you know who she was?"

"Yes. No need to be concerned, Dix. You rest."

"What kind of setup—"

"I know all about it. I'm sure I know who is responsible. I despise the ugliness. No names. I'm handling it."

He didn't need to hear a name. "I can't cope with any more bullying tactics. Something—"

"Will be done. Now that's enough."

Dix, still uneasy, changed the subject. "What are you doing today?"

"Brunch at Jules'. He has a new artist he's being obsessively secretive about."

"Sales technique."

"Sure. But Jules delivers. I'm getting first look, now that he's in a wrangle with the Ushers. They ought to know better than to go behind his back to deal directly with the artist. The whole thing may wind up in court."

Dix wasn't interested. "I'll be back in town tomorrow."

"Don't rush. Your health is everything, Dix. Which we will talk about very seriously when I see you."

"Yeah, I know, I—it was a dumb mistake."

"Can't afford to backslide. Not at this important stage of your career. Your enemies are always waiting. Watching. Who's important, Dix?"

"We are."

"And everybody else?"

"Fuck 'em."

"Attaboy. Dix? I want you to see Mom while you're there."

"Sure. I will."

"I know how you are. The ideas start to flow, time just gets turned off."

"Not too many ideas right now."

"They'll come. Now promise. She'll be so disappointed."

"I said I'd see her. Later."

"I love you infinity."

"Love you, too, Sis."

When the connection broke and her image dwindled to a ghostly spot of light he shuddered lonesomely and felt like crying, a great uncontrollable gush of boyish tears. Gratitude, remorse, self-loathing. He didn't deserve her kindness and compassion. What had he ever done for Esther, but try to please her, and inevitably fail? All she was asking in exchange for cleaning up his latest mess was that he visit their mother, whom he had actively feared and hated in his youth when she had both power and the temper for cruel reckonings. Elnora's outrages. Her sins against the father, culminating in fiery murder. But he'd given his word. He couldn't defy Esther in spite of the torment that would result the moment he crossed the threshold into Elnora's frigid rooms. Esther didn't or wouldn't understand how he could still feel so hostile toward their mother. Nor could she, in spite of her intuitive grasp of the twisty, slippery aspects of human nature, fathom the self-destructive repercussions from any sort of communication between mother and son.

He postponed the visit he dreaded by putting on a sweater and taking a walk.

Day workers were arriving at the funicular station beneath the tapered end of the roof, which covered a full acre of mountaintop, all of it enclosed: the wind on Cloud Horse Mountain sometimes went on for days. Dix had installed a pool and spa in a natural setting, and incorporated rock outcrops in his design of the Great Hall, in which the Trevellian Prizes were awarded every other May. Gardeners, handymen, cleaning women, all of whom lived in the surrounding valleys, got off the automated train, six compact white cars with skylight roofs designed by a Swiss company. The steep ascent took eleven minutes, through virgin forest, across gorges and past the highest waterfall east of the Rocky Mountains, which often turned to an Arctic cataract in harsh winters. Except by helicopter, there was no other reliable way to reach the summit of the mountain. When Dix was a child, before his father had the funicular built, supplies still reached them by pack mule.

His father. A benignly demented man with no interest in his share of the stuffy family businesses that his younger brothers operated, one in Georgia, one in North Carolina. Carpets, textiles. Handeddown, profitable, foolproof businesses. Cy Trevellian was a random scholar, largely self-educated, who coveted status and extravagantly admired talent. He was rightly known as a political crackpot, partly because he sincerely believed there was some good to be found in the basest of men. He chaired hopeless but well-publicized peace conferences and reveled in the attention of the cunning international despots who sucked up to him for their own gain. The Trevellian Prize had been his one inspired idea, designed to upstage the Nobel awards: more prize money, hence more prestige. More time to focus on the prizes (given every other year) thus building anticipation. Cy's brain was shallow, but he had money and looks and couldn't beat the

women off with a stick. The one he married was a penniless international beauty, the niece of an early winner of the Trevellian Prize for
Literature. Elnora Bergendahl was a fashion parasite, tactless, tem-
peramental, and unfaithful from day one of the marriage; yet, like
many promiscuous women, she couldn't abide poaching in her own
preserve.

As for her children, one of whom Elnora had claimed, in a towering
fit of ill-will, was fathered out of wedlock (Scott the most likely suspect, the others thought, although she had never named the supposed
bastard), they were alternately pampered, ignored or despised when
they so obviously preferred the company of their easygoing and in-
dulgent father. Elnora drank like a thirsty moose, stormed society and
fell back, once slugged it out in the lobby of 30 Rock with a network
anchorwoman she had reason to believe was carrying on with her
famous husband. Dix hated her even before the death of his father.
Esther was fascinated and sympathetic; their personalities meshed in
a way that was uniquely feminine and beyond his understanding.
Scott—Scott never said what he thought, his truest emotions never
reached his face, which sometimes had the fragile blankness of the
shunned. One aspect of the overvaulting intellect, the vulnerable early
genius. Dix, eight years older, felt protective toward Scott, but there
was nothing to protect. Scott took care of himself, made no demands
on anyone, was not like anyone else on either side of the family. He
had a good gray head at a very young age. Maybe Elnora had told the
truth. Maybe Esther knew he was the bar sinister, and that was the
reason she loved Scott so much. Because he never really belonged.

Dix, the creative monster of the family, seldom thought very deeply
about anyone except Esther, closest to him in age, his nuturing other
half. Brother and sister as soulmates. Truly he was lost without her.
Esther plucked the thorns from his paws and calmed him during ep-
isodes of debilitating self-doubt. She was his best critic, the only one
he listened to. He had once hunted down and cocked a shotgun to
the head of a gossipmonger rehashing the calumny that Esther as a
teenager had been sexually involved with their father. On those occasions when Elnora was away they all had piled onto that Olympus
of a featherbed for stories, popcorn, fellowship, falling asleep with
their arms around each other and a good fire blazing. The loveliest
moments of childhood distorted by evil voices . . . his mother's voice,
and the punishment she had suffered for her own sick hatred could
never be enough.

If it might be said that Esther had a bad side, Dix thought, walking beneath the sloping elongate roof atop their mountain, it was expressed by the one feature of the house he actively disliked: the eternal flame that burned in a bronze cauldron outside the Great Hall, wastefully wood-fed. Tons of seasoned logs went up in smoke yearly, along with a daily ration of pieces salvaged from the unburned portion of the old log house on Cloud Horse Mountain. A tribute, a remembrance of their father, but vengeful, too, if one wanted to think of it that way. A reminder to Elnora as she was being wheeled into a sheltered place for an hour of sun that she would be cared for by her children, but never forgiven.

He visited the small graveyard where his father and grandfather were buried. Two unpretentious graves, the setting so close to heaven that to have done anything more elaborate would have been an affront to God. His Cherokee girlfriend, Kerry Rogers, had come with him once and played her violin by his father's grave. A lovely thing for her to do. The altitude had been a problem for Kerry. So young to be so sick. Whatever had become of her, he hoped she was at peace.

Dix walked for an hour and a half on familiar trails. The morning wind out of the northeast had diminished to gusts. The day would be a hot one, even at this altitude. Blue sky clearing. Hawk cry. He thought about his projects: an office building in Hong Kong stalled because of *Feng Shui* charlatans; design changes would have to be made to accommodate Oriental notions of harmony dictated by the venal concerns of a handful of so-called masters. As if he wasn't a master himself. At a favorite overlook he let his mind cruise the mountains, eyes soaking in the light. Process would yield solution. Pyramids as a point of departure for the Cairo project. Strong blocks of shadow alternating with desert colors. Purple dusks, crimson and orange flowers after scarce cloudbursts. But throw out the classic principles, the rigid tectonics. Not stone. Concrete, perhaps, sprayed on a metal framework. A flexible approach to his composition. The prows of ships at anchorage, juxtaposed. Windows not practical in that environment. Portlights? Get serious, Dix. The spatial sequence first, and screw Euclid. A mirage in flowing geometrics, that was it. Resonating with the desert itself. The ancient vernacular updated and morphed. His skin prickled, his brow was baking in hard sunlight; he felt powerful, confident again. His lunatic ego a beast unleashed in this wilderness.

Liadan was sunning herself on a long finger of rock over blue air, the wind in her face; she didn't hear him on the trail that came up through mountain laurel to the bald. Blue jeans, moccasins, pale ankles, slender neck, bare nape aglow, a body singing to him. He stopped for breath and watched Liadan, fingers in her flowing hair, the left hand up, little diamond sparkling in the sun. She had a fiancé in Dublin; an actor, she had said. He was coming to visit in a week, before going on to Hollywood to meet with casting directors. Dix imagined her joy at seeing the fiancé. How quickly she would be naked for him, leaping to his touch, so fair.

For the last couple of years Dix had preferred pouring his seed and his contempt into the mouths of whores during those bleak periods when the creative urge had him treed and helpless in a dark psychological wood. Today his psyche was unburdened; he was the genius-god again, and he wanted, in celebration, the girl. Her uncovered flesh, her symmetries, her precious puss, her consecrated bones. There on that rock, tightly astride him, pubic reek and erotic sway, the two of them surrounded by, lighter than air. He wanted her to love him. There was nothing to stop him from taking Liadan. It was custom older than memory, a rule of lordship. She was paid for. Esther had known exactly what was needed for his health and self-esteem.

But if the girl refused him. Fought.

He tasted and swallowed that bitterness, which turned to pleasure hot as brandy in his heart. Seeing her in the air as an eagle, flattened, arms outspread toward him, the loathing in her eyes dwindled to frozen points of terror as she flew, but flew headlong down, always down.

Now he tasted the grief of the fiancé, and was gratified. This was the pinnacle of all power, the power of life and death over another human being: I could do it, but I choose not to. Today I choose to let you live.

Dix put his hand on his hardened penis but did nothing else.

After a while Liadan turned, responding to the pinprick of his gaze. She turned her head quickly back. Her shoulders were hunched. A little more of her tender nape was exposed.

She seemed to be expecting him.

He continued to stand there. Priapian. Luxurating. Doing nothing. Time, and the wind, had stopped; their silence was absolute, it had purity and force.

ELEVEN

CRUEL LOVE

On that Sunday morning, on the South Fork of Long Island famous for enclaves of the summering superwealthy or the merely notable, Jules Brougham drove Sharan around in his top-down Bentley Azure.

They stopped in the unpretentious Springs, a few miles from East Hampton, at the Pollock-Krasner farmhouse, now a National Historic Landmark near Accabonac Creek.

In the barn where Jackson Pollock created his drip paintings, Sharan looked at the stripings of paint—housepaint, her own favorite medium—that remained on the floor.

"Did you know them?"

"Oh, yes, quite well. I met Lee first, when she was involved with those New Deal public art projects. I greatly admired her, even then, for the quality of her draughtsmanship and her incredible energy."

"What was Pollock like?"

"Unknowable. An ignorant lout, but genius has a way of cropping up in people you never would have noticed otherwise. It was impossible to be around him when he drank, which was most of the time."

"You think he was a genius?"

Jules shrugged. "In a manner of speaking. I'm not making a commentary on the durability of his art. Today's revered talents may be the Kmart specials of a later era. Art is a mystery, darling, which I, the dealer as shaman, work very hard to perpetuate. Mysteries entice and agitate the very rich, the *machers*, who are eager to spend large sums on what the dealers assure them is immortal work. Sometimes we even know what we're talking about. Possessing great art further defines the status of the already-privileged in their charmless, vulgar, power-mad universe; it even bestows virtue."

At the Green River Cemetery, where many artists from the New York scene were buried, Pollock's tomb dominated, especially the plot of his wife, who lay behind him.

"Probably still nudging and kicking," Jules said with a smile. "Lee made Pollock, who had no talent for self-promotion, unlike his chief rival and nemesis Bill de Kooning. Bill certainly understood that if one is a genius, it is a big help to be ruthless as well. Lee also knew this, and on Pollock's behalf she nagged and barked and cultivated the likes of Peggy Guggenheim and Clement Greenberg, who was a prominent critic at the time, then hauled Jackson out of his drunken depressions and bouts of self-loathing into the limelight. Which he adored, of course, once he had a dose of it. He adored getting drunk and taking off his pants at Peggy's and peeing in the fireplace in front of her other guests. Rudeness was his other art. Well, it's almost eleven; we should be on our way. Guests will be arriving, and Magda hates greeting them without me."

"Who's invited today?"

"No one. And everyone. It's very informal. I suppose we can count on at least seven blue bloods, six classic beauties, four living legends, three media-anointed geniuses, several billionaires, moguls, pundits, trendmakers. A rival gallery owner or two. Some interesting strangers. A fun mob, generally, if they're not too hung over from last night's do at the Guild Hall Museum. But nothing restores the spirits like the refreshment of a scandal, the narcotic of notoriety."

He looked over at Sharan as he drove—like most elderly men, with maddening slowness and exaggerated caution. "What might it take to restore your own spirits? I feel as if I'm driving you to the guillotine."

"Sorry, Jules. It's just that I don't know any of these people, and I've always been a little backward in social situations." Sharan was unhappier than she wanted to let on. She missed the comfort of her work, the solitude of painting, lovely when it was going her way. She missed her cat. She didn't want to think about Coleman Dane.

"But you're our houseguest, which bestows instant status. Believe me, they will all be curious. And most gracious. A treasured few are friends, and some of our friendships have endured for nearly fifty years. I'm not throwing you into the midst of ogres. I suppose I could fill you in on who is cross-dressing, who has relapsed and is doing heroin again, who is having an affair with her psychiatrist while the psychiatrist concurrently dallies with his patient's husband, which ones are making the S&M scene and which are fetishers, which prominent scion of a noble banking family sleeps with the dead—"

"Are you kidding?"

"Not at all. Laddybuck has a compulsion, usually during the full moon, to share a coffin at a funeral home with a member of the newly deceased. Preferably young, female and attractive even in rigid repose. Nothing happens, he just curls up and goes to sleep with his thumb in his mouth."

"Beside a corpse," Sharan said with a finicky grin.

"I suppose the point I want to make is, those who come on strong may have the most serious human weaknesses and emotional problems. On the other hand, the worst egotists and most rapacious connivers can be passionate about causes, and many have the power to redress serious social ills. Greed and philanthropy, I find, often have a common root."

"What is Esther Trevellian like?"

"Also unknowable, in her fashion. A paragon of confidentiality, even as she makes her rounds, gathering the news, gossip, speculations, like a cat taking a lick of cream from each of a hundred saucers. She was scorned once: a little Southern gal with not quite enough money, diligently working her way toward the top level of world society. The Trevellian Prizes were her entree: Esther greatly increased the scope and prestige of what her father had begun. And of course the money mushroomed like a fucking hydrogen bomb. Great gobs of money assign one to a certain rung on the ladder of respect and approval. But the ability to obtain power and dispense favors is more valuable than a fortune. Esther is down-to-earth, even earthy at times; she is compassionate, wise and circumspect. Her looks improve with age. I'm mad about her. I predict the two of you will get along famously. For one thing, you have your Southern heritage in common."

Jules and Magda Brougham's house was modest next to others scattered along a rustic beach road in their neighborhood. It was a breezy cedar shingle house two hundred yards from the ocean, set on an artificial earthen plinth for elevation and a clear view from the large deck that served as an outdoor living room. There was another stepped-back deck above the ground floor, outside two of the guest rooms. The master bedroom faced the other direction, overlooking a garden with wisteria and azaleas and Japanese touches: calligraphic gates, granite boulders surrounded by river pebbles, a koi pool amid pines to reflect the setting sun.

"That's a lovely cross you're wearing," Nabob Creel said. "Did you design it yourself?"

"No, it was a gift," Sharan said, wondering how he'd react if she added, *from the FBI.*

"Why don't you sit right here," the critic and *New Yorker* essayist suggested to Sharan, "while you tell me all your secrets. I have no scruples about dealing in secondhand gossip, but I often respect a confidence."

"Not much to tell," Sharan said, looking at the vacancy on the painted wicker love seat. Nabob Creel took up a lot of room. He wore resort clothes, including a ludicrous Victorian-era blazer with wide awning stripes that emphasized his bulk. He was unpleasantly hairless, with small eyes and asymmetrical, stuck-out ears—he looked like a tanked-up Nosferatu. Creel patted the seat cushion invitingly. His other hand was holding a plate heaped from the buffet. Sharan sat, smiling at him and at a young woman perched on the side of a table next to Creel. The woman nodded indifferently. Wide Slavic face, unkempt red hair, eyebrows wild as flaming arrows. Her irises were the size of a cocker spaniel's, but a hot sapphire shade. She was barefoot. She wore velvet jeans with suspenders over a T-shirt. Every curve of her body was loaded with carnal impact.

"You're not eating?" Creel scolded Sharan. "Magda is famous for her spreads."

"I don't doubt it. I've been nibbling since I got up this morning. I couldn't stay out of the kitchen."

"You are houseguest?" asked Creel's companion.

"Yes."

"Oh, forgive me," Creel said. "Sharan Norbeth, Nelly. From Dubrovnik."

"Hello, Nelly. Nelly what?"

"Last name Americans hard to say. Why bother. What do you do?"

"Do? Oh, I paint."

"You paint? I am photographer."

"Nelly's having a little show in TriBeCa at the end of September," Creel offered. "Minimalist landscapes. I've been helping her get established in this country."

"How did you lose hand?"

"Accident."

Nelly tapped the right side of her head. "I have metal plate here. From bombardment of the Old Town. Day and night, the guns. Very bad. Our roof fell. My brother has leg like that now, only not so good work as yours."

"I'm sorry."

Nabob Creel paused in the act of cleaning his plate. His fingers were greasy to the second knuckle; he had crumbs on his upper lip. "Nelly, my love, would you mind getting me another glass of the enchanting Chateau Megyer Tokay our hosts are serving today?"

When the photographer had sauntered in the direction of the bar, turning heads like a sexual magnet, Creel sighed. "Ah, the luscious flotsam of Europe. Unfortunately Nelly is without humor, and I suspect she has only a couple of beans left in her jar. Perhaps it was all those one-hundred-twenty-millimeter shells raining down night after night. So, Jules has told me virtually nothing about you and your work, but with the complacency that assures me he is on to something good. What's your forte, Sharan?"

"Pardon?"

"What do you paint?"

"Stop hoarding all the gorgeous women," a man said over Sharan's shoulder, then claimed that shoulder with a squeeze of his hand. She looked up. He had a red, spongy face, hair like the foam on a glass of beer. He smiled. Nabob Creel said with an uncivil pout, "Sharan Norbeth, Tad Broucek. He is everything his former wives have said of him, and should be seen only behind bars in public."

"The choicest comments are sealed by court order," Tad said with a giggle. "Even *I* can't talk. You just have to learn about me from experience." It was a little past one in the afternoon. Tad Broucek was dead drunk. He looked, and smelled, as if he hadn't changed his clothes for three days. "How about dinner?"

"I'm sorry, I can't."

"Eight o'clock. I'll send my car. Looking forward to a wonderful evening. We'll cruise to Block Island." He walked away like a circus bear balancing on a large ball.

"Hedge funds," said Nabob Creel. "Taddy and his associates are in finance the way Hitler was in real estate. Periodically he rapes one of the world's currencies for another half billion profit. Don't worry about the dinner invitation, he's forgotten already. Oh my sweet Jesus. Havelock's here."

Sharan looked, but was distracted by a glimpse of Esther Trevellian in a small group that surrounded her. High-waisted white slacks, sandals, a boat-neck knit shirt, very little jewelry; she made Sharan feel like a fashion emergency. Esther was absorbed in getting that little bit of cream from every saucer, as Jules had put it. Listening with slightly narrowed eyes, giving her head a little amused toss, briefly gripping someone's arm in a paroxysm of intimacy, laughing. Put her side by side with Nelly from Dubrovnik, and Nelly, with all her attributes and blitzkreig blue eyes, would lose on points to style. And, for want of a better analogy, to rank. Esther wasn't wearing the gold stars, but clearly she had rank.

"Nabob."

"Havelock. May I present Sharan Norbeth, a very distinguished young artist. Havelock Blore, and please let us not forget his last name contains an *l*, is a critic-at-large. Which simply means he has bounded from publication to publication, disfiguring egos in every field of the arts with the sleazy glee of Jack the Ripper. But a man's desire to feel superior to something or someone is a craving stronger than lust, which is the reason, I suppose, why we have critics at all."

Havelock Blore was a slight man, awesomely nearsighted, who leaned toward Sharan as if thick glasses were not enough to afford him the scrutiny he required.

"An artist? Delightful. I feel deprived that I've somehow avoided hearing of you."

"Read my column in November's *ArtScope,* Locky. I'll have the lowdown."

"I must say I had no idea I'd encounter you on my return to the States. The rumors of your demise were extraordinarily persuasive this time."

"A minor coronary. I've had four. Two were rather formidable."

"Then I should have sent flowers. But perhaps they don't deliver to the Port Authority bus terminal. I assume you still spend the greater part of your day chatting up those dear little runaways from the Heartland."

"Moral indignation is jealousy with a halo. Quoting Mr. H. G. Wells. What's new in your life, Locky? Have you secured a publisher in England for your massive dissection of Diaghilev?"

"I was very encouraged by the reception my manuscript received. I don't suppose you saw my piece in the *Financial Times* on Fulke Bankston's staging of *Dream* at Stratford?"

"Yes, I did read your review." Creel beamed at Sharan. "Almost a rule of thumb, isn't it? The more extravagant the opinion, the less capable the mind. You should have read *my* review, Locky, before you fouled your britches in public."

Havelock Blore drew himself up to his full five and a half feet and said, "A masterpiece of such coin cannot be debased by your invective."

"Fulke Bankston may once have been your significant other, but that's no excuse."

"You unbearable slut."

"Locky, why don't you take a ten-mile hike through poison ivy?"

Looking after the small furious man as he stalked the length of the deck, Creel smiled wanly and said, "It's called departing in a huff."

Sharan said, "What was your review like?"

Creel peered at the sky. "Let me think. Oh, yes. 'After three hours of the flatulent excesses that characterize Fulke Bankston's retooling of *A Midsummer Night's Dream*, my brain was deader than a coal miner's canary.' "

Sharan almost fell off the loveseat laughing.

Nabob Creel said, "Winning isn't the best thing. It's the *only* thing."

Esther Trevellian, behind Sharan, said, "What did you do to poor Havelock?"

"I pounded his dick in the dust, Esther. What the hell, debating Havelock Blore is like matching wits with an artichoke."

"Hello again," Esther said to Sharan. "This rogue is *not* allowed to monopolize all of your time. Why don't we take a walk down to the beach? Too many bodies here. And I'm beginning to feel claustrophobic, aren't you?"

Her turn to be the cream, Sharan thought.

Where did Jules find you?"

The story Sharan and the dealer had decided on was a simple one. "One of my instructors at the Art Institute of Atlanta sent him some slides. I didn't know. Then Jules came to see me. Just a lucky break."

"Luck? Oh, I don't think so. Jules saw something. He's wonderful at bringing along new talent, when other dealers in his league won't even bother. Very protective, too. I've bought several unknown artists from Jules, and I've never been sorry. Of course I wouldn't have bought if I didn't enjoy the work. I'm not interested in today's fad.

Or yesterday's oversold reputation. I guess I do have a weakness for
Art Deco that makes him wince sometimes. By the way, what commission is Jules charging you?"

"Fifty percent, I think he said."

"More or less standard." Esther wrinkled her nose in a conspira-
torial way. "Jules and I both love to hondle. Maybe we can do a little
better for you." She turned her gaze up the beach. "We're neighbors,
at least during the summer. Our place is so close I usually walk over
to Jules'."

Sharan glanced back toward the house and saw a woman with short
red hair and big thighs on the path behind them. She wore Bermudas
and a loose-fitting shirt over the shorts. She'd been sitting in a lawn
glider shaded by an awning, well apart from the other guests at the
brunch, eating, waving off flies, always watching, eyes unseeable behind dark glasses. As soon as Esther and Sharan left the property she
got up to follow.

As if Esther sensed where Sharan's attention was, she said, "That's
Mardie. Probably my oldest friend. Where I go, Mardie goes. Well,
almost everywhere. We don't have side-by-side bidets."

"Like a bodyguard?"

"Mardie does look after me in that sense. She would give up her
life for me, no questions asked. But it's a much more personal relationship. A kinship, although we're not blood related. Mardie's from
North Carolina, like you. Am I right? The accent is a *little* different,
but I hear similarities."

"I was born at Fort Bragg. We lived on the economy at Benning
for a few years, just across the river in Alabama. My father was career
army."

"How about you?" Esther asked with an appraising tilted glance.
There was about a four-inch difference in their respective height.
"Gulf War? I mean the hand."

"Automobile accident. While I was stationed in Europe."

"I hope you didn't mind my bringing it up."

"No. I don't mind when somebody comes right out and says, 'Hey,
what happened?' It's when they stare, or try not to look at all."

"I understand. I had a—physical problem once. I was hit by a bolt
of lightning when I was fourteen. Until I was about twenty my speech
was messed up. They made fun of me at school, the usual nonsense
that hurts so badly when you're that age. Finally I dropped out of
boarding school and finished my education with tutors. I worked
hours every day with therapists. It was like hell for me."

They walked the rest of the way to the beach in silence, neither of them uneasy not to be talking. Sharan didn't have sunglasses, and the light off the water stung her eyes. The breeze felt good. Windsurfers, the vaporous puffs of sail, made Sharan yearn to pick up a brush. A few slapdash strokes of blue, some dabs of red and yellow, would satisfy her craving. The way she sometimes just had to have Spanish peanuts and a glass of 7Up.

"How long will you be staying in East Hampton?"

She blinked at Esther, her pastels and raven hair against the hard blue sky. "I don't know, Esther. A few days."

"Me too. Then back to work. We do the Trevellian Prizes."

"Oh, yes."

"Nominations for next year's prizes are in. We don't feel obligated to hand out a prize in every category. I suppose it makes the suspense even more nerve-racking." She laughed. "It's a long, tough process. A few weeks before the announcements I have to drop out and almost go into hiding."

"I can imagine there's a lot of pressure."

"So I'm enjoying my time off right now. Jules said I could have a peek at some of your work, but, believe me, I'm not trying to step on his toes. When Jules is ready will be just fine. I *would* like to get to know you better, Sharan." She took Sharan's hand, as she had taken the hands of others while she talked. But it was Sharan's artificial hand. A gesture that to Sharan was more intimate than a kiss, yet earned. Esther had suffered, too. "Look up the beach; do you see the clapboard with the river stone and the different styles of roof? That's us. My brother is an architect, as if he didn't care to flaunt it. Anyway, our house is casual, friends track in sand right off the beach, nobody minds. I hate the fence, but. Not everyone who comes around is a friend, unfortunately. Just ring the bell at the gate if you're in the mood for company. I'm going now, Sunday siesta time after all that good eating. What is it the Irish say? 'Don't be strange.' " A wistful note in her voice, it was like being tickled with a feather. She let go of Sharan's prosthetic hand. "Bye now."

Sharan smiled and watched her go, then stepped aside on the path as Mardie Kregg skimmed by like a rogue swan, without a glance or comment, only a lengthening of her lips that might have been a smile. She was taller than Sharan, probably six feet. Bulwark shoulders, fade-away breasts that didn't need a bra, big but solid below her trim waist. Fair complexion that wouldn't tolerate much sun, axe-blade nose with a dab of zinc oxide on the tip, menacing smoke-blue glasses like the darkness of the blind. Beneath the loose-fitting beach shirt with perspiration blotches at the armpits Sharan saw that Mardie was packing a pistol in a small-of-the-back carry, at an angle to her strong side. A lot of small-time authority in her manner. Sharan didn't feel intimidated. On the other hand, Esther Trevellian's oldest and closest friend wasn't someone she'd care to tangle with.

Esther wakes up in her hammock on the secluded terrace next to her second-floor bedroom, drowsily hearing the sounds of children playing on the nearby beach, and a droning single-engine plane towing an advert banner above the bathers. She knows before opening her eyes that Mardie is close by.

"What time is it?"

"Ten minutes to four."

"I slept too long," Esther complains, stretching. "But it was delicious." She stretches again and drapes her legs over the side of the hammock. "What did you find out?"

"Mr. Hare thinks Wingo must've found the tracker. Says he don't know where Wingo is now."

"Then he did a poor job of placing it on that dump of a Chevy Dempsey drives. I suppose the thing fell off. And Dempsey hasn't been in touch. Damn. I just do not like the way this is going."

Mardie grimaces. "Somethen else about Mr. Hare."

"Yes?"

"He's been to the Plaza Hotel twice already this weekend."

"Why?"

"Mordecai cain't tell. Mr. Hare stays thirty, forty minutes, that's all."

"What else?"

"He's made half a dozen pay phone calls since Thursday week. Different pay phones, but away from Trevellian House."

"Mordecai pick up the numbers he's calling? He'd better, all the money we spend on those surveillance gizmos."

"Two calls to the Plaza, the others long distance. D.C. area code. We checked."

"Washington, huh. Government office?"

"No. The number he calls belongs to a company called Bergen slash McCarthy Properties."

"Which is?"

"Properties. Like I said. Real estate, maybe."

"Maybe. Bergen." Esther sways slowly back and forth in her hammock. An iridescent blue butterfly flutters over the flower boxes of peonies and hanging portulaca. She stares at it in fascination, eyes gradually unfocusing. "Bergen, like my good bud Candy? Her father was a ventriloquist, I'll bet you didn't know that. He had a popular radio show a long time ago. With Charlie McCarthy." Esther grins suddenly.

"Who?"

"McCarthy was the name of the ventriloquist's—*dummy*. The dummy wore a monocle, I seem to remember. Bergen/McCarthy Properties, is it? Somebody in one of those uptight bureaucracies down there has a sense of humor. Defense. Justice." Esther's pulse picks up. "Who knows?"

Mardie says, "Are you thinken that damn nigger—"

"Don't know, sweetheart. But we'll be very careful about Marlowe Hare from this minute on."

Mardie says, grumbling, "Reckon this is my fault. I'll just tell Mordecai to—"

"Not necessary. Have some of the in-group keep a close eye on Marlowe, making sure he doesn't tumble to anything. And the next time he goes down to the Plaza, find out what he's doing there. If he's unzipping for a quickie, she must be high-class." Esther shrugs, then shakes her head. "Mardie, you know what I'd like? A tepid bath, mint tea with crushed ice and one of your great rubdowns."

"Sure."

"Denise call?" Denise is Esther's social secretary.

"Yeah. The wrap party's on the bridge. Wednesday night, they say now. They're shooten tonight, golden hours, but they need to make up time. Studio's senden suits east on every flight."

"What do you suppose Lew would like?" Esther says, looking at Mardie with one eye narrowed. Target shooting.

"Well, he does collect all that old *Star Trek* junk. Props and toys and costumes."

Esther nods. "Mordecai knows where to go. Leave it to Mordecai. And find out which messenger services the studio uses in New York. Needless to say, we don't want our gift acknowledged."

On Monday gloom hid the morning swells; the sea was the unpleasant green of sleep-dragons breathing their fog against the beach house windows. Fog blotted the shaggy trees around the compound in which Sharan spent most of the day with Esther. Telephones rang and rang, were answered by unseen others in the house. They walked together in wet sand, in the mist. Mardie Kregg was not around but Esther carried a pistol in her raincape, a cunning little gold-plated derringer that she proudly showed to Sharan. The derringer had been a gift from the crowned head of Monaco, with whom she had shot woodcock in northern France. Esther liked to go barefoot, encouraged Sharan to do the same. Esther's feet, like the rest of her, showed care; Sharan thought they were as pretty as trout in stony water.

"Are you Catholic?"

"Yes."

"Do you take it seriously?"

"I try to."

"My paternal granddaddy was hardshell Southern Baptist. My mother thought religion was bullshit. But fortunately—she used to say—not all bullshit is religion. None of us were baptised. Maybe I might have turned out differently if I'd been half drowned in a muddy creek when I was a kid. But to the unknowing and the untried, faith is a form of ignorance. I do think about God; I don't know about Christianity. Christians have been responsible for some wonderful music, sublime architecture and a good many of history's cruelest crimes against humanity. I'm still capable of awe, but I have no reverence. If you had one fault you could correct, I mean by wishing it away, what would it be?"

She studied Sharan with the eye of a watchmaker—not clinically, but alert to nuances, the finely wrought meshing of another's psychic works, sensitive to the grit of being.

"Oh—I think I'd try to be more of a mother to my brothers, who still need mothering."

"Like I am with Dix, even though he's older. Scott, although he doesn't want me. That's been hard on my spirit. There are rejections that grind to the core. I never try to correct my failings, I just work harder at increasing competence in other areas. I'm going to be forty soon. I'm becoming part of the family archaeology."

Sharan laughed, and Esther had to smile, but her mood didn't change.

"I dream of being in a room—not exactly a room, it's as blank as a cell. One small window that I find, when I can bear to look out, is really a mirror. A prisoner's mirror in which I see my long-dead face. Nothing else. I wake up with my teeth chattering. That's why I don't sleep with anyone anymore. I mean, spend the night. What would you miss most, if you were dead? But I forgot. You have heaven to look forward to."

"Not at the rate I'm going."

"You have confession. It's as convenient as getting a ticket fixed."

Sharan thought about her most recent confession, and she thought: this is the woman who slept with the man I desire so much. She shuddered.

Esther, noticing, said, "Going on like this, I must be about to get my 'friend.' But you're so easy to talk to, Sharan. Usually I do all the listening. Let's have lunch."

During the afternoon they played chess. Sharan, at her best, could think four moves ahead; Esther's view of the board, and her grasp of strategies, seemed omnipotent. She attacked Sharan's customary open defense with finesse and daring, and won three of four games.

While they were relaxing with tea and brandy, Sharan asked, "How long were you married?"

"Three years."

"Who was he?"

"A bull rider from Oklahoma with a phenomenal gift for play-writing. Talent, but no common sense. Bull riders, you see, are crazy. They have to be to risk the fury, those hooves like anvils falling on their bones. Bull riders swagger and drink themselves into a godlike delirium. Knowing they're going to get busted up, or die. The power of his indifference was an aphrodisiac. It was too thrilling. I had to have him. I suppose we're all entitled to one nightmare obsession in our lives. He knew, when he took me on, that he was going to get busted up, or die, because I have no fear, and the fearless are without limits. When they choose. I knew, when I took *him* on, that if he had an area of vulnerability it was his talent. I had to repay him for my fever, my obsession, my disorder. One way to diminish his potency and stall his talent was to use other men. I was like a roller-coaster junkie. But blood rushing to my head has always made me mean. He kicked my butt until I couldn't sit down. I put an arrow in his back on Cloud Horse Mountain." Through the distance of a decade she studied the ruins of cruel and extortionate love with her tranced un-erring eye. She smiled faintly. "Maybe we're both lucky to still be alive."

On Tuesday Jules and Magda Brougham returned to their twelve-room duplex on Park Avenue. Sharan stayed in East Hampton, looked after by the Czech couple who cooked and did maintenance around the house. Pavel and Iva. After twelve years in the States they had learned enough English to follow the Byzantine television soaps, three of which they watched shoulder-to-shoulder every afternoon and with the intensity of bidders at an auction of souls, but they still refused, except for rudimentary communications, to speak the language. Sharan wasn't lonely. She had Esther for company, books from Jules' large art library. She made some notations in watercolor, her second-favorite medium. She talked to Bessie Chick, her next-door neighbor back home at Rising Fawn. Bonkers, Sharan's cat, missed her and was moping. There were four messages from JimTom Coburn on her answering machine. She called Benning and left a shamefully noncommittal message for him. In New York for a week or so. A gallery interested in my paintings. See you soon, J-T.

The weather was blustery, with showers. When Esther wasn't available Sharan walked by herself on the beach or strolled around in town, which was crowded as the summer season came to a close. Labor Day weekend the last gasp. She fretted about JimTom, how to handle the situation. Stone silence from Coleman Dane. Of course he couldn't get in touch easily. There were times, both on the beach and in town, when she had the quirky feeling she was being followed, or watched. She amused herself by trying to burn the surveillance. Old skills dusted off. It didn't happen. Either they were better than she was, or Dane hadn't bothered, believing there was no need to keep her under constant watch with Dix Trevellian unaccounted for. But she felt neglected, and neglect made her uneasy.

Wednesday morning she woke up feeling dismal. Maybe something she'd injudiciously picked up off an hors d'oeuvres platter at a cocktail party the night before. Esther had wanted her to meet some fellow artists. Who turned out to be a chatty, drunky, unnervingly competitive lot.

Sharan couldn't quite throw up. Instead she practiced tai chi in the garden for an hour, and felt better. A sunny day, not too hot. She stayed around the house, napped, studied great art, daydreamed about fame or at least success, and considered superstitiously what she was doing to get it. But almost everything worth achieving in life had hidden costs. You were Cinderella, or you were the pumpkin.

———

That's hit right yonder," Mardie Kregg says to Esther as they are driving up Redfern Lane toward the Amagansett highway. "That blue Tahoe conversion job parked by the Willets'? Maryland plates."

"What about it?"

"Well, I've been noticen hit round the neighborhood since Sunday."

"Around the neighborhood?"

"Parked in different places. Like hit don't belong nowhur."

"That makes you suspicious? A sport/utility like that one runs into money. Probably some college kid visiting friends."

"Hit'd have a college sticker, wouldn't hit? Or a campus parken permit? Now I never have seen a soul around that Tahoe. Hit's all the time just setten. Monday I swear hit was up the road from us, couple hundred yards off. Last night I'm sure I saw that self-same vehicle drive back and forth at Cal Leyden's while his party was a-goen on. Tinted winders. Never did make out who's inside."

"Okay. Private investigator. Divorce action. Or maybe paparazzi looking to get some crotch shots. We're at the peak of the rutting season hereabouts. What else is old?"

Mardie hunches her shoulders and stops for a blinking light before turning right. "Thur's things I don't know, and don't care hif I don't. This here Tahoe sticks like a burr up my ass. Cain't explain why."

"Look into it then, but don't bother me about it."

"Goddern. What's got you so cranky this mornen, Esther?"

"Dix came back last night, and he's not returning calls. *My* calls. There are times when I could wring his neck."

Sharan stayed on the beach most of Thursday afternoon, sketching. Small children with pails and shovels, sun-striped like candy canes. Adolescents who had reached that gawky age where they all looked like lost causes. College girls moving in prides, in beach thongs and Speedos giving anatomy lessons to heart-heavy hungering boys. The grizzled elderly, dark as old shipwrecks in their umbrella shade, languid from the fevers of the sea, its surface blistered with whiteness in the hale sun. The fever touched her, too, and Sharan went back to the house for a nap, wondering if Esther would phone her. But Esther, even on vacation, was targeted by a hundred calls a day. Friends from the best places on earth, and a slew of lobbyists from distinguished councils and committees and academies wanting to make a case for this or that candidate for a Trevellian Prize.

Dark when Sharan awoke on the terrace that faced the garden. She had that vague stomachache again. Her thoughts were heavy, piled like boulders at the back of her mind. She gazed at a cluster of bird-houses, by moonlight looking like a distant medieval city. A car with a powerful engine came down the beach road, missed the turn that would have taken it on another, narrower lane toward the Trevellian house. The driver found himself confronting the partly open wooden picket gate at the entrance to the Brougham back yard and garden, plowed through it, veered without slowing much and wound up in five feet of pond water, sinking with a burbling sound. The car was a Porsche convertible. The driver sat soundlessly and rigidly behind the wheel as the low-slung car began to fill with water.

Sharan ran barefoot down the back steps and across the lawn, waded out into the pond. The man behind the wheel turned his glistening pewter-gray head slowly toward her, smiled a good-natured, slightly gap-toothed smile and said, "Aw, fuck. Missed it again." He was Dix Trevellian.

"Are you hurt?"

"What's that? No, I don't think so. Who're you?"

"Sharan. You'd better get out of there." She was standing a few feet abeam of the Porsche, the water nearly to her hips, bottom mud over her ankles.

"Yeah, that's a good idea," Dix said vaguely, looking around. He was still wearing his seat harness. "Where's Jules?"

"They're in the city."

A flashlight beam grazed the Porsche and Dix looked away from the light. Sharan saw Pavel, the Czech caretaker, coming from the house.

"Do you need a hand?" she asked Dix.

"No. I can manage." He took the keys from the ignition and hauled himself up out of the seat, threw a leg over the side of the Porsche and eased down into the pond. He leaned on the car for a few moments, shaking his head slowly. "I'm twenty-two hundred in my left eye," he said. "That's why I missed the turn. Can't see it too good at night. Also I stopped off in Quogue to visit friends, and I guess I had more than I should've. Jules is going to be pissed. I wound up in his pond once before."

From the shore Pavel said something incomprehensible in Czech-accented English. Dix waved him away.

"No problem! Tow truck. I'll call somebody. Thanks anyway!" To Sharan he said, "Where did you come from?"

"I was taking a nap. I just woke up when you—"

"Friend of Jules'?"

"He's my—agent, I guess you'd call him."

"Oh, an artist. Sculptor?" Dix began to wade out of the pond, waving his right hand. "That spot over there, I guess, nothing left now but there was a Nevelson like a canary-yellow snowflake or something, and I was driving a Humvee. *No* contest between the Hummer and the iron snowflake. What did you say your name was?"

"Sharan Norbeth."

"I'm Dix. My place is down the road." He shivered. Sharan noticed an inadvertent whistle through the space of his front teeth.

"I know."

"Yeah? Then I suppose you've met Esther."

"Do you want me to call her for you?"

"No, I'm embarrassed enough." Discomfort and embarrassment made his smile all the wider. "Let me catch a breath and I'll walk the rest of the way." He sat down at the edge of the patio amid the green hieroglyphs of ferns, grimacing, and took off his ruined shoes. Sharan turned the garden hose on and washed her legs off. "Good idea," Dix said. He got up and stripped down to his boxer shorts. He took care of his body. "Don't mind, do you?"

Sharan turned the hose on Dix, then went into the house for towels. Dix called after her, "If you can find a keg of brandy, you're in my will!"

The cold air in the kitchen was enough to start her trembling. She wanted something hot, and right now. The coffee that the Czechs kept on all day was still drinkable. Through the garden gate and into the pond, just like that, here he was. Like the so-called requiem snake that pops up alongside African roads as you're driving by, thinking of something else.

Sharan took both coffee and brandy out to Dix. Pavel had already brought him bath sheets and some of his own clothing, including flip-flops. Dressed, wearing a Dacron windbreaker with a hood, Dix drank coffee and sipped brandy, sighing contentedly, looking at Sharan.

"So you're a painter. Where've you been showing, down south?"

"No. I haven't had a show yet."

"You must be the hot property I've been hearing about. Why don't you have some of this brandy? You look cold."

"Okay."

"That's an interesting prosthetic. Realistic. Don't they have flesh tones yet?"

"They do, but it's sort of a candy-pink shade. Didn't go with my hair." Sharan swallowed some brandy wrong, had a coughing fit as she turned away from Dix, tensing all over.

"You okay?"

"Yes, thanks. How about you?"

"Cold lips, warm heart. Surprising how cool it can get out here, August nights. How about a hot tub?"

"Pardon?"

"We've got a big one at the house. Sauna, cold plunge, everything. Why don't you walk me home?"

Sharan thought about her silver cross, all the security she owned, on the bureau in her room.

"Okay, I need to—I'll just be a minute, my shorts got a little wet. Change into something."

"Take your time." Dix looked at what he could see of his Porsche, which was the top edge of the windshield in the pond. "Maybe I'd better borrow the phone, call Triple-A."

Walking along the lane toward the Trevellian house Dix asked her a lot of questions—birthplace, upraising, siblings. Had she ever been sky-diving? No, but she liked motorcycles. He knew a lot about motorcycles, had given up owning them after a couple of close calls, but was still in love with the aesthetics of the machines. They argued the relative merits of Kawasaki, BMW, Harley. Had she ever driven one of the old-time Indians? Sharan felt a little numb walking beside him, wishing for lights, cars, company. Everyone seemed to be tucked in for the night. She made the effort to be offhand, chatty. Half a mile and then, good news, the lights of the Trevellian beach house around the fence line. Dix had changed the subject to paintings and the artists that he and his sister collected.

"I've painted some myself. Esther's always thought I should have stuck with it, but there was never a real choice in my mind. I've been in love with structure since I was a kid. Maybe you'd like to see some of my work. Don't be too hard on me. The last paintings I did, I was on sabbatical in Europe about five years ago. Seven months in France. We'll try not to wake up Esther. She's early-to-bed out here. And I don't want to have to explain about the Porsche yet." He winked at Sharan.

Dix insisted on making them drinks once they were inside the house. Toddies. Sharan asked for mulled hard cider. The brandy she had taken earlier, too eagerly, still had her feeling a little muzzy. She had to remind herself not to keep putting a hand on the cross around her neck.

While Dix was in an upstairs bathroom Sharan settled down in the game room, half a level above and overlooking the main terrace and the silver line of the sea past a garden romantically abloom by indirect lighting. A great deal of wall space in the house was devoted to paintings, none of which Sharan had been able to single out on previous visits as amateurish or tediously semipro, the sort of thing she might expect from Dix Trevellian.

She sipped her cider. The house was quiet except for the muted clickings and murmurings of servomechanisms. Outside, voices in the garden. Nelly from Dubrovnik came into Sharan's line of sight, hair bewitchingly uncombed, eyes as pale as plutonium ghosts. Esther Trevellian, lithe and dark, just behind the larger woman. They made their way to a wrought-iron gate nine feet high, iron trellis arching over it. Climbing roses choked the trellis with their beauty. At the gate Esther paused with a hand on Nelly's arm. They kissed, lingering kiss, full on the lips. Sharan, startled, thought, *Well, what the hell. You knew what she was like.* She'd been giving Esther a lot of thought. A romantic universalist in her sensibility, erotic yet cautiously removed from any sort of wounding involvement—expectable after the shambles she had made of things with her bull rider/playwright nemesis and lover.

Dix Trevellian returned, making enough bustle so as not to startle her again. He'd changed into his own clothes, sailor whites that emphasized the darkness of his tan. He glanced casually at Esther and Nelly by the gate. They had parted, and if he was aware of any sexual afterglow, like an imprint of fallout fireworks on the retinas, he didn't show it.

"Esther's still up. Maybe she'll come in for a nightcap. So, what do you think of my daubs?"

Sharan glanced around at the collection of mostly modern impressionists, American and French. Landscapes, still lifes, a few portraits.

"Some of these are—?"

"Yeah." Dix drank down the cider he had left behind, refueling his already bright eyes and good cheer, then went around the game room pointing out his work. Paris circus. The aerial ballet, mathematics of momentum and trajectory. The astonishment of toned bodies poised in the air, hands reaching for the swung bar, not in desperation but with a certain ecstatic intimacy; hands that have paid their dues.

"That's marvelous."

"This one."

Provençal village. Rain dripping from awnings. The clipped leafless trees soaked, as if they have emerged at dusk from a newly drained sea. Metal shutters glistening by droplet lamp glow. The town is closed. It is closed and looks abandoned to the winter lightning, the drenched pigeon flying low to a sheltered doorstep.

"Your technique is—" She didn't want to rave; he might think she was coming on to him. "Where did you study painting?"

"Couple of old French impressionists who aren't well known in this country gave me pointers. And this one?" Whistling through his teeth again in an agony of pride, relishing her admiration. His ego huge but not oppressive, subject to a childlike lack of pretense.

Frenchman in a small café looking up from his meal, wine fever in his eyes. His beefy sweating face and piranha smile. In the background the maniac motley of caged parrots, each as red as murder.

"My God—his expression, and those parrots. I never would've thought of that! Esther was right—even if you don't want to make a career of it, you should at least be painting more, Dix."

"You tell him," Esther Trevellian said as she came up the freestanding steps to the game room. "I've talked myself blue in the face, but he doesn't hear me. Hello, Trouble. Why the hell don't you return my phone calls?"

"When the hell do I slow down long enough?" Dix said, bantering, an arm around his sister, nuzzling her. He sniffed the hollow of her throat. "Where'd you get that scent, something new?"

"Borrowed," Esther said offhandedly. "Don't think I'm very fond of it. When did you get in, and where did you run into Sharan?"

"Didn't. I mean, I missed her, but I didn't miss the pond at Jules' house."

"Damn it, Trouble! Stop trying to drive at night, or wear glasses." Esther made an exasperated face at Sharan. "What I put up with." She gave Dix a playful slap on the side of his head and he crossed his eyes, reeled around the pool table for comic effect. Esther ignored him. "What are we drinking?" she asked Sharan, sitting next to her. Sharan had a sense of her nakedness beneath the plush warm-ups pulled on casually after trysting. The deeply ravished, cooling body. She recognized the scent Dix had questioned; it was Nelly's rubbed-on perfume, reduced by Esther's lingering musk to a bearable crushed-petal sourness. Esther was not wearing lipstick. Her pupils were big, her lips a little swollen. Sharan smiled slightly, made uneasy by the static orgasmic charge that remained on Esther's skin.

"Hard cider," Sharan said.

"If you're going to the kitchen, will you bring me another cup?" Dix said to Esther.

"Does it look like I'm going to the kitchen? I'm sitting down. You're standing. *You* go."

"Where's everybody who's supposed to be working here?" Dix complained.

"Enjoying a night off. Wait on yourself. Just because we have a few bucks doesn't mean our caca has turned to butter-brickle ice cream."

"Yeah, yeah, yeah," Dix grumbled, and left them to fetch more cider.

Sharan said, "Why do you call him Trouble?"

Esther laughed. "You mean it's not obvious? Dunking a Porsche in Jules' koi pond is one of his milder stunts. Like most geniuses, Dix tries to energize his downtime with kicks that equal his best creative moments. 'Taint possible,' as my grandfather Clydean Trevellian used to say. Daddy Clyde also said, 'Life is like watching a long, dull movie. Death will be the same, but you can't go out for popcorn.' There are sages, philosophers and stand-up comedians all over our family tree. A shrink friend of mine describes creative genius as 'inspired madness.' Which in turn can create a form of luck more potent than blood, as protective as body armor. Dix has had his share of luck, but being a boring old pragmatist I keep a close eye on him all the same."

"He's a wonderful painter," Sharan said, with genuine ardor.

"Those you see here—I think there are four—are exactly half of Dix's entire output. He drew a lot when he was younger, and you have to be born with an eye for color. God knows where the rest of it came from—the tonal qualities most artists slave and bleed from their pores to get. Not Dix. He picked up a brush, he conquered. I could place any one of his paintings in a first-rate museum. But I like having them around."

"What else does he do?"

"Outstanding athlete. Fencing, handball, bar-jitzu, kayaking. He can ride, shoot and hunt. He has a transport pilot's license. We both do. Dix is an inventor, when the occasion demands. We hold patents on half a dozen innovations in heating and cooling systems for homes and large buildings."

Dix returned, overhearing. "I've always wanted to give politics a shot."

Esther shook her head. Tolerant, amused. "You lack guile. You wouldn't last long in an arena where it's difficult to distinguish the truly great man from the consummate opportunist. Did you remember my cider?"

"We didn't have enough." Dix opened up the bar. "How about sherry? Something harder?"

"One brandy, then I'm done for. How about you, Sharan?"

"Okay."

"I'm hungry," Dix said, frowning.

"Look in the freezer. We have complete meals. Italian, French, Jewish, Chinese. We have wild boar with dumplings. We have breast of Icelandic plover. There's authentic rural Southern Negro cuisine flown in from Sweet Auburn. Help yourself. I'm not cooking for you."

"Oh, come on. Let's go out and find us some cheeseburgers."

"Pass. Maybe Sharan's interested. In fact, that's a very good idea. Sharan, keys are in the Gelaendevagen. You drive. If it's not an imposition."

"No, I don't mind."

"Great," Dix said. "Sharan, you're in my will."

It was a quarter to one when Sharan finally got to bed, feeling as if she were, curiously, underwater, but, even more curiously, not drowning; lulled and breathless, after three-plus hours in Dix Trevellian's hectic company. Her eyes wouldn't close for another half hour. When they did, all she saw was Dix, his lit-up face. Hearing him. Three hours of travels, friendships, work, honors, family portraits. Voluble, accessible, excessive in verve. Never touching her, but leaving her in tatters all the same. Sharan needed her rest. She swelled gently into sleep like a cake rising in an oven.

Close to three A.M. when she awoke, sensing that someone was in her room. Nothing she heard or saw, right away. Not an image left over from a dream. Plain instinct, subconscious alert.

She was very still, lying on her left side, facing the terrace doors that had parted, possibly from the pressure of the night wind. Partial moon in clouds thick as plowed earth. Shadows of plantings on the terrace outside darkly feathered the slowly billowing opaque curtains on the doors.

Then, somewhere in the room, an intimate footstep.

Jules had given her the alarm code before returning to Manhattan. She wondered if she had entered it correctly, in the half-dark of the downstairs hall. Not if the terrace doors were open. But maybe someone outside the household knew how to circumvent the silent alarm.

Sharan didn't move, deciding how to handle it. The spot that had iced in her breast didn't spread. Tactical problem. There might be a weapon. Don't think about getting hurt. Maximum action, a lot of screaming. Don't get between the intruder and the terrace. Scare the shit out of him, and let him run for it.

Her eyes were slitted. She saw the beam of a pencil flashlight. Not yet. Not yet. Be cool. You're the stalker now. Surprise is your weapon. *Wait.*

Sense of a figure at the foot of the bed, moving so slowly, coming into shape, printed on the belled curtain of one door. The far-off sound of dogs whuffing in the night. A lonely motoring on the nearby road. Sharan's eyes opened a little more as the flashlight beam traveled narrowly along the edge of the bed. Sharan tensed, believing she recognized the shape of the intruder. Not her worst fear, the man she had left only a few hours ago.

Standing still now, just gazing at the bed, moving the light up Sharan's sheeted body. Sharan closed her eyes, but the light didn't reach her face. The closely focused beam paused instead between her breasts, on the glitter of the silver cross she wore.

Moments later the light went out. Sharan opened her eyes in the dark, and saw the figure slip out onto the terrace, pause to turn and carefully close the doors. Although she wore a watch cap along with her dark clothing, in a torrid moment of moonlight Sharan easily recognized Mardie Kregg.

TWELVE

BIRDS OF PREY

Hello BaDmaN

Words bore me today. Words cold and
featureless as ice cubes. Words that
float in my half-drowned witless mind
like stingless jellyfish. Colliding
amorphously, no sound of chimes, no
thrill of insight. Words without a
language to give them validity. Words
words words boring. Blah blah blah
words. Unutterable sounds. No fury
no substance. They drip shadowless
from unmoving gray clouds. Wordssss.
Dissolving without remorse, containing
no guilt. No words to describe what I
am, to print my name on a blooded
parish wall, in chronicles of infamous
unreachable tomorrows. Words that
define as they condemn. Is the key
to my salvation the blade of a jackknife
?????? Do all God's chillun have
wings

Dempsey Wingo left the Bondo Special in a parking garage on Fifty-fourth west of Eighth Avenue and walked the several blocks to the Plaza Hotel, going in a side door on Fifty-sixth Street.

He took an elevator to the seventh floor. They'd redecorated since the last time he'd been inside the hotel. Shades of gray, apple green and pink. The color scheme made him feel slightly bilious. He'd married Esther at the Plaza, beneath a canopy of ten thousand pink rosebuds. He thought he was a hell of a lucky guy. Still he had to get drunk to do it. As for her motives in sealing their doom, so to speak, Dempsey never had a clue. Maybe she had married his reviews. At the time it seemed he might be a playwright of genius; even Dempsey had been persuaded of that.

He found the suite he was looking for, knocked softly. After about half a minute Marlowe Hare opened the door.

"Mr. Wingo. Right on time. Come in."

It was a two-bedroom suite with a sitting room. Three windows facing the park. A bowl of fruit with a brown banana peel beside it. A Play Station hooked up to the TV. Marlowe Hare stepped over a litter of game cartridges and indicated a love seat for Dempsey. He shook his head and remained standing, arms folded, looking at Mr. Hare, who was dressed head to toe in electric peacock blue today, except for the orchid display handkerchief in his coat pocket. Dempsey heard a child complaining behind the bedroom door. He didn't recognize the language. Probably Dutch.

"Miss Miranda be right out. They getting ready to go to Pittsburgh this afternoon. To visit her folks. First time her father ever see Timothy. But he's had two strokes in the past year, and a change of heart, so I understand."

"What does a suite like this run, five hundred a day? Miranda seems to be doing all right for a working girl."

Marlowe said in a hushed voice, "Well, her grandmama, who doted on her, left a goodly sum for Miranda when she passed into the hands of her Creator couple years ago."

"A goodly sum? Is that equal to a tidy fortune? A shower of shekels? How big *is* Miranda's boodle, in round dollars?"

"About four million. So you see, it ain't a question of money, I mean, Mr. Scott's money. She just want to—"

The bedroom door opened and Miranda Leland came out, immediately closing the door behind her. The boy inside threw something, a toy, that hit the door. Miranda smiled a rueful strained smile as she crossed the sitting room to Dempsey, her hand extended. She was dressed casually for travel: white jeans, Doc Martens, a sleeveless knit top.

"Hello, Mr. Wingo. Thank you for coming."

Dempsey decided, on quick appraisal, that he liked her. He unfolded his arms and shook her thin cold hand. Miranda Leland was tall and almost hipless, with low-slung breasts. She had an oval face and a pokey nose, but her chin line was strong, her eyes a smoky hazel shade. Her chestnut hair was pulled away from her face, tied off in back, a glossy comma between her shoulder blades.

He refused the offer of a drink. She said, "I'd like to smoke," and took a French cigarette from a small pack on the table with the bowl of fruit. Dempsey helped himself to an orange from the bowl and, still standing, began peeling it with his fingernails. Miranda shook out her match and exhaled and said, "Have you heard from Scott since you and Marlowe met?"

"Yes."

"By E-mail?" Dempsey nodded. "How did he . . . what did he have to say?"

"Not much. He was depressed."

"How depressed?"

"I can't judge degrees of depression from the way he expresses himself."

"Have you looked for him?"

"I'm about to."

"Where?"

Dempsey shrugged, and glanced at Marlowe. "Did you bring the photos?"

"Yes, sir. I found a couple that ought to do."

Miranda said, "I also have some Polaroids. Of course they were taken several years ago. Scott must have changed."

"They might still be helpful." Dempsey ate a segment of orange, looking steadily at Miranda.

"I'm sure Marlowe told you I'm willing to pay whatever—"

"I don't need money. I get royalties from my play. It's a classic of the American theater. Still being performed all over the world. Translated into fourteen languages."

"Yes, I understand that you—"

"When I'm bored I hunt fugitives for the INS. I'll find Scott, but not for your sake, Miss Leland."

"Miranda," she pleaded, looking anxious.

"Miranda. I'll find him because even though it's a one-sided kind of friendship, I've grown to be fond of Scott. I look forward to hearing from him. And lately I've begun to worry about him. I think he badly needs treatment."

"If only he could see his son."

Dempsey was going to object, to be ruthless in refuting her hope; but Marlowe Hare cleared his throat in an admonitory way, and Dempsey bit down on another section of orange. He smiled at the young woman, feeling both envious and ill at ease, resigned to Miranda's belief that Timothy was the talisman, the center of her assurance that bad years could be repaired. She was young, she needed to believe. Miranda was someone he would like to love, and knew he couldn't. He felt heartsore. So give what little you can, Dempsey, he thought.

"Like I said, I'll get right on it."

Miranda smiled gratefully. "Would you like to meet Timothy? Then you can tell Scott about him?"

"Sure."

"He's not having a real good day. He doesn't want to go to Pittsburgh. But my father—well, there's no telling how much time he has left."

She went into the bedroom with the boy and was in there for a while, negotiating. Dempsey finished his orange. Marlowe Hare said, "Something worrying you big-time, Mr. Wingo."

"Scott may be suicidal."

"Oh, my Lord."

Miranda came out with Timothy, guiding him, a hand lightly on his shoulder. Timothy stopped as far away as his mother would allow him, facing Dempsey as if he were a hard lesson, or an unsafe ledge. Emotions otherwise hidden in his round and mildly dreaming eyes. Not robust, but tall for his age. There was, in the boy's smooth face, the germinating image of Scott Trevellian, or the Scott whom Dempsey had known ten years ago.

"They call me Badman José," Dempsey said to Timothy.

Timothy looked up from his sneakers and said, "Why?"

"I used to get into fistfights over girls and ride bulls in the rodeo."

"What's that?" Timothy said, still hanging back in his mother's semiembrace.

"Rodeo is cowboys. Roping calves and riding broncs. Wild horses."

"Oh." Timothy looked at his mother. "That was on ESPN."

"Yeah, sometimes," Dempsey said. "I brought you a present." He took from a pocket of his vest a silver belt buckle in a tarnish-proof jeweler's cloth. It resembled the buckle he had on, with a little more engraving. He held the buckle out to Timothy, who, after a few moments' hesitation and encouragement from his mother, came across the sitting room to Dempsey.

"Thank you." He looked the buckle over carefully. "What is it?"

"A prize. Best bull rider. That was Tucson, I think. I've got a lot of them. And a broken bone for every buckle. Make that two broken bones."

"Why?"

"Those bulls are pure meanness. If you have the time, I'll tell you how I outsmarted some of them."

Timothy's fair face scrunched. "I have to go to Pittsburgh."

"When you come back," Miranda said. "In a few days."

"Okay. When I come back." He looked at Dempsey.

"It's a deal, partner."

"How will I get in touch with you, Mr. Wingo?" Miranda asked.

"You can't. When are you leaving for Europe?"

"My plans are flexible. I have some vacation time left." She handed him a business card. "The number on the back is where I can be reached in Pittsburgh. The other numbers are for my office in Amsterdam. My secretary will always know where I am."

Dempsey rode the elevator to the lobby with Marlowe Hare.

"Can't thank you enough, Mr. Wingo."

"This isn't going to work out, Marlowe. I feel it, like I feel changes in the weather. In the broken places."

"But you'll do your best." Just past the elevator doors Marlowe's step faltered for an instant. He breathed harshly. "Oh-oh."

"What's wrong?" Dempsey said, thinking Marlowe might be having a coronary.

"I seen somebody I don't want to see. Just a glimpse. But I know he made me."

"Who?"

"Wearing a white bandage over the ear that was sewed back on."

"Woodrow Kregg?" Dempsey looked around. "Where'd you spot him?"

"Going down the steps to the Fifty-seventh Street door."

"What's he doing at the Plaza Hotel?"

There was misery in Marlowe's eyes. "Maybe I ain't been so sharp as I likes to think."

"You go on. I'll see if I can find Woodrow."

"Wouldn't do that, Mr. Wingo," Marlowe said, stopping him. "No, sir. Make matters worse. Reckon I can explain, if I have to, how I come to be seen in your company."

"What if you can't?"

"Then the fluctuations will likely be severe."

"Sounds like trouble, all right. Does any of it have to do with Miranda?"

"No. They can't know she's in town. I always used pay phones to call her."

"Then I'm your problem, Marlowe. You told Esther you couldn't find me, right?"

"That's right."

"So she's going to learn you double-crossed her. Marlowe, take some advice. Terminate your employment. Don't bother with your last paycheck. Do a fast fade, Marlowe. And for God's sake, change your wardrobe. Do it before you leave the hotel."

"Yes, sir. I get your meaning."

"So long, Marlowe."

"What you got in mind, Mr. Wingo?"

"No telling how many Kreggs are outside. Three or four of them can cover all the ways out of here. How long for you to change clothes?"

"My friend Yancey's the head shine man downstairs. Some gray polish for my hair, one of his jackets, leave here bent over like a tired old man. Ten minutes."

"Use a service entrance. I'll be on Fifty-seventh."

"Doing what?"

"Getting my ass kicked, probably."

Lunchtime crowds on Fifty-seventh. Sunny, temperature only in the high eighties, not much humidity for the time of year. Across from the Plaza Hotel there was a lineup of horses and carriages. Dappled grays, blacks, chestnuts, a couple of them wearing feedbags. Another carriage with four Japanese tourists pulled out of the line and headed into Central Park. Over the rooftops of yellow cabs at the taxi stand Dempsey saw a familiar blue Suburban van, illegally parked on the opposite side of the street. But it had DPL plates; whichever Kregg was driving could have parked in the hotel lobby if he'd wanted.

Dempsey stood on the steps leading down to the sidewalk for almost a full minute, letting them get a good sighting. Then he went down the remaining steps and crossed the street at the light, not looking in the direction of the van until he was on the opposite curb. Then he saw Woodrow Kregg, one side of his head a cocoon of bandages, standing on the sidewalk beside the Suburban.

Dempsey smiled and waved and started walking briskly past peddlers selling T-shirts and junk jewelry and artwork toward Woodrow, who seemed momentarily unable to believe it. Then Woodrow turned and appeared to speak to someone in the front seat of the van, still keeping an eye on the oncoming Dempsey. Woodrow was wearing his flat-crowned black hat and a Latino-style shirt that flashed in the sun when he moved his arms and shoulders. His pants were tight on spindly legs so he wasn't concealing a boot gun, but he wouldn't have pulled it anyway. There were a lot of people on the wide brick sidewalk, fifty percent of whom looked, like Woodrow, as if they traveled with a carnival. Colorful city vagabonds. Dempsey kept moving until he could see clearly the wen in the middle of Woodrow's forehead, the thready whites of his eyes. He stopped.

"How're you, Woodrow? Ear healing up okay?"

Woodrow's mouth worked, producing spit instead of words. His jaw was wired together. Around the waxen wen fury stained, then drowned his face.

"Where's your big brother?" Dempsey asked him, glancing at the closed tinted windows of the Suburban, seeing no one inside. The engine was running.

Under the best of circumstances, Woodrow had never been articulate. His IQ, Dempsey reckoned, was about equal to his hat size. He'd had a harelip once and still couldn't express himself without stumbling like a three-legged dog. Dempsey grinned at him, which made Woodrow's agitation that much worse. He backed up, toward the rear of the van, producing gagging sounds but still no words.

Low IQ and not a bit of cleverness. Dempsey was meant to follow him. Instead he turned and picked up an NYPD barricade on the sidewalk, a sawhorse six feet long, and as a side door of the sixteen-passenger van slammed open he turned holding the sawhorse by one end, swinging it hard. Kregg kinfolk were trying to jump out of the Suburban. He drove one facedown and sprinkling blood into the curb with the end of the sawhorse, jammed the other back inside the Suburban. Turning, still swinging the sawhorse, he backed Woodrow up. Then he smashed the sawhorse against the sidewalk, breaking off the legs on one end, pulled the gray two-by-four free, feinted at Woodrow with a jagged end. Turning again, he saw the window on the driver's side of the Suburban gliding down, revealing Mordecai Kregg's turbaned head.

Dempsey reached the window in two steps, the six-foot length of wood raised, and drove it through the open window as Mordecai yelled. The two-by-four passed through the steering wheel and wedged solidly against the underside of the dashboard. Dempsey let go, saw a taser in Mordecai's left hand, ducked and ran into the street as a white carriage with a fringed sunroof clattered by, empty.

Dempsey jumped aboard and hauled himself into the high seat beside the driver, a slim woman with dark hair going gray beneath a tatty old straw hat. Her horse was a shaggy-looking Morgan, forelegs white to the knees.

"Let's see how fast old Dobbin can hoof it," Dempsey said, taking the reins from the startled woman.

"What?"

"There's a hundred in it for you." He looked back. Kreggs running after him, led by Woodrow. Also he heard the blurting of a police siren.

"Two hundred, and don't get Slyboots killed!"

"Ma'am, I'm wonderful with horses. Yee-up, Slyboots!"

She almost fell off the seat, and grabbed her hat. The horse took off with the empty carriage, straight into Fifth Avenue traffic, which was momentarily snarled. Slyboots found room to squeeze everything through, then Dempsey drove him up onto the sidewalk in front of the Sherry.

"Are you officially kidnapping me? Just so I'll know what to tell the cops."

"That left rear's a little wobbly."

"It was okay til you ran over the curb with it. Three hundred. Watch that old Jewess with the walker!"

"We're not going that way," Dempsey said, taking Slyboots around the corner on Fifty-ninth.

"Who's that chasing you?"

"Bad guys. I needed to get them off a friend's behind."

She looked back. "Still coming on."

"They can be persistent." Dempsey relaxed a little. The sidewalk was clearing rapidly in front of the running horse. Most of the people getting out of the way looked blasé about it. "Where're you from," he asked the woman, having picked up on her accent, "Sallisaw?"

"About nine miles west of there. Where're you from?"

"Salt Fork of the Red. Born and raised. I'm Dempsey."

"Mikki. You want to go uptown on Madison."

"I know it."

"*Damn*, let me drive if you can't be careful!" Dempsey had clipped a trash receptacle with the right front wheel.

"Sorry."

"That'll be three hundred and fifty dollars, plus all applicable fines and legal fees I'll have to pay to get my license back. You want to be in the street now, there's room."

"I see there is. What're you doing in New York?"

"I'm in show business. I just drive a hack for a living. Okay, we've got the lights." She looked back again. "Gaining on them. Those old boys are just not in shape. They'll never catch up to Slyboots. *Good* boy, Sly," she called to her horse.

"Sorry to give you a scare, Mikki."

"I'm not scared. If I was I'd've shot you." She showed him the small old revolver in her right hand. Smooth walnut grips, worn gray steel. Thirty-eight, probably a family hand-me-down. "Daddy wouldn't let me come to the Big Apple without it. I've got a permit, too. I wouldn't have done a day's worth of time for plugging you in the liver."

"You're part Cherokee, I'll bet."

"Sureinthehell am. One-quarter, anyway."

"I'm Comanche."

"No kidding."

"And Irish."

"It gets worse."

"Mikki, I think I'm falling in love."

She said, with a not unkind curling of her lip, "You Staked Plain cowboys fall for every woman you meet."

"But darlin', I'm faithful while it lasts."

"I'm not doing anything Friday night," Mikki said.

Esther Trevellian met Coleman Dane for lunch at one o'clock. The restaurant was Brio, on the East Side just off Park Avenue in the mid-Fifties.

Luncheon at a socially important Manhattan restaurant was no affair for any but the flagrantly beautiful, the respectfully coddled and the custom-tooled, Dane thought, while waiting at a favored table for Esther to show up. The waiters earned the kind of money dentists used to earn before fluoride toothpaste was invented, the wine was straight from Bacchus, the food too gorgeous to insult by eating any. There was always that ritual preamble before the regulars settled into their chairs when the energy level was high enough to send men to Mars and out-of-towners were sniffing at one another's status like dogs visiting a fire hydrant.

Brio was decorated like a prelate's coffin in swagged silks and burnished rosewood, with a fountain obtained from a Renaissance villa in the middle of the large main dining room. Esther's banquette was on one of the little balconies at the four corners of the room (the closest to the entrance) where she could observe and acknowledge, from a distance, without being troubled by crass table-hoppers.

He had his usual Scotch while waiting. When Esther arrived she was delayed in the foyer for about ten minutes before ascending the freestanding staircase to her table: greetings, fawnings. She seemed to know everyone at today's lunch. Retired statesmen hanging on and on in the sun, making a living off public deference. An older member of the British royal family: sedate, stilted, too dull, like most of them, to be called quaint. A fiftyish rock star with sulky-hip mannerisms and a face nearly as cute as a hemorrhoid, a singing style as easy on the ears as someone breathing through a cut throat. An aging Jewish novelist lusting after a literary prize. His ego had long been an eyesore, like Quasimodo's hump. Numerous semistarved women exhibiting themselves in memorable and expensive mistakes of dress by coterie fashion twits. Tanned and manly media kings with overly neat teeth, the sort who are in everyone else's little book of very private phone numbers. Most of them looked as if they had just flown in from L.A., the world's longest, meanest back alley.

Dane smiled wryly, and thought about having another Scotch. In Washington, he wouldn't have dared. The rumors would fly, the knives would come out. But he needed to get well primed for Esther.

"Cole. I *am* sorry. How long have you been waiting?"

He leaned over the table to kiss her cheek. "Not long." His pager went off discreetly. He sat down and checked the number. Office, not a hotline number. It could wait.

"It's really good of you to see me. I know how busy you must be."

She wore a long silk coat, nude tank shirt, a simple strand of pearls. He smiled at Esther, his throat closing a little. It seemed like a fantasy that he'd once bedded her. He wondered how many others had had a similar reaction, long after the affair. *Got you, under my skin.* He was a difficult man to fluster, but Esther could do it. The majesty of her silence. So pleased to be with him again, as if meeting him for lunch was the highlight of her month. Or year. Gracious, no hint of nerves, although he knew very well what was on her mind. The most fascinating personalities, he thought, have that rare ability to maintain a presence without saying a word, while all others talk themselves to extinction.

Esther ordered wine. He skipped the second Scotch. She wanted to know about his new career in the Justice Department, the plum she had obtained for him. He didn't say he was already hating the job. He delivered the fresh Washington gossip she was eager to hear. Intrigue and peccadilloes. He found himself working hard to entertain her. He was rewarded with looks of arch amusement, light laughter. On their private balcony time flowed swiftly, and Dane no longer wished he were somewhere else.

Esther ate for maintenance; food was neither therapy nor entertainment. Salad with a teaspoon of dressing, baked fish. They didn't have dessert. Espresso for two. The bill, Dane knew, would be stupendous, but it was a form of self-aggrandizement. Cachet, as everyone dining at Brio well understood, was the thing itself.

"I haven't been home in a while," Esther said thoughtfully. She had never considered the city, in spite of her prominence there, as "home." "I'm looking forward to bow-hunting season. It begins in two weeks."

"You hunt deer?"

"Yes."

"It must be a lot more difficult with a bow and arrow."

"You have to be within fifteen yards to ensure a kill. Practically breathing down the buck's neck. Except you don't dare to breathe. Bow-hunting requires nerve and discipline. My granddaddy Clydean taught me, beginning when I was ten. He also taught me that only a few people bother to acquire much self-discipline until it becomes a matter of survival. By then it is usually too late. I can be very quiet and very still for a very long time, Cole."

"Yes," he said, fixed in her gaze, the quarry now.

"I don't want us to be enemies, Cole. But I can't be quiet any longer about your vendetta with Dix."

"Your brother is—"

"*Don't,*" she said sharply, giving him a momentary chill. "Don't presume to know anything at all about my brother."

"I know that he dated or had affairs with six women who have disappeared from the face of the earth."

"He can account for his whereabouts in every instance."

"Not accurately. In most cases the disappearances can be timed to within a few minutes—a half hour, at most."

"Are those poor women dead, Cole?"

"They must be."

"But *are* they? Where are the bodies? How difficult would it be, Cole, for a man acting alone to dispose of six bodies in four different countries, in places where he barely knew his way around, dispose of them without a trace? Do you know how difficult it is to deal with a deer you've killed in the woods? I know. A dead, human body, Cole! Philadelphia, Buenos Aires, New York—*think* about it. What do you do? Most murderers leave them where they lie. Not only because disposal is so difficult, but because they *want* the bodies, their work, to be discovered. That's true, isn't it?"

"I suppose it is."

"My brother is a lousy deer hunter, Cole. I won't go fishing with him, either. You know why? No patience. He gets bored easily. He gets bored with his women, too, but he doesn't kill them."

"Just breaks an arm now and then."

Her eyes narrowed at that. "He's done some terribly impulsive, wrong things while under great stress—as have we all."

"I never beat up women. Don't try to apologize for Dix's mean streak, and don't tell me he doesn't have one."

"He has a temper, which gets the best of him during periods of creative frustration. It's hard, Cole, what he does, what he goes through to excel—it takes such a mental and emotional toll. Your ugly persecution of Dix has no basis in evidence. I see it as a threat to his work and his life, and I won't permit that."

Dane was silent, he had to be. Love, any kind of love, was the unanswerable insult to reason. Love had fed on Esther's eyes like blackbirds at a gallows, until nothing was left but blind and ruinous idolatry. The silence he maintained might have infected the luncheon crowd; it seemed as if nearly everyone in the restaurant had paused in their prattle to catch a breath.

Someone was coming slowly up the stairs to their table. Not a waiter. More like a bum off the street who had made an earnest attempt to dress for the occasion. He wore a loosely knotted tie with sailfish on it. His dress shirt had a frayed collar and a button missing.

His loud soiled lemon blazer was long on him. He had his left hand in a pocket of the blazer. He was wearing a rucksack on his back. His face alarmed Coleman Dane. It was stubbled and looked awry, as if recently stepped on. Graying untidy hair reached his eyes. He was one of those street people who seem to be all nerve endings and psychic knots.

Esther, realizing that she had lost Dane's attention, turned slowly to see what was looming up behind her. She looked stunned, then, swiftly, delighted.

"Scott," she said.

Scott Trevellian paused at the top of the stairs. The restaurant's maître d' and a captain were behind him, aghast. Scott turned with an air of slightly exaggerated travail, no will to see them, only to discourage their presence with the stone-dead eyes of an archaic curse.

"It's all right," Esther said, now perfectly composed. "This is my brother Scott. We'll need another chair." His head came around again; their eyes met. "You are staying for a little while, aren't you, darling?"

When Scott didn't move or speak she got up slowly. "Take my seat. You look hungry. We'll order something for you."

He looked at her and through her. He was very thin, and in spite of the loud mismatched clothing seemed as insubstantial as Banquo's ghost.

"We love you, Scott," Esther said. "And we've been worried. Do you want to go home?"

She took a step toward her younger brother, touched his shoulder diffidently. Touched his cheek. A muscle twinged there.

Esther kissed him.

"Please don't run away again."

Scott took his right hand out of the coat pocket. The hand was red and dripping. Through the unbuttoned cuff Coleman Dane saw the wound on the inside of his wrist. Esther looked stunned.

Scott raised his bloody hand slowly and placed it firmly on Esther's cheek.

She rocked a little, and tried to hang on to him.

As if he had inducted himself into a state of grace, Scott put his hand back into the pocket of the blazer, turned and walked back down the stairs. Esther sank into her chair and reached for a napkin on the table, knocked over a water glass instead.

Dane handed her his handkerchief and got up to go after Scott.

"No," she said. "Leave him alone! I don't want a scene."

The bloody handprint on her face blurred and ran. Blood dripped on her pearls. Esther held the handkerchief to her face, hiding it. Her lips were parted. He thought she might be about to faint.

"Poor Scott," she said. "Why do we do what we do to each other? It was only love. Nothing else has ever mattered."

... And ... cut," Dickie Highburn says from his tall director's chair on the Verrazano Bridge set of *Wolfpack*.

The actors in the scene, Lew Carbine and Livia Kane, hold their places. Livia is crouched protectively over the bloody form of Carbine, who lies near a crashed and burned-out helicopter. FX smoke drifts over the bridge. Livia looks up expectantly at Dickie, who says nothing more, seemingly lost in contemplation of the take just concluded. After a few seconds, Lew, without moving, rolls his brown eyes questioningly in Dickie's direction. Everyone else on the set, from the continuity girl to the lowly PAs, are in suspension. All watching the director.

Dickie Highburn rubs his long nose with a forefinger, musing. A smile forms. At last he turns his head to the assistant director nearby, and gives a nod.

"Print it! And that's a wrap!" the A.D. shouts; the set erupts with cheers. Eighty-one days, and except for a few retakes (Highburn is known for getting it right the first time), *Wolfpack* is safely in the can.

Lew Carbine gets up, his arms around Livia, whose three-quarters naked body is slippery from simulated sweat, kisses her, flings himself at Dickie Highburn and hugs him, shrugs into a purple satin robe with The Big Shot embroidered on the back and says, "My place, you guys."

Twenty minutes later, at the private wrap-party-within-a-wrap-party in Lew's stateroom aboard his luxury bus, Lew smokes a Cohiba cigar, hands out presents and receives presents. The stateroom is crammed: three suits from the studio, relieved that *Wolfpack* has come in for only eighty-five million (already presold in enough territories overseas to be in the black); Dickie Highburn; seven of the film's nine producers; Lew Carbine's agents and business manager; his newest girlfriend, this year's major presence in the fashion world, a tall, straight child with savage good looks and the dark, wide-awake, unfazed eyes of a raptor on a Mongol's fist; Livia Kane; and the screenwriter, a squat bearded man with shoulder-length gold locks who looks like a B-movie Viking named Ragnar.

Lew loves presents. In addition to a couple of pre-Columbian figures and a small beautifully framed Roualt drawing for his art collection, there are a couple of obscene gag gifts and items for his *Star Trek* memorabilia: a script of the first TV show autographed by all of the principals and the show's creator, and a model spaceship in a sturdy blue Tiffany's box.

"Hey, who's this from?" Lew says, lifting the enameled metal Klingon battle cruiser from its tissue wrapping. "Mickey? Jass?"

"Don't know."

"What is it, Lewie?" Livia asks.

"It's a Klingon Bird-of-Prey. Didn't you ever watch the show when you were a kid?"

"I'm still a kid. I watch MTV."

The Klingon Bird-of-Prey makes warlike whirring and clicking sounds in Lew's hands as he turns it around, examining the wealth of detail. The model is heavy, weighing about eight pounds.

"No shit, I love it."

Lights begin flashing on the Bird-of-Prey.

"*Warning . . . warning . . .*"

"Hey, it talks."

"Look out, *Enterprise*."

"I'll bet Shatner doesn't own one of these."

"*Warning. This battle cruiser is now armed. I contain two kilograms of RDX and TNT explosives with a lead azide initiator and a pressure-sensitive detonator. If you let go of me, I will explode.*"

"Jesus Christ!" Lew Carbine screams.

It is suddenly very quiet in the stateroom. Everyone is looking at him.

"Did you hear that?"

"*Warning . . . warning . . . if you put me down, I will explode. I am not a toy. I contain two kilos of high explosives. Enough explosive to blow a hole eight yards in diameter through a reinforced concrete wall three feet thick. If you put me down, I will explode.*"

Lew stares with sick eyes at the Klingon Bird-of-Prey, which is making a humming sound while its red lights flash.

"That's a pretty stupid joke," the scriptwriter says, scowling as he looks around for a culprit.

"Grotesque," Livia adds, but she takes a step away from Lew's side. She can't go any farther; too many people in the room.

"Wait a minute," Lew says, beginning to tremble. "Wait a minute. Who says it's a joke? This thing's heavy. It could be—Jesus. Somebody better call the cops. Sick people out there, man! Sickos. I'm not taking any chances."

The Bird-of-Prey says in its matter-of-fact robotic voice, *"If you put me down, I will explode."*

The head of the largest talent agency in Hollywood, and Lew's mentor, says calmly, "I think it's sensible to take this seriously."

Now everyone is looking at him as Lew screams, "Well, what am I supposed to do with the fucking thing?"

"Hold on, Lew. As long as you're holding it nothing will happen."

"You want to guarantee me that, Bryan? You absolutely want to guarantee it won't blow up in my fucking face?"

"Steady, Lew."

"Steady, *fuck*. You hold it!"

The agent's smile hangs from his cheekbones like a man dangling by his fingertips from a cliff.

"Don't panic. We'll get help. Be calm."

"If you put me down, I will explode."

"I think we ought to clear the room now," Dickie Highburn says, with a grimace of reassurance for Lew.

"Are you serious? Leave me alone with a fucking *bomb*?"

"Lew. Lew. Don't get agitated. Okay, everybody. One at a time. Who's calling New York's finest?"

"There's six of them on the bridge already," somebody says.

"All right," Dickie says. "Go out there and have them hustle up the bomb squad."

"Wait a minute, wait a minute! Get Gunther for me. He's our pyro guy. He can probably disarm this thing!"

The stateroom door is open. Lew's guests are leaving, in an atmosphere so poisoned by terror that Lew's girlfriend is vomiting on herself as she jostles for position. She had crab legs for dinner. Only Dickie Highburn stays, looking casual, even relaxed, with his arms folded.

He says, "This is probably out of Gunther's league. Hang tough."

Lew says with a tickle of hysteria in the throat, "I don't fucking deserve this, Dickie."

"You're gonna be okay, big man."

"I don't deserve this!"

"If you put me down, I will explode."

"Smells like barf in here. That stupid cunt Kolaya, puking all over herself. It's making *me* sick." Lew is trembling, as if the weight in his hands has become unsupportable. "Aren't you scared, Dickie?"

"I survived a plane crash when I was scouting locations in Africa for *Catacombs*. Nothing really gets to me anymore."

Lew says passionately, "Nobody'd know it to look at you, but you've got stones, Dickie."

"This is gonna work out. You're gonna walk out of here, rifleman."

Outside the cops are audibly ordering everyone to back off to a safe distance from Lew's bus. The exodus causes Lew to feel abandoned. Lew begins to moan, rolling his eyes. He is shaking so badly he has to hold the Klingon Bird-of-Prey close to his body to avoid dropping it. He appears to be blinking nearly twenty-four times a second. His mind shifts over to a safer locus of make-believe and scripted climaxes.

"I could throw it over the side of the bridge! Like I did with the bomb in *Take It to the Limit*. Remember, Dickie? It'll explode in the fucking water, no harm done."

"You might drop it on a tugboat. Wait for the bomb squad, lovey. They'll know how to deal with this."

"But I got to get *rid* of it, Dickie. I got to."

"Why don't you sit down? It'll be easier for you."

"Yeah. Yeah."

Lew moves backward to the wall, bumping into the blow-up of Uhuru, those great cheekbones and that ghostly look of command, and slowly slides down to a sitting position on the carpet. He is stunned and sweating, holding fast to the Bird-of-Prey.

A cop sticks his head in the door, checks things out swiftly.

"Okay, okay."

"What do you mean, okay?" Lew says, his voice a whine.

"Bomb squad's coming." The cop withdraws.

"Believe I'll have some champagne," Dickie Highburn says, and drinks from a bottle he retrieves from an ice bucket.

"Dickie?"

"Yeah, Lew."

"This thing isn't talking anymore."

"That's a blessing."

"It's just ticking. Honest to God. It really is ticking. I hear it."

"It's not talking, but it's ticking."

"That's not good, is it?"

"I don't know."

"If it's, you know, rigged to explode if I let go, why does it need to tick."

"Don't get scary, Lew."

"I mean, that could be part of it. The whole stinking game. What I'm saying, it's trying to trick me. The Klingons—they were *always* treacherous. I'm asking myself—I'm saying to myself now, what would Kirk do in this situation?"

Alarmed by Lew's tone of abject terror, Dickie says, "Don't be thinking that. Don't think anything at all. Just wait. The bomb squad—"

With a wild scream Lew gets to his feet and runs for the stateroom door.

"No, Lew—!"

"I got to get rid of it! Oh, Jesus, don't kill me, oh Sweet Mother, I don't want to die!"

As Dickie Highburn drops and huddles on the carpeted floor of the stateroom, hands joined on the back of his head, the Klingon Bird-of-Prey speaks for the last time:

"Fuck it. I am going to explode anyway."

Dempsey Wingo had spent most of the afternoon and part of the evening in the Bondo Special, making his way slowly north on the New York side of the Hudson River (Scott had remarked on the sunsets), stopping at driving ranges and golf courses (*I watched a Japanese gentleman in pink knickers and white golf shoes practicing wedge shots on the west lawn*). He also paid visits to every computer store he could find in phone books from Yonkers to Hastings-on-Hudson, showing the photos he had of Scott Trevellian. He ate dinner around nine o'clock at a steakhouse south of Ossining. At a few minutes before ten he was relaxing in a motel room with a six-pack of cold beer, watching a Mets-Cubs game from Chicago, when the first news flash came on. Channel 9 News had a helicopter a mile or so from the Verrazano Narrows Bridge, as close as they were permitted to fly. Even from that distance it was easy to tell that two-thirds of Lew Carbine's luxury bus had been devastated. The upper deck of the bridge was chock-a-block with police and emergency vehicles. Dempsey turned off the TV and then the lights in the second-floor room, sat looking out at the Hudson Canyon and the prison called Sing-Sing. Dempsey recalled that Lew had once made a prison movie that hadn't done any business. He turned the TV back on for the eleven o'clock news. The bomb had got Lew, all right. Dickie Highburn was in critical care at a Brooklyn hospital. Expected to recover. The same distant views of the hazy bridge were repeated. The actual tumult, the shock and hysteria, could only be imagined. A superstar reduced to a butcher's pail of unidentifiable body parts. Ordinary people would shudder tonight. Some obscure terrorist thing. Nobody knew yet. Dempsey turned the TV off again, and went to bed.

Thinking, *I stole his luck.*

Shower? he asked her, and she said, No, bath, not wanting to remove her prosthesis, an act of nakedness she wasn't yet brave enough for. The lights in the bathroom of the luxury East Side hotel were dialed so low they cast no shadows undressing. He walked up two steps to the rim of the gold and black onyx tub, turned and held out a hand for her. Hair slicked back, that patrician slimness. Delirium in her breast, common sense had nothing to do with it. They touched, he held her, the penis she'd judged to be on the small side could really get up there. Midnight radio, almost subliminal, the old hits, plaintive voices from the graveyard of doo-wop and soul rock. *Be my, be my baby.* One-handed, she helped him wash. Loofah. The skin of his chest, hairs in tight wet coils, shone redly. He used a telephone shower to shampoo her. It seemed at times he could barely keep his eyes open. She shaved him with a quiet prickling elation. The scrapings of the safety razor along his bony jaw, the soft lapping of the foam-dappled dark water louder than any sounds either of them made for a long time. Men's bodies. The scars of childhood and adolescence. Broken shoulder, he whispered. Rugby. And that one? Ran into a jagged branch on a fishing trip. The hollows of his temples pulsed beneath her lips. His weariness and vulnerability made her ravenous. The moment was biologically ordained. The faucet ran slowly. He cradled her. His hand cupped her pussy, gentle pressure that made her wild. He would not be too rough, or perverse. He was starved, too, but reserved, respectful of her body, her feelings. Not one of those men who just wanted to get on board and drive you to Tucson. I know I may be a damn fool, but please. Be my, be my lover.

Bathsheets piled thickly on the cool tile of the floor. Fan blades whispering unseen overhead, a steady beat. She mounted and fucked him while he dried her tangled hair.

There haven't been any bodies," Coleman Dane said. "I haven't wanted to think about that. Felicia, dead. The ritual of funerals has always disgusted me. I feel actual loathing. Solemn observances, periods of mourning. It condemns her to the fate I don't want to acknowledge. I dream about Felicia. Usually when she was a teenager, and had all of her toes. We still play tennis in my dreams. She had a slashing two-handed game. Good enough to be ranked in the national fourteen-and-under group. When I beat her, she raged; but she never sulked. Then she'd do something to get even, like water-bomb me. When she was sixteen she cut her hair punk-style, and dyed it parrot-green. Felicia made herself over into one of those kids who look like the close-outs at every high school graduation. It was ridiculous. Her spirit, her intelligence, shining through that putrid adolescent camouflage. I think she also lost her virginity about the same time, so it may have been some sort of penitential theatre. The new look and lifestyle lasted about a month, then she got bored with it. Felicia enrolled at Wellesley, had a saintly vision of a useful life, but got married first. One of those Englishmen who flick the language at you in a manner that makes you want to carve out their tongues. We, the rest of the family, hated him. Felicia's marriage lasted only a year, then she discovered her true passion: remote, nearly uninhabitable regions, the lapsed places of earth, as far from the triviality of inherited money as it is possible to get. God bless Felicia. I miss her so. What did you do today?"

Sharan shifted her weight slightly against his body, two fingers cozy on his throat, the pulsebeat there. Pale breast like moonrise on his chest. Troubled breathing, as if his lungs were saturated with fog. Sharan heard dim voices in the hall outside their suite; the rattling of a room-service cart.

"I found a church I liked. Just happened on it. Red-brick, crammed between brownstones uptown. Not much light. English the third or fourth language of all the priests. The confessionals are dark and tight against the walls, like sarcophagi. How was your lunch with Esther?"

"Her younger brother showed up unexpectedly. An Ancient Mariner of the streets."

"Scott Trevellian? He's—"

"I know, schizoid. Looks it. He'd cut himself, maybe deliberately. Right wrist. His hand was bloody. He put his hand on her cheek. Something passed between them. Something final." Dane moved, too, his dormant penis against her thigh, glistening, red as a newborn from their last lengthy lovemaking. Her prosthetic hand was on his naked hip. She made a slow fist.

"What did Esther say?"

"She said, 'Why do we do what we do to each other?' "

"Was she frightened?"

"Despairing is more like it."

"Of course she loves him. But she hasn't had much to say about Scott. Dix dominates her conversation."

"No wonder. So the three of you have had the time to get acquainted."

"It's all on tape, isn't it?"

"Yes. I haven't been free to listen. I'm going back to Washington in the morning. What have you found out?"

"About Dix? Not much."

"What are your impressions?"

"He's—not what I expected."

"Does he like you?"

"Yes. He hasn't come on to me. But he calls. He sent two hundred dollars' worth of flowers to Jules' duplex today. Obviously a courting gesture. We're having dinner tomorrow night. Then the private showing at the gallery on Saturday."

"Excited about that?"

"Yes. I am. Jules has had everything of mine framed, but he won't let me see them yet. I'm meeting the gallery staff tomorrow. Oh, Nabob Creel will be there. I met him already. I've got my fingers and toes crossed. I think he likes me, but Jules says he's very impartial when it comes to making a call. If he hates my work, he'll say so. Then it's back to obscurity."

"Never," Dane said, and he was smiling for the first time since he'd opened the door of his suite to her.

"Cole, something scary did happen, out on the Island. It wasn't Dix."

"Who?"

"Mardie Kregg. She came into my room at Jules' beach house. It was about two-thirty in the morning."

Dane let out a long breath and sat up slowly, looked down at her. "Were you transmitting?"

"No."

"Are you sure?"

"Yes. I was told not to waste—"

"Okay. She came into your room, and—"

"I don't know how long she was there. Dressed like a burglar. Pen light. She didn't take anything. Not that I had all that much to take."

Dane whistled thoughtfully, without tune. An electric concern had made his body all angles, uncomfortable for Sharan. He asked her if she wanted a cold beer.

"Share one."

He walked naked into the sitting room of the suite, took a beer from the full-size refrigerator behind the bar. Sharan admired the length of his back and his pale behind, visible in many mirrors. She went into the bathroom to wash. She felt chilly and put on a hotel bathrobe, lay down on the king-size canopied bed again, in the warmth they had made together, coupling and dozing.

They drank a can of beer in silence, huddled against each other in the middle of the bed.

"It's Mardie's job to be suspicious of strangers, I guess. But it isn't as if I've tried to worm my way into the family. They've adopted me."

"What's your impression of Mardie Kregg?"

"Bad news. Mountain stock. Worse than garden-variety rednecks. Rednecks are predictable in their habits and follies; rough, slovenly people, but endearing somehow. Mountain people have this malevolent rectitude. Their blood is darker, their mysteries more intense. They live in the hollows and heights of forbidding places. When mountain people get into beefs the outcome is usually lethal, and they usually win. If they have religion, and many do, it's the speaking-in-tongues, rolling-on-the-ground-in-fits kind of religion. Mardie Kregg gives me the clammy creeps."

"Dix does not."

"The night I met him, I was jumpy as a stray cat. Then the nerves just kind of faded away. I saw some paintings he'd done. Remarkable. What a talent he has! We went out for cheeseburgers. He's easy to talk to. Like Esther. Old friends in an hour, best friends in two."

"He'll make a play for you."

"I know it's coming. Another couple of dates, time to jump her bones."

"How will you handle Dix?"

"Maintain his interest in me without giving him what he wants."

"But how?"

"Damn, Cole, it's a woman's thing. Don't ask how, we just know."

"Tricky, Sharan. This guy has violent mood swings. Not long ago he broke a hooker's arm, smacked her around." Dane paused, then said, "Somebody sent the hooker to Dix, chosen to resemble my sister. Face and build, the eye patch, the limp. That's what touched him off. Esther thinks I set up the sting. She accused me at lunch. She was more than a little bitter, and a lot less friendly, after Scott left a bloody palm print on her face. She was worried about the tabloids, but I doubt if anyone got pictures to sell. Happened too fast."

"But you weren't responsible for—"

"Dix's hooker? No, although it's something I have the resources for, and Esther knows it. Black Ops intrigues. The new motto of the Justice Department should be, *Stilus virum arquit*."

Sharan, having forgotten most of her high school Latin, shook her head irritably at the digression.

"Who else, then? Was the hooker a blackmail attempt?"

"Hard to say. But obviously someone else knows, or suspects that Dix is a mass murderer. Yet Esther brought up an important point. One I haven't thought enough about. The bodies. Where are all the bodies? The disappearances are almost professionally managed. Organizational. Dix might well have killed that hooker, a broken neck instead of her arm, but then what did he do? Climbed up on the roof of his workshop and sat there crying with his arms around a lightning rod until his sister arrived to coax him down. Crafty of Dix. Nerves of steel. Conscienceless killer."

"You're beginning to have doubts?"

"*No.* It couldn't be anybody else. Dix is the only connection between the missing women."

"I know. Something else about him. Dix confided this. He puts himself through intense bouts of creative work, and afterwards he can't remember what or how he accomplished something. There's a cognitive gap, a loss of memory. Hours, even a day or two. Dix believes it's a form of epilepsy, but he's afraid to find out. To be treated. Because drugs might put out the creative fires, he says. And he would rather be dead." She stared pensively at Dane's face, thinking, not really seeing him. "He's so afraid, of so many things. I already know that much about him."

"Maybe we all are. Afraid of using ourselves up, and leaving no monuments."

"*I'm* afraid morning will come, and we won't have made love again."

Her lover, sleeping, was a mild, intermittent snorer. Nothing she couldn't learn to live with. By this time (2:50 A.M.) Sharan ought to have been asleep herself. The city was as quiet as it ever got outside the thick walls of the old luxury hotel. Her body limp from pleasures, but there was a light in her brain that wouldn't go out. The hotel robe felt heavy as chainmail, but outside of bed or bath she didn't like being naked. Catching glimpses of herself in too many mirrors, not enough butt to suit her and of course the truncated right arm, the clunky Frankenstein look of the prosthetic device. A loss that could still devastate, or swamp her with fury, when her morale was low.

Dix had loaned Sharan his author-inscribed copy of *The Fountainhead*, which she'd been carrying around with her and reading dutifully. It was about an incorruptible architect, probably Dix's hero, who blew up his own creation because the purity of his ideas had been compromised by others. At times the novel seemed like a long-winded exaltation of a classic sociopath with unearned pretensions. She'd been skipping a lot. Tonight she couldn't get into the novel at all.

There was always television. Lucille Ball, Dick Van Dyke, manic infomercials. A motivational huckster descending from heaven in his own helicopter to inspire the masses with an expensive set of tapes (money-back guarantee), telephone psychics, sullen puppy-fat teenagers with complicated sex lives on some media whore's talk show. A movie she hadn't seen about West Point. Flawless marching phalanxes under a brilliant blue sky. She didn't need to be reminded of square-jawed American boys barely old enough to shave who had called her slut and bitch and left condoms filled with piss and cum in her bed. Or the physics instructor, a captain, who made her sit knee-to-knee with him in an empty classroom and felt her up while he calmly went over an assignment. Not all that much of a surprise, of course. Life in and around the Southern army camps could be just as rough for a growing girl. Her roommate at the Point had been a street-smart ghetto kid from Oakland, so terrified during their first three months she literally had been unable to speak. Doing fine now, Sharan thought, a major assigned to the Pentagon, and she owed Rosalie a letter . . .

Sharan turned off the TV and went back to bed, but didn't lie down. The light in her head burned pitilessly.

She put her hand on Coleman Dane, stealing warmth from him. He didn't move.

What scared her tonight was the fact that there were no bodies, six women simply gone, they had vanished. Her sole line of defense was the microtransmitter in the cross she never took off except to bathe. But if they had died, then how? And would she be prepared, would there be enough time for help to get to her? It was driving Sharan nuts, yet her lover slept, and she wondered. Was he so confident that she could defend herself, or did he only care about the incriminating tape he would have, the killer's voice, the victim's screams . . . if she screamed at all, if there was time to scream. *Absolutely the most morbid you've ever been, Sharan; so turn it off, off now, I mean now. You're tougher than this. Lie down beside the man you've chosen, lie in his arms and do not doubt him or his motives. Lie with him and understand that you can love many men for many different reasons; but for the sake of your soul you must never love a man you don't trust.*

THIRTEEN

GOD LIVES IN YOUR EYES

The Jules Brougham Gallery was a four-story building on Fifty-seventh Street east of Lexington, a neighborhood that was a hotbed of ultraexpensive antique and art dealers. During the last decade Jules had brought in three young associates to help him run the gallery and another on West Broadway in SoHo, a lesser hotbed but still commercially important. The associates cultivated and advised a younger, newly monied crowd—brokers, lawyers, entertainers—just beginning to acquire works of art selling in the low-five figures. Jules continued to deal with the world's preeminent collectors and curators, and had a good working relationship with three of the most celebrated American painters. He represented the estates of two others. There were, by Jules' estimate, more than fifteen thousand painters currently studying and working in New York. The figure, casually mentioned, made Sharan feel like an ant from the wrong nest. The number of galleries exhibiting contemporary art was probably a shade less than three hundred, and the smaller galleries often disappeared in pools of red ink when times got a little tough and discretionary spending dried up. Few galleries had either the exhibition space or the time to deal with more than two or three dozen artists. It was virtually unknown for a major gallery to sponsor a new artist, no matter how gifted. One-man shows were the Holy Grail of the art world. There were painters with established careers who did not have a New York show to their credit. He said all this to Sharan en route to the Fifty-seventh Street gallery on Friday afternoon in his Bentley Azure, which he preferred to drive himself in spite of the rigors of Manhattan traffic.

Jules said, glancing at Sharan, "You don't look at all well this afternoon. I hope I haven't made you faint-hearted talking about your competition."

"No, it's my stomach." A bus spouted diesel fumes at them. She held her breath momentarily. "Wondering how I fit in up here, I guess."

"You don't fit in. But you stand out."

"Artistically?"

"Of course. Now we've had this discussion. What you must do at this stage of your career is focus. Be ruthless in eliminating distractions, go back to Georgia and work very hard. Otherwise, frankly, my efforts will be wasted. No matter how completely you may have ingratiated yourself with Esther and Dix Trevellian."

"Do you think that's what I've been doing?" Sharan said, hurt and indignant.

While traffic stood still he studied her. "No. That wasn't fair of me. It isn't your nature, as I've come to know it. I suppose I have no business asking if you and Dix are having an affair."

"What? Absolutely we are not."

"Yet you didn't return at all to our house on Wednesday night. That worried me."

"I'm sorry. I should have let you know. I was—some friends came down from West Point, and we really made a night of it. I stayed with one of them, at her parents' apartment on West End."

"The best falsehoods contain at least a grain of truth, Sharan."

"Jules, I'm thirty-five. I had a military career. I love that you're concerned, but—"

"There's nothing you can, or will, tell me. So I'm left to speculate on the forces that contrived to bring us together in the first place. I had a visitor from the Justice Department offering a deal that seemed out of proportion to the favor I was asked to grant. I'm getting a very good break in a tax case that would have cost me millions, resulting in public censure and, more than likely, bankruptcy. Not that I was willfully dishonest. But it would have been better if I had paid in the first place, and not tried to slip a few deals through the fine mesh of the tax laws. God said everything that was necessary for the perfection of human beings in just ten commandments. The Internal Revenue Service Manual consists of two hundred and sixty closely printed volumes that no one understands, and which makes victims of us all. I'm rambling today. A phrase of yours continues to rattle around in my head. You said you were a means to an end. I think what I would like to know is, are you working for the Justice Department, Sharan?"

"I can't talk about that, Jules."

"Is it dangerous? Is that why you seem so tense to me?"

"Jules, I—"

Her attention was caught by a middle-aged man on the sidewalk less than half a block from Jules' gallery. Once a banker, maybe, or an insurance executive, someone of probity if not distinction, sedate, truthful wardrobe. Cinnamon-colored hair, medium height, watched his weight. His shoes were polished. He had no briefcase. Lacking expression, turning slowly around and around in the middle of the wide sidewalk, turning with precision and not as if he'd drunk so much at lunch that he had lost his bearings. He held over his head a soiled placard, block letters on stiff white posterboard. SOON YOU WILL BE GONE, said the placard, and underneath, in smaller letters, ACCEPT JESUS NOW.

A ponytailed messenger on in-line skates flitted past him with that loose-jointed swaying motion, leaning in, leaning out. A Japanese man with a face like a pumpkin muffin paused, grinning to take a snapshot, resumed strolling with his companions. Well-dressed women looked him over as if whiffing burnout, a willful snub of status that blurred their own definition of well-being or perhaps reminded them of whatever it was that made them uneasy about their own husbands. The proselytizing man never made eye contact. He had no leaflets to distribute. He wasn't collecting money for a suspect religion. This aloofness made him seem all the more potent, though no less eccentric in his ambition to inform. Others in his vicinity with ties to the block—doormen, truck drivers on daily delivery routes—ignored him, as if he were a regular on the street. He was afforded his space.

His arms must get tired, Sharan thought.

"Two years he's been on Fifty-seventh," Jules said. "He used to be farther west, near Park. In the rain he tapes dry-cleaners' bags to his sign. Wears a yellow slicker with a hood. Eight hours, ten hours a day. Turning around, turning around, like a lighthouse beacon. He takes a lunch break at the McDonald's on Third. Half an hour for lunch. A woman came up to him one day, and tried to talk to him. I don't think she was his wife. But a close relative, perhaps. He wouldn't speak to her. She went away with tears streaming down her face. A fall day, the wind whipping her coat."

Jules signaled for the door of the garage on one side of his building to rise. Sharan watched the man with the sign. He wore a white button-down shirt. His tie was perfectly knotted. She pictured him getting up from behind a desk in one of those high offices all over the city, getting up with a little sigh and frown, walking outside and down the hall to the water cooler. Not a word to anybody. Then walking past the water cooler and stepping onto the elevator, not thinking, just going. Never returning. She had thought him expressionless, but that wasn't it. There was a density of feeling in him beyond any reasonable means of communication. What he felt was open to interpretation. Grief, she decided. Grief had formed on him like mold on bread until it changed the nature of what he had been, as time changes sediment into stone.

On a hill in public parkland with a vista of the river and the estate founded in the 1600s by descendents of one of the first families of the Hudson River Valley, Dempsey Wingo frittered away a long afternoon pretending to be a bird-watcher while he waited for Scott Trevellian to show up. He listened to Gene Autry on headphones. Then the complete recordings of Hank Snow, the Singing Ranger.

His third day on the job. He had begun to wonder if he had the right place, after all.

Dusk.

Alive or dead. Just give me a sign, Scott.

From the near calm of a humid evening a thunderstorm blew up in less than twenty minutes, blotting out the stars, chasing a few fishermen ashore. Lightning glimmered above the surface of the broad river, which showed a few whitecaps. Wind but no rain yet.

He saw a figure walking among the swaying cedars on the north side of the estate, near a fin de siècle conservatory. Dempsey raised his binoculars and zeroed in. There he was, moving pensively, barefoot and with lowered head, toward the edge of the bluff, a bundled blanket or bedroll under one arm. Dempsey watched as Scott spread the bedroll and lay down, fingers laced behind his head. A few big drops of rain splattered on the windshield of the Bondo Special. Dempsey watched Scott until the rain came sweeping up the river valley, clouds like the smoke from a dump of burning tires. The oncoming rain didn't seem to be a threat to Scott. Maybe it represented some sort of cleansing that he welcomed. Dempsey got into his car and drove back to the city.

Dix Trevellian called for Sharan at eight-thirty at Jules' co-op on Park. Small talk in the mirrored elevator going down. Sharan wore a shade of blue selected by Esther's color consultant. Esther's stylist had done Sharan's hair. She felt worthy of a night on the town.

Rain was coming down steadily on Park. Two dog walkers, a nanny with a couple of children and an elderly foursome waiting on their car made a crowd under the canopy over the sidewalk. Three of the dogs were lowslung hairy yappers, dogs for other dogs to despise. The kids wanted to pet a Great Pyrenees, still looking undernourished from its summer shearing. The nanny, a black woman with the upper body development of a stevedore, stared at Dix as she tried to get the two little redheaded girls, both as implausibly exquisite as waxworks children, inside the building. Sharan had seen her in the lobby a day or two ago with the girls. The woman had a low-pitched voice, a Jamaican accent, a dark and lurking temperament.

Dix's driver was a Kregg; Sharan couldn't recall his name. His jaw was wired shut and he had a lump of bandage on one side of his head. He took Sharan to the double-parked car beneath an umbrella, returned for Dix. Sharan looked back: a scene she wanted to fix in her mind, possible painting. The Jamaican nanny was still there, a child in each hand, her eyes on Dix. She didn't turn to go inside until their car was pulling away. If Dix had noticed her at all, he didn't comment.

His choice of restaurant was a packed noisy celebrity hangout where he seemed to be popular. A few faces were familiar to Sharan from the Hamptons. There was the famously irascible actor, balding and bearded and in his sixties but somehow more attractive than he'd been when he played secret agents. A senator, one of the last survivors of a large, boisterous self-cursed family, confounded by fortune yet too stubborn to be broken by epic tragedies and his own misadventures. Both men were surrounded by women who looked like sure things.

A mantra dominated the conversation Sharan overhead as she and Dix were shown to their table. The news event of the week.

"Lew . . . Lew . . . Lew."

Dix said it probably had to do with a former manager, with mob connections, whom Lew had stiffed in some way. No facts, only gossip. On the other hand, the bombing had the earmarks of a terrorist statement. Tremble, Great Satan. No one is beyond our reach.

After ordering the wine, sparring with the sommelier and winning on points, Dix presented Sharan with a watch from Cartier's. It was inscribed on the back *God Lives in Your Eyes.* Just a little something, he said. Sharan tried gracefully to refuse. Dix wouldn't hear of it. He made her put the watch on, then kissed her hand. The most popular TV interviewer in the country stopped by the table, leaned on it and looked at them. He wore suspenders and had the shrewd narrowed eyes of a ghetto pawnbroker dismissively fingering someone else's idea of an heirloom.

"If the sex act is, as the French call it, 'un petit mort,' then is masturbation to be considered incremental suicide?"

"You know everything." Dix asked the interviewer, "Who did Lew?"

"I heard it was the studio. His last two movies tanked. They wanted out from under that big contract."

A bisexual fashion designer with an aw-shucks haircut paused to kiss both men.

"Lew had inoperable cancer. Pass it around."

"You mean he blew himself up?"

"Isn't that just like Lew?" the designer smirked.

"Nobody actually saw him get it," Dix suggested. "Maybe what they have left isn't really Lew."

"You're saying he did an Elvis? That's not really Elvis buried in Elvis' grave, you know. I did a show on that. You should have heard some of the call-ins. He's planning to reappear when they name a country after him. Ratings went through the roof that night." The interviewer picked up Sharan's wine glass and drank from it. His smile was as gray as tombstones. "What's your name?"

"Sharan."

"Sharan's a painter," Dix said.

"Love to have you on the show sometime," the interviewer said slyly. Everything about him seemed sly and slippery. Probably the most odious man she'd ever had breathing on her.

"Thank you," Sharan said, with enough show of teeth to make him go away. She wondered if the evening could get much worse. She put on her game face again, trying to give Dix the attention he evidently felt he deserved. Thoughts stealing off, to her paintings, framed now and hanging in the homelike surroundings of the Brougham gallery. What a kick. She could have hung around all afternoon, goosebumps, looking. Seeing what she was in the process of becoming. Nothing, not even graduation day at West Point, had ever felt so good.

Saturday morning Sharan woke up with a case of nerves she decided to walk off. The day was partly cloudy. The block where she had found the Church of St. Lazarus was closed for a children's play day. The church doors stood open, and she went in for a few minutes of solitude.

She was sitting with her hands joined over her rosary, studying the elaborate reredos with its many paintings of the annuciation and the resurrection, when a burly woman moved with difficulty into Sharan's pew and sat down next to her, breathing as if she had a badly deviated septum. She should have had plenty of room without crowding Sharan; except for the two of them the church was empty. Sharan glanced at the woman, and recognized her: the nanny from Jules' co-op building. She had two shopping bags with her and was dressed as if it were her day off. The woman was looking at Sharan with eyes that seemed terminally tired. They had an Oriental slant.

"Thought I see you come in here."

"Don't I know you?"

"My name is Portia. But you don't know me."

"I'm Sharan."

"I don't need to know your name," Portia said firmly.

Sharan looked away, checking, the church still empty, looked back at Portia when an elbow nudged her. Portia's breath was scented with cloves, her skin with lilac. She was holding a gun in her lap, a nickel-plated, tackily made Saturday night special. It wasn't quite pointed at Sharan, but Sharan's breath hung up in her throat.

"Don't shoot me," she said. "I'm finally in love."

"Let me look at the watch you wear."

"All right." Sharan used her prosthetic hand to pull the Cartier's watch off her wrist.

Portia said, "Soon as I see you with him, see you was a infirm woman, I have a terrible feeling. Because I know you the kind of woman he prefer."

"What do you mean?"

Portia took the watch with her free hand, ran a blunt thumb over the back of the gold case.

"There's writing on it. Don't have my reading glasses. Tell me what it says."

"The inscription? 'God lives in your eyes.' "

Portia started, then her mouth sagged and her eyes closed. A sob, and her heavy breast trembled in a series of aftershocks.

"The words. The very words. That chile so much in love with him."

"I don't understand."

"When the mon give you the watch?"

"Last night."

Portia nodded mournfully, raising the watch to see it better in the dim light of the church. Tears glided down from the inside corners of her eyes.

"It mebbe be. It mebbe be."

"What, Portia?"

"The same watch he give my chile. Three week before him disappear forever."

Chile. "Are you Robin Smallwood's mother?"

"No. Robin mama die when him a pickney. I take him in, raise him like me own chile. But I never adopt Robin. And like a fool Robin don't make out no will. True, sah. Them prize money, all them money Robin fetch to write him books? Matter of fact, I never see none of it. But I spend my lifetime savings anyway. Give all my money to private detective, you know. Try to find me Robin. You see, the *babalon*, the police, they don't give attendance. Robin been gone since ninety-two. Walk down the street in Philadelphia with him blind white cane, gone to the vet to fetch him eye dog. My Lord. My Lord. How my heart suffers. I know Robbie is dead. And I know that mon's the one who kill him."

Apparently there was no pronoun for the female in Jamaican patois. Sharan cleared her throat and said, "Are you talking about Dix Trevellian?"

Running footsteps, echoing. Men running into the church with drawn guns, all of them aimed at Portia, who looked around in terror. Another man came from Sharan's side and yanked her out of the pew, thrusting his body in front of hers. She didn't resist him, realizing instantly who he must be, not understanding that quickly what they were all doing there.

"Drop it, mama!"

"Put the gun down!"

"Now, *now,* do it now!"

"Stop!" Sharan yelled, as she was hustled up the aisle toward the vestibule of the church. "She wasn't going to hurt me!"

Portia, screaming, three men pulling at her, dragging her into the other aisle. The narrow old church reverberating with their efficient violence, Portia's hysterical protestations.

"I bring pistol for the cripple lady! I mean to give *him* the lickle pistol! Him need protekshun from the blackheart mon!"

They wrestled Portia down in the aisle, snapped on handcuffs, pulled her to her feet and half-carried her up the aisle and out the door. Portia wailing and crying foul all the way.

"Wait, I want to talk to her!" Sharan called, and was ignored.

A Justice Department hard rock with a sweaty face came up to Sharan and handed her the Cartier watch. He had a badge pinned to a loop of his belt.

"This is yours."

"For God's sake! Did you have to be so rough with the poor woman?"

"She had a gun. We heard you say 'Don't shoot me.' We hit the bricks running."

"Thanks," Sharan muttered, a hand on the silver cross. "I guess it works. This is the first time—" She drew a long breath. "I was never sure there was anyone around."

"We've always been around."

"What are you going to do with Portia?"

"Ice her, as long as you're in town."

"She'll lose her job!"

"Yeah? Sorry. Not our problem. A car will be by in a few minutes to give you a lift wherever you need to go."

"Never mind. I want to finish my walk."

"Wait until we've cleared the block and nobody's curious anymore."

"I know."

Another agent was talking to a priest attracted by the commotion. The priest looked at Sharan and went away. She sat down in a rear pew, rosary and watch in her left hand. When it was quiet again in the church she turned the watch over and traced the tiny inscription with the tip of her little finger. Wondering. Robin Smallwood. Legally if not completely blind, Sharan recalled from the reports she had read; thus it was either a thoughtlessly cruel or very beautiful sentiment. I know you cannot see, yet God lives in your eyes. Maybe it was something Dix said to all of his lovers or would-be conquests, the same words inscribed but not personalized on expensive jewelry that dozens of women, most of them very much alive at the moment, still valued.

Sharan listened to children playing ball in the street, their uncomplicated games, morning laughter.

Or else the watch was unique, and once had belonged to Robin Smallwood, as Portia had insisted. No way to prove that, of course, unless she'd been in the habit of marking her jewelry for identification and insurance purposes. If Robin had been that careful, however, then she also would've drawn up a will to protect her estate and provide for the future of her foster mother. According to Portia, Robin had had only three weeks to enjoy Dix's gift.

Even if it could be established that the watch Dix had given to Sharan, looking like new in the Cartier box, had once belonged to Robin Smallwood, there was no evidence that he had thriftily removed it from Robin's dead body. Revulsion gripped Sharan's diaphragm until it was pressed as hard as stone. She would have to continue wearing the watch while trying to ignore the sensation that she was linked by it to a chain of baffling disappearances, to a murderer who may already have announced his intention while proclaiming his invulnerability.

God lives in your eyes. And it is power over God that I seek.

FOURTEEN

THE WILDCAT'S SIGNATURE

Dix Trevellian, keeping a lunch date with his sister in her suite at Trevellian House, found her in a touchy mood. He had passed Mardie Kregg in the hall, and Mardie barely spoke. She looked taut and sulky, probably from a lengthy going-over by a master of the verbal knout.

Esther was sitting at a table set for two, looking out through the windows that faced Central Park.

"Sis." She didn't look up. He kissed her nape. Esther responded with a grudging smile. "What were you and The Kregg scuffling about?" He ostentatiously dropped a portfolio of architectural drawings on the chair next to her. She barely glanced at it.

"Not doing her job."

"What job?"

"I've given her twenty-four hours to locate Dempsey. No fooling around. They had him Wednesday at the Plaza, they let him get away."

"Why are you so interested in Dempsey all of a sudden?"

"Because I'm damn sure he knows where Scott is. And I must find Scott. He's desperately ill. I didn't tell you, I knew you were working. Scott showed up at Brio when I was having lunch the other day. Oh God, Trouble. He looked so awful. He'd cut his wrist. I'm sure it was no accident."

Dix put his arms around Esther. "Well, why didn't you—"

"I couldn't keep him there. He came to paint my face with blood."

"Jesus. You don't say."

Esther looked up at Dix, her eyes a little red from lack of sleep.

"I had *blood* on my face. In Brio, for God's sake. Scott turned and walked out. He never said a word. But if you could have seen him. Our brother. I called Dr. Epperson right away. Epperson agreed with me that the wound on Scott's wrist was probably self-inflicted. He said the disease, if not treated, takes unexpected, bizarre, sometimes lethal turns. Scott's always been schizoaffective, but now—"

"He was telling you he wants to kill himself?"

"That may have been his message. Or he was putting blame where it doesn't belong."

"Blame for what?" Dix said, easing into a chair and reaching for a decanter of wine.

"The way he is. His illness. And he's always thought I used his genius badly. Making so much money was just another computer game to Scott, not all that interesting. He probably thought I should have given the money back when he got bored playing."

"Scott the idealist."

"He can't reason, he's in a deep pit with the sides crumbling down on him. I've got to get to him quickly. There's always hope, with some of the psychoactive drugs they're using now. The least we can expect is a high-functioning schizophrenic. Says Epperson." She looked as if she had bitten into a lemon. "A *manageable* schiz. But if that's all we have to look forward to—"

"Getting back to Dempsey. What's his relationship with Scott?"

"Oh, they ran into each other a year or so ago. And of course Dempsey is always looking for ways to—get back at me. As if a marriage like we had was anyone's fault. It was arranged for us by the god who arranges train wrecks."

Dix sipped wine and passed the glass to Esther, who took it in two hands like a child.

"It'll work out, Sis."

She looked at him as if she sensed he wasn't all that interested in Scott's dilemma, which was true. Dix wanted her to look at his drawings. He was disappointed that she hadn't opened the portfolio right away.

"Where were you last night?" she asked him.

"Went out with Sharan. We had dinner, listened to jazz, saw some people. All anybody could talk about was Lew Carbine."

"I called his mother right away. She didn't understand, it was like another movie to her. To a lot of people, I expect. He lived a fantasy life, so the manner of his death doesn't seem very real, either. The script needs work. There's a memorial service Monday in Los Angeles."

"You going?"

"How can I, with everything else? By the way, what are your travel plans for next week?"

"I don't know yet."

"Mom's birthday party is Thursday night. You *will* be here."

"Yeah. I know. Okay."

Esther turned to the portfolio. "Is this the Cairo project?"

"Uh-huh," he said, feeling a pleasurable tightening in his chest.

Lunch was served while Esther, head down, sorted through the drawings. Nothing finished, nothing in color yet. She nodded, she smiled. Once she frowned. He hated Esther's frowns.

"How is Sharan?" Esther asked as she continued to study his embryonic Cairo project.

"Seemed a little nervous to me."

"Tonight is very, very important to Sharan. I hope we like her work. Have you made love to her yet?"

"No. You?"

"No. But I want to."

"Maybe the three of us—"

"Oh, I don't think so. A ménage is not Sharan's style. Besides, I think she already has a lover, someone in town."

"Really? Who?"

"I don't know. Jules may. I'll ask him tonight."

Esther put the drawings back in the portfolio and sealed her approval by leaning over to kiss him.

"Brilliant, Trouble. You're going to win."

"Thanks, Sis. Love you infinity."

"Something wrong with the omelette?"

"The lobster was a little tough."

Esther nibbled, and agreed. "I'll have Romero fix us something else. Oxtail soup?"

"And garlic toast."

"Perfect." She summoned one of the stewards standing by in her sitting room. "By the way. Did you know that Sharan was a career army officer?"

"No."

"She was with the Criminal Investigation Division, until her accident. It wasn't really an accident, poor girl. She had her hand cut off in the line of duty."

"How did you find that out?"

"How do I find out anything? I'm a snoop." Esther laughed delightedly.

"Sharan was like a cop, you mean," Dix said, pouring more wine for both of them.

"Yes."

"Well, she's very interesting. Don't you think?"

"The more I learn about her," Esther said, "the more I'm anxious to know."

Nine-thirty P.M. on East Fifty-seventh Street, the rain coming straight down and hard on the dark blue stretch Lincoln parked in front of the Brougham Gallery. Mardie Kregg is behind the wheel talking on the phone to the chief of the security detail at Trevellian House and listening to Callas on CD. To the surprise of those who don't know her well, which is nearly everyone in the world except Esther Trevellian, Mardie is an opera buff. She has good seats at the Met and for the Brooklyn Academy of Music's opera season. Her greatest thrill in life is rising to her feet after three-plus hours to pound her palms ecstatically in honor of the stout beaming tenors and divas who reappear for curtain calls, wading like musk oxen into that warm sea of applause.

Not many people on the sidewalk in this weather. Those who must be out are in a hurry, hunched beneath umbrellas carried low enough so as to make them appear nearly headless.

The drunk, however, doesn't have an umbrella.

Mardie was first aware of him leaning against a marble-faced wall by the chromed standpipe that marks a division between the gallery and the building next door. He wears a cheap, shiny, military-green parka that comes down to his knees. The hood is pulled tight around his face, leaving only a dark oval. He has a quart liquor bottle in one hand, remnants of a paper sack clinging to the wet glass. Occasionally he stumbles away from the wall with a palm rudely outthrust to a passerby, who avoids him with an indifferent change of step and hurries on in the pelting rain. The drunk nigger stands there for a few moments, unsteady, looking around, then retreats to his wall and leans there, sinking lower each time as his knees begin to give out. She sees him, his presence registers, peripherally, something more than dogshit but less than human that will wash away before the rain quits.

Having completed her call, Mardie sings along with Callas, a portion of a favorite aria in Italian she has painstakingly taught herself. Mardie's mezzo voice, her pride, although no one ever hears her sing, is surprisingly true but lightweight. She doesn't have the diaphragm for classical singing.

Tapping on the curbside window.

Mardie turns her head, glimpses the drunk, hunched over, trying to claim her attention but not looking directly at her; the beggar's attitude of sham contrition. One eye appears to be swollen shut, or missing. She shakes her head curtly. After a few seconds he stumbles away along the curb, toward the rear of the long car.

Mardie wonders if she wants to hear *Alceste* tonight.

Another call on one of the limo phones. Trevellian Security again. The woman named Mikki, whose horse and carriage Dempsey Wingo drove recklessly through the streets of Manhattan a few days ago, says that Wingo left a message for her on her answering machine, breaking a date but promising to call back. Mikki, last name Sullivan, also gave them a copy of the personal check Wingo wrote to her for wear and tear on her nerves during his getaway. The address on the check a mailbox service in Brooklyn. Mardie says, Stake the place out and stay with Mikki Sullivan, twenty-four hours. And feels a little better. Now she has something positive to report to Esther.

Thump.

Ka-Thump.

The drunk nigger, banging his fist or something on the trunk of the Lincoln. Looking in one of the mirrors, she can barely make out his form back there in the rain.

Just when she was beginning to ease out of the dumps into a reasonably good mood.

Mardie thinks about calling the cops, but she knows she can count on a response time of about twenty minutes, unless she exaggerates the drunk's presence into an emergency. So she reaches for a ten-dollar bill and an umbrella instead.

Outside into the rain. She can't see him. He isn't on the sidewalk, so he must be crouched down behind the limo, or passed out in the gutter. No way is she going to move him. If he's unconscious, let NYPD handle it.

But he's on all fours; seeing him this close he's bigger than she had thought. He is shaking his hooded head side to side, moaning, but not as if he's in pain. Just trying to communicate with himself.

"Here's ten dollars. Take hit. Go buy yourself a bottle."

"Haaummmmmmhummmmmummmm."

"Mister? You listen. I said I've got ten dollars for you. Git you a bottle and git out of the rain somewheres. You caint be lyen down in the street, you'll get runt over for sure."

Mardie nudges him with a rubber-booted foot, has a fraction of a second to reconsider her mistake of getting too close and tries to withdraw as he lunges up from his knees. She sees something, a silvery whisper of light in the down-splashing rain, a loop swung from his right hand, then the filament swishes down over her close-cropped head, stinging both ears, and is pulled tight around her throat. She freezes instantly under the umbrella, his fist a foot from her chin, holding a sawed-off rod and reel, the instrument of the snare with which he has captured her. Eyes going to his dark face and seeing that the darkness is high-gloss liquid shoe polish, impervious to rain, the concealed eye undoubtedly not a match for the other, brown eye that confronts her unwinkingly.

"Know what it is around your neck, Mardie?"

"Fish line," she says, or whispers, not wanting to move the throat muscles unnecessarily, thus causing the filament to slice, just a little, through the skin. He has her; she forces herself to relax. "What you want?"

"We'll get in on the right-hand side. I'll let out some of the line I have on this reel, enough so you can drive."

"Drive whur?" She wants to swallow, can't help herself; the pain is intense. "Too tight," she breathes.

"Tough shit."

"Pay you. For this." Her fury causing her neck to bulge against the filament.

"Put it on my bill, Mardie. And get going. Think of a chicken flopping around with blood spurting from its neck all over the chopping block. That's how quick it'll be if you give me problems."

She can feel that she is already bleeding, a slight trickle. Dempsey gives her a little push and she takes a couple of careful steps, head up, still sheltered by the breadth of the umbrella, feels for the curb with a booted foot. Can't look down, or turn her head.

Dempsey opens the front door of the limousine, takes the umbrella from Mardie, companionably close, right fist near her shoulder. In the

rain no passersby, if they should pay attention at all, would be able
to see how neatly she is ensnared.

Sliding in slowly across the plump leather seats. The engine running. Dempsey gets in beside her, keeping the line taut.

"First Avenue. There's a parking garage on Seventy-fifth between
First and Second. Drive in. Second level."

"I said. What do you want?"

"We're going to have a pow-wow. Now shut up and drive."

The attendant on duty at the parking garage doesn't look up in his
booth opposite the entrance when Mardie slowly eases the limo into
the tight drive. Sweat mixing with the blood on her neck as she nurses
the big car around a tight turn to the second level, managing not to
scrape the wall on the curve, as a hundred other cars apparently have
done before tonight, leaving a colorful strata of paint streaks on the
concrete. With his free hand Dempsey has loosened the hood around
his face and removed the wad of blackened bandage taped over his
green eye.

"Next to the Bondo Special."

When parked the limo sticks out four feet, but the garage is quiet,
no one coming or going right now.

"Turn off the ignition."

Mardie does so, sits rigidly with one hand at her throat, her fingertips bloody. Tears of pain leak from her eyes. Dempsey pats her
down, locates both of the pistols she is carrying, and takes them.

"Mardie, do you know how Lew Carbine was killed?"

Mardie makes no sound.

"Military-style bomb. It was a sophisticated device."

Mardie sighs. She is trying not to swallow; saliva drains from the
corners of her mouth. She looks straight ahead, giving him no satisfaction.

"When I was married to Esther and we were down at the home
place for R and R, I used to drink with Mordecai and some of your
kin. A few of them, those that never majored in safecracking at one
state pen or another, worked the quarries, the mines, they worked for
the railroads in the glory days. They all knew explosives. Hell, I don't
think there's a mountain boy that ever grew up not knowing how to
dynamite a stump."

"Fuck you," Mardie says hoarsely.

"Noose not tight enough for you?"

"Fuck you, Dempsey Wingo."

"But Mordecai's the real expert. Wouldn't you say? At least when he had enough corn liquor in him he'd brag how he was. Learned armaments in the military service, which was his alternative to the crossbar hotel when he was age nineteen. Have I got the story right? Don't say 'fuck you' again unless you want to be headless."

Mardie chooses to say nothing. She turns her eyes on him, spreads her knees wide and there is a sudden sound like a can of coffee being opened. Mardie is pissing in the seat. Watching him, so he will know she isn't pissing from fear. It is a deliberate, symbolic act, a wildcat's signature of her contempt for him.

"That's choice," Dempsey says. "So I've got the story right, and I know it's right. Mordecai has the ability to rig a bomb like the one that whacked Lew Carbine. What we need to establish is, why did Esther want Lew whacked? Because, of course, it *was* Esther. Had to be."

From a potential guest list of thousands, Jules Brougham had carefully chosen sixty of his best friends and frequent clients for Sharan's introduction to the New York art world. Her first jury. In addition to Esther and Dix Trevellian, there was Nabob Creel; the only TV news personality in the country who had any claim to good taste; his wife, an art scholar; the curator of an important university's art collection; philanthropists; a composer; a theatrical producer; a biographer; a publisher of fine arts books.

Jules had explained that Sharan was to be seen but not sold, at least not yet. Her paintings were hung in two rooms on the third floor of the gallery, a paneled library and a living room furnished with classic Italian and French pieces from the late 1940s: curvy, quirky, colorful stuff in satins and faux suede. No intrusive track lighting here, no clichéd salesroom look. And no other painters. Despite the gallery setting, the reminder that an event might or might not be happening, the evening succeeded on its own merits because Jules was—Esther said to Sharan—"just a fabulous party-giver." The food was wonderful. Nabob Creel ate until his upper plate came loose and his mouth looked tortured. He was with another beauty, a megamodel who said not a word all evening. Her reticence enhanced a shadowy hint of death in her allure, as if at the age of twenty she had already become disconnected from her soul.

An aging actor came on to Sharan. A peppy sort, with a hairpiece and a freckled hijinks face. He was apt to break into dance steps to punctuate his monologues, like Donald O'Connor in an old MGM musical. She found him fun, the way flea circuses are fun, for a while. Nabob Creel gossiped in a circle of brand-name faces while pretending not to notice Sharan's paintings. Sharan tried hard not to observe him not noticing, but all the social slickery got on her nerves.

She said to Jules in a private moment, "He hates me."

"Don't think so. Out of the corner of his eye. Always out of the corner of his eye. But missing nothing. He's particularly taken with the black boy lounging against the side of the yellow school bus. The impact of all that sun, the angularities, the lettering on the bus that you choose to reveal. *Far Hills.* A potential destination, an unfulfillable dream. Always a story to go with your image, the strong emotion. Hopper, of course, but High Victorian as well. Tissot comes to mind. Incidentally, Nabob considers himself a master of that difficult period. I should mention your teenager lounging in the bathtub with her hand to her face, peering at us through spread fingers. Such cheekiness. My personal favorite. She fascinates, like an odalisque. Where did you find her?"

"That's Becky McNabb. She lives in the mobile home park. Most of my subjects do."

Dix said to her later, "You're a hit."

"How do you know?" Sharan asked, trying to keep the avidity out of her voice.

"I know all of these people."

"But what do you hear?"

"They ask a lot of questions about you."

"So? Nobody's talked to me, really. Just polite chat."

"Relax. You'll be hearing from them. Invitations to lunch, their own parties. They'll be vying to show you off. That's the true gen. You'll be hot. Jules has probably already revised his estimates of what you should go for."

"What should I, uh, go for?"

Dix grinned and shook his head.

"I'm not talking. I intend to be a buyer. By the way, Esther was negotiating with Jules ten minutes after we got here."

"Negotiating what?"

"Let Esther tell you."

Sharan didn't have the opportunity to talk to Esther right away. She had no appetite, but the wine was good. She began to feel the effects of drinking and not eating. After the final curtain the bug-eyed female star of the Broadway producer's musical revival hustled over from the Majestic Theatre to make a smash entrance and entertain with a medley of songs from her hit shows.

Sharan overheard Nabob Creel say, "I may have been too harsh, but I was in the mood to sink my fangs into an overpraised book."

Oh, Lord, she thought. The famous malicious wit. You don't have to like me. Just let me off easy.

Esther found Sharan in the ladies' lounge.

"You okay?"

"Sinus headache."

"I could use some air. The rain's let up. Why don't we slip out for half an hour, drive around. Jules won't mind, and I wanted to talk to you."

The blue stretch Lincoln was waiting outside. Esther said, "Truth is, I don't think I could suffer another evening of Sugarpie's chirping. How long has she been doing that tired old musical? Since I was a kid. God, she looks just like she did thirty years ago. Of course you'd have to run a sander to get all that makeup off." She held the back door of the limousine open. "After you, Sharan. Mardie, just take us through the park for a little while."

Esther settled into the seat beside Sharan. The door locks clicked into place. The black glass privacy panel separating the front seat from the rear compartment slid down halfway. Sharan saw a dim dark face in the rearview mirror. Now there was an odor of whiskey in the limousine. And a slightly stronger reek of urine.

Dempsey Wingo said, "Mardie's in the trunk, Esther. How're you all doing tonight?"

After a long pause, during which she instinctively tried the door handle without success, Esther said, "What did you do to her?"

"Duct tape. Some chloral hydrate. She'll be semiconscious for a few hours. But she can breathe okay."

"Let us out of here. *Right now.*"

Sharan was staring at her. Esther shook her head in annoyance, put a hand on Sharan to reassure her.

"My crazy ex-husband," Esther said with a tight grin. "Dempsey, this is my very good friend Sharan Norbeth."

"Hi," Dempsey said. He was behind the wheel. He didn't turn around. Sharan couldn't see his face. "What's going on at Jules' tonight?"

"A little party for Sharan. She's a painter. Dempsey, didn't you hear me?"

"Lewie went boom," Dempsey said disconsolately, and Sharan had the impression he'd been drinking. A lot. "My fault, wasn't it? I took his luck away from him. His protection. Isn't that what it was, Esther? That little golden hand reminding him always to bless his good fortune and keep his mouth shut."

"I don't have any idea what you're talking about." Esther had opened her purse. Sharan involuntarily reached up to her cross. Watching the mirror. She sensed he was watching her, too.

"What have you got with you tonight, Esther, that gold-plated derringer? Now I wonder if you have the guts to shoot me in the back of the head."

"I have every right to shoot you," Esther temporized. There were weak thumping sounds from the trunk of the car. "Get out now, cut Mardie loose and we won't make any more of this. But you're on thin goddamn ice, Dempsey."

"Why did Lew have to go, Esther? Because he talked to me? Because he said too much about Thursday Childs? Were you afraid he was going to say something incriminating about Thursday and your brother? Not Dix. Scott."

"You miserable bastard. Nothing that *ever* went on between us justifies this continuing persecution of my family!"

"I'll be seeing Scott pretty soon. I'll ask him about Thursday Childs." Dempsey paused, drumming fingertips thoughtfully on the steering wheel. "Could be he wants her off his conscience after all this time."

Esther held up the derringer from her purse and clicked the hammer back.

"Hear that, Dempsey?"

"I heard it."

"You have gone way *way* too far tonight. Not to mention that you're full of shit. I know nothing about Lew Carbine. Or that actress. This is so absurd. You're such a fool. Get out of this car *at once* or I'll kill you."

The black glass panel closed noiselessly. The door on the driver's side opened, closed. Through the tinted window on her side Sharan saw the figure of Dempsey Wingo striding through eastbound New York death traffic toward the other side of the wide street. Jammed brakes, swerving cars, multiple collisions. Dempsey deftly kept going.

Esther lowered the derringer's hammer and slipped the .44 caliber pistol back into her purse. There was a niche between Esther's brows. Her darkly austere eyes studied Sharan for a reaction, which was sympathetic and concerned.

Esther shrugged.

"Always these little melodramas. Once I thought he had talent. You see what I've had to put up with, all these years."

"Yes."

Esther seemed to be waiting for Sharan to ask questions. She looked bemused when there were none. She shrugged again.

"Sharan, would you mind helping me get Mardie out of the trunk? I wouldn't want her to smother." She sounded as casual as if she were asking Sharan to lend a hand with some shopping bags. Sharan admired her cold-forged nerve. "Oh, I almost forgot! Why I wanted to talk to you. I've commissioned you to do our portraits. Dix and me. That is, of course, if you're agreeable." She leaned over and kissed Sharan lightly, just brushing Sharan's lips with her own. And Sharan felt how alive she was, her own heart jumping from the passed-on charge excited in Esther by the encounter with her ex-husband.

FIFTEEN

A PRISONER'S MELANCHOLY

Sharan," Coleman Dane said, "remember that you're not talking on a secure line. Now go ahead."

"How are you?"

"Okay," he said, after a moment's hesitation, a trace of impatience in his voice. "Mondays are always jammed up."

"I miss you."

"I miss you, too. Closed-door hearings. I can't get away just yet. This week sometime. I listened to Saturday night's tapes."

"Could any of it be true? I mean, Younger Brother and not Older Brother?"

"Younger Brother may have had a brief relationship with the actress. She wasn't all that exclusive, obviously. But there's no substantive link between Younger Brother and the other women, at least not in our files. You have to consider the condition Younger Brother has been in for the past few years. A lot of planning was involved, something schizophrenic personalities find difficult if not impossible. Withdrawal, diminished function—they're too paranoid, usually, to maintain even a short-term relationship. Also they're almost never violent, although some will do violence to themselves."

"But Younger Brother probably knows something about the disappearances."

"I almost had my hands on him, last week at Brio. I wish I'd known then, I could've had him taken into custody."

"The Ex-Husband talked as if he knows where Younger Brother is."

"We've been trying to have him picked up. He's done some bounty hunting for the INS, although not lately. How're you doing? Do they like your paintings?"

"Yes. I think so. Big Sister offered my Angel seven thousand for two portraits. Angel suggested fifteen. They'll go back and forth for awhile. He thinks they'll close at eleven thousand. In the meantime Angel said go ahead and get started. I'm looking forward to doing some real work again. And their faces! Especially Big Sister. Something I notice in those dark pupils, a ghostly shadowing, an ancestral image . . . you know how the great portraitists capture not only a likeness, but a history? That's what I want to get—"

"Yeah, well. Congratulations on your first commission."

"You sound so tired."

"Misty had a bad night. Her right shoulder's hurting."

"Oh. And that's not very good news?"

"No. I'm afraid it isn't. She's back in the hospital for a couple of days. And I'm trying not to—you know. Get nuts."

"Wish you were here wish you were here wish you were *here*. I need to know something. The Cartier watch? Did any of the others have personalized jewelry from Older Brother with that particular inscription?"

"Checking on it. What are you doing the rest of the day?"

"After I hang up I'm going to sit on a bench here at the zoo and eat the lunch I bought at this wonderful deli around the corner from Angel's. At two o'clock Big Sister and I are going to what she tells me is one of the western world's great antique establishments. Tonight we're having dinner with some foundation people."

"Older Brother included?"

"Busy, but he invited me up to his workshop later to show me around."

"You're like one of the family."

"The thought chills me to the bone. *That* family? God."

"Something else going on?" Dane asked alertly.

"No," Sharan said, remembering the quick affectionate kiss bestowed by Esther, wondering if she could possibly explain her own, complex reaction. A thank-you, shall-we-later kiss? Women had come on to Sharan before. Never much interest, not since she was a teenager with a crush on her art teacher and volleyball coach, just a glimpse of her tightly curled head in the high school halls could send a comet streaking through Sharan's adolescent breast. No real interest now, either, but curiosity, part of her absorption in her subject, the desire to know Esther so completely that the finished portrait would contain everything of her, the vessel of her face brimming with vitality and mystification.

Sharan ate her lunch near the show-off seals and did some sketches in crayon of faces that circulated through the zoo plaza. Two well-dressed black women of a certain age and standing, their faces bred for haughty. A pigeon-feeder with a snowy beard, a sleeveless V-neck sweater that had been food for moths. His was a chipped and damaged face, like a dropped decanter; but still with such a regal shape to it, an antique gleam. Derelicts dressed like zombies. Tattooed youths with cigarettes and that dicey look, no integrity in their bones. A large man with a shaved head, a gold hoop earring, gangsta sunglasses. He occupied a corner of a bench not far away, was sunning his bare ankles, eating popcorn and listening to Jimmie Dale Gilmore on his headphones. Gilmore's ghostly ascetic face was easy for Sharan to make out on the labels of the CD boxes when he made a change. He seemed interested in what she was doing, smiled when she lifted her head and looked his way—very white teeth, one of the front ones badly chipped—but he didn't approach her.

Twenty minutes to two. She had a date with Esther, and Trevellian House was a brisk twenty-minute walk up Fifth Avenue. Sharan put her materials away and left the zoo grounds.

She was at Seventy-seventh when she happened to look back. She saw the tall man with the big shoulders and shaved head on the park side of Fifth, standing at a bus stop, looking her way. No reason to make anything of it, but it crossed her mind that he might be one of Dane's people, keeping an eye on her. Not that he resembled anyone who had come storming into St. Lazarus Church the other day. But it was comforting to believe that the JD agents might be on the job in various modes of street dress. She resumed her walk uptown.

Dix Trevellian, like his sister, had an eye for antiques. He collected architectural models, and half of the third floor of the mansion across from Trevellian House was devoted to an exhibit.

"The model building probably began in ancient Greece or Egypt, although nothing survives," Dix explained to Sharan. "All of my models are late- or post-Renaissance. But as early as the 1400s designs had become complex and more expensive to execute. Brunelleschi and Michelangelo almost always used them to give their patrons a preview of what the finished structure would be like. For instance, this little cupola someone, I don't think it was Michelangelo, made out of wood and lead. Look at the technical work—models also served to give exact instructions to woodcarvers and masons. A good many models were commissioned after the fact, like the Duomo di Milano here. It took five hundred years to build the original. Every detail of the miniature is exact and to scale."

Dix paused to pour himself another glass of wine from the bottle he'd carried around with him. He was having a good time. He pointed with the nearly empty bottle and said, "There you have the greatest cathedral that was never built." He waited amiably for some word of recognition from Sharan. "Christopher Wren's first design for St. Paul's, the cathedral that was to take the place of the one that burned in the great London fire."

"It's incredible. The workmanship."

"A work of genius," Dix said lovingly. "It almost gives me the stutters, I'm afflicted with artistic penis envy. I've spent entire days studying Wren's model, lost in it. Learning from it, I hope. The problem, the reason why it wasn't built, is that the great model is too spectacular. Oh, it works, it would have worked, but the design is centuries ahead of its time. It wasn't properly 'English.' So Wren tossed out the beautiful fantasy, the dreamlike undulations, the smaller Roman dome, and gave the cathedral committee the trite Latin cross they wanted. Everything works, of course. St. Paul's is still there; the central dome, which was a staggering feat of engineering for its time. Staggering. But I've often wondered how Sir Chris felt when they nixed his grand design. Needless to say, I fucking hate architectural committees." He enlarged his animus with a sweep of his free hand. "Committees of any kind. A committee is never anything more than the asshole of status."

Dix sat down with his arms across the back of a black Chinese Chippendale chair, facing the model, musing, his head unsteady on his wine-wilted neck.

"I know how I feel when it happens. Some of the most brilliant work I've done has been flushed because a few untalented nonentities thought it was ugly or too innovative."

"How do you feel?"

"Like I've stepped off a cliff. And I just fall. Down, down, down I go, blackness rushing up. So far I haven't hit bottom. Esther's always been there to catch me, and bring me back up. Light and air. Prod and push, on your feet, 'Get to work, Dix.' I work, hell I work like a dog with the rest of the population in heat. But I have this ominous feeling now. I'm working on a project for an Egyptian consortium. Monufuckingmental. What I do best, I debunk. I have a keen sense of disrespect for the familiar and the revered. But my work may be too good, too advanced. I just never can bite down hard enough on the goddamn silver bullet. Deliver what I know in my heart they're going to want."

He turned his head slowly, looking back at Sharan, his eyes simmering and not tracking too well. "I wish I had the strength of, let's say, Picasso. You don't like Cubism? Well, here's more of it, more and more and in your face and *I will prevail!* That's what I said with Trevellian House, you know. Not in your face—more like, up your withered old asses. All the trustees of the Metropolitan who complained I was making fun of their hallowed institution. They tried to keep us from building Trevellian House. Esther twisted some arms. Well, that's not exactly what she twisted—" His dirty grin turned to a scowl that froze in place, too long. Sharan wanted to snap her fingers. Then Dix shuddered slightly. "But I love my sister and I won't ever say a word against—I won't *hear* a word against her. Anyway, three or four days a year in the mornings the shadow of my obelisk goes straight to the heart of that museum. Up their asses, too. We got back at them, didn't we, Sis?"

"Hey. I'm Sharan."

"Of course you are. Apology apology. Slip of the tongue." He was whistling between his teeth as he became drunker. "Gonna paint me, Sharan?"

"Yes."

"Well, damn, let's get started then."

"Can't, Dix."

"For an extra ten bucks I'm willing to pose in all my natural-born naked splen—you can't paint? Why's that, you bucking some kind of artist's block?"

"I don't know where to put you, yet."

He thought about her meaning, nodded.

"Oh, yeah. You're right. The setting. Very important."

"And I don't know you well enough."

"You've never painted people you didn't know?"

"Maybe I haven't said that right. I can 'know' people in a flash. They just come to me . . ."

"Sure, sure."

"But I always want to think about my first impressions, make sure I'm right. Otherwise what I paint doesn't emerge. It's lousy."

"Let me tell you something about Dix Trevellian."

"I'd love to hear."

"I am not attracted to very many women. Fact."

"Not the way it was told to me, Dix."

"Sure, sure. I've *had* a lot of women. Getting women in bed, that's easy as pie. You have to be interested in women. And I am. So that's all there is to it, basically what women want is *interest*. More important than sex to them."

"I don't disagree."

"But what *attracts* me to a woman? 'Nother story. Do you really want to hear this? By the way, is this the first or second bottle I opened tonight?"

"Second."

"Thought so."

"What attracts you, Dix?"

"Quality. I don't mean good looks. I love good-looking women. I love plain women. Just as long as they have quality. That can be anything. Intelligence. Education. Talent. First things I look for in a woman. Then, the other thing . . ." He swallowed and looked vague for a time. "What I mean is . . . flawed. Hurt in some way. Like you. Breaks my heart."

The silence in the little museum began to weigh on Sharan's eardrums, like a pressure of depths, as she looked around at the antique models Dix Trevellian had collected. Worm-eaten wood, dry rot, cracked plaster columns, a broken spire, faded colors. The imperfections of beauty or someone's cherished ideals, caused by time or accident.

Dix was looking at her prosthetic hand.

"Do you have bad dreams, Sharan? About . . . it?"

"Yes. I have bad dreams."

"Are you angry?"

"Yes. Sometimes."

"Your pain. My pain."

"No, Dix. That isn't true. You could never assimilate my feelings. I wouldn't want you to. Pity is no basis for a relationship."

"But I would never pity you! When you paint me, then I know . . . you'll understand me. I empathize, Sharan. I can accept all of your pain. I want to take it for my own. Relieve you of that burden."

Her shoulders stiffened. "Dix. It's getting awfully late; I've enjoyed this so far but I don't care to be with you when you've had too much to drink."

The low flicker of his drunkenness, transit of desire in a still room. Sharan, her skin prickling, recognized a mood flammable as straw. Draughtsmen were working late upstairs, coming and going on the stairs outside the museum, shadows seen on opaque glass. She had no sense of danger. Dix held the wine bottle at a downward angle, regarding it sadly, the taste of the last drops fading on his tongue.

"But there'll be another time for us. Won't there, Sharan?"

The birthday party for Elnora Trevellian, of uncertain age, was a gala. Five hundred seriously overdressed guests filled two levels of the ballroom in Trevellian House. There were four chandeliers fifty feet above the ballroom floor, inverted crystal domes to echo the massively strutted bronze bowl that anchored the twenty-eight story obelisk above it. A staircase in red circled the ballroom twice, spiraling to a gallery with doors that opened onto the terraces. The night was clear and breezy and the doors had been opened.

Sharan wore a tight satiny black dress that flared with some flounce above the knees and rustled like dry leaves when she walked. Esther had picked out the dress for her at MoMo Abreggio's salon, one of three designers currently competing for her business and endorsement. All three designers were among the guests. Elnora Trevellian, the honoree, was not there. She hadn't been seen in New York for twenty-five years. Few of the guests at her birthday party knew what she looked like.

Two bands played for dancing. Sharan allowed herself to be picked up by an unassuming young man with almost no shoulders and a lonesome-looking face not enhanced by a gunfighter's droopy mustache. He said his name was Alex Bard Owens, and he gave her a business card to prove it, as if he was accustomed to the indignity of authenticating his presence.

"Alex or Bard?" Sharan asked him.

"Bard, if you don't mind."

"Has kind of a ring to it."

"I'm from Richmond originally. And you're from—"

"Way south of Richmond, podner."

"It's the mustache, isn't it? I'd shave it off, but then I wouldn't have any face at all."

Sharan smiled and glanced at his business card again.

"Says you're president of the Experimental Unit of Trevel Resources. You're young to be a president."

"Well, it's a small unit. Just a few of us, actually. The fabrications are all subcontracted out. Would you like to dance?"

"I'm a clunky dancer."

"So am I. I just wanted to talk to you anyway. Somebody said you were a painter."

"Uh-huh."

"Have you shown in New York?"

"Not yet. Next spring. Jules wants more paintings."

"Jules Brougham? Wow. You must be terrific."

"I haven't heard anybody say 'wow' since I got to New York."

"I used to say 'gee' and 'gosh' a lot, but I conquered the habit with the help of my twelve-step support group."

"Trevel Resources? What are you working on, Bard?"

"Oh, our main thrust is environmentally friendly waste disposal. There's this mountain down in North Carolina that the Trevellian family owns. A lot of virgin forest, unspoiled wilderness and so on, but airborne industrial pollution is playing havoc with the red cedar and other indigenous trees there, and in widespread areas of the Great Smokies. Esther feels very strongly about implementing new methods of neutralizing harmful vapors and toxins that are killing off valuable forests, polluting the ground water, ruining our air and contributing to global warming. She's invested quite a bit of money in my father's research."

"What does your father do?"

"Pop's a physicist. Trevellian Prize winner. He designed the first practical portable plasma furnace."

"Plasma being an extremely hot gas?"

"It can be hot or cold, depending on the method used in exciting a primary, rarefied gas. We can produce plasma temperatures of ten thousand degrees Celsius, which is eight thousand degrees hotter than conventional incinerators that use fossil fuels. And plasma furnaces burn much more cleanly; only one-fifth of the emissions. The extremely high temperatures break down hydrocarbons, PCBs and any other contaminant known to us. The by-product is an inert form of glassy rock suitable for paving roads."

"You're saving the planet and rebuilding it at the same time."

"Well," Bard said a little proudly, "as a species, human beings just don't seem to have much common sense. For every bad action I like to think there's a good reaction to be found by science. But there's always a bottom line to human endeavor. The method is efficient; we're simply not cost-effective yet. We've had prototype furnaces operating in Germany, England, Argentina and New Jersey for several years, and we're installing one at a toxic landfill site in North Carolina this month. That's a very exciting project; we're going to use plasma torches in boreholes in an attempt to neutralize the entire site."

"It does sound exciting, Bard. Where in England?"

"Pardon?"

"You said you had a prototype furnace operating in England."

"Oh. It's in Nottinghamshire, a little place called Chudley Market. About halfway between Nottingham and Sheffield in the industrial north of England. But as I said, it's portable, about the size of an eighteen-wheeler. We do move them around."

"Uh-huh. What about Argentina? Where would that facility be?"

"It's near a large dump outside of Buenos Aires, on the expressway to the airport. Are you interested in plasma furnaces? I could show you the one in New Jersey. It's down the Turnpike about ninety minutes, right outside of Glassboro."

"I know I'd be fascinated. Did you say something about champagne, Bard?"

Exactly at eleven o'clock the lights in the ballroom were dimmed and with no fanfare Esther and Dix Trevellian took their places on the bandstand. Esther did all of the talking.

On four big screens around the ballroom images of childhood appeared. The Trevellian children at play, parents usually in the background. Christmas and other holidays at numerous resorts. School occasions. Birthdays. Esther read from poems by Dylan Thomas. "Fern Hill" and "In the Beginning." Sharan concentrated on what could be gleaned from the faded old eight-millimeter images of the adults. The father was a tall shadow-man with deep-set eyes, a brushy mustache and a slightly bucktoothed grin. The sort of unpretentious guy children felt good about hanging around with, confiding in. The best shot of Elnora Trevellian, probably in her early thirties at the time, lasted six or seven seconds. Handheld zoom-in. She was posed in a doorway, sliding glass door, a sunlit alp reflected on the pane.

About a third of her face and figure were behind the door frame. She was looking to her right, at the unsteady camera. Breasts the human equivalent of alps, barely covered by a zippered something; that was the peasant in her lineage, but for her cheekbones alone Elnora's beauty deserved to be called classic. It wasn't the perfection of features that interested Sharan the painter. It was Elnora's look of intelligent disdain, of amused stubbornness along with a clarion sexuality that defined her. *I am going to do exactly as I damn please, and the rest of you can suffer the consequences.*

Through all of this portion of the birthday tribute to his mother Dix fidgeted like a small boy who had been combed, spit-shined and told to be mannerly.

"Everybody. We're downlinking now, and in just a few seconds Mom will be with us from Cloud Horse Mountain. She'll be able to see and hear us, just as if she were here tonight. I'd like a big joyful 'Happy Birthday!' from all of you, so let's practice a couple of times, all right?"

They all shouted Happy Birthday, Elnora!

"That was wonderful," Esther enthused. "Thank you. Okay— we're ready? Here she is."

Flickerings on all four screens, then the mother's face appeared.

Elnora Trevellian, thirty years or so later.

Very soft tight focus, subdued lighting. No sense of background. After a few moments Sharan decided that Mother Trevellian was being photographed from a low angle, and that she was propped up in bed on several pillows.

"Hi, Mom!" Esther turned to the marshaled guests and raised her hands slowly as Happy Birthday! rose from five hundred pairs of lungs like a blimp leaving the ground. The emotion labored, and to Sharan's ears heartily false.

Elnora's lips moved, but it wasn't conclusive that she smiled.

"Thank you," she said, in a scratchy voice. She blinked a couple of times, but otherwise nothing about her face was animated. Her hair, her eyes, the imperishable cheekbones; she had the same coloring Sharan had seen in the films, perhaps slightly overdone by the cosmetician and hairdresser who had prepared her for tonight's celebration. But everything else was missing, beginning with the go-to-hell spirit. Of course she had to be—late sixties? And not in the best of health, Esther had confided to Sharan with a regretful sigh.

Dix's expression of stiff furious ordeal, of unconnectedness, contrasted with his sister's determinedly upbeat mood.

One of the country's enduring balladeers, gray but still full of twin-
kle, took the mike from Esther and sang a few of his best-loved songs
for Elnora, whose multiple images seemed as distant as Andromeda
outside the rosy spotlights that contained the song stylist.

At one point during the medley a frail hand rose to one side of
Elnora's face, middle finger extended toward the cheekbone in silent
bitter commentary. Sharan wasn't sure she was interpreting this correctly. Maybe Mother Trevellian was wiping away a tear.

When Sharan looked for Dix again, he had disappeared.

hello BaDmaN

there was a fabulist with a dreambook.
in his book, memories of days
I still live for and study
with a prisoner's melancholy.

what sort of creature is the human heart?

the lost fabulist spake a rosier
sentiment, but the mistress of Mr. Morph
revels in the erotica of wounds.

Jesu, a very tall man and a very good
whore!

All tragedy, in time, becomes comedy
to the crueler mind.

another day, BaDmaN?

SIXTEEN

FINDING HUMMINGBIRD

The restaurant Coleman Dane had chosen for their meeting was on West Eightieth, two doors from Columbus Avenue and diagonally opposite the Museum of Natural History. Sharan took a cab across the park. The restaurant was a narrow floor-through, up a steep flight of steps from the street. Low lights, brick walls, sawdust on the floor, a line of booths along one wall opposite the bar. Uptown arts crowd, young professionals with degrees from good colleges, vivacity and nonchalance, most of them still with an air of expectancy about their lives; they stood two and three deep at the bar. Dane told her the pasta was exceptional. Sharan decided on linguini with white clam sauce. They held hands across the lacquered plank table, clinging to each other like survivors after a torpedo attack. She'd been biting her nails, but he didn't say anything. Beefy darkness under his eyes, a constant wearied smile she found romantic. Misty's white count had stabilized on an altered drug protocol and she was out of the hospital; no further talk of a bone marrow transplant. Full recovery from acute leukocytic leukemia still appeared to be in the girl's favor. They didn't have anything else to talk about until they'd finished that first bracing drink. Sharan was learning to like the Mac-Allen, smoothed with an ounce of Dr. Brown's cream soda.

"How much of it did you hear?" Sharan asked him, speaking of the events that followed the party at Jules Brougham's gallery.

"Nothing. Apparently there's a jamming device in the Town Car."

"I'd better remember that. My God but they're cautious people."

"What happened?"

"This is how I put it together. Mardie Kregg was driving that night. Dempsey Wingo somehow drugged her and locked her up in the trunk—"

"On Fifty-seventh Street?"

"He may have taken her somewhere first. Listen, I didn't want to ask too many questions, Daner. Anyway, he was behind the wheel when we got into the back seat. Couldn't see him very well; he didn't turn around. I caught him watching me in the mirror a couple of times. He locked us in. Esther pulled a gun. I'm telling you, it got very tense. I think she might have shot him."

"No. Esther hates scandal. Plugging her ex-husband in the back of the head, justified or not, that isn't just bad publicity to Es, it's a potential plague. What did he say to rile her so bad?"

"Accused her of having Lew Carbine murdered."

"Are you—?" He hunched his shoulders and glanced around, as if he were afraid everyone in the place had homed in on this tidbit. He leaned across the table until their faces were a foot apart.

"Verbatim. 'Why did Lew have to go, Esther? Because he talked to me? Because he said too much about Thursday Childs? Were you afraid he was going to say something incriminating about Thursday and your brother? Scott, I mean.' By the way, he sounded a little drunk. I smelled liquor in the car. Also I'm sure somebody had, um, relieved himself. Herself, could have been Mardie, depending on what he dosed her with. Chloral hydrate, I think Wingo said."

Dane closed his eyes momentarily, meditating.

Sharan kissed the bridge of his nose. His smile flickered like heat lightning, but he didn't look at her.

"Then he said he was going to see Scott soon, and I could feel the hatred coming off Esther's skin, she was burning up with it. He said he was going to ask Scott about Thursday Childs, something about getting it, her, off his conscience after all this time. That's when Esther cocked the hammer on her little gold pistola. Do you want another drink? Go ahead, you're going to need it, there's a lot more."

Dane opened his eyes, savoring a revelation. "You should see your face. You're into the chase now. You love this stuff, don't you?"

Sharan said, with her offputting grimace, "The more I find out, the more fascinated I am. Think about what I've told you."

"I know, I know."

Sharan looked around for their waitress, saw someone familiar in the backbar mirror. Shaved head glowing frostily in the nimbus of a neon beer logo, gold earring flashing as he lowered his head to listen more closely to a petite blonde in a peasant blouse. Coleman Dane's man on the street. He raised the beer in his fist, then their waitress cut off Sharan's view of the Justice Department undercover watchdog.

Sharan decided she could handle another Scotch herself.

"Esther denied she knew what he was talking about. Of course."

"But, from her reaction?"

"I don't know, Cole. I'm not sure. Wingo got out of the car then, caused a couple of fender-benders as he crossed Fifty-seventh against traffic and disappeared. Then Esther sort of shrugged the whole thing off, and—"

"For your benefit."

"Again, I'm not sure. Horns blowing, cars squealing into cars, not enough light to read her eyes. Then she—kissed me."

"Kissed you." He touched his own lips, as if sealing in a forbidden notion. "Uh-huh. What kind of kiss?"

"Friendly. Caring. Like, I'm sorry this shit happened, but hey."

Dane sat back, breathing out, nodding.

"Esther is never easy to read."

"Wingo may only have been taunting her."

"But he got pretty damn rough with Mardie Kregg. I really want to get my hands on that guy."

"I would call it a priority," Sharan said. "Do you want to hear about the furnaces now, or after we eat?"

He was beginning to smile at her smug expression when his pager went off. He fished for it and checked the number.

"AG himself. Gotta do this." He took his cellular phone from an inside pocket of his suit coat and began punching in numbers. Listened and frowned, looked around. Unfinished ceiling, a lot of pipes painted silver. "Need to go to the car," he said.

"It's a living."

He mussed her hair and left the booth. Sharan watched him go, smiling fondly at the man who had filled her eyes and altered her vision; no atoms of regret or caution adrift in the heart tonight. She folded her hands and waited. Two more shots of the MacAllen came, soda on the side for Sharan. She blended, stirred, sipped.

"Sharan?"

She looked up. The man with the big shoulders and shaved head was standing beside her, looking concerned.

"Yes?"

He spoke softly, close to her ear. "We have to get out of here. Right now. Come with me."

"What? Where's—"

"There's no time to explain. He's left already. You're meeting him somewhere else. Let's move."

A hand on her elbow. She rose from the booth, turned toward the front of the crowded restaurant.

"No. The back way. Through the kitchen."

"Cole is—"

"I have my instructions. Don't worry about him, he's safe."

That was a shock. What was the situation? A death threat against Cole? "All right," Sharan said, but she had a creepy sensation. It was the watchdog's voice, insistently whispered. He didn't want to be overheard, but maybe that wasn't the only reason. Whispering didn't disguise the regionalism. A westerner, Texas or—

Hadn't she heard his voice somewhere else?

"Hurry."

Sharan had no doubts that something serious was going down. Cole's line of work, someone with a grudge out to get him. But the watchdog had said he was safe. She took a couple of quick breaths as the tall man with the shaved head—recently shaved, she'd observed—escorted her firmly to the kitchen. He wasn't muscling her, but she had more than a hint of great strength. A relentless intensity. Someone she could count on if she were in real trouble. She glanced back at him. He was alert, protective, eyes flickering here and there. Mismatched eyes. One green iris, the other dark brown. Again the creeping sensation at her nape.

The kitchen was sweltering, noisy. She was reminded by the steamy aromas of how hungry she was. Oh, well. They squeezed past stoves and tattooed cooks wearing T-shirts and cheesecloth snoods and went through a door onto an iron stairway.

"When we get to the alley, walk beside me. Don't look around."

"Can you tell me—"

"Don't talk any more. *Vamonos*."

Nothing else for her to do but follow the scenario. Quick exit, escape route. Cole waiting for her in another location. He would explain, when she saw him. Then maybe they could do something about dinner.

Two drinks on the table, no Sharan.

Coleman Dane looks around the crowded restaurant, not seeing her.

He starts to sit down, then frowns and grabs a waiter by the elbow.

"Have you seen my—the woman I'm with?"

"I'm sorry, this isn't my section."

"Whose section is it?"

"Janet's."

Dane hasn't paid much attention to who was serving them. "Which one is Janet?"

"By the bar, picking up an order. The long ponytail?"

Dane takes four seconds to swallow half of his drink, then crosses the sawdust-covered floor, peanut shells crackling underfoot.

"Janet?"

"Yes, sir?"

"My, my *wife,* did you happen to see her leave the booth? Did she go to the bathroom?"

"Oh, that's you, number sixteen? She has the, the—"

"Yeah, prosthetic hand."

"No, sir, I don't think she—they were going to the kitchen, I'm pretty sure, but I just had a glimpse—"

"*They?*"

"She was with a man. About your height, shaved head. Shoulders out to here—"

Dane starts for the kitchen, pushing through the bar crowd, taking out his cellular phone. He punches in a number.

"Unit four."

"This is Dane. Where the hell is Hummingbird?"

"Outside."

"Outside where, goddammit!"

"Uh, we were picking up footsteps. Traffic noise. That's all. She was, uh, breathing a little heavy. A little while ago—here's the read-out—nine-twenty-three oh six, she said, 'Can you tell me—' That's all we've had for a while, we weren't picking up inside the restaurant. Uh, assumed Hummingbird left with you."

"She's not with me! What the hell is— *Find* her."

In the kitchen Dane nearly runs over a little man in a tall chef's hat.

"Sir, you're not supposed to be—"

Dane raises his voice to a shout. "Tall woman, about five-ten, strawberry blond hair, right hand is a prosthesis. She was with some guy who has a shaved head. Did they come through here? Who saw them?"

One of the kitchen workers points with a wooden pizza shovel.

"Out that door, man."

"How long?"

Shrug.

Dane goes outside and clatters down the iron steps of the service stairway, cellular phone to his ear.

"What have you got?"

"Hummingbird is on the move. CP is tracking her northbound in the park, east side."

"Meet me on the street; what's closest, Eighty-first? *Now*."

"Hummingbird's at Ninety-second: five, maybe six minutes away from us depending on traffic. Do you want NYPD in on this?"

"Yes. Patch me to Blue's liaison officer in the post. And *get* here." Dane is running now.

"Sir, we've been informed that the L.O. has stepped out for a few— Jesus!"

"What? *What?*" Dane shouts as he runs.

"The guy. First time we heard him. He was, like, whispering before. He's faint, almost out of range. But he just told Hummingbird to get out of her clothes. Everything. Take *everything* off, he said."

You ou want me to do *what?*"

"I said clothes. To the skin. Jewelry. All of it, out the window, and do it now."

"Stop the car and let me out!"

They were in the park, northbound, east of the reservoir and close to Fifth Avenue—so close that through the trees Sharan could see the furnishings in empty Art Deco lobbies of old apartment buildings. But not a soul in sight. Then Mount Sinai Hospital. The old car doing fifty, fifty-five. Too fast to bail out, and there was no door handle on her side. The car rattled at that speed, but cornered well, and the engine sounded powerful. Instead of stopping he ran a light at the Ninety-sixth Street transverse. He had not looked at her, nor had he looked back for possible pursuers. Their speed increased. They passed taxis, a slow Cadillac motley with religious emblems and bumper stickers. *Jesus Salva*. Spanish Harlem. The drive curved away from upper Fifth and back into the park.

Observing, absorbing herself in detail to keep her emotions out of this predicament, Sharan studied him and tried to figure out his game. Kidnapping already, possible assault—actual assault if he made her strip, even if he didn't touch her. He'd been planning this, watching her. His profile, the high cheekbones, hadn't she seen him once before, from almost this same angle? She shuffled probabilities with intuition and played a hunch.

"You're Dempsey Wingo."

He produced, with a magician's ease and deftness, a wicked-looking hunting knife in his right hand, blade angled above the steering wheel.

"I'll do what talking is necessary. You don't talk until I'm sure it's a private conversation we're having."

"Put the knife away," Sharan said desperately. "I'm afraid of knives."

He replied by yanking the wheel and driving them off the roadway, up a wooded slope and along what might have been an equestrian trail, in what seemed to be a nearly lightless, desolate area of Central Park. Rough going. Sharan's head hit the unpadded ceiling of the Bondo Special and she bit her tongue. The car jolted to a stop. Sharan held her head with both hands, as if trying to keep a grip on her courage. But he had her nearly petrified.

Dempsey transferred the Green River knife to his left hand, opened his door, reached for Sharan and pulled her out of the car. She stumbled on the ground and fell to her knees. She couldn't see anything of Manhattan from where she kneeled. Except for the noise of a jet heading for LaGuardia and more distant city sounds, they might have been deep within a primeval wilderness.

"Don't," Sharan said, in a strangled voice.

"Sorry. Just do what I tell you from now on."

Sharan looked up, at the point of his knife.

"Oh, God. Not that, please, Jesus and Mary, don't, not ag—no, *no, what are you doing to me?*"

NYPD is on the scene first, in that part of the park known as the Ramble. Coleman Dane is four minutes behind them, traveling in a three-car caravan filled with Justice Department special deputies, plus loaners from the FBI. Two NYPD helicopters are in the vicinity, at three hundred feet, scouring the woods with searchlights.

A little distance from the spot where the Bondo Special leaked oil, still warm to the touch on a warm night, Sharan's clothing is flung in tatters: the remains of a blouse and twill pants, her underthings. Her shoes are untouched. A pair of earrings, costume jewelry, has been ground under someone's heel on a rock. Her handbag has been emptied. Her Cartier watch and her Mexican silver cross, still transmitting, hang from the tip of a leafy branch of a sapling.

Dane retrieves the cross and stares at it, wordlessly.

"No sign of a body yet," one of the cops reports to him.

Dane stirs, a little shiver across the shoulders, and continues staring at the cross.

The coveralls he'd had her put on smelled of the sewer. Sharan slumped in the front seat of the Bondo Special, arms folded, no longer trying to talk to him. He hadn't said a word since they'd left the park. Now they were almost across the Queensboro Bridge. Her mouth was completely dry, she felt wrung out from tension but not in any danger. For now. He'd had her where he wanted her, nude and vulnerable, and had shown not the slightest interest in her body. Except to get her dressed again, once he made sure she wasn't wearing a wire. Blue work shirt, stiff with dried sweat at the armpits, a railroader's billed cap, clunky steel-toed shoes that didn't halfway fit. But maybe he'd made a mistake, the steel reinforced toes—Sharan had resolved to go for his shins and his knees at the first opportunity. When he was down, clog dance on his balls.

At least he'd put his knife away, after quickly slashing the clothes from her body. It was an eight hundred and fifty-dollar blouse, from Bergdorf's; Esther was an impulsive gift-giver. Sharan would have taken it off, but he was in too much of a hurry to give her the chance.

In Queens he took Atlantic Avenue to the BQE, then south. Staying within the speed limit. No hurry now. Sharan sighed a couple of times.

"So your name is Sharan Norbeth, and you're Esther's newest pet."

The sound of his voice, after so much worrisome silence, startled Sharan.

"I'm not anybody's pet," she said.

"Then why do the Feds have you on a leash?"

"You must be crazy. Did a bull stomp on your head and spill half your brains?"

He grinned slightly. "Esther tell you all about me?"

"Where're you taking me?"

"Home."

"Where do you live?"

"I live in Brooklyn. Your date tonight is the number two man at the Justice Department. Fate or coincidence?"

"What are you talking about?"

"The Feds have you, did have you, under constant surveillance. So the transmitter, now that I've had time to think about it, is probably in that good-looking cross you wore, that you fiddled with all the time. If I noticed, Esther has probably noticed. Or Mardie. Those two you don't want to fuck with, I don't care how smart you think you are. The fact is, you're probably an amateur. It's the prosthetic hand, isn't it? That's what the job required—another crippled sister, easy prey for somebody as bent as you think I am."

"Bent? I said *crazy*. Kidnapping me while Cole was away from the table for five—"

"I went to a lot of trouble, you'll have to agree. Why? Maybe for nothing, who knows. We'll talk. We've got plenty of time. At least you're not in danger anymore."

"Oh, *really?*"

"I could as easily have come up to you in that restaurant, slipped a knife blade into your armpit and down through the heart, then walked out with no fuss while you quietly lay there, head on the table, swelling up from five quarts of loose blood."

"What you're saying—some twisted thought process you think is perfectly logical—you've saved my life?"

"Could be. The point is, I got to you and so could anyone else, so much for your guaranteed protection. If that's how they sold you in the first place. One more thing. My thought processes are a lot more linear than those of Scott Trevellian, and probably his brother, Dix. One of them may be partly responsible for the disappearance of five or six other crippled cuties. Also I believe I'm thinking more clearly than that cynical asshole at the Justice Department who has set you up to be next, little darlin'. Yeah, I'd say I did you a good turn tonight."

"Thank you. These clothes stink. You couldn't find better?"

"Where we're going, you'll blend right in."

"What did you mean, *partly* responsible?"

"Still on the job? You've got good ears."

"I was CID, Germany, four years. Military police before that. I know how to—"

"Take care of yourself? You're in the wrong orbit already. Gravity will pull you down, pull you toward the constellated fire, until there's nothing left, no star for the Seventh Sister, just a cinder in space."

"Interesting you should put it that way."

"What way?"

"Burning up in orbit."

"What about it?"

"Nice imagery."

"I mean, what *about* it, Sharan?"

"I don't owe you anything."

"I think you do. I opened your eyes tonight, Sharan. What is it worth to you?"

"I've been kidnapped. I'm a hostage. This is a hostage situation. We are not going to get on a first-name basis."

"Call me Dempsey. You're not a hostage. That presupposes a demand for something or other. The late lamented rifleman would have described this as a get-acquainted kidnapping."

"Cole is looking for me. The FBI. Everybody. You don't stand a chance."

"Lotsa luck," Dempsey said nonchalantly. "Coleman Dane, right? Do the stars come out in your eyes when you speak his name? Yes they do. He's your lover, isn't he?"

"I am not going to discuss—"

"He's your lover. That makes it worse. What a prick. One of these days I'll go to the trouble to tell him so."

"We have nothing more to say to each other."

"Would you like to meet Scott Trevellian?"

After a few moments Sharan said cautiously, "Why should I?"

"Put it this way. I think Scott should meet you. It might be worthwhile. Or it could blow what's left of his functioning mind past the Pleiades. But I lean toward catharsis. In a way, Scott just might have been expecting you for some time now."

Sharan made a fist with her prosthetic hand. "What makes you think so?"

"The Pleiades. Scott's referred to them before, in the E-mail I get from him. Seven daughters of Atlas, who placed them with the stars in the constellation of Taurus, the object being to keep them away from the lust of Orion. But only six of them can be seen. There's another, the Lost Pleiad, who seems to be hiding. Why don't we call the missing one—Sharan? Scott's expecting you, all right. Fate, not coincidence."

"Esther said you used to be a playwright. What's this, *Grand Guignol*?"

"Uh-uh. There's no reason to be afraid of Scott. He's a victim himself, not a murderer."

"So you think it's been Dix all along."

"No," Dempsey said. "It's not Dix. It's Esther. The only thing I don't understand is, why?"

Given the event he'd staged, and his obvious paranoia, Sharan wasn't all that surprised to be escorted by Dempsey Wingo down into the abandoned rail tunnel, to an underground station unvisited by trains for more than a century. Into chill silence, where rumblings from other deep tunnels were so muted she felt rather than heard them.

He'd said something about dinner. He opened two cans of chicken and dumplings and heated them in a dented pan on a two-burner stove. He made hot tea, and gave Sharan a ratty quilted jacket to wear because she was trembling in the fifty-five-degree air. She forced herself to express gratitude for each intended kindness, but ate very little out of the pan they shared, like subterranean hoboes hoping to hear a ghostly whistle, waiting for an eternal journey to resume.

Esther, Sharan thought, had been accurate in all of her explanations and judgments of her former husband. Berserk love had turned him into something slightly monstrous, and never mind how he looked with his head shaved. She wasn't afraid of Dempsey. All of his animus was directed at Esther. He couldn't stop talking about her; rather, the baleful, homicidal Esther he had invented while in thrall to her strongly erotic influence. But as he talked, or rambled, Sharan drifted into a fogging dolor, wondering if Dempsey's irrational claim that he'd rescued and was keeping her from certain harm would translate into a term of captivity. She'd tried to memorize the way in, down a manhole and through a long utility run, but the distance underground was considerable, the light poor, making any kind of break looked like a losing proposition for now. Better to get something out of the relationship he wanted to establish. But when she tried to redirect Dempsey to his offer to take her to Scott Trevellian, he hedged, wouldn't talk about Scott, renewed his efforts to convince her that only Esther had had a motive to bomb Lew Carbine to smithereens. *Grand Guignol* again. Characters, no convincing plot. His obsessions the smouldering residue of a failed talent. She only half listened to Dempsey, because his computer was printing out something on a desk in a corner of the old railway station.

Four big vans parked on a Brooklyn street, engines running. One van contains an FBI hostage rescue unit Coleman Dane is determined not to use. Another is filled with sophisticated equipment that can detect and provide an image of living bodies through walls or beneath city streets.

Two-twenty A.M.

The Bureau's SAC in New York has one of those sculpted death's-head faces: bleached long teeth, very little flesh, skin the color of barely cooked pork. His eyes are as bitter as poisoned wells. He isn't pleased to be under Dane's direction, and so far has made a bad show of hiding his disapproval.

In the NYNEX van an area operations manager for the telephone company and a Brooklyn Union Gas Company supervisor are viewing tunnel schematics on two computer screens.

"What sort of alarm system does Wingo have?"

Dane and Mr. Marlowe Hare are sitting knee to knee in the cramped interior of the van. Marlowe blots his forehead with a banana-yellow silk handkerchief.

"None that I knows of. But he has sharp ears, Mr. Wingo, and he's always on the alert."

"Does he carry a gun?"

"Don't reckon that's his style."

"But you wouldn't know for sure."

"No, sir."

Dane turns his head and looks at the infrared images of Dempscy Wingo and Sharan Norbeth in the restored Long Island railroad station, two blocks south and thirty-five feet beneath Court Street. They haven't changed positions in twenty minutes. He wonders if she's tied to something. If Wingo is asleep.

"Mr. Dane?"

"What."

"Why don't you let me go down there by myself, try to talk to him. He ain't going to do me no harm."

"You're sure of that."

"Unless something happen, and he be completely round the bend."

"Well, give it some thought, Marlowe. Has Wingo acted rationally so far tonight?"

Marlowe gives it some thought. "I know he must have his purposes, even if it don't seem entirely copacetic to us. But I truly believe I wouldn't be in no danger from Mr. Wingo."

The Special Agent in Charge says, "Would like to convince you this is a situation that demands a BSU-trained negotiator. We can't be sure what type of sadistic nutbar we're dealing with here. To my mind, slashing her clothing was an act of protomutilation. Sounds like a regressive necrophile I talked out of a sorority house in Philadelphia a few years ago. You should've seen what he did to a couple of those young girls with a carpenter's auger."

Marlowe sighs and raises his eyes to heaven. Dane ignores the SAC and says to the NYNEX manager, "How many ways out of that underground station?"

"That we know about? Dozens."

"That you know about," Dane says grimly. "He hears something, he vanishes. With Sharan."

The SAC says, checking the computer schematics, "If you feel there's no time to talk, there are places where we can post snipers. We can disconnect Wingo's power source at any time. Wadcutters, minimum ricochet potential."

"No guns, for the last time. *No fucking guns.*"

Silence, except for brief transmissions between the NYNEX command post and the other units on the street.

"He knows I'm up here right now, with all of you," Marlowe says. "Think he don't?"

"What does that mean?" Dane says, with renewed interest in Marlowe Hare.

"He's put his trust in me, that I won't do something to get nobody killed. Please, Mr. Dane. I can deal with Dempsey Wingo. Let me try to calm the fluctuations."

Dane stares at Marlowe for five seconds. And makes up his mind.

They took a break. Dempsey made coffee, his back turned, while Sharan, having lasted as long as she could, used his small toilet. No privacy made her highly nervous, so she hung a curtain of chatter.

"What made you do it? Ride bulls, I mean. There can't be much money in it."

"Day money will add up, if you're consistent. And if you make it to the National Finals Rodeo, which I did four times, there's big prize money. Nowadays they have a pro bull riders' circuit with a million-dollar payoff in Vegas every year. Rodeo's changed since I've been out of it. The champion cowboys have sponsors, like golf pros. A few of them fly to the big rodeos in private jets. I drove pickups, none of which had less than a hundred and fifty thousand miles on the clock. Slept in the truck most nights to save money. My best year, I made thirty-one thousand bucks. My medical bills and other expenses ran about half that amount."

"So—"

"I liked bulls. I liked their meanness in the arena. I liked the fear, and the competition. Four nights a week, as often as I could take the pounding. They have the power; all you need is the will to get up there in Wranglers and chaps with your crotch stuffed full of maxipads and ride for eight seconds. The bulls average about two thousand pounds apiece. They come out of the bucking chute like an earthquake tearing loose. You can study the great bulls and know their moves, but you never know enough. The technique is simple. Keep the right arm bent and the back straight. Stay in the middle. If he slings you backward, you'll hit the deck just in time to meet his hooves when he spins around. If you get forward on the bull with your head down, there are bulls who will head-butt and shatter every bone in your face. Yee-hah! You seldom get a really high score on a ranked bull. Even if you make it all the way to the whistle, he's left his mark on you. I can lie awake at night in pain and think about the pins and compression plates that hold my bones together and the kidneys that aren't likely to get me through a normal life span, and then I remember the faces of the bulls who did all that to me—bulls with names like Annihilator, Tuff Enuf and Twilight Zone, and I'll tell you true: it's like remembering the faces of long-gone lovers. What do you like in your coffee?"

"Sugar," Sharan said, refastening the straps of her grimy coveralls. She drifted toward the rolltop desk where his computer, modem and printer were plugged into a surge protector. The cartoon on the laptop's screen, when she was close enough to see it, was a cute mailbox with the red flag up. Dempsey had E-mail waiting.

"What does your friend from the Justice Department take?"

"Coffee? He doesn't drink coffee. He likes chocolate milk. Why?"

"He's probably upstairs by now. With an FBI SWAT team. Now I'm thinking: does he have the nerve to come down here after you, all by his lonesome?"

Conceit, cowpoke posturing, paranoia. Sharan drew her shoulders together, wondering if this time Dempsey knew what he was talking about. How could Cole have found her? She walked toward Dempsey, who was pouring coffee into thick diner mugs.

"Bad ride tonight," Sharan said. "Time for it to be over, don't you think?"

He handed her a mug, smiling skeptically. She briefly considered throwing the coffee in his face. Blinding him for a few moments. He was at arm's length. Didn't look to be on his guard, but, beat-up bones to the contrary, she knew how strong he was and she assumed his reflexes were still pretty good. The coffee in her mug was hot, but not scalding. Her chance of making a break: next to nothing.

Patience, Sharan told herself. And don't let him intimidate you again.

"I thought we were starting to get along," Dempsey chided.

"Have I had a choice?"

"You haven't told me much about your investigations."

"I don't have anything to tell you."

"You need to find out where the bodies are buried, don't you? One body. Before it's your turn."

"It's never going to be *my* turn."

Dempsey shook his head.

"Haven't learned a thing. You're going to die, all right. Then disappear without a trace. It's how they keep up appearances in the Trevellian family. If you don't believe that, then nobody can help you. Darlin', I have tried my best."

"Maybe Scott Trevellian can help. You were going to take me to him. It was my fate, you said. But you can't seem to make up your mind about Scott. Victim, murderer. Victim of what? Oh, right. Esther, of course. Evil personified. But I don't see her that way. It's Dix. Why? Because the longer I know him—the closer I come to the heart of Dix Trevellian—the more I don't understand. Artist's intuition. I can't draw him. I've tried to do a few sketches, from memory. I get the look, the charm is mostly there, but there's something else that refuses to be known. Hiding. It chills me."

Dempsey said, after long, somber moments, "Why don't you just get out of there?"

"Why don't I get out of here, first? Maybe we can talk—some other time, in a place where I feel—a hell of a lot more secure than I do right now."

Dempsey shrugged, and smiled regretfully.

"Too late. Didn't you hear? We've got company. It appears the Feds have arrived to take ol' Dempsey out."

They have used the hooded flashlights and then the night vision goggles to get this far, to the bulkhead of the abandoned railroad tunnel.

Now the glasses are no longer necessary. Sound carries down here. Dane has heard their voices, coming from the station platform that lies perhaps two hundred yards from the bulkhead.

"Far enough," Dempsey says, scarcely having to raise his voice for his words to reach them. "That you, Marlowe?"

Marlowe Hare stops, a hand on Dane's elbow. Movement on the station platform; two insubstantial shadows flicker across the vaulted tunnel ceiling.

"Yes, sir, Mr. Wingo. I'm sorry. But you must have knowed I'd have to do it when they come to me."

"Don't fret, Marlowe. It's the way the world works."

"Thank you, Mr. Wingo."

"Who's with you?"

"Mr. Coleman Dane is here."

A few seconds pass, a whispered conversation, then Sharan says calmly, "Cole? I'm all right."

"Wingo?"

"Yeah."

"What the hell are you thinking about?"

"Come on down here, Guv. I've got the coffee on. We'll have a talk. I'd like to get acquainted with your mentality."

"My what?"

"It's the way he talks, Cole," Sharan says with a touch of weariness and, possibly, amusement in her voice. But distance and a slight reverberation in the tunnel is hard on nuance.

"I don't think I like you," Dempsey says, "but I could be persuaded to change my mind. Oh, I forgot. You're not a coffee drinker. Got that covered, Guv. How about a beer instead?"

Dane shakes off Marlowe's hand and walks a few feet into the tunnel.

"I want you to let Sharan go. Right now! I want to see her."

"I'm not holding her. But I have the notion she wants you to come and get her. Because you were kind of careless leaving her unescorted tonight. You know how women can be."

"I'm not armed," Dane says.

"Wouldn't mean a thing to me if you were. Come on. You're invited too, Mr. Hare."

"I'm humbled by your forgiveness, Mr. Wingo." And what irony there may be in his words is lost in the distorting acoustics of the old railroad tunnel.

They listened to the two men approaching the station, following the beam of an electric torch down the rounded middle of the packed dirt floor. Dempsey took two brews out of the refrigerator. Sharan watched him.

Whatever was wrong with Dempsey Wingo, still he had nerve to spare. She was almost forced to admire him.

"Last call," he said cheerfully, turning to catch her eye. She wouldn't look away. "You can walk with the Guv, or you can leave with me. Either way, you're out. But only one way, as I see it, do you have a chance to go on living."

"With you?"

"That's right."

"You poor, demented, son of a bitch. They'll kill you before the night's over."

In the broken notch between his front teeth, Dempsey pulled the cap off a beer bottle and spat it on the floor. Then he did it again. One of the beers spewed some foam. The foam dripped from his chin. He stood there grinning as Coleman Dane came into view, and stopped below the station platform, Marlowe Hare standing a little behind him, shadowy. He looked from Dane to Marlowe, and a flare of recognition appeared in his green eye.

"*Et tu*, Mr. Hare?" he said, as the Teflon-coated Sig Sauer automatic came up in Marlowe's hand. Dempsey's grin got bigger.

Because he didn't seem to understand that he was about to be shot, Sharan took a quick first step and aimed for Dempsey's knees.

"Sharan, look out!" Dane warned.

The lights in the station went out. Simultaneously Sharan jolted Wingo with a rolling block, moving him out of the line of fire as Marlowe Hare was squeezing the trigger of his pistol.

Gunflashes. Two shots, echoing through the tunnel. Beer and glass from the shattered bottle Dempsey had been holding rained on Sharan's head and shoulders. She was flat on the station floor, a hand on him. Then he pulled quickly away from her. Seconds later the beams from two electric torches swept across the station platform.

"Where'd he go?" Marlowe Hare said in bewilderment. Sharan stayed down, looking at him. Marlowe was crouched in the tunnel, his flashlight in his left hand, gun hand extended, describing a precise arc with the barrel of the Sig Sauer, right to left and back again.

Sharan shook her head to get rid of some of the glass fragments, looking too, wondering.

"Stay down!" Dane made an angry move toward Marlowe Hare, who shifted the black handgun cautiously in his direction.

"Sorry, Mr. Dane. Forgot to tell you that I done left your employ."

Dempsey's laughter drifted to them, from another level, a deeper tunnel, a loner's mysterious space.

"I'm a playwright," he boasted. "Don't you think I know how to stage an exit?"

SEVENTEEN

THE DEAFENING
CRIMSON

It wasn't *my* idea," the Special Agent in Charge insisted. "I had nothing to do with it. He had a gun, sure, we knew he was carrying, why not, he worked for you, didn't he?"

"I want him. I want his ass, right now!"

"We don't have him."

"Telling me you don't have him. Where did he fucking *go?*"

"Hare," Sharan said dispiritedly.

Coleman Dane glanced at her. "What?"

She raised her eyes, an unfriendly look. She was nursing a bruised elbow from hitting the floor a little awkwardly. Also there was something wrong with her prosthetic hand; it wouldn't work. Battery terminal jarred loose, or something.

"If he knew where to find Wingo, knew about his hideout, he had time to do some exploring down here, didn't he? Find a convenient way out, if he needed one? The hare has gone to ground. Does anyone want coffee? It's still hot."

One of Dane's men said from the station platform, "Found it."

Sharan walked a few steps and looked down at the recessed switch, the size of a silver dollar, in the station floor. She pressed down with the toe of a work shoe. The lights went out again. After a couple of seconds she turned them back on.

Voices in tunnels and utility runs around them as the manhunt continued. Voices on walkies. Dark blue body armor, forage caps, assault weapons, men poking through a maze and finding nothing. Sharan sat down and removed the work shoe, which rubbed in the wrong places. Someone had brought her own shoes from the Ramble in an evidence bag, very thoughtful. She put them on, walked over to Dempsey Wingo's computer station and began sorting through un-labeled storage diskettes.

"Better print out everything," she said.

"Why?" Dane asked her.

"Wingo knows where Scott Trevellian is. That's where he'll turn up, eventually. Scott sent him a lot of E-mail, it's how they stayed in touch. Some of it may be on these disks. If we're finished here, I need to get a bath and change clothes. Some breakfast would help, my stomach is growling. Then you and I have to talk. Privately, Cole."

At five-thirty they had soft-boiled eggs and Belgian waffles in Cole-man Dane's suite at a small expensive hotel off Park Avenue South.

"You can't protect me. Wingo proved it."

"What do you want to do now, Sharan?"

"I want to sleep most of the day. Then I want to pack up and go home."

"I don't blame you."

"He doesn't blame me," Sharan said with a wry smile, finishing off her waffle with a jolt of Napoleon brandy.

"I still think we can ensure your safety. We've learned something. There's additional measures we can take."

"I said I want to go home. I didn't say I was going to."

He looked at her for a few seconds, baffled, reached for the brandy snifter in her hand, added to what she had poured and drank it down.

The phone rang. Dane talked for a little while. Sharan went to the bathroom and brushed her teeth. The brandy had helped, but she still felt a little early-morning nausea. She came back and sat on a love seat beside him and laid her head on his shoulder.

"Marlowe Hare gave us the slip."

"Maybe Wingo is right about his ex-wife. Maybe she is the monster he claims. But I don't see it, Daner. I just don't believe it."

"She hates Wingo enough to have paid Mr. Hare a considerable sum to bump him off."

"Is that the way it was?"

"No other explanation makes any sense."

"What about Lew Carbine? Where's the motive? Speaking of motives, why kill six seriously impaired, helpless women? Why and how? No. None of it works. Scott Trevellian may be able to provide a link, but where is Scott Trevellian?"

"You have that glow again. Can't let it drop and go back to Georgia, can you?"

"What time are you due back on Capitol Hill?"

"Nine o'clock this morning."

"Is that why you haven't taken your shoes off?"

"I'll be back tonight. Get some sleep. Wait for me."

"Maybe. If I need to know something, I mean some research your office could provide, who would I call?"

"One of my horseholders. I'll leave you a couple of numbers. What are you going to do?"

"When I wake up? Go through Dempsey Wingo's E-mail. That should keep me busy for a while."

"We've already looked. Nothing useful there."

Sharan picked up a folder of printout from the floor, glanced at the top sheet, handed it to Dane.

"How do you say this?"

"*Omnia mutantur, nos et mutamur in illis.*"

"Meaning?"

" 'All things change, and we change with them.' "

"Scott Trevellian's last E-mail message, received last night. I wonder what he's thinking. I'm really dying to meet him."

Dane yawned. "Bad choice of words. I'd better shower and shave. Car's picking me up in twenty minutes. Don't let anyone know where you are. Maybe you shouldn't go out again until I get back. If you do, just leave a message, Hummingbird."

Sharan closed shining eyelids, shining like the rest of her brutally scrubbed skin beneath a hotel robe, and she touched the silver cross as if she were meditating.

"Cole."

"Yes."

"Is there any chance you wanted Wingo shot, because he made you look like a fool?"

When she looked at him again, eyes slow to focus, somnambulant, he was rubbing his stubbled jaw as if she'd let fly with her fists.

"That is a goddamned ridiculous thing for you to say."

"I don't say ridiculous things. I had a very bad time tonight. My clothes were removed at knifepoint in Central Park. I stood there feeling like a dim-witted whore in a slasher movie. His blade never touched my skin, but if it had I know I would have freaked. And I'm telling you if I'd had a gun in that tunnel I would have shot him, Cole. No hesitation, like the last time." She closed her good hand over the passive prosthesis. "Shot and killed the motherfucker myself. So if you set it up I really don't care, but I had to ask; it's not the time to let any question go unasked, is it? I have to look long and hard in all the dark corners. Too much is at risk for me not to. Oh, more than I can tell you right now, lover. So you weren't responsible and you haven't lied to me. Then hurry back. Because I need you. All things change, and we change with them. And hope for the best."

Sleep, but not what she'd longed for. Too many reality dreams, replays of incidents of the night before. She had to go back and do it again because she'd been careless the first time. The matter of identities. Faces. Dempsey Wingo, Dix Trevellian, Coleman Dane. Prove who you are, or I will not go with you, she said to all of them. But it was already too late.

Waking up with a backache that required a tai chi adjustment. Then half an hour of near-blankness and inertia, looking out at a city brassy bright and cooking in its humidity, wishing vaguely for a cat in her lap, Georgia's rolling pine green, homely things. House paint, an old frayed shirt, some sense of accomplishment as she studied the nub of an image growing, expanding like a foetus on sheets of rough heavy drawing paper. Paint on the tip of her nose, in her eyebrows. *Who I am.* The intensity, the sense of calm and balance amid chaos when work was going well.

But nothing felt right today. She'd been taken for a ride. Called Dane a fool, but she knew rightly who the fool had been.

Her pain returned. She needed a church and she wondered if she needed to see a doctor. But her discomfort might have been psychological. She was angry, very angry with herself. She settled for a drugstore on Third Avenue and a chat with the pharmacist, a droll Jewish girl who, it turned out, was married to a guy from Conyers, just a hop and a skip away from Jubilation County. The pharmacist made some recommendations about what Sharan ought to take and what to avoid. Sharan had always mistrusted drugs, even aspirin.

Back in the hotel suite, quiet, the sun on the other side of the narrow street now. At last peaceful, able to concentrate, she read through the collected E-mail of Scott Trevellian to Dempsey Wingo. Scott's psychic pain became too much for her after a while. She had jotted down some observations, a couple of questions. Esther could easily have answered the questions for her. But there was no way.

She decided to construct a portrait of Scott, whom she had seen only as a half-grown boy in home movies, from those images and from Cole's description of what he now looked like. It was something to do, and working on the portrait, however inaccurate it might turn out to be, was a form of meditation that might uncover a spark or two in the ash heap of Scott's own bitter meditations and recriminations. Her tools were colored pencils and an unlined pad of paper from the stationer's on the corner.

From Washington, Coleman Dane called the hotel suite at one forty-five and again at ten minutes to three. No answer either time. He checked with his office at the Justice Department to see if Sharan had been in contact with one of the assistants whose names and numbers he had given to her. She had not. The surveillance team on the day shift reported that Hummingbird had taken three short walks in the early afternoon. Her last visit was to the library. She was now back in the suite, presumably napping. Not transmitting. Dane called the hotel again, left a number where Sharan could get back to him, and went off to an early dinner with his two children and his ex-wife, who had just announced her engagement to the former Secretary of State Misty didn't much care for.

The New York Public Library was six blocks from the hotel. Sharan spent forty minutes there, researching everything that had appeared in print about Scott Trevellian. *Business Week, Fortune, Who's Who*. No interviews, no photos. A total of about eight paragraphs, five sentences of biography.

Harvard graduate. Two months shy of his twentieth birthday. Double major, Asian philosophy and Japanese literature. He had written his senior thesis on Bashō.

The mind of Scott Trevellian, slowly becoming more accessible to Sharan in spite of his illness.

Hi, Rosalie. How's my old roomie?"

"Sha-rann! Good Lord, gal, I thought you'd dropped off the face of the earth!"

"Didn't you get my Christmas card?"

"Noooo."

"Damn. Time I revised my Databook. I was hoping you'd still be at old Fort Fumble. When did you move up to the Joint Chiefs, Major? I am some kind of impressed."

"Six months ago, and, girl, I am loving it. Just finished an NMCC exercise, so I'm out of the barrel for a few days. How *are* you? *Where* are you, Washington? Can we get together?"

"I'm in New York, Rosalie. I'm going to have a show."

"You are? When? Am *I* invited? Can't believe this. You're having a *show* in New York! You gonna be famous or some thing?"

"Too early to tell. Maybe I'm just a three-minute egg. But you'll be there."

"It is so *good* to hear your voice. Know who I ran into the other day?"

Sharan chatted awhile with her West Point roommate before getting down to business.

"Rosalie, who do you know would have access to the Japanese community in the New York area?"

"You needing an introduction to somebody?"

"What I need is, oh, a correspondent for one of the Japanese wire services or networks who knows everybody. Maybe a military liaison to the UN delegation."

"I see. Let me mull that over. What are you up to?"

"The Japanese are starting to buy art again."

"Say no more. What I'll do, call the Japan desk at DIA. Ask Eddy Nazzarro to work on some names. Need this right away?"

"COB, if it's not asking too much."

"Sounds like an easy request. Let me have your number in New York. Did you hear Connie Berkmar went to work for Raytheon? Executive Vice President. Oh, does her shit smell? Not likely."

"Only a few of the group still on active, I guess. But good for Connie. Thanks for the favor, Ros."

Jane reached her at ten forty-five.

"At long last you answer the phone."

"Sorry, Daner. I've been in and out."

"I know."

"Yes, of course. You would know. You're not coming tonight."

"Just can't get away. I'm sorry. Tomorrow for sure. What are you doing?"

"Oh, sketching. Missing you."

"I'm sorry."

"You're sorry, I'm sorry, we're sorry, just get here. Please."

"How are things with the Trevellians?"

"Dix is out of town, so I'm not being pelted with roses and gifts of expensive jewelry. Esther, I don't know, I haven't wanted to call her. I'm taking a time-out, waiting for you. Why do I love you so much?"

"I love you, too."

"I'm scared."

"Nothing's going to happen to you."

"What do you mean? It's already happened. Goodnight, Cole."

She read herself to sleep. Bashō, Buson, Issa, translations of haiku in a book she had bought at Barnes and Noble. Cozying up a little closer to the mind of Scott Trevellian.

> *honeysuckle*
> > *silence*
> > > *of*
> *hummingbird's wings*
> *the deafening crimson*

It was six-thirty the next evening when Coleman Dane slumped into a seat in his Agusta helicopter and catnapped on the flight to New York. There was an equinoctial storm front moving in from Pennsylvania, dropping temperatures nearly thirty degrees from the sweltering highs of the past few days. Turbulence woke Dane up fifteen minutes before they landed. He was met at the East Thirty-fourth Street Heliport by a Justice Department car and driver. On the way to the hotel he tried to call Sharan again. No answer. The team leader of the surveillance unit assigned to Hummingbird reported that she had gone out a couple of times earlier in the day, stocked up on magazines and art supplies at a Madison Avenue store. Sharan had sequestered herself a little before noon. She had obeyed Dane's instruction to leave her transmitter on, even while sleeping. Right now all it was picking up was the laugh track from a rerun of *America's Funniest Home Videos.*

The flight from Pittsburgh had been delayed for over an hour due to bad weather in Western Pennsylvania. Thunderstorms, hail. It was now due in at ten-fifteen.

Dempsey didn't mind hanging around LaGuardia. He had nothing else to do, and he wasn't worried about NYPD making him. He had hair again, gray, a short Roman cut, and a gray mustache. His eyes were bright blue. The art of theatrical makeup had always interested Dempsey, and he'd long been friendly with a couple of the best makeup artists in the business. He'd ditched the gold earring and recapped his front tooth. He wore tinted glasses halfway down the bridge of his nose and carried a spare laptop with accessories. He had four thousand dollars in cash tucked inside an elbow brace, not visible beneath his farmer-boy checked shirt. He also wore a tweed jacket and Levi's.

Under his right arm there was a bandage covering the three-inch-long furrow left by the first of the nine-millimeter bullets Marlowe Hare had fired in his direction. The wound was clean and closing, the pain negligible.

He wondered what flight Mr. Hare had caught out of town, and how much bounty he had collected from Esther. Of course by now she knew Marlowe hadn't been successful. Dempsey had phoned in the glad news himself.

Esther, Esther. Goddamn they were *on* again, and how he loved it! Just possibly the excitement of having her skizzerfrantic brother safely home would do for Esther's libido what a near-miss bullet had done for him. Anything for Esther. His battered sense of honor, his flickering chance for heaven—every chip pushed to the middle of the table. Esther's bounty, her escalated desire to have him killed, only fanned Dempsey's ardor and his competitive spirit.

Draw your last card, Esther. Play for my soul, win if you can. As long as we go to hell together.

Dane let himself into the hotel suite and found it empty. In the middle of the king-sized bed a folded note lay beneath her silver cross and chain.

Hope you won't take this the wrong way, Cole. I did some looking around and I think I know where Scott Trevellian is. Also I think given his mental state I should go alone, no big police escort that would only serve to intimidate or frighten the poor guy. Dempsey Wingo said that in a way Scott is probably expecting me. We know he doesn't have a capacity for violence. So I'll be okay. As soon as I've seen him I'll call you.

Much love, S.

After leaving the hotel Sharan had taken a taxi uptown to the New York bureau of NHK, the Japanese government–owned television colossus. There she had a deli lunch in the office of the assistant bureau chief, whose name was Johnny Chiba, L.A. native and recent Columbia J-school graduate.

"That's a West Point ring? You're pretty well connected, I don't get calls from the Pentagon very often. Would this be official business?"

"I'm just doing a favor for a friend."

"Who?"

"If you're able to do me any good, Mr. Chiba, then I could mention a couple of names. But it's only a small sad story, a family thing. Not of interest to a television audience. FYI only. Agreed?"

"If I don't quite agree with you?"

"Then you'll miss out on having a friend who can be a very powerful friend."

"Or a serious enemy."

"Oh, I'm not sure I'd go that far," Sharan said, with a smile that implied otherwise.

Chiba smiled, too, and turned to his computer terminal. "Let's see what we can find out. What's the name again?"

"Hideo Kuhara. Harvard, class of Seventy-eight."

Scott Trevellian watched the storm as it approached, then crossed the Hudson River, stood in it near the edge of the bluff until he was drenched and shaking from the sudden drop in temperature.

Was it possible, as D. H. Lawrence had said, for a soul to get to heaven in one leap?

Yes, Felicia answered him. *But he also said, you leave a demon in its place.*

She was the only one of the Lost Ladies who had remained at this crucial hour. All but Felicia disapproving, unwilling to be a part of the necessary ritual. One by one they had left the phenomenal world for the clouding sky, dimming as they rose, disappearing with the other celestial lights. Their place of waiting. He would never see them again. But there never had been anything he could do for them, anyway.

The slashing rain drove him with his burden of failure back to the conservatory, where he stripped to the skin and took a hot shower, scrubbing himself until nearly every inch of his skin was red. Felicia was still there, but she had nothing else to say. Having dried himself, Scott lay faceup on his spartan bed. The palm of his left hand covered his navel. His right hand gripped the nacre hilt of a knife, thin blade wrapped in fragile silk, very old, in a sandalwood sheath. A gift, years ago, from his friend Hideo Kuhara. The storm passed and it was quiet except for a drip of water from a skylight where the caulking had worn away. It made a splash puddle on the moonlit tiles near his bed. Felicia kneeled beside the puddle combing her hair, watching him. The motions of her hands, the passage of the tortoiseshell comb through mildly crackling hair: the essence of *fūryū*. Her artful femininity and elegance. He thought of a line of Japanese verse he had translated once: *Before me, the mountain pass: my heart holds the moon tonight.*

Felicia paused and smiled at Scott, knowing what was in his thoughts. *Home.* She laid her comb aside and courteously turned her back to him, dark hair flowing, head bowed.

By the side of the highway Sharan waited out the worst of the rain in her rented Toyota, then drove on to the Hudson River estate of Hideo Kuhara's father, where she found a gatekeeper on duty. Japanese, limited English. But Johnny Chiba had anticipated that.

On the back of his business card Chiba had inscribed ideograms. The guard read the message, and nodded.

"Messer Scott. Yes. You must go that way, then that way. Conservatory. You see from here." He pointed.

Rising above a windy silhouetted line of deodars, the conservatory's central vault with its decorative iron filigree shone against the sky.

"Thank you."

The serpentine drives that connected all corners of the nineteen-

acre property were of crushed red-brick, so well shaped and maintained there was little standing water after the deluge. A sloping
treeless lawn behind the main house afforded an uninterrupted vista
of the river and Bear Mountain, which was immediately south of the
military reservation where Sharan had spent four years of her life,
working harder than a blacksmith to prove her worth. Wind gusts
rocked her compact car. She passed a couple of stone cottages, the
drive bearing right, away from the river canyon, and passed through
a grove of cedars. The conservatory appearing in isolation just ahead,
a gorgeous anachronism lightly misted, at its best by moonlight, a
dream structure for a Renaissance masque.

Sharan closes the door of the rented Toyota and stands looking at the
entrance to the conservatory. There is a stone walk around the building, a fleur-de-lis in flagstone in front of it, sundial at the point. The
wind prys and pushes and bumps her like a big clumsy dog. There
are no lights inside the glass conservatory. She has the prickling sensation of being observed. But most of the panes are opaque from
condensation. Her ears are cold. She hears nothing but the insistent
wind.

Hands in the pocket of her nylon raincoat, she walks slowly toward
the conservatory. The narrow wrought-iron door of the vestibule,
eight feet high, is standing open a couple of inches: heavy, even the
wind can't budge it.

Sharan pushes with both hands, the hinges groaning.

As she sets foot inside the vestibule, a scream goes through her like
a spear.

Footsteps, running.

Out of the dark, something comes at her. As the footsteps reach
the other end of the vestibule, she sees by moonlight the terrified face
of a small boy.

Seeing Sharan he stops, looks around wildly, then reverses direction
and runs back into the dark of a corridor at the rear of the conservatory.

"Mo-ther!"

"Oh, God!"

Responding to the hysteria in both voices but scared to the bone,
Sharan runs, too, toward the rear of the conservatory.

Not as dark as it seemed from the entrance, but only a quarter of the moonlight raises the level of illumination in a shedlike addition to something approaching deep gloom. Agonized sobbing. She trips over the boy, who is sitting against a corridor wall opposite several doorways, feet outstretched. He screams as if attacked.

Sharan picks herself up, turns to him. The boy huddles against the wall, trembling.

"I'm sorry I'm sorry what's—"

He shrinks from an outstretched hand. "Nono. Nono. No. No. *No!*"

"Help. Please. God help us, he's dying!"

Sharan follows the voice.

In a small room, furnished like a monastery cell, the last room down the corridor, two figures: one kneeling, another crouched. The moaning of the wind outside doesn't quite cover the sounds of a dying man struggling for breath.

A woman's face, turning to Sharan.

"Who are you?"

"Who are you?"

The woman shakes her head impatiently. "Do something! He's— Oh, Scott. Oh, Scott. We'll help you. Don't. Don't do this. Don't die."

Odor of fresh blood in the room, a lot of it. Sharan remembers, sickens. Her own blood, the crimson horror on a butcher-shop floor. The pulsating stump pushed hard into her other armpit to stop the bleeding. Kneeling on the floor and swiftly going cold. As Scott Trevellian is kneeling, naked, slumped, hands on the small hilt of the knife he has used for disembowelment. His eyes open, close. With every harsh breath more of his intestines coming out, piling around his knees.

Sharan puts a hand on the woman's shoulder. She is jolted. She resists being pulled away. Her hands stream with Scott's blood.

"Where's my son?"

"Outside."

"He saw this. He saw his *father* like this. What will I *say* to him?"

"It isn't too late. Hurry. Run to the house. Get help."

"I can't."

"Do it."

Scott's eyes have opened again. He seems to have noticed Sharan. He forms a smile.

"You're all here," he says.

The woman is backing toward the door. "*Go*," Sharan says urgently, with a motion of her prosthetic hand, and the woman is out the door, calling to the boy.

"Miranda," Scott says, through the blood thickening in his mouth and on his tongue.

"Scott, my name is Sharan."

"Sharannnn," he breathes.

"Why did you do this?"

"Tired."

"I know you must be. I'm sorry." Tears stinging her eyes. "Oh what. How am I going to tell Esther?"

"The demon. Leave behind."

"You're—I didn't understand you."

"Stop the pain."

"I can't. Oh, God, I'm so s-sorry."

"Dying. Makes me thirsty."

"I can't give you any water! Please just hang on. Maybe. M-maybe a chance, God, I don't know."

"Don't want to. Hang on." He is shuddering. She touches him. He is cold to the point of hypothermia. The blood flowing out.

"Can't see you. Are you there?"

"Scott. I need to know. What happened to them? Thursday Childs, Kerry Rogers, Felicia. The others. Do you know where they are?"

"Yes."

"Tell me."

"Why?"

"I don't want to go too."

"That's right. That's right. Because—I leave the demon behind."

"Where are they? What happened to them? It wasn't you, was it?"

"Can't see you," he says, softly. He has fallen over toward her. Sharan holds his head.

"Scott, *Scott*."

"Felicia. Robin. I don't know. So many. Esther sent them."

"Where?"

"To the furnaces."

"Oh dear God. Sweet Mother of Christ! I knew it."

Scott moans and shakes and dies in her hands, only a scalding whisper escaping him.

"Esss-therrrr!"

"*Sharan.*"

She looks up in terror as her own name is called.

In the doorway. Filling the doorway. Changed, but the shoulders are recognizable. His twangy voice.

"Oh no. Oh no."

"You have to get out of here."

"What are you doing here?"

"I brought Miranda. And Timothy, to see his father."

"They saw *this*!" Sharan groans, trembling with rage and pity.

"I didn't know. Get out now. You're already at risk. Don't make it worse for yourself."

"Help me hold him."

"I can't. Put him on the goddamn floor."

"I have to pray for him, he's—"

Two strides, he has Sharan, who is looking down; he yanks her ruthlessly off the floor by the scruff of her neck, fingers digging into her carotid artery.

"I said get out of here! Forget what you heard. Go far away while I deal with Esther."

"You?"

Dempsey pushes her out into the corridor, letting go of her bruised neck. Sharan almost falls, recovers quickly. When he comes at her again, Sharan meets him with a tai chi form called Parting a Wild Horse's Mane, and Dempsey, astonished, flies into the wall. Sharan steps back gracefully, making a forty-five- degree turn, Hands Moving Like Clouds according to the Peking form. Simultaneous blows to his ears as Dempsey staggers off the wall.

"Don't touch me again," she warns him.

Dempsey shakes his head gingerly, a little groggy. He doesn't move.

"Popped me pretty good. I think you busted an eardrum."

"One more step, I'll show you what else I can pop."

"Okay, let's make peace. We—"

"We're letting Scott die in there!"

"He's dead already. Nobody can do anything for him now. Understand? And you butt out of this. Esther is mine. My wife, my business."

"Where did they go? Miranda, the boy?"

Alarms on the property. Dempsey raises his head, listening for a couple of moments, then backs away from Sharan, toward the conservatory's entrance.

"That's it. We're out of time. I'll take care of Miranda. Get moving, if you know what's good for you."

Dempsey turns and runs. Sharan is frozen for a few moments, then goes back inside the spartan room and kneels beside Scott. His eyes are half-open, but there is no movement of the pupils, no flicker of eyelids as she leans close to him, two fingers trying to locate the pulse in his throat. Her own face is hot, flushed with the deafening crimson.

It is not for her to hand him over to God, but there is no one else. Sharan says what she can, her throat too clogged for many words, and gets out of there. Behind the wheel of the rented Toyota, she backs up in a frenzy, headlights flashing across the conservatory glass. She finds the way back to the open gates. The alarms are still whooping, lights have come on all over the estate. She can barely see for the tears in her eyes.

EIGHTEEN

AT RISING FAWN

Nothing much in the media about Scott Trevellian: dead at thirty-seven, by his own hand, following a lengthy illness. Several investigative reporters attempted to follow up; the Trevellians were always news. But an hour after Scott's death was reported to his brother and sister the law firm dedicated to the preservation of the family's privacy was hard at work, making certain that only the basic facts were released by authorities. The Kuhara family was even less interested in publicity.

There was no service. Scott was buried on Cloud Horse Mountain beside the man whom no one, except Elnora Trevellian, knew for sure was his father. Esther and Dix remained at Cloud Horse after the funeral. Secluded, presumably in mourning.

Sharan had called Esther as soon as the news was out; all of Esther's calls were being taken by secretaries. She wrote a note of condolence, messengered it to Trevellian House. The rest of the day after Scott's suicide she spent, tensely, with Coleman Dane. He needed to be in Washington, but he stayed with her. They did a tourist routine: no chauffeured car or his-and-hers bodyguards. Ordinary citizens for the day. They even rode the subway. Lunch in Chinatown. Afterward they took the ferry to the Statue of Liberty. It was cool for September but bright, the wind from the sea. He was not quite angry; nettled would be the word. A bundle of nettles pricking at her own nerves.

"Scott was a father, and we don't have a clue as to who they are. But Dempsey Wingo knows. God damn him."

Sharan was wearing a coffee-brown turtleneck knit jersey to hide the bruises Wingo's fingers had left on the side of her neck. Her voice raspy today. She had never hated anyone as much as she hated Dempsey Wingo; not even the army captain who had abused her at West Point.

"Three of them traveling together. Maybe they're still together. I did get a good likeness of Miranda, considering the available light."

"It'll take time. We'll need some luck."

"Meanwhile."

He shrugged.

"Scott's dying declaration."

"Worthless. We already knew, suspected."

"You have to examine those portable furnaces."

"Working on it. The one in Glassboro, we'll do some OSHA shuck-and-jive to gain access. But we won't find anything. Ten thousand degrees Celsius, nothing remains. Vapor."

Sharan wiped salt spray from one cheek with her sleeve and stared at the island as the approaching ferry slowed. Waiting for that thrill of recognition, a rousing sense of pride. Belief in America. The faceted stone in the captain's West Point ring had hurt her, hurt her clitoris. She had looked him in the eye while it was going on, maybe not even blinking, holding her breath but shedding no tears. He wore rimless glasses and parted his graying hair on the left. In memory she was related to him as if by marriage. One of those jagged little pieces of memory that litter human souls like shrapnel and can never be fully absorbed or rejected. She felt a little sick and feverish—the ferry ride, Dane's hard hand locked on hers, did she want him or didn't she.

"What Scott said was, Esther sent them to the furnaces. He didn't say she killed them first."

"Tidying up after Dix. Or *do* you think she killed them?"

"She might as well have. She let it go on, she's guilty, too."

"I wonder if Esther and Dix are lovers."

"Physically? What would it matter? What's between them is something more compelling, and awful, than mere perversion."

They went ashore but stayed outside, on a bench looking back at Manhattan, sharing a box of popcorn.

"Cole, there just isn't anything more I can do. Call it off."

"No."

Sharan had a long look at him, feeling more feverish and unclear than before. Oppressed. "If Dix is a murderer, it happened during blackouts. What he doesn't remember he can't confess to. Esther is too tough and cunning for me to handle. Scott knew what was going on. Who else knows? Mardie Kregg? Her clan? As long as there was a possibility that bodies existed, then you had a means of building a case. I'm not volunteering to be the next corpse. I've reached the limits of my usefulness, and you know it."

"I don't have Marlowe Hare anymore; he sold me out, which he'll regret. I need an insider. You're practically family now. You can't back out on me, Sharan."

"Why?" she said quietly, but alert to the threat that would destroy any hope she still had for them.

Dane got up and walked slowly away from the bench, scattering popcorn to some seagulls hovering on the wind. Most of the popcorn was snatched in midair.

"Wingo," he said, turning back to Sharan as if he meant to surprise her.

"What about him?"

"He's gone out of control; his obsession with his ex-wife will do him in."

"Good."

"The point is, he'll be back. I think he already knows enough to put both Trevellians away. I want him, Sharan."

"He roughed me up last night. So much for saving his life in the tunnel. I don't want to deal with Dempsey Wingo. Dix Trevellian is a model of predictability compared to Wingo."

"But you won't have to deal with him. Just be there when he does show up. We'll do the rest. Don't leave your Mexican cross lying around again, where it can't do either of us any good."

Sharan thought of silver, and silver-tongued devils. Not fair, but she was in that kind of mood: brooding, exhausted. Dane came back to the bench and sat beside her. A large family of Scandinavian tourists posed nearby with the Manhattan skyline behind them. Sharan glanced at the tall men with muted suspicion, seeing Dempsey Wingo everywhere today, in yet another theatrical disguise. The Scandinavians were having a good time. Their fine spirits began to turn her own mood. She knew what she needed.

"Nothing's going to happen for awhile," Sharan said finally. "I'd like to go home for a week. See my cat. Tinker with my Harley. Get some work done, maybe. I need to paint."

"You're having a show." Pleased, proud of her.

"I'm having a show. By the way, Esther is paying me twelve thousand to do her portrait and Dix's, so I'll be going back to New York whenever Esther's ready to resume her life. Oh, and Jules gave me a check for three thousand dollars this morning."

"Congratulations." Beginning to relax a little himself after the edgy morning, when a black penumbra seemed to surround him; now only traces appeared to her eyes. He offered to kiss her. She wasn't sure she wanted it yet but the sexual feeling was back, a cat-clawing of the groin. Of course she wanted it, forgave him. Sharan felt relieved, and snuggled. The Scandinavians rearranged themselves with Miss Liberty behind them, jostling, cutting up for their Camcorders.

"Do me a favor?"

"Sure."

"The woman named Portia, Robin Smallwood's foster mother? What happened to her?"

"Revoked her RA status. She's being deported to Jamaica."

Sharan winced. "Has to be that way?"

"She brought it on herself."

"Portia was only trying to protect me. Look, I want her to have the money. Most of it, I've got a few bills to pay. Can you arrange that?"

"I'm the great arranger."

"And before long, maybe we'll take a trip down to Jamaica? Visit with Portia. Tell her the news that Robin's death didn't go unpunished. I'd like that." Her troubled eyes, in a shadowed face close to his own, were a deep blue.

Dane nodded. His fingers were light on her temples, in her wind-streaky hair. Building a pleasurable tension, lifting her heart.

"When do you want to fly to Atlanta?"

"Tonight, if possible."

"I'll take care of it. See that you get to Newark. And I'll have a Federal marshal meet your flight at Hartsfield."

"Okay. But—Daner, please? No watchdogs at Rising Fawn. I just want to be myself again, for a little while."

"I know it's been rough; rougher than we could have anticipated. But I've learned a few things."

Sharan laughed, leaning away from him, shaking her head. "I hope I have. What time is it?"

"Quarter past two."

"How long would it take us to get to the hotel?"

"Forty minutes."

"Too long. The other ferry's coming. Let's do it in half an hour."

"Are you going to make love to me?" he said, moving nearer with a little questing tilt of his head, wanting to be playful, his grimness fading in raw sunlight. How much of him could be considered reclaimable from a damaging marriage and the ordeal he seemed obligated to make of his life was still an open question to Sharan.

But her eyes were lighter now. Make love to him? She quoted from a Welsh poem, learned in childhood.

" 'Til you gleam the magic, and weep the tears of love's beginning."

Her first morning back, Sharan slept soundly until eleven in a familiar bed, then went looking for her Harley. Buddy Scope had retrieved the iron from Prexy's Hawg Heaven after the repairs were made and was keeping it for her. She went for a long test ride and had only minor criticisms of the job Prexy's mechanics had done. The rest of the day she puttered around, returned calls, chatted with her mother, wired her brother Lyle a hundred dollars in response to urgent messages left on her machine. That night she had a long halting conversation with Jim Tom Coburn about what was left of their relationship, and he accepted her conclusions with hurt silences. She got a little drunk after the call, with Dardy Jeff Kimbro and Allison Bonner, reprimanded herself severely for that and swore off liquor for the duration.

Dane called at two A.M. Sharan was boozy and missed him and cried a little about matters she couldn't bring herself to talk about. He'd had his usual tough day but he listened patiently and said all the things she needed to hear. The conversation got very sexy, even for lovers apart at a late hour. Then she curled up with Bonkers and had another long, healing sleep.

Esther Trevellian said to Miranda Leland, after breakfast following Miranda's late arrival at Cloud Horse Mountain, "Would you like to see the gravesite? It's very beautiful up there. Where Scott is."

"Yes. I think I would."

The mist on the mountain, with intermittent rain, had been heavy the day before. At ten o'clock the mountain was still shrouded, only an occasional disc of lightless sun showing through the swirls. Esther loaned Miranda hiking shoes and a mountaineer's thick sweater, the oil of the sheep still in the wool, making it waterproof. Esther wore a white ski outfit and boots, a white Stetson and earmuffs. The temperature was only in the high thirties when they set out for the summit, several hundred feet from the house.

"I'm glad you wanted to come," Esther said, leading the way.

"Thank you for having me."

"Actually I've wanted to talk to you for a long time."

"I see," Miranda said, in a doubting tone of voice. There was a noticeable taint to the white mist that enclosed the mountain. Miranda commented on it.

"Industrial pollution," Esther explained. "The jet stream brings it to us when it bends this far south. Sometimes the mist doesn't lift for days, particularly in the winter months. Just in the past ten years we've lost thousands of susceptible trees. Fraser fir, red spruce. You might call it devastation. Not only Cloud Horse, but all through the Smokies and up along the Blue Ridge. Mount Mitchell has been badly damaged. We've spent a lot of money looking for a solution. We hope there is one. You should have seen how beautiful, thirty years ago. When I was a girl. How's my nephew? Did you speak to Timothy this morning?"

"Yes."

"I wish he could have come. I want to get to know him."

"Well. I wasn't sure. If either of us was really welcome."

"Put that thought out of your mind. I don't send my plane all the way to Pittsburgh for unwelcome people. Did you get psychiatric help for Timothy?"

Miranda stopped on the path; Esther continued walking slowly, beginning to disappear although she was only a dozen feet away.

"What do you mean?"

"You know what I mean. Try to keep up with me, Miranda; it's so easy to get lost in the mist, take a wrong step if you don't know the way."

"I'm coming."

"I mean he must need help, after what he saw that night."

"I still don't—"

"Miranda. Don't shit me, dear. You were there, at the Kuhara estate. With Timothy. Tim? Do you ever call him Tim? No? Timothy, then. My nephew. Scott's son. He saw Scott dying. So awful for him. And you, of course. If you loved Scott, even worse for you."

Miranda caught up to Esther.

"But how could you—"

"Oh, Miranda. Am I such a dummy? I *have* kept up with you, all these years. I was told ten minutes after my nephew was born. I did a thorough investigation, the day after Scott killed himself. Young woman, your description, with a boy, approximately Timothy's age. Screaming for help. Suddenly whisked away by an older man, short gray hair. I want to know who took you to Scott, although of course I have my suspicions. Gray hair! How ironic, when I think about the gray hairs he's given me. The security cameras didn't provide much of a likeness, but there are certain physical attributes you can't disguise. You're going to tell me about him, aren't you, Miranda? For my peace of mind. Oh, yes. I almost forgot. The other woman who showed up. I'm *very* interested to learn who that might have been. Did you know her?"

Miranda was silent, shuddering in spite of the bulky sweater, the knit ski cap pulled down around her ears. Esther stopped again. They had reached an enclosure on the summit, a low rock wall. Inside were two simple graves with granite markers. Flame azalea and mountain laurel grew all around the mountain cemetery.

"Here we are," Esther said. Her cheeks were the only spots of real color in the midmorning murk at the summit of Cloud Horse Mountain. "Do you want to be alone for a little while, with Scott?"

Miranda stood with her knees turned in and her shoulders hunched, but the deep shudders were beating her up anyway. Her gray eyes smarted.

"Yes."

"By the way, what name did you put on my nephew's birth certificate?"

"Tim—Timothy Leland Trevellian."

"Officially an heir."

"I don't give a fuck about your money or *anyone's* money! Just leave me alone now! Don't you see I want to be with him?"

"I *know*, Miranda. I'm grieving, too. Stay as long as you want. We'll have plenty of time to talk. Not much else to do but sit by a roaring fire when the mist is on the mountain, drink mulled cider, open our hearts to good friends and family. The telephoto pictures I have of Timothy aren't all that good. You must have better ones to show me. I'll be back for you after awhile."

Sharan was hard at work on a portrait in her storefront studio next to the DUI school, and paid little attention to the motorcycle that had pulled up outside, except to register it as a Harley.

Knock.

"Sharan?"

Oh bejesus.

Without turning or putting her brush down, she invited him in. It took a few moments to prepare a nonchalant smile from a chilled heart.

"Look who's here! Where did you come from?"

"Oh, I had some business in Atlanta," Dix Trevellian said. "And I've missed you. But are you ever hard to find."

Sharan looked past him in the doorway, at the red line of sunset. She'd been working almost without letup for more than four hours, and now she was aware of the stiffness in her neck and shoulders. She put her brush down and fell automatically into the basic tai chi stance, facing him. Relaxing, but also on the defensive. She couldn't just blow Dix off, but she was anxious to leave and find a crowd, the common human herd available at any mall.

"Dix, you don't know how sorry. I tried to call. I sent a note to Esther. One of her secretaries said there wouldn't be a service, he was going to be buried right away."

Dix nodded, with a glint of sorrow.

"He was; and it's over. The last few years, seemed like we were waiting for the worst. Esther's taken it very hard. But Scott and I— never much of a relationship." He was carrying a touring helmet with a smoke-bubble visor and wore biker boots that looked new. He walked gingerly, as if saddle sore, across the bare concrete floor, eyes on the rectangle of paper Sharan had tacked to her easel board, where the portrait of a child was taking shape.

"Hey. Who is she?"

"Her name's Kaylyn. She's Lozelle Orlander's granddaughter. Lozelle and Wilbur live a couple of doors from me over at Rising Fawn."

"Down syndrome?"

"A mild case. Kaylyn's precious. It's just an exercise, really, a birthday present for Lozelle."

"How often do you work from photographs?"

"It's something I've tried before. But I have to take the photos, myself, a lot of them. Three or four rolls of film, at least. Until something clicks in my head. That old cliché."

"Artistic truth. I've spent weeks looking at a site. Looking and sketching, discarding ideas. Here's an idea. Barbecue ribs. I've worked up an appetite on that Harley I bought this morning."

"You bought a *Harley*? Man, let me get a look at it."

Low-Rider Shovelhead, rebuilt, luscious in pink and turquoise: Mitchell wheels, chopper styling, gutted pipes, probably a rejetted Bendix carb that looked like an original to Sharan. Lots of chrome. Seventy-eight, seventy-nine. Righteous.

"You bought it this morning?"

"I remembered how you went on and on about your own Harley, so I said, have to have one, Dix, if you're going touring with Sharan."

"We're going touring?"

"Why not? Tomorrow. I'm feeling a little beat up right now. Take me to your nearest rib joint."

"Big 'Un's, over in Osbia. About five miles. Let me lock up."

Dix wasn't new to motorcycles, but plainly he hadn't done much riding during the past few years. They went side by side to the rib joint, a log house with rusted metal advertising signs all over it—Gold Cup Bread, Bull of the Woods, Beechnut, Double-Cola—a front porch full of rocking chairs that overlooked a churchyard and a patch of thick green croaking swamp. All the rockers were occupied by the habitually sedentary and customers were standing in chatty groups in the gravel parking lot waiting to be summoned by pagers to tables. The Big 'Un was violating a local ordinance by selling beer out of wash tubs to the overflow crowd. It was a warm mellow night. Randy Travis and Trisha Yearwood on the outdoor speakers, UGA football on a couple of portable TVs sitting on barreltops. Dix had a beer while they waited and Sharan, remembering her recent resolution, drank a Dr. Pepper. They talked motorcycles.

"Your iron seems to be a little flukey at low speeds, Dix. One of the tendencies you'll have with a hard-raked bike. I think you'd be better off with broomstick bars, you know, for front-end stability and extra leverage."

"Is that a big job, to change the handlebars?"

"No, I could do it for you."

Dix looked around. "What's all the cheering?"

"Bulldogs must've scored. This is Bulldog country. Their mascot is named Uga. Uga the fourth or fifth or something."

"Where am I, anyway?"

"Heart of Georgia. A little east of the heart, I suppose."

"I must have got lost a dozen times today. Nobody seemed to know what Rising Fawn was. An old Indian legend."

"I can't explain, either."

"Would you look at that moon," Dix said with naive enthusiasm.

"How much did the bike set you back?"

"Twelve thousand. I picked up a copy of *Cycle Trader* and there it was, right out of my dreams. One owner. He shed tears. But he needed cash."

"You just happened to have twelve thousand cash with you?"

"I never carry money," Dix said, perplexed by the question. "I call somebody, the money shows up."

"Buff the lamp, out pops the genie." Sharan put on a regretful face. "Say, I don't know if I can go touring with you, Dix. I'm kind of beat. New York is not restful. And Jules said, Get to work."

Dix wagged a finger at her, disallowing the alibi. "Jules told me where to look for you. Since you've impressed the hell out of me, I want to show off *my* best work. It's an ego thing."

"Not a tour you have in mind; an ego trip."

"Right," he said, with his gap-toothed, self-indulgent grin.

"To Cloud Horse Mountain?"

"You'll love the house."

"I'm sure I would, but I don't want to intrude right now."

His mood shifted unexpectedly; until then everything about Dix—his new modish biker's gear, his full ripe hedonistic face, the way he moved or stood around with his thumbs outside his belt—had as usual shouted *cock, cock, cock*. He looked at her with a rather hangdog expression, not typical of Dix at all. Randy Travis sang through his nose. Sharan watched a plump blonde in a short skirt and cowgirl boots go berserk when her boyfriend put a dead baby bird in her frizzy hair. Watching her antics, Sharan thought, *Honey, if you only knew what this guy I'm with does with dead things.* Because she had come to the conclusion, after worrying about it for days, that it couldn't only be Esther. Whoever was responsible for the actual killings, afterward they must have worked as a team to get rid of the principal evidence. The sultry windless night was saturated with meaty pit smoke, the tang of vinegar that distinguished North Carolina–style babybacks and pulled pork. Sharan knew she would throw up before the evening was over.

"I could use your help, Sharan. I don't know what to do."

"About what?" Sharan said remotely, gazing at the churchyard.

"Esther. She's taking Scott's death hard. Very hard. As if it were her fault. She scared the hell out of me, a couple of days ago."

"What did she do?"

"I'd rather not say. Maybe I ought to explain that Esther has no fear, she can't experience fear because of—an accident when she was a kid. Doesn't recognize fear in others. But her lack of fear has always been balanced by good judgment. I've depended on that, on Esther's control and common sense, because God knows I've had *my* moments—"

"Like driving into Jules' koi pond."

"That's a minor example. I'm a big success, a huge goddamn success. But my other life. Things just seem to happen to me. I guess people have talked to you. You were in New York long enough to hear a lot of bad mouth about Dix Trevellian."

"I don't let gossip tell me what to believe, Dix."

"I know you're not like that. One very good reason why I'm so attracted to you. The artist's eye. You believe what you see and feel. I've always been on my best behavior with you, Sharan. None of my usual tactics. Because I admire you so much. Your show? I'm going to buy it out. I don't want anyone else owning Sharan Norbeth."

Sharan felt a soul flutter, a superstitious alarm.

"About Esther," she said.

Dix hesitated, decided to come out with it.

"Crying jags. That's not Esther. She's scaring me. Biting her thumb until it bleeds and crying, doesn't want to see anyone. My God. Esther has to snap out of this." For a few moments his eyes were fixed, expression lagging the emotion that was swelling into panic. There were fracture lines of light in his dark pupils, reflected from a parking-lot flood. "She likes you. She's told me more than once, 'Sharan's someone I can talk to.' How many people would like to be Esther's close friend? But they all want something. The prestige of being seen with Esther Trevellian. The Prizes. There isn't a pussy on earth as seductive as those damned Prizes. You're not like all the others. You could be her one true friend."

"What about Mardie Kregg?"

Dix wiped at a gnat that had worked its way into one corner of his mouth. "Mardie, that's different. Mardie's basically indentured, depends on Es to tell her what to do. It gives her emotional security, justifies her existence."

They were paged. They went in to eat. A plate of ribs and a baked potato soothed Dix. Sharan ate some cole slaw and two bites of a pork sandwich. A baby in a highchair at the next table contentedly snacked on french fries, smiling a lot, ton of personality, she even drooled cute. Sharan played eye games with the ruddy charmer, smiling, too. Wondrous. When they turned out that beautifully.

"I'm jealous," Dix said. He was uninterested in babies.

Sharan drank tea and tried not to look as lonely and fearful as she was feeling.

"Dix, I'd really like to help. But I can't just go flying up the mountain, bust in on Esther in her time of mourning. What would she think of me?"

"No problem; but if you'd feel better we'll give her a call first."

"Dix, let me sleep on it. And, uh, where're you staying tonight?"

"Oh, I don't know," Dix said, casually; Sharan gave him a long bland look and suggested the inn at Stone Mountain Park. He accepted her brush-off with good grace. But with a slight wise tightening of the eyes she didn't much care for.

M r. Marlowe Hare has had one too many rum swizzles at his favorite watering hole, Moko-Jumbie. Too much rum to get up and dance again with Marcella, his Thursday-night girl. Down here in the tropics, with money to spend, he's had a different girl every night of the week since he arrived. Marlowe is taking what he feels is a well-deserved vacation, far away, safely away, from the pesky fluctuations.

"Honey," Marcella says, the long nails of her brown fingers tickling beneath his chin, "don't you think it's time to get started on the loving?"

Marlowe smiles, the diamonds in his teeth flashing at Marcella. The fat candle in the hurricane lamp on their terrace table has burned to its last puddling half-inch. The Zouk band is still game, but the off-season crowd at Moko-Jumbie has dwindled to half a dozen diehards, Marlowe and Marcella included. Marlowe may be a little squashed, but the knot of his passion-flower print necktie is still precise, the long pointed collars of his strawberry-pink dress shirt are unwilted. Marlowe knows how to make an impression on the local belles, beginning with his clothes and continuing with the half-inch-thick fold of currency in his platinum money clip, all new bills. He hasn't let any of them down in bed yet, either. But tonight he has trouble keeping his eyes uncrossed. An unexpected indisposition. Marlowe, keen on his prowess, able to make love until the sun rises, keeps track of his drinks. Maybe the two fairy bartenders, Cary and Beau, identical blond crewcuts and gold lip-rings, have been going heavier on the rum tonight, a way of thanking him for his patronage and the generous tips he's laid on them during his stay.

"I need to have a cup of coffee first. My eyes going back on me tonight."

"Oh, honey," Marcella says, draping her thin arms around his shoulders, "I'll do the driving. I know how."

"For a fact?"

"Sure." She fishes in his jacket pocket for the keys to the rental, waggles them in the air above his head like a cat holding a mouse by the tail. Marlowe grins and grins foolishly, seeing double. At last he is able to consolidate Marcella's image. She is gaudy as a firedrake in her island gladrags. He can't remember where he found her, or if she found him. Henna-streaked hair in a rigid Psyche knot, hibiscus bloom behind one ear as provocative as a war-bonnet, haut-couture cheekbones. Her white teeth jut slightly, but he has always found that erotic. The silk handkerchief puffed between her breasts she has wiped across her pussy more than once tonight and held to his nose like a flag of surrender after a wild fling on the parquet dance floor.

Only three cars left along the road near Moko-Jumbie. Marlowe has been driving a Mitsubishi Galant. Automatic transmission, but even so Marcella seems totally unfamiliar with the simple procedure of starting it up and shifting into drive. Marlowe leans unsteadily toward her and puts the car in gear, then is flung back into his seat as she takes off too precipitously, squealing the tires on the heavily pocked, lane-and-a-half blacktop road.

"Easy, gal."

"Where's your hotel?"

"South Wind Cove. Going the wrong way."

"No I'm not."

Marlowe isn't sure himself. His vision is blurring again, and he is sweating. The air conditioner isn't working.

"How do you let down the windows?" Marcella asks him.

"Watch the road. I'll do it."

The night wind flowing in feels good. But they are heading up into the lightless hills, away from the beach. The road is worse than ever.

"South Cove," Marlowe says again.

"I know the way," Marcella says stubbornly, going too fast around a curve. "Oops." She laughs, trying to center the car in the middle of the erratic road, hedged in closely by flamboyants that join boughs overhead, by traveler's palms and lime trees. The moon is tinged with red. They pass some shacks in the hills, goat pens, the skeleton of a wrecked bus in a ravine, half-smothered in jungly creeper and plumbago. The road turns and twists toward a dark volcanic peak in the luminous sky. Behind and below them, the sea.

Marcella jams on the brakes; the road has diverged. Marcella studies her choices with an outthrust lower lip.

"We lost, honey? Thought you said you was borned here."

"May have done, but I lie a lot. Actually I'm from Lucia."

"We're lost, then."

"Can't get lost on an island small as this one is. Look, there's the sea, and *there's* the sea. Anywhere you look from on high."

"Yeah, and ain't it a beautiful sight tonight."

"Like it's all diamonds. How do you feel, sugar?"

"I'm good."

"Little walk in the moonlight would be *so* romantic."

"Yeah."

"Then this car, look like it have plenty of back seat room."

"Oh, yeah. I'm with you."

"I've got a yen for you, honey. Which won't wait much longer. I'm about to howl at that big old moon."

"Oh, yeah. Me too."

Marcella looks around again, more leisurely than he might have imagined from her impassioned declaration, her heavy breathing. Marlowe closes his smarting eyes, calming the gyroscopic spin in his brain. The car moves on, bumping downhill. He isn't aware of when it leaves the road, but the scrape and swish of vegetation against the sides causes him to look out.

They have stopped on a rocky hillside facing the sea. Hurricanes have stripped everything except scrub vegetation such as Antigua heath, century plants and the quick-growing poinciana, a few lignum vitaes too tough to die, and a single wind-twisted cannonball tree, so-called because its spherical fruit is nearly rock-hard.

Marcella gets out of the car and takes off her dress in the headlights. What he thought, no underwear. She leaves her sandals on and the flower in her hair. She is small-breasted, shaved all over, glossy with good health. Her eyes so big she looks hypnotized by lust. She gets into the back seat, turns on the light and slouches with upshot knees, opening her pussy with her fingers, Marlowe getting an eyeful over the seat headrest.

"What you got?"

"What you been whiffing all night long. Disappointed?"

"Huh-uh."

"You don't want to get your suit all wrinkled," Marcella advises him, opening her pussy again like a jeweler's plush box on the pink pearl it contains. "Or anything on it."

Marlowe gets out of the car, staggers a little but catches himself, and undresses. Carefully folding and laying each article of clothing down to his garters on the front seat. He leaves his shoes on, too, for now: sharp rock and hard-to-see things with sawtooth leaves and pincushion centers cover the hillside.

"Step away from the car, honey, and let me see if you're worth my time."

Marlowe clenches his buttocks and walks away from the car, stands in profile with the sea and the starry sky for a backdrop. Clenched all over now, posing proudly.

The car door opens, closes. Marcella approaches, hands behind her back, giving it a flavor of revel, a little hokey-pokey.

"Oh Lordy, *yes*. Is it real? It can't be real. You foolin' me."

"Let's hop back in that car, you'll find out what dick is."

"Lover *man*. But we can't go back in the car right now."

"Well why not, baby?"

"Just stand still and never you mind," Marcella says, shaking her head slightly as she brings the nickel-plated revolver around from behind her back and points it at his manly joy.

"Whoa, now," Marlowe says with an aggrieved moan. "What's this here?"

"Three-fifty-seven Magnum. It sure would spoil the hang of your tackle if you make any kind of move at all."

"What you want, gal?"

"Money."

"I got all kinds of money. You don't have to go and pull a goddamn pistol on me! I'm a generous man!"

"The money you have don't rightfully belong to you, Mr. Hare."

"What's that? What you talking about?"

"You got paid to do a job you didn't do, would be my understanding."

The Magnum fires; Marlowe Hare jumps, yelps, freezes, one hand between his legs.

"That's better. Hold just that way, or I promise I *will* have to shoot it off. I mean, I won't be leaving so much as a nub for you to pleasure with."

"Well shit. Take what's in my pants. Take my watch and chains and leave me be."

"Oh, honey." Marcella grins and shrugs. "I get a paycheck, too. Thing is, I'm known to deliver, and I don't want my sterling reputation spoiled. What's the matter? Something I said? You need to throw up? Don't turn your back on me. Just bend over, but keep your hands where I can see them."

"God damn. I'm sick. You dope my drinks? God *damn!*"

"Won't be too long. We're here just a little ahead of time."

"Time for what?"

"Wait and see."

"My head hurts. Bitch, what you want I'll pay. Just don't be doing this shit to me!"

Marlowe makes retching sounds, but nothing comes up. Marcella hears a four-cylinder engine that badly needs a tuneup laboring in their direction. She doesn't turn her head. Shaky headlights eventually find them on the hillside. Now she sees, out of the corner of her eye, an old Econoline van. Smells it. The van pulls up a dozen feet from her. It is painted all over, not crudely but with considerable flair: Epic jungle beasts, lush Rousseauean foliage.

Two black men get out of the back of the van; they are joined by the driver. There is a white woman—Marcella thinks it's a woman— in the front seat. She stares through the cracked dirty windshield until Marcella steps to one side and reveals herself more fully in the van's weak headlights; then she looks away as if offended by Marcella's nakedness. The men surround Marlowe, who closes his eyes despairingly, chokes and spits up vomit. For a while no one seems to want to be the first to touch him, as if they are abashed by his pervasive daze, his aura of near-swoon. A few insects flick in and out of the headlight beams. Marlowe looks at the face behind the bug-smeared windshield of the van. He tries to speak, but is raspingly inarticulate.

Marcella steps a little closer to him, alertly.

"What did you say?"

"Give me another chance."

"Did Jesus get another chance? And you ain't Jesus."

She backs away. Marlowe Hare is pushed to his knees. His hands are lashed behind his back. A jute coffee sack is pulled down over his head and torso. He is trembling and sick again. They wait until he stops vomiting, then get him up; two of them guide Marlowe farther down the hill, where some palm trees, left permanently bowed by savage winds, fronds sweeping the ground, provide concealment. Marlowe hooing and moaning and stumbling all over the place. The third man begins gathering fallen fruit from the cannonball tree, which he drops into another coffee sack. When he has collected at least a dozen of the fruit he slings the heavy sack over one shoulder and with bent back trudges after the other men into the palm thicket.

Marcella hears Marlowe Hare cry out, once. Then a succession of sounds like croquet balls smartly struck. Marcella's lips part over her pretty splayed teeth. She puts the gun back in her purse and cups her breasts, playing with her nipples, star-gazing. The rhythmic striking sounds fade after a couple of minutes until they are little more than punky thuds. Pretty soon it's over.

Marcella puts her dress back on.

Once she is no longer naked, Mardie Kregg gets out of the van, glances at her, walks on down the hill.

Marcella lights a cigarette and waits until she sees the men coming back up the hill, single file, one of them carrying the now-empty coffee sack.

Marcella takes something from her purse and passes them on her way to the palm thicket. None of them speak to her but she feels the heat from their recent exertions, their glances saying they remember her nakedness. Blood on their hands, her own nostrils reacting, the rancidness she craves sometimes; it could be interesting but she's got better things to do.

Mardie Kregg's head turns against the mercurial southern sea.

"What you looken for?"

Marcella holds up a pair of pliers. "The diamonds in his teeth," she says.

Mardie just stares at her, annoyed.

"I have a thing for diamonds," Marcella explains, with another display of her girl-can't-help-it grin.

Where are you, Cole?"

"San Francisco. Addressing the Bar Association meeting. Then I'm delivering the annual Asbury T. Brasher Lectures at Cal Law School. Immigration and International Law." He drew a long breath. "Promises to be a spellbinder."

"How long will you be there?"

"Four days away from the office. Weather's drizzly, but the food's wonderful. What are you up to?"

"Not much. Resting. Dix is here."

Coleman Dane said sharply, "Why?"

"Said he had business in Atlanta. Said he missed me. He bought a motorcycle so we could go touring."

"Where?"

"He wants me to spend a few days at Cloud Horse Mountain. Apparently Esther is taking Scott's death very hard, and—"

"You told him no."

"I've been trying to."

"There is *no way*. I can't provide you with protection on Cloud Horse Mountain. They own it. It's private property. You're not to go, understood?"

"Yes. I didn't want to anyway. I'll make up an excuse. How's Misty?"

"Mil wants her to be in the wedding. Misty's making a stink. I told her I didn't feel it would be disloyalty on her part. She said I was stupid. The joys of being a divorced parent. Oh, Misty's asked about you. Three times."

"Hostile?"

"Not at all. She's curious about your career. I told her you were having a show in New York in the spring. She has Griffin curious, too."

"Could I drop her a note? You know, just hello, how's it going?"

"Sure. I wish you would."

"Cole. Did you write Milly love letters?"

"Milly? Are you kidding? Her malicious wit. I'd have been pieces of quivering flesh all over the floor . . . what did you say?"

"I said, I'm sorry for Milly. And you have a lot to learn. You can start learning by writing me a love letter. I badly need one."

After a long pause he said, "Two dozen yellow roses wouldn't—"

"Nope. Love letter. Have you ever written one?"

"I was fourteen, for God's sake."

"Um-hmm. Why not be fourteen again for a little while? Nobody's looking. Remember what you said once about 'that nearly forgotten adolescent astonishment refreshed in the blood'?"

"Did I say that?"

"You have a natural eloquence when you get rolling. I don't want roses, they bloom from horse shit anyway. I want stellar sentiments. I want you to glow on the page for me. Notes to tie up with a purple ribbon and put away in my trunk for my great-grandchildren to read. And know that I was loved, way back there. Cole? What are you doing?"

"Looking for stationery. Six-hundred-dollar-a-night suite, they don't have any stationery."

Esther said on the phone to Dix, "I do want to see Sharan. More than anything, and right now."

"Her mother fell and broke her pelvis, Sharan says. She has to go to San Diego for a week or so. But she'll see us in New York."

"No, I said, *right now*, Dix."

"What am I suppose to do, kidnap her?"

"Don't be an ass. Just persuade Sharan. There's not a woman alive who can resist you when you're being persuasive. Get her out of that trailer park and up to the mountain."

"What's going on, Esther?"

"Something I don't like. Sharan is not to go to San Diego, or anywhere else. I must talk to her. Don't let her out of your sight, Dix. Oh, hell. Maybe I *can't* depend on you. Maybe I should take care of this myself. Call me back in the morning. Make sure you use a secure phone."

Wearing a stockman's straw hat, a denim jacket with leather fringe, his comfy old boots with the bulldogger heels and one of his PRCA prize belt buckles, Dempsey found it easy to get rides down south. He took his time on the secondary byways, enjoying mild early fall weather and the company of farmers who liked hearing his stories about the circuit and some famous rodeo cowboys he knew. Athletes who put up their own money for entry fees at every venue. Earning every dime they made, no overinflated multiyear contracts and Pepsi commercials for bouncing a ball around indoors. He hung around small-town cafes and poolhalls, flirted with waitresses, slept on hay bales under the stars a couple of nights. On the road again. But it was colder after sunset in the mountains, so he would put up at motels off the trodden path, as long as they had cable TV, and watch Western movies. Some of the good Audie Murphy films they were showing on AMC, when young Audie was in there with pros like Jimmy Stewart, Burt Lancaster and Walter Brennan. Audie, a Texan, was the most decorated soldier of World War Two. Before he turned twenty-one. In the fifties, a bullshit TV actor who was making a name for himself in a western series had challenged Audie to a quick-draw duel, the latest fad out in Hollywood. Audie said, Sure, as long as we use real bullets. Real bullets. He meant it, too. That was the terrific thing about Audie Murphy.

Dempsey had all of Scott's diskettes, prudently removed from the conservatory before he whisked Miranda and Timothy away from the scene. One of them held all of the keys to the family's security: en-crypted E-mail files, bank and brokerage accounts in a dozen coun-tries. Scott had stored all of the cellular phone account numbers; he had the means to unscramble secure lines. Dempsey tested the fresh-ness of Scott's information by calling Esther at Cloud Horse Moun-tain. Not all that certain she was in residence. Maybe sunning herself at the villa in St. Bart's. But he knew Miranda had flown there, to the mountain, last week.

"Yes?"

"I'm coming."

Dead silence.

"I'm coming," Dempsey repeated. Real bullets, this time. No more fooling around.

The silence continued. He knew Esther wasn't going to speak again, but she seemed oddly reluctant to hang up on him.

"Leave the light on," Dempsey advised her, and hung up himself.

NINETEEN

BLACK EMPRESS OF GOSSAMER

Just past shooting light, the mist at three thousand feet on Cloud Horse Mountain was already thinning to a haze, and enough of a wind had risen across the grass-heath bald nearby to lift the black thread tied to Esther's longbow, flutter it against the knuckles of her left hand. The wind blowing toward her. She knew there would be deer on the bald, but she was only interested in the buck she had heard earlier, not twenty yards from her place of concealment. There she had noticed fresh rubs on some trees about six inches in diameter a day or two earlier. She hadn't seen the buck yet, only the quick gleam of antler as he moved through the understory. Esther also was moving downhill through the hardwood swale, mostly white oak, on the east side of the mountain below the sheer metamorphic-granite face of Standing Wolf Cliff. Moving slowly, like a snail on sandpaper. Wearing scent-neutralized rubber boots, Fall-brown camo clothing and a combination of face-camo colors: gray base with streaks of brown and green. Esther never hunted from a tree stand or blind. The bow she carried had been a gift from Clydean when she was twelve, crafted from ash, not much different than the bows that had been in use seven hundred years ago. The bow had a sixty-pound draw; she'd spent ten years becoming dead-accurate with it. The shafts of her feathered arrows were made of hickory by an old-timer who had taught her as much about the art of the hunt as her own grand-daddy.

The buck seemed to be following an old scrape line that ran from the bald three hundred yards away up into some higher timber, mixed with hemlock, at the base of the four hundred-foot cliff. A month early, at least, for any rutting activity; and the acorns, a favorite food, hadn't begun to fall from the oaks. Flying squirrels were up and soaring in the trees, which included red maples and basswood. It was too cold for timber rattlers to be out of their dens. She guessed the buck was moving from habit, not from compulsion, stopping often to lift his nose, have a look around.

Something caught in the branches of a purple catawba rhododendron at the edge of a creek wavered and glinted in the wind. It looked like the wrapping from a dehydrated food package. She'd already seen messy evidence of campers and backpackers. Cloud Horse Mountain was private property, and posted; the Trevellians employed a force of twenty-seven rangers, naturalists and conservationists to patrol their woods on horseback and by spotter plane. They maintained a full-time fire-fighting crew in the critical months. But all they could do was hold down the number of trespassers, not eliminate them. Esther didn't mind the occasional backpacker who knew his way around the woods and didn't leave a polluting campsite behind. Poachers were inevitable, but seldom a nuisance; Esther didn't care as long as they killed to eat. When her rangers culled the deer on a yearly basis, Esther contributed thousands of pounds of meat to the Salvation Army and other programs designed to feed the hungry in a four-state area.

The firebugs and other troublemakers, the novice climbers who were poorly prepared for the hazards of Cloud Horse Mountain, were an ongoing headache. Kids trying to hitch a ride on the funicular railroad had been injured; climbers above Spearfinger Falls had lost their footing and died. In all cases, a lawsuit. Then a trial and like as not bad publicity, but Esther always refused to settle, and she had never lost a case, although two were still pending before the North Carolina Supreme Court. Then there was the fortune paid out over the years to legislators on the state and national levels who were eager to seize their holdings, nearly twelve thousand acres, pay a few cents an acre and turn Cloud Horse over to the public trust, whose conservators were anything but trustworthy. Or, when that didn't work, attempt to tax them into the poorhouse so they would be forced to sell. Every couple of years, a new crop of greedy legislators came along, eager to exploit the vulnerability of the Trevellians, who just wanted to be left alone and maintain the beauty of their mountain home, fight off the ravages of toxic winds, fire, disease and insects that in combination could turn virgin and old-growth forest into a wasteland.

She needed to cross the water, but stopped in midcreek when the buck came into view in a birch thicket about twenty yards downwind. Short-haired Southern whitetail with an impressive rack. He was moving away from her; she had a glimpse of shoulder but the angle was poor, and he was at the perimeter of her killing range anyway.

It occurred to Esther that he might recross the same creek she was fording. Mist moved over the surface of the water but the light had strengthened. There was a giant mist-beaded web stretched between branches of a dead alder that hung over the water, the huge spider with its pronglike legs off-center in the web. Black empress of gossamer, waiting in languor for a morning victim.

Esther backed up to the bank and resumed moving downstream until she saw the buck's head and graceful rack again, in profile. He was drinking. She gained another two yards, nocking a broadhead as she moved. The wind was still blowing her way, clearing off the last of the mist.

The buck lifted his head and listened. Esther continued to raise her unglazed bow, not liking the angle yet but aware of possibilities if he turned away instead of stepping out into the creek. She didn't think she was near the buck's line of scent, but something had alerted him. For sure he couldn't see her, against the background of an embankment of gray-green moss, windfalls so old and decayed that orchids grew on them, leaf-filled hollows and rock outcrops that were part of a mountain known to be two hundred and fifty million years old.

Caution defined the tawny buck's attitude; patience defined hers. Esther was flushed with buck fever now, willing him to present himself at an angle where she knew she couldn't miss the heart. He wasn't a trophy buck; the rack was asymmetrical, with one shattered tine. Didn't matter to Esther, by the time she was twenty she already had all the trophies she would ever want. The speared heart of the buck, blood erupting, death a tribute to her strength and nerve. Twinkling of birds, the motionless spider, round body like the pupil of Esther's eye, web swelling in wind rush on what would be a fair warm morning. She was rigid but not tense, the drawstring back, the arrow steady along her line of sight. She tasted old metal on her tongue. Knew it was going to happen.

The buck turned his head downwind, ears flattened and quaking.

Took a regal step and then another out of the sparse creekbank cover and there was the right shoulder, where she wanted it. Range about eighteen yards. *Twing*. The broadhead went through him, probably cutting the heart in half. He bounded twice in the creekbed, sending up spray that was colored with nostril-blown blood, reached the opposite bank and dropped, antlers ringing against a windfall. The birds were suddenly still.

Esther breathed through her mouth and trudged along the bank to where the buck lay with wisps of steam rising from his long blood-flecked muzzle. She kneeled and ran a gloved hand along his backbone, wary of ticks but needing the feel of her kill. Good-looking old dodger, hefty, scarred from rutting battles, maybe two hundred twenty pounds.

She remained hunkered for a few minutes, cooling down herself, until the first flies showed up in the dawn light. Then she got out her pocket GPS navigator, noted her position—error factor of about three hundred feet—and sent the coordinates by cellular telephone to the ranger station. She planted a Day-Glo orange flag on a telescoping pole beside the buck, having decided not to wait for the ATV retrieval team; it might take them a half-hour or more. She was close enough to the midmountain tram station at the base of the falls, and company was expected.

Her first deer hunt of the season had helped her, for a little while, not to dwell on Scott's unnecessary death. But only for the duration of the hunt. As she walked through the brightening woods it wearied her just to think about her next, inevitable convulsion, what dreadful course her grief could take. Uninfluenced by fear, nonetheless she was susceptible to her rages, a danger to herself. Each occurrence made emotional control a little more difficult to grasp, a slippery line in a battering sea. She conceded the possibility that she needed help, but no drugs: the pharmaceuticals that were routine with Dix. Coming out of a binge-sleep, she'd observed, was like returning from the grave. And she would be at the mercy of doctors whom she paid but had no reason to trust.

Esther had never minded being the lonely one, the family bulwark, the logical center, the last resort, the caretaker. The giver of love, in all of its beauty and its blight. Esther, on whom all things depended. As long as she retained her strength and resolve. But she would soon turn forty. What weakness did that imply? In her dispassionate judgment, she was better in so many ways than she'd been a decade earlier. But had she trembled there, at the edge of the creek, while lining up the buck? Esther methodically replayed every split second of the action, every response of her body to the imminent kill, and gave herself top marks. Then became aware that she had taken the glove off her left hand, was chewing again, chewing the tight bandage off the thumb she had already savaged and gotten infected. Biting down hard for the grim thrill of pain, but also for the taste of the corrupted flesh, the drop of blood on her tongue. Loss of control. Where had she dropped the glove, how many yards behind her? Losses, losses, Scott interred on the mountain beside her daddy, and *she couldn't afford any more losses.*

Esther put the bowstring in her mouth and drew it back with her teeth. Maximum tension, her jaw muscles aching. Like a filament of web; through it she could feel the vibrations of her known and suspected enemies. Just come on then. Come on. It's my mountain. And I do not tremble at your approach.

TWENTY

Sharan had told Dix that she was going to visit her hospitalized mother in California, which was not the truth; Caitlin had an herbal consultant, a numerologist, a spiritual advisor named Prakob Mandalay and a fitness trainer; she was feeling sunny-side-up these days. But Cole had called and asked her to take a flight to San Francisco to spend a couple of days with him down at Big Sur lounging in warm mud, inhaling vapors and intensifying the relationship. Sharan could hardly wait. Dix claimed he had business in Washington that required him to take a late-evening flight himself, but there was time for lunch at one of his favorite restaurants, in the hills of North Georgia. Only about ninety minutes from Jubilation County on their bikes, he assured her. The day was sunny, temperature in the mid-eighties. Fine touring weather. Sharan didn't exactly hate the idea. Her flight was at ten-thirty that night. And, she rationalized, the lore and mechanisms of biking gave them a language to speak through which she could maintain their relationship without putting herself on a more intimate, riskier level.

She decided it would be wise to let Dix lead on his newly purchased Harley, in case he had mechanical problems, or something worse happened. Although Dix had proved he wasn't a novice biker, Sharan didn't know how good he might be on winding hilly roads. But the route they took to the old gold-mining boom town was a divided four lanes; midweek traffic was light and Dix sailed right along. It was one of those days when she would have enjoyed riding without a helmet.

The wind in her hair. But brushing the bugs out afterward could be a chore.

The restaurant occupied a stone-and-frame house at one corner of the town square with its homely nineteenth-century buildings, roofed sidewalks and tourist shops. The first floor of the restaurant was a museum: gold miners' gear, a moonshiner's still with its crude glazed jugs and coils and battered copper kettles. Some Civil War artifacts, although the region was well to the east and north of the major battlefields in Georgia.

Sharan and Dix sat outdoors on the second-floor dining porch of the restaurant, shaded by two huge poplar trees. A mannequin in faded Confederate uniform stood sentry duty at one end of the porch, facing the hills and college buildings with his chipped blue gaze and small lonesome chin, the bayonet of his rifle rusted to a nub. Down a side street of the town logs were planed in a sawmill, the saw making the keen eerie music Sharan didn't mind listening to.

"How did you know about this place?"

"Family made some money here in the boom times. I forget just which of my kin were involved, but they all knew how to grab a buck. Second-generation carpetbaggers. My father used to bring us kids down this way, after a rafting trip on the Chatooga or the Horsepasture River. He always liked the food in this place."

"What's special?" Sharan asked, studying the chalkboard menu.

"I recommend the buffet. Try the spiced peach sauce, chicken giblets gravy with biscuits, pan-fried mountain trout with a dab of chow-chow or pepper jelly on the side. Don't pass up a slice of baked ham with crushed hazelnut and honey glaze." The description of tempting food brought out his complimentary side. "You look fantastic today, Sharan."

"Why, thanks, Dix."

"New York appeared to be getting you down, when I saw you last."

"The most convivial mood of New Yorkers seems to be suppressed hysteria." She tossed off New York with a shrug.

"The city of cities. Big town. Big Apple. Babel-on-the-Hudson. Even before we set foot there, New York is an experience we've all filtered through our perceptions too many times, until reality is removed like caffeine from coffee. No matter where you look, you've seen it before. Times Square. The Gay White Way. All those dancing feet in movies. The Bronx is up, and the Battery's down. I brought the magic with me, all of New York that was stuffed into my imagi-

nation. God, I was feverish. My first day in Big Town, I couldn't race
around fast enough, confirming that it actually existed. Technological
events, engineering marvels, the street-level excesses and asylum
tempo of the subways culture. But I couldn't respond. My sense of
astonishment had been blunted by too much mythic input. My capacity for rapture was diminished by photographic familiarity. I was
disappointed. I felt real bitterness. How do we repossess our childhood dreams? Restore our crippled faith? Good question. I designed
Trevellian House. I put something in Big Town that wasn't there
before. I gave it *my* touch, my sense of romance. If I had to describe
myself, and thanks for not pressing me on that point, I would say
Romantic Nihilist. Would that be a tautology, or a synechdoche?"

"Oxymoron, I think."

"Anyway, one of a kind. Also a lonely guy, Sharan, in spite of my
success. The recognition I've received. I guess you're surprised, hearing me say that. But willing to be sympathetic." The S's were whistling
through the space between his front teeth. "I like being with you."

"I've had a good time, too." So far. While smiling, Sharan felt the
pressure again, hard as a doorknob, under her diaphragm. And reminded herself: tonight she would be with Cole.

"Friendships," Dix mused. "I've never devoted enough time to
friendships. Just to sit and talk with you without looking at my watch.
That's a new Dix Trevellian, is what I'm saying."

He had looked at his watch at least five times since they arrived at
the restaurant. Sharan said, with a defensive lift of one shoulder, "I'm
highly flattered."

The ride up to gold country had given her an appetite which she
nearly lost when she saw a familiar face in the restaurant: Lew Carbine's.

The local weekly paper had devoted half a page of photos and interview space to Lew when he had been in the vicinity a few years
back, filming a *Deliverance* knockoff. There was Lew with both arms
around the proprietors of this very restaurant, his familiar lopsided
grin of menace, the lank curl on his high forehead.

Dix turned to point out an item on the buffet to Sharan and saw
her looking at the laminated interview framed on a butternut-paneled
wall.

"Lew. God rest." He lamely attempted to cross himself, then
smiled worriedly, as if he'd somehow imposed a curse instead.

"Were you good friends?"

"No. Esther had a thing for Lew, though. Once upon a time."

"Wasn't all that serious, I believe you said."

"Did I? Esther can't get serious. All of her love has been for us. I don't know what I'll do if she cracks up." His eyes had the stark lightless look of doomed worship. "I have to do what she says, that's all. Of course she feels lousy about Scott. Believe me, I do, too. But it'll pass. And there's still the two of us. There always has to be, you know, Sharan?"

"Yeah. I understand."

"I think you do." For a few seconds it seemed that he was going to weep, right there at the buffet table. His bleakness was real to her, unactable. Sharan surprised herself by putting a steadying hand on Dix's arm. So tense.

"It'll be all right, Dix."

"Thank you, Sharan. That's a great relief to me. Thank you."

They ate, for the most part in silence. Butterflies visited the climbing wisteria on the porch lattice. They were the color of the sun. Dix's vigor had diminished. A few of his anecdotes about notable people she'd heard before. She tried hard to put a shine on his mood, and eventually that seemed to help.

"We still have some time," Dix said, when they were downstairs putting on their helmets. "Want to take a look at the family glory hole?"

Sharan was thinking double entendre, an old whorehouse for miners she had seen posing in exhausted rummy-looking groups, the mother lode having forever escaped them.

"It's a gold mine. Defunct now. But the view up there is worthwhile."

The road into the hills was not much to Sharan's liking. Badly designed to begin with, and not well maintained. Switchbacks, worndown asphalt buckled in places and patched with long snaky seams of tar, crumbling shoulders, no shoulders in places where the faded white wooden guardrail had been breached above ravines, the hillsides and tall trees shrouded in kudzu like mysterious stage sets stored for a green eternity. And Dix, out front, was intent on pushing it. Showing too much confidence for conditions. She lost sight of him for up to ten seconds at a time as the road climbed and the ravines, now free of the kudzu that overwhelmed the lower dells, were deeper, darker, rockier. Faded signs and a small billboard reminded of the nearby Rutland Glory Hole. Country store on the left, a hicky frame job with a tin canopy painted yellow, then miscellaneous imploding cabins that had no windows, and daylight roofs.

Almost a minute without a glimpse of Dix.

She abruptly reached the overlook parking lot of the Rutland Glory Hole and gold mine museum. Half a dozen vehicles there, some tourists panning for bits of gold beneath the roof of a long wooden sluice, but no other motorcycle: she'd lost him. Somewhere.

Sharan made a slow circle of the parking lot, then accelerated and went back down the hill. She couldn't recall any turnoffs for the last five miles or so. He hadn't stopped at the general store, which was close to the road with only minimum parking space, hard-packed red clay and glittering mica. Maybe he had pulled off behind a shack to do some business—riding a bike greatly stimulated the bowels and kidneys.

She kept her speed under thirty. A pickup truck flying a Confederate flag from the radio antenna passed her on its way up to the Glory Hole. She was looking mostly at the right—downhill—side of the road and almost missed the skidmark again, on the other side. Where gravel had washed across the road from the hillside in a recent downpour. Not enough gravel, however, to have caused her a problem earlier.

The skidmark.

It looked fresh to Sharan. Almost to the edge of the pavement, then tire tracks across three feet of cruddy shoulder to a jagged gap in the guardrail, and blue yonder. Her stomach seized up. She saw a thin veil of dust in the air, lingering over the ravine.

Easy to imagine it happening to him. The gravel, a skid, panic-braking but too much throttle and over he'd go, helplessly.

Sharan parked her own bike off the road and ran to the gap in the guardrail.

The pink-and-turquoise Harley lay upended a hundred or more feet below, near the wooded bottom of the ravine. She could see the trail it had left once it hit: metal and taillight fragments glinting in the sun, a torn road map fluttering on a bush.

But no sign of Dix.

She looked up and down the road. Nobody coming, no help in sight.

Her skin was flushed, but her heart felt cold, a lump the size of a freezer roast. She began to pick her way down the steep slope, sliding in hillside dirt and rubble bladed off the road by snowplows in winter.

"Dix!"

Sharan heard a hawk cry, and the distant, intermittent sound of a helicopter. She paused for a few moments, leaning downhill, sus-

pended by her prosthetic hand from the limb of a dogwood growing
almost horizontally. Hoping to hear a sound out of him from
wherever he'd fetched up in the jumbled brush that lined a cove and
shallow stream below.

No traffic on the road. A few noteworthy birds on a telephone line.
A couple of flies landed on her bare arm, and she twitched them away.
Her own breath was the loudest sound she heard.

She found that the customized bike, when she got to it, had been
seriously torn up. Gasoline reek; a couple of tigerish butterflies staggered through the tainted air. But there was no blood sprinkle on the
savaged chrome or shattered mirrors. He should have been cast off or
left behind on the side of the ravine when the bike slammed down,
pinwheeled off an outcrop where she had seen fresh gouge marks and
tumbled the last fifty feet to rest with bent front wheel and shocks
uppermost in a clogging mass of vine and brush. She looked around
desperately, calling Dix's name again.

And heard him respond with a cough, somewhere off to her left
and in the cove.

"I'm coming, Dix!"

A thin whippy branch raised a welt below her right eye. Then she
tripped over something partly buried in bottom trash, sprawled and
cut the heel of her hand on the jagged point of a small windfall. Heard
him coughing again. And then, as the mild breeze shifted west, the
faint dull clopping of the helicopter sounded nearer.

"Where are you?"

Sharan got up, looking at her gashed palm, momentarily distracted
by the sight of blood.

If it hadn't been for the rising racket of the incoming helicopter she
would have heard him, because he was moving clumsily out of the
bottomland wildwood in his rush to get to her.

Just as Sharan noticed his shadow and began to turn, the butterfly
net swished down over her head and shoulders, covering her nearly
to the waist. He gave a strong yank on the long handle. Sharan tripped
and sprawled again, on her face.

Rolling over, bleeding, arms pinned to her sides by the aluminum
rim of the cloth net, Sharan saw a short man with coarse black hair
and Sino-Tibetan contours to his coppery glistening face. Peering at
her as he kneeled. He wore welder-style sunglasses so dark she
couldn't locate his eyes, and several strands of bright beads. She tried
to kick him. He straddled her at the waist, knees clamping her ribcage
tightly, and produced, with the hectic anxiety of a door-to-door sales-

man selling an unloved product, a ceramic jar from the fanny pack he wore. Around the squat lidded jar was the fancifully elongated, painted image of a tiger with wings.

"Don't worry," he said nonsensically, in British-accented English. "I am a doctor. This won't harm you."

Sharan cursed and ranted and bucked.

At arm's length he removed the domed lid from his little jar, averting his own face as if from a threat of fire. When she tried to crawl away in terror on her back he sat down hard on her pelvis, holding the tilted jar within an inch of her nose beneath the net.

She couldn't have described the complex odor that came from the jar. It wasn't unpleasant. Sour but peachy, ashes, too. Acrid, a moment after she inhaled involuntarily. Stinging her nostrils and the membranes at the back of her throat. After the first whiff Sharan held her breath, but he knew just where to poke her, two stiff fingers to the diaphragm, to get her to inhale convulsively again.

"Breathe deeply," he said. "Don't struggle."

The tops of the trees were thrashing in a violent rotor wind. Helicopter thunder. She saw it, green and white, hovering a hundred feet above the ravine, sideways to her. Too much agitation, dust devils, for her to get a good look. The closely woven net half blinding her.

Butterflies.

The man sitting on her gave her another poke. Sharan gasped. Fighting back seemed to have become less important. What was the use? She just didn't want him poking her again. So she breathed in, breathed out, beginning to feel calmer, dissociated from the event, removed from the solar-hot maw of pure calamity. She closed her eyes.

"How do you feel?"

Why was he still bothering her? She had visions to attend to. The little Confederate sentry from the upstairs porch of the restaurant was coming toward her across a sunny field through clouds of rainbow butterflies, waving, calling to her. He had put his rifle down, somewhere. The war was over. It was time to forget. Just forget the unpleasantness. No more fears. Be content.

"Leave me alone," Sharan said, and followed with a yawn.

He continued to sit on her, but he put the close-fitting lid back on his jar, and the jar in his fanny pack.

"My name is Dr. Dorji. It is useful for you to know that now; later it will not be necessary for you to remember that you have ever met me. I want you to know that you have nothing to fear from me. Do you understand?"

Sharan winced.

"What's the matter?"

"Noise. Can't hear you very well."

"Yes, the helicopter. It will land in a few moments. I'll help you not to hear the noise any longer, only the sound of my voice. I will count to three. On three, you may see the helicopter, but you will no longer hear it because you wish not to."

"Fine."

"One, two, three, the noise is no longer there. Blink twice if you don't hear it."

Sharan blinked twice.

"But your hearing is in no way impaired. Your reflexes are normal. Why don't I remove the net now? Do we need it?"

"No."

"And you have nothing to fear from me. Is that right?"

"Umm-hmm."

"In point of fact, I am now the only person you recognize, have ever known, will ever need to know, unless I advise you otherwise. Who am I?"

"Dr. Dorji."

"I'll help you sit up. Good. And now the net is gone. No need for you to remember that it was ever there." A few moments later he asked, "Have you seen my butterfly net, Sharan?" He was holding it, collapsed, in his left hand.

"What net?" Sharan asked, mildly puzzled.

"I want to attend to that cut on your palm before we leave. It might become infected."

"What happened to my hand?"

"You were in a cycling accident. You were riding alone. Fortunately you had no severe injuries. The cut is nothing. You could heal it yourself, in a matter of minutes, through meditation to accelerate the body's natural restorative power. However, at some point in the future you will need a physical reminder that the accident did occur."

"Okay."

"Later you will be told about the accident. And when you wake up, you will remember the details just as the accident was described to you. I'm going to get my emergency medical case now. You wait here for me."

"Okay. I'm thirsty."

"I'll also bring you a drink of water." Dorji rose, looking through the trees at something or someone. The helicopter was on the ground. Sharan sat in the attitude in which he had placed her, with her cut hand palm up in her lap. She studied a mote of sun on the torn sleeve of her shirt, endlessly and earnestly, until he came back.

Dorji wasn't alone.

"How is she?" Esther Trevellian asked.

"Cloud nine. Or is it cloud eight, Sharan?"

"Cloud ten," Sharan answered, and laughed. She had not responded to Esther's presence or the sound of her voice. She drank all of the water that Dorji had brought to her in a plastic cup.

Esther gave the doctor a perplexed look.

"Does she know I'm here?"

"You exist for Sharan; she sees you, but not as a distinctive entity. It's a little complicated to explain."

"What *is* that stuff?"

"Botanical-sourced hypnotics, in combination with various hallucinogens that bear biochemical relationship to well-known substances found in the West, peyote being most common. The drug has been known to *lunggom* masters for centuries, some of whom are said literally to walk on air. I haven't seen this, myself. Those monks wishing to achieve oneness with Rimpoche without also tumbling off a cliff use a milder form of the vapor with which I've released Sharan's mind from the temporal. As for a name, it is simply called Tiger Breath, in the Jhomolhari region where many of the specimen plants are collected from crevices at very high altitudes."

"Uh-huh. Who or what is 'Rimpoche'?"

"The most holy guru who brought Buddhism to my native land in the eighth century."

"How long can she be maintained like this?"

"How long is necessary?"

"I need to get some true statements out of her."

"For that something more prosaic will be required; an IV drip of that old standby, sodium pentothal."

"Dix is coming. Let's get her aboard the helicopter before we attract more attention than we may have already. Sharan's hand can wait. You say she won't remember any of this?"

"No."

Esther shrugged.

"It may not matter anyway."

"I'm still thirsty," Sharan said, now watching, with a toned and rapt eye, a bumblebee cruising around her.

Esther found her mother in her customary place, taking late-afternoon sun near the commemorative flame on Cloud Horse Mountain. A middle-aged Bavarian nurse with severely braided hair and unplucked eyebrows sat nearby doing needlepoint. Esther stood beside Elnora's wheelchair, the wind at their backs. The wheelchair was outfitted with numerous devices that measured Elnora's vital signs, analyzing and updating by the second, displaying graphs and flow charts on screens the size of credit cards. In addition to her many sensors, some implanted, others taped to her withering skin, Elnora wore a cashmere sweater-coat with a hood, sculpted hair like frozen slush visible at the edge of the hood. She wore the kind of sunglasses you see on cruise ships, jaunty plastic frames in primary colors. Her frames were red. Plain dark lenses, no prescription. Rouge was thick and dark on Elnora's cheekbones, like scabs forming on skinned knees.

The cloud show was on. Thunderheads in the southeast with tridents of lightning, swift movement, distant torrents. No horse's head today, but the thunder-horse above the mountain was a frequent occurrence. Due west the clouds were huge and roly-poly, with a pink blush. Nothing much near the mountain yet, only a few silkworm streaks picking up a tint of gold from the sun. The sky too pale for Esther's liking; change in the weather soon, and it would turn colder. At eventide the moon would rise one day from the full.

"Was that you in the helicopter?"

"Yes, Mom."

"Why didn't you crash?"

"I'm a very good pilot. I won't ever crash."

"Curse my wretched luck."

"Now, Mom."

"I've written to *Sixty Minutes*. Complete exposure on national television. The disgrace you so richly deserve."

"You didn't eat your lunch, did you? Your blood sugar is low. That's why you're in such a feisty mood. Low blood sugar."

"Feisty? That's what you call it?"

"You have to eat, all there is to it. Or you get this way."

"I have no taste buds left," Elnora said, her stridency suddenly reduced to an impoverished whine.

"You'll have to go back on drips again. You don't want that."

"No end to your cruelty."

"You're just feeling sorry for yourself."

"I want to call *Larry King Live*! There's a sympathetic ear. I'll reveal your true character to the world. Why can't I have a telephone in my room?"

"For that very reason."

"Ursula!"

"Ursula's busy with her needlepointing. If you want something, I'll gladly get it for you."

"I want one of her needles, to stick in my eyes! I might as well be blind, too!"

"Then you couldn't watch *Larry King Live*. Or *Geraldo*."

The old woman's hand darted out from beneath her lap robe, and she seized Esther's left hand. Esther snatched it away.

"Don't."

"What's the bandage for?"

"I said don't touch."

"You're doing it again, aren't you?"

"What?"

"Biting your thumb. You always bit your thumb when things weren't going your way."

"It's a little infection, that's all."

"Can't stop yourself, can you? We had to tie that hand behind your back, so you couldn't get at it. The crazed look in your eyes. You'd scream and scream. Little monster working herself into a frenzy, trying to get that hand free. Don't think I didn't enjoy it."

"I hate hearing you talk like this."

"Eat! That's right, Esther. Chew and chew until you're bloody rag and bone. Until you've devoured your own black, evil heart. Won't I be glad! Things aren't going Esther's way. Isn't that wonderful?"

"Just shut up, Mom."

"I didn't invite you to hang around. Go away and chew on your thumb. But it won't bring *him* back. Your nutty half-brother."

"Have some pity. Show some compassion. And Scott was my *brother*. Not partly. Not half."

"Little you know."

"Why do you have to be so—horrible. Horrible, horrible, all the time. I'm taking away your TV."

"Esther's mad! Esther's going to *punish* me."

"No, I'm not mad. Hurt, maybe. The TV goes until you apologize."

Elnora's narrow jaw set itself. She sat stiffly in the wheelchair, her only hand stirring in her lap like a feeding lobster's claw. Nothing more was said for a few minutes.

"Can I apologize now?" Elnora said.

"Sure, Mom."

"But I will *never* tell you who Scott's real father was. I will say this much. He was one hell of a fuck, a potentate of cock, unlike your *own* father. But of course you know how poorly Old Saggy performed. Darling dearest bitch of mine."

Esther turned and walked away from the wheelchair, bandaged thumb going to her lower lip. She froze and whipped her gaze toward Ursula, who was looking down at her needlepoint with the exaggerated indifference of one who has been eavesdropping. Ursula's comprehension of English was suspect and there was little chance she could have overheard more than scraps of conversation because of the wind's direction, but. Get rid of her tomorrow, Esther resolved, before wheeling and going back to stand behind Elnora's thick tired motorized chair.

"Do you know where the brake is? Then get a good running start," Elnora advised. "We'll go over the side together. I've made my peace."

"You're a package, Mom. Now, listen. You're not going to die. Dying is not on your schedule in the foreseeable future. You're completely monitored. Every heartbeat, change in respiration, blood pressure, brain waves, skin temperature, drop of tinkle. Every moment, waking and sleeping, thoroughly analyzed. Nurses on eight-hour shifts, specialists on call, replacement organs in storage. But they're just insurance. A long life is programmed into your genes. Your heart has the vigor of a mountain goat's. And I intend for you to take every last breath that, genewise, you have coming to you. Can you last another ten years? You'd only be seventy-five when you blow out the candles at that celebration. Could it be fifteen years? Wait, how about *twenty*? I really believe we can keep you going for at least another twenty years! And they said you wouldn't last more than a few days, when I dragged you out of the smoldering ruins. They didn't know my mom. Twenty more years! Go for it. Meantime, I think we should make up. What d'you say? No hard feelings."

"Daddyfucker."

"I guess you aren't hearing me too well."

"Even between your sweet lips he couldn't get it up all the way, I bet."

Esther said, in a voice lethal for its lack of tonality, "What I think, it's high time for another keepsie, Mom. Remind both of us what you mean to me."

Elnora was silent. After a couple of minutes Esther moved to the side of the wheelchair and went down intimately on one knee, looking her mother in the face. Elnora trembled. Some saliva had leaked from one corner of her sunken, puckered mouth, as crudely colored as if she had used a child's liquid crayon for lipstick.

"You did hear that, didn't you?"

"No more."

Esther reached for a handkerchief to wipe her mother's seamed chin. Elnora cringed.

"Another keepsie. A little remembrance. Hasn't it been such a long time? How long? Oh, I think it must be almost fwee years now."

"Stop. Don't."

"I do it for *you*, Mummy-wummy."

"I said . . . no. You *can't*."

"But our whole relationship *depends* on the keepsakes." She placed a cold finger on the pulse in Elnora's throat. What a healthy, fascinating pulse. The dark mainstream of their lives. "All six of them. Soon to be seven. For you, Mommer. All dedicated to you. How much love do you need, or want? Never mind. I don't expect a show of appreciation. I'll keep it coming anyway. Keep my luvvy-wuvvy coming. While your amazing, one-in-a-million genes keep you ticking, just ticking away. So many more years to go. Haven't I demonstrated my love for you? Believe me, after what you did, it wasn't, hasn't been easy. But I'll do what I must do as many times as *I fucking have to!* Lay them all to rest, while you, you, *you* go on living! Momsie? Try, for my sake, to have a little cheerier, more positive outlook. The time passes so much more quickly. I'll have Ursula take you in now. Oh, chicken curry for dinner. With wild rice. Don't tell me it's not one of Momsie's favorites! And I want you to make a special effort to clean your plate for me. Now pwomise Essie you'll clean your plate tonight. Pwomise. Pwomise."

TWENTY-ONE

WHISPERING DEMON

Dempsey Wingo was having steak and hash browns at a truck stop off Interstate 26, just south of Asheville, when the all-white tractor-trailer rig appeared, glow of sunset on its tinted windshield. No trace of chrome anywhere to interrupt the flowing, curvilinear appearance: the wraparound bumper, the aerodynamically styled cab roof. Nor did the rig have the usual stickers on the driver's door required for commercial hauling across state lines. The small logo was in green. A *T*, with the right crossbar of the T ending in an arrowhead. He'd seen the logo before.

Two drivers, both of them wearing handlebar mustaches. Exhibition quality. They were mustache hobbyists. Waxed points in rapier attitudes. While they ate their dinners they placed bets on pro football games by cellular telephone. It sounded like a complicated business. Dempsey had never understood the jargon of sports betting. But he wouldn't have wagered a plugged nickel on a game controlled by seven men wearing prison stripes.

Dempsey ate a piece of mom's apple pie with a slice of cheddar and watched the drivers for Trevel Resources have fun arguing about weighted offenses and other arcane statistics. When they were down to their after-dinner coffees he paid his bill and sauntered over to their booth. Names in script on their shirt pockets said Rusty and Pistol.

"Fine-looking rig you boys have there."

"For sure," Pistol said.

"Primo," Rusty said.

"Trevel Resources. Has a familiar ring to it."

"Pollution control devices," Rusty said.

"Smog, that sort of thing?"

"That's catalytic converters. What we're hauling is designed to break down toxic waste that can't be got rid of by other means. Hazardous bios that trickle out of dumps and contaminate aquifers. It's still kind of experimental, so we're told."

"Sounds promising. How does it work—or is that a trade secret?"

Pistol said, "Don't think so. It's proprietary, but no secret about it. You ever hear tell of spontaneous combustion?"

"Human beings bursting into flame? I think I read about it in *Fortean Times*."

"Yeah. But they burn so fast and so hot, nothing around them even gets scorched. That's the principal of the furnace we've got inside our van there. Shoot, you wouldn't believe the temperatures—ten thousand degrees Celsius. Almost twice as hot as the surface of the sun. Has to do with passing electrons through a gas. Partner, that bitch-demon *burns*. But they ain't hardly a sound, just a whisper. You can watch it, as long as you're wearing protective glasses. Put your hand on the outside of the furnace, won't so much as raise a blister while she's operating."

"But whatever's inside?"

Rusty snapped his fingers. "Gone. That quick, nothing left, not even a smell."

"Sounds like a boon to mankind. Where're you taking it?"

"Simon the Rock County, for some tests at a dump site."

"That's a hell of a coincidence. I was about to head down that way myself, visit my old granny. If you've got room for one more."

"Reckon we could find a place for you," Rusty allowed. "Where'd you come by that good-looking buckle?"

"Rodeoin'. I always have been a fool for hard times."

Esther found Dix outside at two in the morning, huddled in a sealskin coat and studying a comet with his twelve-inch telescope and Astro-Search computer software, containing more than 64,000 programmed stellar objects. It was a fine night for stargazing, but she wondered how he could see anything: she accidentally kicked an empty brandy bottle he'd left lying around and sent it skittering off the viewing platform and across the bare rocks. Dix had another bottle beside his leather director's chair. He drank from it before acknowledging her presence.

"How does it look for the human race, Dix?"

"This one won't hit us," he muttered. "But it's only a matter of time. A near-earth object nudged out of orbit will be picked up by electronic light detectors. It's already penetrated deeper than the orbit of Mars. Mass and velocity like nothing we've known before. A thousand kilometers in diameter. Tunguska was a firecracker by comparison. Long before it's bright enough to be seen with the naked eye, they will have done all of the calculations at Kitt Peak and JPL. There can be no mistake. It's headed right for us. Eight months to impact. Six months. The object can be seen now, in the night sky. Brighter than Venus. Panic conferences around the globe, conducted in secrecy. But total secrecy creates its own sinister aura. People intuit that something is going on. Naturally they assume the worst. Governments don't hold secret meetings for benign purposes. World-renowned psychics convene in haste to employ their powers in an effort to divert the incoming object from its collision course. The word is whispered around the globe. *Asteroid.* Now it's visible in the daytime. Three months. All human endeavor, except for eating, drinking and screwing, comes to a standstill. Our helpless leaders and astrophysicists are forced to reveal what they've kept from us. The jig is up. Sorry. People begin fleeing the cities. Looters take over. Now they can have that TV, the washer and dryer they've always coveted. Half the population of the world becomes a wailing, wandering horde, heaping ashes of contrition on their heads, besieging shrines, vowing next time to invent more capable gods. The other half step up their screwing. One month. The sky is on fire."

"You're a joy to be with tonight. I bought you the telescope to give you some perspective on our earthly muddle. Please pass me the goddamn brandy." Esther had a satisfying slug, then blew into her cupped cold hands. Dr. Dorji had fixed her up with another bandage, tightly taped over a thin cushion of foam rubber. But still she felt it with a pang that mimicked the onset of orgasm: the snug imprisoned lure of thumb, abused and corrupted flesh.

"How's Sharan?" Dix asked.

"Sleeping. We had a nice chat first."

"What did you find out?"

"You won't believe this. She has a Federal prison rap hanging over her head, courtesy of Coleman Dane. He set her up so she would have to spy on us. That louse. I don't know what I'm going to do about him yet. But something dire, depend on it."

Dix shrugged away any notion that he might care to know. "What about Sharan?"

"How can we blame poor Sharan? I don't. There's more to the story."

"There is?"

"Sharan's fallen for him. Cole is the mystery lover I was convinced she had tucked away somewhere."

Dix had no comment, other than a pressing-together of his lips. He scrutinized a readout on the telescope's keypad, hunched his shoulders and sought the otherworldly serenity available in the eyepiece.

"Again, although I might question her taste in men, who can really blame her?"

"Would you like to see the Veil Nebula? It's stunning. The whole loop is visible with the new UHC filter."

"Not tonight, Dix."

Dix sat down in his chair and rubbed his tiring eyes.

"Does Sharan know where she is, Sis?"

"No, not yet. She'll wake up tomorrow with a headache and that cut on her hand. I'll explain about the accident. Sharan was knocked unconscious, you called me, and because we're only seventy miles away as the crow flies, I came with Dr. Dorji and brought you both back to the mountain. Fortunately you were only shaken up. And you'll be in the Big Apple by breakfast."

Dix said, with a rib-level twinge of fear, "Esther, it's the middle of the night!"

"You have important business to attend to, and my feeling is we'll be socked in again by daylight. Mardie got back an hour ago—"

"Where was she?"

"Quickie vacation; she was looking a little peaked to me, so I insisted on a change of scenery. Anyway, Mardie will fly you to the Asheville airport, and Kip is standing by to whisk you up to Teeter in the seven-thirty-seven. I want you to get some sleep, and then back to work. You've been a little morbid lately. I guess we both have."

"What about Sharan?"

"Oh, Sharan. We'll have a nice brunch when she wakes up. Then I'll send her by limo home to the trailer park, and we won't be seeing her again."

"She's not going to do our portraits?"

Esther said, with enough irritability to make him flinch, "Dix, your brain has crashed. I said she was *spying* on us. I don't socialize with known enemies."

"Was it because of Felicia Dane?"

"Yes, of course. Has Cole ever bought himself a *load* of grief."

"I told you," Dix said tensely. "He'll never leave us alone."

With her right hand Esther massaged the back of his neck; his skin crawled pleasurably.

"What do I always say?"

"It's a hill of beans."

"And?"

"Ten thousand years from now none of this will matter."

Esther sighed. "My definition of paradise. When you look at the stars through your telescope, oceans and oceans of stars, how do you feel?"

"Not so anxious. Relieved. Sometimes I feel myself falling—up. From darkness to light."

"To Eternity."

"To *something* that's blessed. Primal infinity. The harmony of the Beginning."

" 'Wherever poor Eulenspiegel fled in terror, he saw nothing but heads on stakes, young girls put in sacks and thrown alive into rivers, men broken on the wheel with iron bars, women buried in ditches and the hangmen dancing on their chests to break their ribs.' "

Dix cringed in horror. "Esther, don't."

"I remember that from a novel Cole gave me to read. He had a college crush on the German Romantics. What I'm saying, it's the way of flesh on earth. It's what goes on here. You and I—what we are is not our doing, and some day we'll escape. There are no flaws or failures that seem so terrible from the perspective of the stars."

She continued to rub his neck. The heat generated by her hand rose to his temples; his skull felt aglow.

"Am I right, Dix?"

His eyes swam in luxurious unshed tears. He nodded slightly.

After a minute or two Esther asked cautiously, "Would you look in on Mom before you go, Dix?"

"Oh, God, do I—"

"We've made some changes in her medication. She's a pussycat now, I solemnly pw-promise."

"I never know what to *say* to her, Esther!"

"I think a glimpse of your face will do her a world of good." She withdrew her vibrant fingers and made a fist, giving him a no-

nonsense nudge. "I'll have the telescope put up for you. Why not leave the rest of the brandy with me? A sauna on the flight to Noo Yawk might be a good idea too. You'll want to be tip-top for your meetings this afternoon. And don't take any shit from the sand niggers."

Sharan wasn't on the Delta flight from Atlanta, which arrived in San Francisco at eleven-fourteen Pacific Daylight Time.

By a quarter past one Coleman Dane was aboard an air force passenger jet out of SFO, en route to Atlanta.

Already a good many citizens of Rising Fawn Mobile Home Park had been awakened and questioned by FBI agents and federal marshals. The fax machine coupled to Dane's Thinkpad had printed out enough information to confirm that Sharan had gone biking with Dix Trevellian at around ten-fifteen the previous morning, and hadn't returned.

In Asheville, a flight plan had been filed for the family 737, ETA Teeterboro at six fifty-seven A.M. One passenger, and that was Dix.

Dane got the director of the FBI out of a bed he wasn't supposed to be in, in a Boston hotel suite.

"Kidnapping? There's not enough to go on yet, Cole."

"She's missing, and I haven't heard from her." Dane gestured to Fitzie, his good right arm, to bring him some Alka-Seltzer. "She was last seen in the company of Dix Trevellian; that's a positive ID. Dix may be on the move right now from Cloud Horse Mountain, expected at Asheville Regional Airport within the hour. I don't want that plane leaving the ground until I've talked to him."

Michael Harms groaned softly. Dane heard another, female voice chirping in the background. She sounded very young.

"Okay," Harms said. "I don't know if there's enough time, but I'll try to delay the seven-thirty-seven's clearance through Atlanta Center."

Dane picked up the telephone beside his seat and spoke to the pilot, telling him to refile for Asheville, North Carolina.

Fitzie brought him a brimming glass of Alka-Seltzer. "That stuff is no good with an ulcer, Boss."

"All I have is heartburn, Fitz."

"You have an ulcer. Fourteen years I've worked for you, have I ever been wrong about the state of your health? See a doctor, before the wall of your stomach blows out like a bad tire."

"She may already be dead, Fitz. Godammit! Has that surveillance van left Atlanta yet?"

After a shower and a shave Dix made his promised stop in his mother's dwelling place, a room he hated for its automated strangeness, perpetual twilight. There was also the tropic pungency of sickroom bouquets, aroma-enhanced vapors jetted periodically into the air, and the medical electronics creepily keeping tabs on her functions. For all but a couple of hours each day she lived in a chromed bed with rollbars like a dirt track racecar that slowly rotated and plumped-up beneath her into new computer-plotted positions, making whooshing and clicking sounds. Lifting buttocks, lowering a shoulder, changing the elevation of her head. An old folks thrill ride in a medical Disneyland. The point of it to prevent her blood from pooling or tissue from wasting on any part of her surgically foreshortened body. The half-cremated limbs long ago pruned away. Two inches above one knee, midshin of the other leg. Her right arm well past the elbow.

The nurse on the eleven-to-seven night shift was a Sudanese woman with a long neck and piquant slanted eyes. Lime-colored irises with a splatter-dash of rum: she had some Creole as well as Dinka blood. Karmika put down a copy of *Elle* and left DisMed when Dix walked in, giving him a familiar little pat on the way out. Maybe the gesture was meant to be reassuring. He'd had Karmika twice during this, his most recent sojourn on the Mountain. In the equatorial heat of his sauna it had been like trying to hold onto an armload of eels. No matter what position they assumed, his less-than-rigid cock kept slipping out; after a while it seemed pretty funny to both of them. Karmika had a nice chest-deep laugh.

There were three TVs on in the room, tuned silently to different channels. On one screen a dozen skydivers held hands in circular freefall. On another, a female evangelist with a face like puff pastry and a mauve wig with curls a foot deep was weeping softly in close-up. Elnora's black eyeshade lay across her forehead as if she'd been hastily censored. She regarded Dix blankly.

His gut feeling: say nothing, smile a little, nod respectfully, leave. He had a belated, skull-busting headache from the brandy, which the cold night air had postponed.

"To what do I owe the honor?" his mother said.

"How're you, Mom?"

"I'm living dead. What else is new?"

"Well, I'm on my way to New York."

"Don't take Karmika with you; she's the only good nurse I have."

"I won't."

Elnora said with a wan smirk, "I saw that horny look she gave you."

Dix watched the skydivers fall; it made him queasy. "I wanted to know if there was anything I could do for you."

She gestured. "Bring me a gun. Loaded, of course."

Dix's shoulders slumped. He looked at the floor, like a man who has heard a bad diagnosis.

"Dix."

"What."

"I never have liked you."

"I know."

"But I don't hate you. My living death isn't your fault. I know you would have found mercy in your heart to put an end to it long ago. Except for Esther."

He nodded bleakly, unable to commiserate with either of them. Elnora wore a nasal canula, oxygen to refresh the dreariest hour of her night. She seemed to monopolize most of the breathable air in the room. His lungs filled with the lugubriously sweet vapors from the flowers in their crystal vases. Fresh flowers every day. Nothing was allowed to wilt, stale or grow old in DisMed.

"Come closer. I have no voice."

"I really should be—"

"No, no, no. Something important."

Dix trudged a little closer to the bed. A priest wearing a wide-brimmed hat and an ankle-length soutane crossed an empty plaza in a small Mexican town. The skydivers opened their rainbow parafoils. Mary Tyler Moore was young again, putting a casserole into the oven at the Petries'.

Elnora changed channels with a bored frown.

Dix waited, bracing his forehead with one hand, shielding himself but alert for something unpleasant, the treacherous *bon mot*, the small well-placed knife in the ego.

"It's keepsie time again. She told me so."

Dix reacted slowly.

"You're lying."

"You know the symptoms. The distracted drifting air. The down-hearted silences."

"Esther's in mourning, for Christ's—"

"Then the thumb. Have you seen her thumb today, all wrapped up like a mummy? Don't tell me *that* isn't meaningful."

Dix breathed harshly, and trembled.

"I know you're a yellow-belly. But I still have three fingers left on my hand. I can do it. Just bring me a gun."

A long-legged girl with bare breasts ran bobbingly along a beach.

"Don't talk like that."

"It's somebody you like, to be sure. Maybe you're in love with her. Like the last girl, what was her name? I'll remember in a minute. Right over there. Bottom drawer of the armoire, thrown in with all of sister's other keepsies. An eye patch? Yes, it *was* an eye patch. And her name—it's coming to me."

"Don't you say it!"

"No need to get snarly. Who else can I talk to? Hasn't it sunk in *yet*? Esther has a real serious *problem*."

Dix cast his eyes helplessly around the room. He saw Geraldo's toothy countenance in a life-size blowup, autographed to Elnora. His throat convulsed like a man forced to breathe under water. He ran a hand over his lower jaw to suppress nervous giggles, and tasted cast-up brandy.

"No, no, no," he admonished his mother.

"You're as much to blame as she is. There are sins of omission as well as sins of commission. Don't you know your sins will catch up to you? It's already festering in your gut, I can tell by your expression. Next, your brain. You'll start making mistakes in your designs, because you know you *want* to be punished for letting your incestuous sister get off scot-free! That new ball park will collapse and mangle a thousand people in broken concrete and twisted girders. A skyscraper will fly to pieces in a high wind. Maybe you've already made that one careless mistake. I lie here feeling this humble abode shaking in a good blow. The steel creaks, Dix. The bolts are loosening in the granite. I know you've heard it, too. God forbid that this *house* you're so proud of should come loose from the cliff and we all plummet two thousand feet to our doom. Is that in your dreams, too, Dix? Do you wake up screaming? Failure. Repudiation. Disgrace. Don't let it happen to you, son. Put an end to your own torment, before the next keepsie. Push the monster out of the helicopter if you have to; drown her in her bath, sprinkle strychnine on her mashed potatoes. But don't let her kill another poor cripple as a stand-in for her own mother!"

Real-life open-heart surgery. Chimpanzees wearing suits and ties and carrying attaché cases. A man in a desert setting, pointing to Biblical ruins.

"Look at me, look at me, at *me*, Dix!"

With a strangled sound in his throat that would have blanched any but the living dead, Dix bolted from his mother's presence.

Elnora stared nervelessly at the door space, waiting for Karmika to return. The machines around her responded in their efficient ways to physiological changes. Five minutes went by. Ten. Karmika was taking her time, having coffee, using the john. The mechanism of the computerized bed clicked several times, changing her position; minutely, ever so gently. Elnora's thumb and remaining fingers crept up to her forehead. She pulled the shade down over her eyes.

"Yellow through and through," she said disgustedly. "The bitch wins again."

Dix looked in three empty bedrooms before he found the one in which Sharan lay sleeping.

The fiberglass shades were up; there was a drifting mist outside the convex windows, star fields fading from view. A change in the weather, but sudden changes, for better or worse, were the norm on Cloud Horse Mountain.

"Sharan?" he said, moving closer to the circular bed in which she lay sprawled on her back, relaxed arms at four and ten o'clock, lips parted, her breathing sibilant and very deep. Her tanned face was composed on a yellow silk pillow, skin looking a little jaundiced in the light from four dim ceiling spots. She had a slight cut and a bruise under one eye. Well concealed, he had watched her fall, several times, scrambling down into the ravine, calling his name. Afraid for him. *Caring*. The "accident" he'd staged good enough to fool anyone. Hated to do it. He was enjoying the bike he'd pushed over the side, throttle open. Total wreck now. But Sharan—some hope left.

Dix sat down beside her; her body moved to the shapely rhythm of the warmed water-filled mattress. He gave one shoulder a hard shake, and her head came up from the pillow, mouth opening a little more. But her eyes remained closed. Dorji had really put her under. This was no use. He was trembling so violently his ribs ached. Try again.

"Sharan? Wake up. It's Dix. Open your eyes. You've got to wake up, you're c-coming with me."

His own movements had the water bed rocking. *Get up, wake up. You don't know what's happening.* Already nauseous from too much brandy and deadly fear, his efforts to rouse her popped sweat on his brow and made him dizzy. Black spots before his eyes, disorientation; he slumped across her body, sobbing drily.

"What's going on, Dix?"

He made thick, gurgling sounds, forcing down vomit.

"Es-ther."

"Mardie's waiting in the helicopter. We're going to be socked in soon. What are you doing?"

"I was—I wanted to say good-bye to Sharan."

"Obviously Sharan is sound asleep. She can't hear you. Sit up, Dix."

He felt Esther's hand on his shoulder. A light, concerned grip.

"Are you sick?"

"No, I'll—be all right."

"Come on then. I'll go up with you. We'll leave Sharan to sleep it off. Okay?"

Dix nodded and blotted his mouth on the bedsheet. He rose slowly, unsure of the strength of his knees. His body a void, all of his energy crackling at the tips of fingers, the top of his head.

"Esther, don't you think—"

He turned around. She was wearing an old red terry-bathrobe, one he recognized as having belonged to their father. Cy Trevellian, a big shambling man. Like a child, she was lost in the droopy robe. His teeth chattered from the shock of seeing Esther's face painted in neo-savage camouflage colors. She had pinned up her dark hair, meaning business.

"Wha   w why did you—"

"What is the *matter*, Dix? I told you I was going hunting this morning. It's already four o'clock, and I still have to dress. Come on." She studied his expression for a few moments, then leaned forward to kiss the tip of his nose. Her own nose wrinkled, leaving striations in the thick greasepaint. "Oboy. Do you ever need a breath mint."

On the water bed Sharan raised her false arm and moaned dreamily. Esther gazed at her.

"She is *quite* a dish. And very talented. I'm going to miss her, too, Dix. Really. But it just can't be. We're strong, Dix, because we defend ourselves."

She put a hand inside his elbow, interlocked fingers, walked him gently from the room. Diverting him with little hugs and squeezes; with whisperings and playful animal bites. Never allowing him to look back. Because, as she had told him often enough in the past, nothing would be there.

Nothing worth remembering.

TWENTY-TWO

HANGING JUDGES

Dempsey heard the woman, could smell her in the dark, long before she got to the kitchen. He wondered what she was doing up at four-thirty. It couldn't have been on his account. Both Mordecai and the woman had been snoring in a back bedroom when he entered the house by way of the screen porch, slicing through the nylon mesh screen with his hunting knife and just walking in. Knowing Mordecai Kregg depended on his Redbone and Plott Hounds to raise alarums and his shotgun for protection; his bullwhip was for intimidation. Nobody in Simon the Rock County was feeble-minded enough to mess with a Kregg anyway. The dogs were sound asleep after feasting on the hamburger Dempsey had doctored and lobbed into their kennel an hour ago, and Mordecai was still razzing away in his bed. Maybe the woman was just an early riser, or had a complaint of some sort that got her up at odd hours.

She was holding her lower back with one hand when she appeared, yawning, in the kitchen doorway. She wore a flannel nightgown, probably gray or light blue. Hard to tell in the illumination afforded by the stove's pilot light. The odor that accompanied her was a miasma of dried love-sweats and unwashed hair, lingering perfume and a case of the farts. She farted again while trying to find the light switch with an outstretched hand. Dempsey had unscrewed the bulb in the porcelain fixture above the sink. The woman cursed spiritlessly. Dempsey watched her from the porch, to where he had retreated when he heard her get up. No moon or stars behind him; fog filled the hollows at the base of Cloud Horse Mountain.

The woman grumbled to herself, cleared her throat and opened the refrigerator door. Darkness inside; Dempsey had thought of that, too. Finally she picked up a charcoal starter and used it to light a candle in a Bell jar lid on the counter beside the sink.

There was a box of the Colonel's fried chicken on the kitchen table along with two uncorked wine bottles, a bowl of fruit with blackened bananas and a pile of chicken bones on a plate. The woman looked into the box, took out an extra-crispy drumstick and chewed on it as she turned back to the stove. She opened a cannister of coffee, put a fresh filter into the coffee maker, then primed a sink pump. Electricity and cooking gas, but no town water this far out.

Dempsey took advantage of the noise she made getting the well water to flow, and reentered the kitchen. He paused at the table, selected a piece of chicken himself from the box, crusty breast meat, went up behind the woman and tapped her on the shoulder.

She jumped and looked around sourly, probably thinking *Mordecai*. She had a bruise on one cheekbone and a complexion like wet newspaper. When she saw Dempsey her mouth opened wide; he crammed the breast of chicken inside before she could scream, spun her with the other hand, picked up an iron fry pan and rang it flatly off the back of her skull. She sank to her knees against the kitchen cabinet, tilted, fell sideways to the floor, her eyelids fluttering.

Dempsey made sure she was breathing all right, then trussed her up with clothesline from the porch. Through all of this activity Mordecai continued to rattle the windowpanes in his bedroom with salvos of snores.

After the woman was secure, Dempsey visited the bedroom and took away Mordecai's shotgun. He turned on a light. Mordecai's head was buried between pillows and his sleep was not interrupted. The sheets had needed changing for a week. He wore long johns, spotted yellow at the crotch. He hadn't shaved for awhile. The transplanted skin taken from the back of one thigh was hairless where so much scalp had been removed.

Dempsey looked for other weapons in the bedroom. A .45 automatic on the closet shelf that looked uncared for, slide and trigger guard flecked with rust. He took the pistol, too, then had a look around the house.

Mordecai's workshop was of great interest. Two benches held the tools of a sophisticated bombmaker. Microelectronics. Explosive materials and detonating cord, by the case: black powder, ammonium nitrate, fulminate of mercury, commercial-grade dynamite, RDX and PETN. Some yellow-brown nitroglycerin in a refrigerator, cooled, according to the temperature gauge, to just above nitro's freezing point of 56°F. Hobbyist's shelves and drawers of computer chips, audio-sensitive detonators, timers, pressure plates, spools of coated and uncoated wire. He had a microscope that cost as much as the trailered bass boat sitting in his front yard. Mordecai could build bombs that would explode on hearing the song of a woodland canary, bombs that reacted to changes in atmospheric pressure, bombs that could be set off by laser beam. Bombs in tubes of lipstick, bombs in office staplers. A bomb activated when you picked it up, that would explode if you set it down. Concealed in a child's toy.

Looking at the explosives cached in a small room next to Mordecai's own bedroom, enough power to dig a football-size crater in the earth a dozen feet deep and level mature trees all around, Dempsey wondered with a shading of rue if there was anything the man was afraid of. Which could make for difficulties getting him to admit that he had built the bomb that killed Lew Carbine.

Dempsey went back into the bedroom and shook Mordecai awake, which took some doing. When Mordecai raised up groggily, unfocused, and before he had an inkling of trouble, Dempsey hit him over the ear with the butt of the shotgun, sending Mordecai to a deeper dreamland.

The air force jet bringing Coleman Dane from San Francisco landed at Asheville Regional Airport at 7:36 A.M. Federal marshals came aboard and he spoke to them for a few minutes before disembarking. They escorted Dane to a windowless office in a hangar on the south side of the field. Unpainted concrete-block walls, a concrete floor, fluorescent lighting, three padded, steel chairs, a gray office safe, matching gray steel desk with a hard black vinyl inlay. A pinup calendar on one wall, nearly nude coeds posing sweetly with phallic sports equipment: hockey sticks, baseball bats, a catcher's mask worn like a chastity girdle. Dane took the calendar down. There was nothing else to look at in the room. It was as monolithic and isolated from the world as a prison cellblock. The right atmosphere for what he had planned.

"Bring him in."

Four minutes later Dix Trevellian, wearing denim pants and jacket, a chamois shirt and Eurotrash gold jewelry, came scowling to the door, giving the marshals plenty of lip. He stopped at the threshold and stared at Coleman Dane. An unexpected displeasure, from Dix's expression. Dix cast aside a crumbled Styrofoam coffee cup with a snort of annoyance and put on his threat display. He could get red from the neck up in a hurry. Even his tightly curled hair seemed to go bouffant.

"Could you please tell me by what authority you've held up my flight to New York for the last hour and a half?"

"There may be controlled substances aboard," Dane said with mild disapproval, then patronized Dix with a slight sneer of amusement.

"Controlled—are you nuts? Have you totally lost it, Cole?" He looked around quickly as the door was closed and locked behind him. He had to make an effort not to twist the door knob, but couldn't stop the first, furtive gesture of the unwittingly trapped. His failure got him madder. He faced Dane again. "What's going on here? What do you think you're doing? None of this is remotely legal. You've really overstepped any authority you might have. Wilton Hardesty—" Dix blew off to a new level of power-jiving. "Fuck it, *forget* Hardesty, this outrage is going straight to your boss!"

Dane shrugged. "Or your aircraft may be unsafe. For your own good, it should be thoroughly inspected before you take off. While you're waiting, Dix, have a seat."

"My ass. I mean, *your* ass, and I'm walking out of here. Get that door open now!"

"Better do what I tell you," Dane said, with a significant change of tone.

Dix turned and began hammering on the steel door with his fist.

"Unlock the door. Unlock it! I demand you unlock this door!"

Dane watched him carefully. Too much bluster, tantrum creeping in, altogether a bad showing for a man of Dix's wealth and stature. The hour and a half he'd been forced to wait around the airport, kept maddeningly in the dark about the delay, had exposed some badly frayed nerves.

Dane said, "Nobody's listening. Go ahead, beat your hand bloody. You don't go anywhere until I say so."

Dix clenched and unclenched the hand he'd hurt in his burst of rage. He turned away from the door, looking around the room, confirmed there was no other exit. He took a couple of steps toward Dane, leaning, shoulders aggressively forward.

"Your job—this is going to cost you plenty. I'll sue."

"Take the job. I don't want it anymore. Maybe I never wanted it. Your sister convinced me it would be a great career move. I don't know why I listened to her; but who among us can resist Esther Trevellian when she's being persuasive?"

Dix said, suddenly wary, "What is this about? Esther? I don't want to talk about my—"

"It's about Sharan Norbeth. Are you going to sit down?"

"No," Dix said, with a sudden avoiding sideways step, as if he imagined the chair was going to slide toward him. "What about Sharan?"

"Where is she? What did you do with her, Dix?"

"Do with? More of your nonsense? She was sleeping when I left this morning."

"Asleep where?"

"Cloud Horse."

"Why is she there?"

"Is that any of your—"

"Yes, it is."

"I don't—"

"Answer me."

Dix drew down an aggrieved breath. Let it out. "We were touring yesterday, on our bikes. North Georgia. Sharan's Harley hit some loose gravel, and she took a spill, down into a ravine. My heart was in my mouth."

"Your heart was in your mouth."

"She was knocked out, but thank God not seriously—no, she's in good shape. A cut or two, some bruises."

"A fall like that, she ought to be in a hospital."

"But Esther—"

"Esther what?"

Dix spread his hands. "I called Esther. After the ac—"

"Why didn't you call the cops?" Dane said, now clipping Dix off at every opportunity, pressuring him. He was sure he was hearing lies.

"I don't know. I thought—kind of a remote area, who knew how long the response time—we have a helicopter, at Cloud Horse. A doctor for my mother, full-time nurses. But I'm telling you, Sharan is—"

"And you always call Esther, when you're in a jam?"

"Jam? What do you—? It was an unavoidable accident, I didn't—"

"Have I accused you of anything, Dix?"

"Well, you sound—"

"Get Sharan on the phone for me. I want to talk to her."

"She can't—"

"Can't what? Didn't you say she was okay?"

"Yes, but—"

"Then make that call. *Now*. So I'll hear for myself that Sharan's not badly hurt."

"I think, I'm positive that Sharan is still asleep. The doctor gave her a sed—"

"Then have Esther wake her up. What's the big deal?"

"Esther, I'm pretty sure she went deer-hunting this morning. I know for a fact—"

"*Somebody* there can wake Sharan up. Can't they? Dix, godammit, *sit down*. Why are you so nervous?"

"Because I, I should've been in New York by now. You have no right to— Okay. Look, I'll forget about this. I'm not sore at you, Cole, sorry I got so upset. My time is—"

"Sharan's *not* okay, is she, Dix? What have you done to her?"

"Done to Sharan? My God. Stop this. I told you! She was asleep when I went in to—sound asleep, I couldn't—"

"Wake her?"

"No. I c-couldn't."

"Why? What kind of shit did you give her?"

"Me? I'm not a doctor."

"What did the doc shoot her up with?"

"I don't know! Whatever Es—it's not important."

"Not important. But you couldn't wake Sharan up to say good-bye when you left? What time was that?"

Dix had to think about it. Thinking made him tense.

"Four, ten after."

"At ten after four this morning she was asleep and helpless?"

Dix tried to look incredulous, but his lips trembled slightly. His chest rose and fell.

"Helpless? Cole, you have no idea what you're—"

"I know exactly what I'm saying, Dix. Sharan wouldn't be on Cloud Horse Mountain at all unless she was kidnapped. A kidnapping you took part in. I'm also saying that exactly one minute from now I'm going to blow your pitiful brains out the back of your skull."

Dane reached into his lap and picked up a .40 caliber Smith and Wesson automatic that one of the marshals had loaned him. He laid it on the desk. Then he unfolded several letter-sized sheets of paper and slid them across the desktop toward the empty chair.

"For the last time. Sit down. Read this."

Dix looked in panic at the locked door, as if a fist had struck there, a deathblow to his ears.

"The plasma furnace is there, Dix. In a truck at the foot of Cloud Horse Mountain. I suppose you didn't know that Esther had the furnace sent down from Glassboro."

Dix's head sagged. He made a shaky whistling noise through the space between his front teeth.

"Probably three women were consigned to that particular furnace, a no-trace mop-up after their deaths. Thursday Childs would have been the first." Dane drummed his fingers on the desk. "Then Robin Smallwood, who disappeared from a street in nearby Philadelphia." He drummed more softly. "The last one was my sister. Read the letter."

Dix said, looking at the matte-finish black automatic, "You won't kill me. You might as well shoot yourself."

Dane said with a show of cheerfulness, "But I like myself too much, Dix. And I have the resources to disappear, new identity anywhere in the world I choose. What's your fortune worth at this particular moment? My life has been devoted to the law, but I'm afraid it was ivory-tower ethos too much of the time. The last twenty months have exposed me to every pathology that the system, our bureaucracy of law, has to offer. The interminable and inflexible codifications, perversions of intent and wisdom, tyrannies of ideology that flourish like weeds in what was once a pretty decent republic. It feels good to be back at the beginning, the common law that deals with human relationships on an equitable, no-nonsense basis. If you do me wrong—and you have, Dix—*you will be punished.*"

He raised the automatic, cocking the hammer. The sound was loud enough to provoke a disastrous twitch from Dix Trevellian.

Dix more or less crumpled into the chair opposite Dane, agape with dread. He tried to clear his throat. His eyes drifted over the pages of the letter unfolded in front of him.

"What's this? I'm not—I will not sign anything unless my lawyers—"

"This letter has nothing to do with you." Dane smiled slightly, thumb on the hammer of the Smith, finger light on the trigger. "It's a love letter I wrote to Sharan. Once I got started, I wrote a hell of a lot, as you can see."

"A lot— You and Shar—?"

"Didn't you hear? Are your ears ringing, Dix? Are you that frightened?"

He fired a shot, inches past Dix's head. Soft-nosed slug that buried itself in a puff of gray dust in the wall. It was like a cannon going off in the small room. Dane was prepared for the crush of noise, and his expression changed only a little. Dix was not prepared. He jumped and his mouth fell open. Then he grabbed his crotch, too late. All he could do was sheepishly try to cover the wet spot with his cupped hands.

Watching Dix's expression was like watching a crack spread across a stressed pane of glass. The fracture deep, and beyond repair. Dane was fascinated, but he felt no satisfaction.

He had told the marshals not to interrupt, no matter what they heard. He stared at Dix.

"Now the letter."

"I don't w-want to read it." Dix seemed to be trying to make himself smaller in the chair. Sitting with his shoulders hunched forward, his elbows tucked in, knees tightly together. His eyes were deeply troubled, then went out of focus. His lips would not come together in a way he found comfortable. He made clown mouths.

"My letter to Sharan is all the proof you will ever need, Dix, that I'll kill you without a second's delay if any harm has come to her. Is Sharan all right, Dix?"

Dix nodded, looking at Dane to see if he was believed, reduced to silent pleading. Dane glanced at the letter on the desk. Dix's wet fingertips touched the pages, withdrew. He rubbed eyes that seemed suddenly sleepy.

"Promise me something," he said in a reedy but earnest voice.

"What is it, Dix?"

"*Promise* me. It's important."

"All right. I promise."

"Don't *ever* tell Esther I peed. She'd be so ashamed of me."

Dane's jaw felt stiff, his chest filled with inappropriate laughter. He took a deep breath.

"You have your promise. Is that all you wanted to tell me?"

Dix shook his head slowly, and wiped his fingers on his chamois shirt, leaving dark impressions.

"It was never me," he said, as if each word were dragging through his throat like fishhooks. "I loved all of them. Esther didn't like that. She was afraid I would run off and marry Felicia. That's how serious—oh. I love Sharan, too."

"Not as much as I do."

"Then—*do* something. I can't. The furnace. Oh, God." Dix made a sudden gasping noise. "I saw it once, when it was operating? Esther *made* me watch. Oh, my God. I haven't thought about it, for such a long time." He cast a beseeching eye on Dane. "Some things you just don't want to remember. We've all done things we regret, haven't we?"

"Don't worry about the furnace, Dix. We've impounded the truck already. What I need from you now is a complete statement, beginning with Thursday Childs."

"Esther and Lew were screwing Thursday together. Sometimes it was Esther and me with another of—of them, but never Felicia. I think that's why she was so jealous, I kept Felicia for myself. It was a *sacred* love."

"Let's get back to Thursday Childs."

"Okay. Well, you see, it got kind of rough, Lew told me. Thursday had arthritis. I think her bones, you know, weren't very strong. Esther broke her neck when Thursday was down on her, you know, head between her legs, Esther riding her shoulders like a horse. Squeezing, writhing, while Thursday made her come. Esther had Lew help her get rid of the body. That's how it began. Esther just came too strong, I guess, and twisted—I told you. I will never sign anything. Never. Esther wouldn't find it in her heart to forgive me."

"Dix, you should be grateful. The burden's off you. It's finished. Whatever she did to you, made you swear never to talk about, there's no reason to be afraid of Esther anymore."

Dix looked up slowly. The light in his eyes like the lonely glitter at life's end.

"You don't know *Esther*," he said.

A low hiss of flames, odorless burning.

Twittering. Parakeets, or some other small captive birds.

A distant, dirgeful, operatic voice.

Someone humming along.

Coffee cup clinking against a saucer—

These sounds on awakening.

Sharan emitted a breathy tuneless humming of her own, and yawned deeply.

Awake, looking at what she thought was the night sky; constellations of tiny lights easy on the eyes. She moved involuntarily, buttocks clenching, and felt the voluminous sway of the water bed beneath her. Something of a shock, as if she had discovered herself adrift at sea. The aftermath of a dream, no image of storm or shipwreck remaining. She raised her hand to her eyes, gently touching, lashes crummy at the outside corners. She wiped them clean. Soreness under her right eye, the texture of a trivial cut. Band-Aid patch covering the heel of her palm. The bed undulated again, her heart constricted, she explored with her artificial hand. Warm to the touch, apparently she'd slept very soundly, but what water bed? Where? She raised her head. Another small shock. Daylight, full in the face, but through tinted glass. A lot of window space, the elongate convex windows glazed by high-altitude sun. A dark bird, large wingspan, soared through her field of vision. The belled steel ribs between windows were like the ornate bars of a cage. The ceiling wasn't really the sky, only an elaborate lighting scheme. The flames were contained inside an antique tile stove that warmed the room efficiently. The water bed was round, and in the middle of the oddly shaped room. There was a good-sized ficus tree growing in a ceramic planter by the windows. Next to them, the green-and-yellow birds on several levels of a tower cage. Then a couple of small plump sofas and a low stone table, the pedestal of which looked like part of a column from a city looted and abandoned before Christ. A figure, dark against the incoming sun. Big package of headphones contributed to an otherworldly look, low-budget invader from space. But the bare callused feet propped against the edge of the table were human enough. Mardie Kregg was painting toenails tough as paving stones in the focused light from a gooseneck lamp while she listened to opera.

Sharan was wearing a short-sleeved pair of woman's pajamas. There was a large tan Band-Aid on the inside of her left arm just below the crook of her elbow. Also sore to the touch.

Mardie's head was turned toward her. She capped the bottle of nail polish and turned a hair dryer on her toes.

"Mornen."

"Where am I?" Sharan said.

"Cloud Horse."

"How did I—" Sharan had difficulty getting her voice right. Also she was aware of another difficulty, the morning queasiness, which was becoming habitual, and which the motion of the water bed intensified.

"They said you wouldn't remember."

"Remember what?"

"Bike accident."

"I had a bike accident? I've *never* had a bike accident."

"Had one yesterday. Fell on your head. Knocked you clean out. You been out for some time. Don't get to stirren around yet. I'll fetch Dr. Dorji when my toenails are dry."

"I'm all right. I don't have a headache." Sharan put her hand to her head, back and front. Her neck seemed okay. She remembered nothing but lunch with Dix, on a porch overlooking the square of a North Georgia town.

"Where's Dix?"

"New York. I coptered him over to Asheville at four this mornen."

"But how did I get here?"

"The same. Helicopter."

It wasn't adding up to Sharan, but the queasiness had most of her attention.

"I need to find a bathroom."

"It's thur. Off to your right."

Retching left her feeling haggard and miserable. There was a plush robe hanging up behind the bathroom door, felt slippers in one pocket. When she returned to the bedroom after washing her face and wondering about the welt that had drawn a trace of blood under one eye, breakfast was waiting on a trolley, and so was Dr. Dorji, in a white jacket and black bow tie. He had coin-slot eyes and a youthful pudginess. She felt that he was ill at ease.

"I don't remember crashing."

"Not unusual," he said, checking her vital signs, looking into her eyes with his penlight. "Probably it will come back to you, in only a few days."

"I don't understand why I'm here."

"I flew with Esther to the scene when Dix called. Of course if there had been severe trauma you would have gone straight to the nearest large hospital."

"I was unconscious?"

"Yes, but your pupils were reactive and you had no broken bones. Your reflexes were within normal parameters. Modern motorcycle helmets are wonderfully constructed. I had no reason to suspect a hematoma, but I monitored your progress all night. You simply slept."

"I'd like to go home. Where's my bike?"

"Seriously wanting repair, I'm afraid."

"Oh, not again! Damn it, I'm jinxed."

"Esther arranged for you to be driven back to Georgia when you're feeling up to it."

"I feel up to it now. Where is Esther?"

"Hunting. Do you wish to have breakfast?"

"I don't know. I just want to sit here a minute."

Dr. Dorji rose and held out his hand. "Safe journey."

"Thanks for—"

He looked admiringly at her prosthetic hand as he gripped it.

"Most amazing. Such sensitivity." For a few moments he looked into her eyes as if he wanted to say something smooth and memorable, but Western women confounded him. Most of them were taller. He was one of those men who smile as if they've just stubbed a toe, and feel they deserve the pain.

Breakfast was fresh fruit and country biscuits with butter and jam. Pork loin instead of bacon, two firm eggs. Good coffee. Sharan ate everything. A rawboned country girl in mint-green coveralls brought her the denim Harley duds she'd been wearing the day before, washed and pressed. Her underwear and motorcycle boots.

By the time she was dressed Mardie Kregg was back.

"Got a car waiten. I'll go with you on down to the flatland."

Mardie was wearing burnt-orange corduroy jeans and a khaki bush jacket. The work she had done on her toenails was buried in heavy red-topped wool socks turned down over her hiking boots. Sharan wondered if she was also carrying a gun.

"Esther back? I'd like to thank—"

"No. She hain't here yet. Now hif you're ready."

The house was stepped back into mountain granite. There was a glass elevator in a cylindrical shaft that rose three floors to an atrium level with a stunning view of blue mountains half-sunk in low-lying clouds or mist. The house seemed to live up to the brag Dix had put on it. And she hated it. So aloof, so precariously pretentious. She couldn't leave fast enough. As Dix had left, apparently, in the middle of the night. Not showing much concern for her well-being. Sharan didn't feel like she'd been tossed off her bike. There should have been deep-seated aches, scrapes, bruises everywhere. Bullshit, the accident story. More than eighteen hours of her life were missing (maybe the small blue puncture mark beneath the Band-Aid on her arm had something to do with that), and she had to work hard to squelch the fear that had been skittering around beneath her skin from the moment she woke up. But she was on her way out. No one was stopping her. Mardie seemed bored to be an escort.

They crossed the atrium and went outdoors under a slanted roof like a huge seashell. Terraced stone-paved patios, a flame that burned brightly in the clear air. Sharan remarked on the flame in the Olympic-sized stone cauldron.

"Hit's dedicated to the everlasten memory of Esther's daddy," Mardie explained briefly.

"What was he like?"

"Never knowed him."

"Where's the car?"

"No roads up here. Only the tram. I'd fly you down, hit's a sight faster. But the fog's bad this mornen. Halfway down the mountain, cain't see feet ahead."

"What's the tram?"

"Funicular railway. See the tracks right yonder whur the cable house is? Thur's two trains on cables that kind of balance each other. One goes down, huther one comes up. Five thousand feet down the mountain to the station at the huther end. Hit's all automated, too. Don't take but a few minutes."

The car bringing Coleman Dane from Asheville had to slow to less than twenty miles an hour once they reached Simon the Rock County. The marshal driving, a man named Axelberg, had been raised in western Carolina. He knew the roads and he knew where the morning fog would be so thick they were virtually blind in the coves of the mountains east of Cloud Horse. There were two bubble lights, blue and red, on the roof of the otherwise unmarked government sedan. The fog reflected the lights back into the sedan. The windshield wipers were going. Visibility lessened from two hundred feet to half that. They found themselves in a crawling caravan of other vehicles westbound. Axelberg took chances on the narrow highway, nudging pickup trucks aside with his siren, coopting the other lane when he thought they wouldn't meet head on with a logging truck on a blind curve. But the road was nearly all curves. Everyone in the car was tense, but Dane was like a maniac. Pounding on the seat back with a fist when there was a break in the information filtering back to him from the surveillance van at Cloud Horse Mountain. Radio communications were intermittent in the mountains. This had to be explained to him a couple of times.

"Mist is better than fog," Axelberg said. "Except when it freezes. Freezing mist, that's the worst."

"Would you describe this as fog or mist?" another marshal asked him.

"I don't know if there's a meteorological distinction. Fog, to me, is just a damn thick cloud. You can't see your hand in front of your face sometimes. Mist, you've got some visibility. It's more like a drizzle. You can have both. A fog bank in a heavy mist. I've seen it, plenty of times. I allow I've seen everything in these mountains. I've seen blizzards with thunder and lightning."

"How far?" Dane said through clenched teeth.

"Oh, we should be picking up the sheriff's escort any time now; said they'd be waiting on us by Settler's Fork. That's a couple miles."

The radio in the car gave them something, a few staccato words.

"What was that? What did he say?"

Axelberg glanced at the Deputy Attorney General in his back seat.

"Didn't hear it all. 'Gunfire.' That was clear. He sure enough did say 'gunfire.'"

Sharan rode with Mardie in the front car of the funicular railway, which lurched slightly moments after leaving the summit station, then abruptly dropped over the brow of the mountain and plunged noisily on its cable down a nearly sheer cliff with some blighted spruce growing on it. Momentarily she felt almost weightless. "Hold on," Mardie recommended. The sun was bright on the crest of a waterfall that fell in rocky steps to a more heavily wooded area. Mardie sat opposite her with folded arms and a brooding look in her pale eyes.

"What kind of hunting does Esther do?"

"Hit's deer season. For bow hunters."

"I'm sorry I didn't get the chance to—"

"Esther don't want to see nobody right now."

"I understand that."

Mardie nodded, as if it didn't matter. She tightened her arms over her small breasts and brooded further as the little train swayed and plummeted. Not going all that fast, but the steepness of the decline gave an illusion of speed that could be chilling.

Mardie said, "What kind of a woman would pull the teeth out of a dead man with a pair of pliers, to get the diamonds from his teeth? Now I'm asken you."

"Diamonds in his teeth?" Sharan said.

"No respect for the dead. Hit was sorry behavior. I shouldn't have stood for hit, and I'm ashamed that I did."

Sharan looked at her without comprehension. Mardie was gazing off, lips so tight together they had disappeared. Sharan maintained her silence. It was darker on the train, the twin tracks having entered an area of old-growth forest with trees reaching a hundred and fifty feet in height.

Mardie said, "Hit's pity of the cripple and respect for the dead that makes us different from the savages. You know that?"

"I guess so," Sharan said, resisting an urge to shudder.

Mardie turned in her seat to watch her.

"Esther's the finest human being hit's been my privilege to know. As a child I was beaten. I was treated like a vessel for men's wretched sins. Only Esther loved me. I walk with her through the Valley of the Shadow, because someday I will lead her to the huther side. This is the task God has set for me to accomplish in this life. I see that you don't have with you the cross you oft times wear."

"No, I—it's at home."

"Never mind. Hit's your love of the Lord that matters. You love Him, don't you?"

"Y-yes."

"Don't you tremble, now. I don't want you to have no fear. In the beauty of these woods I give you back to God. You know, hit's a sight brighter, thur on the huther side with its streets of gold." Mardie smiled enticingly. "You won't suffer. I don't believe you have done anythen in your lifetime that deserves you to suffer. But if thur be somethen a-weighen on your soul at this hour, you can confess hit to me."

"Mardie, what are you—"

Mardie stood up. From one of the cargo pockets of her safari jacket she took out a length of knotted silk rope. She wrapped it behind the horny knuckles of her large hands, leaving a ten-inch-long piece between the hands, the biggest knot of them all squarely in the middle.

"Oh, no, Mardie, no."

"Hit won't pain you, hardly atall. You just go to sleep, like, and after hit's done, why we pay the deepest respect to your body. I mean hit don't lie in the earth rotten away. And your soul, hit rises up straight to heaven in a burnen cloud a glory."

Seeing her against shrouded trees in the fog, Sharan's creative mind composed a Renaissance painting, and was numbed by the terribilità.

"You, Mardie? It was you who killed them?"

Mardie said thoughtfully, with a little uncomfortable hitching of her shoulders, "Esther done the first one, but hit was purely an accident. Lew Carbine and Esther and Thursday Childs, playen their rut games in bed, games I don't want to ever hear nothen about. Hit don't concern me, only matters of the spirit is worth payen attention to. But later, when she said to me, Mardie, I cain't help myself, I got to do hit again, I said—no. Not you, Esther. You're too fine a person. I'll do hit for you. Just tell me when and whur. We walk through this Valley together, Esther. Together we will find our way—to the Glory a-waiten on the huther side."

Her nostrils pinched together from the force of the breath she drew into her lungs as she jumped at Sharan, who was badly positioned to react. A tai chi master could have handled the assault, but she was years away from such proficiency. Her reaction, a parry with her prosthetic hand, failed. The streamlined knotted silk captured her neck.

Sharan's next, instinctive reaction at close quarters was a shoulder strike, then a hooking heel behind Mardie's leading foot that failed to take her down or loosen her grip. She was, as Sharan had suspected, very strong. Both of Mardie's fists were together at the base of Sharan's throat, the knot in the silk pressing deep. She felt her tongue swelling in her mouth. Sharan remembered the tai chi precept of "investing in loss" to keep her body from going rigid, which would have meant her death in another few seconds. Be supple. Carry the Tiger Back to the Mountain. Her favorite exercise, but she had no air. Although she recognized a look of contrition in Mardie's pale watery eyes, there was no letup.

Without warning the train slammed to a stop, throwing both of them a dozen feet against the observation glass at the blunt front end of the car. The rope loosened as Mardie lost her grip, and Sharan gulped air. One breath, then Mardie struck her on the side of the face and took a new purchase, sawing the slim rope against Sharan's neck, the knot sliding back to the notch below her windpipe.

Fog was all around them but the sun seemed to have burned through like a welder's torch at track level below them. A bright showering cloud of flame, rolling greasy smoke. The left side of Sharan's face was pressed against the convex window. As the fog was consumed, burned away by whatever was on fire between the funicular tracks a hundred and fifty feet away, Sharan thought she recognized the shape of a man, sitting upright as if bound to a stake.

Mardie screamed, a hoarse, desperate sound, and her hands fell away, the silk rope going slack around Sharan's abraded throat. She dropped to one knee, reaching for the noose, and pulled it off as

Mardie jumped from the train and went shrieking toward the ferociously burning man.

"Mordecai!"

Sharan dragged herself to her feet, gasping for air, and followed.

The heat of the flames, fueled, unmistakably, by gasoline, kept Mardie from getting within a dozen feet of her charred unmoving brother. How she had recognized him at all was beyond Sharan's understanding. His head, like a large sunspot in the celestial inferno, was deeply bowed, as his sitting body leaned at a fierce take-off angle from the metal fence post to which his hands had been bound. Mardie scrabbled in the roadbed for handfuls of dirt and gravel, pelted the swirling flames in an effort to save him while her own hairline frizzed and her eyebrows shrank to ashy ridges, her fair skin blistering from the heat. One of Mordecai's eyeballs exploded, perky as popping corn. Mordecai had compacted, in only a little more than a minute of ferocious burning, to half his original size. Sharan turned away and sat down heavily on a mossy rock, unable not to watch as Mardie stumbled like a dancing zombie around the remains, gesturing, raving hysterically.

"Who did this terrible thing! Whur are you?"

"I did it, Mardie," Dempsey Wingo answered from the fog. "I gave Mordecai what he deserved! I did it for Lewie."

Sharan heard two quick shots before she realized Mardie had a gun in her hand. One of the shots whanged off the side of the funicular car not ten feet away, and Sharan dived off her rock.

Mardie was screaming, firing shot after shot blindly into the fog.

"God damn you, Dempsey Wingo! I'll find you! I'll kill you for this! Devil! Devil!"

Sharan, remembering the noose around her smarting neck, kept low and began working her way uphill along the tracks, away from the stink of gasoline and burned flesh, the wild gunshots. Grateful for clinging fog.

A hand she never saw grabbed her by one shoulder.

"Stay down," Wingo said. "And don't make any noise."

"Mardie's stone crazy. She tried to kill—"

"All Kreggs are living proof that cousins shouldn't fuck. Let her empty that gun, then I'll take care of Mardie."

Sharan thought Mardie must have fired at least fifteen shots. Then there was no more shooting. And Mardie had stopped screaming. Except for the faint burning crackle down-track and the sound of the waterfall unseeable in the fog, it was very quiet. Sharan started to get up. Dempsey gave her a push.

"Wait."

She tried to look behind her.

"Where's Mardie?"

"Hard to tell. I think I see her."

"What's she doing?"

"Sitting down, looks like."

"Let me up, damn it."

"Careful."

Sharan sat up beside Dempsey, who was hunkered behind a large outcrop next to the funicular right-of-way. Fog drifted around his head. She cautiously massaged her sore throat, which felt half-crushed inside. Couldn't raise much more than a whisper from her larynx.

"What happened to you?" Dempsey asked.

"She was strangling me when the train stopped. She would have killed me. God, she was strong, I couldn't—" Sharan was trembling badly, and she couldn't keep herself from sobbing. He put an arm around her; not much comfort, he smelled like gasoline. "How could you just set him on fire like that?"

"Because he enjoyed blowing people up. Because he was vermin. It was napalm, by the way, Mordecai's own private, illegal stock. Be grateful, I apparently saved your life. What did I tell you about hanging around these people?"

"Thanks a l-lot, they kidnapped me."

"Again? Where's Dane?"

"He's—I d-don't know. Don't blame *him*."

Dempsey got slowly to his feet.

"Where're you going?"

"She's just sitting there. Hasn't moved."

"So?"

"Not trying to put out the fire. I wonder why, it's manageable now. Maybe she's snapped."

"A l-long time ago. For God's sake—can't *you* put it out?"

"Why? Did you forget the marshmallows?"

He left her and went down beside the tracks in a half-crouch, somehow not making a sound. Sharan held her breath. After a dozen feet Dempsey lost definition in the charnel-smelling fog. Mardie Kregg was only a blur another twenty feet away. Dempsey approached her still form as if he were trying to sneak up on God.

He stood two feet from and—as far as Sharan could tell—behind Mardie, like someone in a dim museum studying a piece of sculpture. A little time passed. The low flickerings and sudden puffs of flame from the shrunken dead man redefined Dempsey's shape, glazed a cheekbone taut as a tribal drumhead. His hair had been growing back, but there was just barely enough of it to be called a nap.

Sharan heard a creaking in the woods, as if two bare branches of a tree had rubbed together. She looked around cautiously. Not even a hint of wind to disperse the fog and cleanse the air. The train remained stalled. Apparently there was a sensor aboard that stopped it when something was on the tracks.

Dempsey reached out and nudged Mardie. She fell over and rolled softly, as if she had no bones, a few feet down an incline, away from the tracks.

Dempsey said, "Ricochet, most likely. Caught her under one eye and exited by way of the hind brain." He bent down again and picked up the handgun Mardie had been slinging lead with in her frenzy.

Sharan started to rise, desperate to get far away from there. Follow the tracks down the mountain, she knew she couldn't get lost in spite of the fog.

Behind her Esther said quietly, "Get out of my way."

Sharan turned, flinching, her marrow freezing after the first convulsive reaction. Esther stood a dozen feet away, head to toe in camouflage clothing, only her open eye and the shape of her face confirming her identity. She held her longbow at an angle of ten degrees from the vertical, arrow nocked. A little sharp gleam of broadhead in the faint light from the beacon of Mordecai, as the last of his fatted flesh was consumed. Esther hissed a final warning between her teeth. Sharan ducked, hearing the hard twinging sound of the bowstring a split second after the swishing passage of the feathered arrow a foot from her ear.

Dempsey Wingo uttered a short, not very loud sound, as if he were urgently trying to interrupt someone.

Sharan looked up and saw him erect, hands half-raised, chin lifted in surprise. He stood like that for several seconds. All but about eight inches of the arrow's shaft had been driven into him, high in the chest, not far below his right collarbone.

He coughed, spraying blood six feet into the fog, and staggered, but he didn't lose his balance. One hand seemed to wave acknowledgment.

"Missed the heart, Esther!" he called to her, and then he laughed, but it wasn't a happy sound, bubbling through blood in his throat. "I told you—you needed glasses."

Sharan heard Esther take a couple of steps onto the graveled right-of-way and glanced back. Another arrow nocked, tip of her tongue caught expectantly between her even teeth, enamel gleaming in the mud tones of her face. The strength of her slender arms, the quick, sure aim. Sharan didn't see the arrow leave the bow. But this time she heard it hit the target.

And Dempsey Wingo was down, his head starkly elevated by the broadhead out the back of his neck, the long shaft protruding from the center of his throat. All movement involuntary, a dumb-show jerking of hands and feet like the last vestige of a primitive communication.

"*Why?*" Sharan cried.

"Because he was asking for it. Scott would be alive today, if not for Dempsey. Dempsey kept Scott from me. And look at poor Mardie! Would you just *look* at her?"

Esther jerked her right thumb toward her mouth. Sharan hadn't paid much attention, before, to the streamers of bandage darkened with blood. Three bodies behind her, the violently deceased, she would not have expected to have any more capacity for shock. But the sight of nearly bare, gristly thumb bones, the flesh and ligaments mostly gnawed away, sickened her. A wild animal had been at work. The animal that Esther had always kept close to her, that sometimes looked—carnal, casual—out of her eyes.

Esther bared her teeth in Sharan's direction. A strangled lament deep in her throat turned into a howl of rage.

"What am I going to do without Mardie? She breathed the life back into me. But the lightning keeps coming, and I don't have Mardie anymore!"

"Esther—please. Listen to me. Mardie tried to choke me to death on the train. She said she was doing it for you, like she did the others. Because you, *you* were too fine a person to have their blood on your hands."

"Bless her heart," Esther said mournfully, looking past Sharan for a time, eyes focused in hardship farewell on Mardie's body. Then, when Sharan moved cautiously to one side, Esther looked furiously into her eyes. She smiled, nodded as if acknowledging some unfulfilled pact between them, reached for another arrow in the quiver at her side.

"Don't. You'll n-never be able to explain any of this. Don't make things worse for you than they are already."

"I don't have to make explanations," Esther said, frowning slightly. "I have two billion dollars."

She was drawing back the arrow, bow half-raised, when Coleman Dane's amplified voice stopped her.

"Sharan! Where are you?"

Esther looked around alertly, trying to judge the direction from which his voice had come. She looked back at Sharan.

"It's Cole. Isn't it?"

"Sharan!"

The two women stared at each other, Sharan with goosebumps and trying not to be elated. It seemed to her that Esther had become easier to see, as if the fog had thinned and was taking on a faint sparkle from the sun. Possibility, though still remote, of a better day.

"Cole knows everything I know," Sharan said. "So fuck your two billion dollars, Esther."

"Sharan!"

A different voice this time, then there were simultaneous shouts echoing from the cliffs of the mountain. And the sound of a helicopter flying above the fog.

"Just be still," Esther said. "Be very still. We'll wait for Cole."

"No, Esther."

"Esther! Are you there? I've got Dix, Esther! I've got a confession!"

The grayish knucklebone of Esther's right thumb danced against her front teeth. Bloody ragged bandages hung beardlike down her chin. Her camouflaged head seemed a gross fabrication, like a papier-mâché head in a Mardi Gras parade. Her eyes were large with fascination. Sharan was still, as Esther had requested, relaxed in the beginning tai chi form, the Qi Ji, from which all movement flowed. But Esther was five yards away, uphill, a broadhead arrow on her bow.

"Take Dix away from me?" Esther said quietly. "Oh, no. I don't think so. Show yourself."

"Esther—"

"Didn't you see what happened to Dempsey? Didn't that teach you anything? Say another word *and I'll kill you first.*"

Sharan swallowed, then worked silently at expelling all tension from her back, her legs. Eyes on Esther, alert for any distraction that might provide a chance to disarm her. It was a bow and arrow, after all. But, yes, even though she knew remembering was a mistake, creating tension in her body, she couldn't forget how swiftly Dempsey Wingo had died.

A slight catch in Esther's breathing, quick movement of her eyes, she had seen something.

"Following the tracks," Esther whispered.

Sharan turned her head slightly. She saw Coleman Dane, or the figure of someone who could be Dane, taking shape, but still an ashen smudge in the fog below. Moving slowly toward the darker stain of smoke surrounding the unidentifiable hulk of Mordecai Kregg between the funicular tracks. Pausing. He had something that might have been a bullhorn in his right hand.

Too far away to be the can't-miss target Esther wanted.

"Say hello," Esther suggested. "Tell him to come up to the train."

"No," Sharan said.

"Sharan! Where are you?"

"Do it," Esther said.

"Who's there? What's going on?"

Dane took a few more steps alongside the tracks. He stopped and looked at the huddled char of Mordecai Kregg and said sonething half-whispered Sharan didn't catch. Then he spoke sharply into a walkie, but there seemed to be an interruption in communications. The helicopter came back, unseen, with a noise like wild horses running through a canyon. Rotors churned the mass of fog into a slow whirlpool above their heads.

Dane now moved nearer the body of Mardie Kregg, further reducing the distance between himself and Esther.

Esther raised her bow slowly, drawing back the arrow with two fingers, cords in her neck standing out like the ribs of a kite swelling in the wind.

The helicopter, motionless, released a powerful shaft of light. It illuminated Coleman Dane, and he looked up with the newly incandescent face of a prophet. He raised the hand with the walkie to shield his eyes, trying to talk again. The helicopter was making so much noise Sharan knew that he would never hear her scream.

Instead she sprang at Esther, in a movement that brought her right hand up with the palm turned toward her face, the elbow slightly bent.

Sharan didn't see the arrow as it flew from Esther's bow, but she felt the jarring impact of the broadhead cut squarely through the prosthetic hand, spinning her half way around, staggering her in the loose gravel of the ballast beside the funicular tracks.

The beam of the searchlight was floating their way, burning with a laser's power but unfocused, lighting up the fog all the way to the trees beside the railroad cut, a hard fuming light that struck Esther full in the face and blinded her as she swiftly attempted to pull another arrow from the quiver at her beltline.

Sharan got to her first with a sweeping kick that upended Esther and dropped her on her back.

But the footing wasn't level and Sharan lost her balance, fell forward, instinctively throwing out a hand to break her fall: the hand pierced by an arrowhead with three razor edges.

Instinct also caused Esther to jerk her head aside, a split-second of movement that cost her her life.

The broadhead punctured the side of her neck below the ear and was driven hard through the muscles, all of Sharan's sprawling weight behind it. The arrow sliced laterally across the top of Esther's spine, shearing it from the brain stem. There was no convulsion. Her body merely slackened as her lips parted in an expression of surprise, something in the brain still in motion, though waning; the body absent, as remote from final thought as a fossil in solid rock.

For a few seconds Sharan didn't fully realize what had happened. Her face was inches away from Esther's. She smelled greasepaint, a last exhalation from Esther's lungs as she pushed hard with her other hand against Esther's breasts, a rising stink of bowels. Then Sharan in panic tried to sit up, but the arrow was locked in Esther's neck. Esther's head and face came up with her. The face like one of the clay-balls Sharan had made as a child, mixing gray and green and brown in a swirling mass, daub of nose, crease of mouth, fingernail dents for eyes. The pupils of Esther's eyes were small and fixed, already dimming from dark to utter blackness, emptied of secrets, no longer involved. Sharan moaned in distress. She made a cushion of one thigh and rested Esther's head on it. Trembling, she closed Esther's eyes with her left hand. Then she closed her own eyes, the trembling now like shock waves.

The helicopter had drifted off, and she heard scrunching footsteps.

Coleman Dane kneeled beside her.

"My God. *What happened here?*"

Sharan looked up. His face was indistinct, as if she were trying to recall it from a dream.

"I didn't mean to. It was an accident. I lost my balance."

"Hey. Nobody's blaming you. Are you hurt?"

"Break it off, Cole. Break the arrow off! Get me loose from Esther."

Help was arriving. More shadowy figures, some with powerful flashlights. Dane rose, borrowed a knife from a marshal and hacked off the arrow where it protruded beneath Esther's ear. Some blood welled out of the agitated wound. Sharan looked away and got clumsily to her feet. In the act of rising she had a rushed sensation of leaving the earth to soar in fog and darkness, a tingling deep in her wrists, the rest of her like cold, boiled fish.

Dane gave her his fleece-lined black leather coat to wear, then put his arms around her.

"This place is hell," Sharan said earnestly, "and I want to be out of here *now*."

"Can you walk?"

"Yes. Of course. I'm all right."

Sharan pulled the shaft of the arrow from the ruined prosthesis.

"Look at this. How am I going to explain? This was an experimental glove." She wasn't tracking too well. Tears drained down her face. "They p-probably won't give me another one," Sharan said bitterly. It was all she could think about. "I damaged government property."

Dane smiled and said calmingly, "But I can buy you a hundred just like it."

Three steps, her knees weakened. She was as out of breath as if she had run down the mountain.

"Just lean on me. That a girl."

Sharan turned gratefully to press her cheek against his, tried to kiss him, but she was trembling too badly, and her lips were numb. She began slipping from his grasp, and sat down again.

Dane called for a medical kit. Someone broke a capsule of amyl nitrate under her nose. Her head snapped up, eyes wide.

"Dix," she said. "What happened to Dix?"

"We've got him. He had a lot to say about his sister. He'll have a lot more to say before they finally commit him."

"Dix didn't kill anybody. That was Mardie, acting out some aspect of a stark and merciless religion. But Dix isn't innocent. It was the three of them, but mostly Esther. They were a little dark circle of demons, doing Esther's will. Even Dempsey Wingo. He couldn't break away from her, he had to keep coming back and back, and look what it got him! God, what *was* it about that woman? I know I felt it too. An attractive evil. Where did it come from? How did it start?"

Her voice was listless, her head nodding slightly as she stood. A four-wheel-drive Bronco filled with sheriff's deputies came uphill toward them, straddling the funicular tracks, roof-rack of lights blazing. They moved aside. Sharan looked at Dane, then for the last time at Esther Trevellian, where she had fallen, the fog leaving her still-humid body in slow streams, swags of fog like dirty ermine.

I didn't want you to die, Esther. I wanted you to live. I wanted you to tell me, explain it away, so I don't have to dream about you for the rest of my life.

"What is it, Sharan?"

She looked at her ruined prosthesis, at her other palm with drying blood in the creases, ingrained along the lifeline.

"I don't know. Esther—where? Not quite gone, but soon she will be gone. Nothing remaining except—how did you put it once? A stain of superstition."

"We walk away. We turn our backs and walk away now."

"Yes."

"No one really knew her. If you can't know someone, you're not responsible for their memory."

"But we have some duty toward the things we kill." Sharan held out the bloodied hand in protest, not remembering how blood had come to be there. Dumbly afraid it wouldn't wash off.

"I need to find a church."

"All right."

"Quickly. To deal with this. I can't deal with it, any other way."

He took her hand in his, held it tightly until it wasn't shaking anymore, and walked with her like that the rest of the way down the mountain, following the tracks, to the empty station that was a scaled-down replica of the lodge that had burned on the summit of Cloud Horse Mountain twenty-five years ago, and the emergency vehicles parked beside the platform with wide doors open. Waiting, once again, for Trevellian dead.

ACKNOWLEDGMENTS

I'm indebted to Dr. John Pervis Milnor and Dr. Charles White of Memphis, both of whom have been extremely patient in answering numerous queries for this and other books; their range of interests and knowledge beyond the confines of their profession is truly impressive. They are Renaissance men who somehow manage to cram thirty hours into every twenty-four-hour day. Also thanks to my sister Su Mead, who is never too busy to hunt up those arcane facts that are catnip to this novelist; to Michael Hurst for his lawyerly input; to my wife and head cheerleader Mary Ann; and to Tom Doherty and Bob Gleason, whose patience and endurance over the years have, I hope, in some measure been rewarded.